In a World of Nuclear Terrorism, There's Always Enough Time to Die.

Raul Valenzuela: He was a war hero in Vietnam when, on his last mission, he disappeared. Now he's a man Delta Force will do anything to recapture . . .

Sergeant Major Matt Jensen: The Green Beret NCO knew Valenzuela in Vietnam. Now Jensen is the team leader on a crucial Delta mission to snatch him from El Salvador . . .

Major Dave Ames: The Delta Force operations officer is known as the team's top lover-boy. But his magic touch has gotten him mixed up with two beautiful spies—and a special mission for the CIA . . .

Captain Rachel Brown: As a Delta Force officer, she's proved her strength under fire. Now she's on her way to Cyprus to hunt down a terrorist—and find out how far her courage will take her . . .

Command Sergeant Major Dick Salem: He led a Delta team to the terrorist Hakim Nidal once before. But someone tipped off Nidal—and he slipped away with the KGB. Salem won't let it happen again . . .

Hakim Nidal: He's killed innocent men, women and children all over the globe. Now he's made the ultimate terrorist deal, and Delta has to take him down . . .

"Burruss is a great storyteller and an extraordinarily good and refreshing writer."
—Colonel Charlie A. Beckwith, U.S. Army (Ret.),
former commander, Delta Force, and author of
Delta Force: The Army's Elite Counterterrorist Unit

A MISSION FOR DELTA

L.H.Burruss

AN AUTHORS GUILD BACKINPRINT.COM EDITION

A Mission for Delta

AN AUTHORS GUILD BACKINPRINT.COM EDITION

Published by iUniverse.com, Inc.

For information address:
iUniverse.com, Inc.
5220 S 16th, Ste. 200
Lincoln, NE 68512
www.iuniverse.com

Originally published by Pocketbooks

ISBN: 0-595-16525-7

Printed in the United States of America

for Rachele

If all the world were just,
there would be no need for valor.

—Plutarch

For our sort of war you need shrewd, cunning men
who are capable of fighting far from the herd.
Who are full of initiative, too . . . Sort of civilians
who can turn their hand to any trade, preachers and
missionaries too, who preach but keep one hand on
the butt of their pistols in case anyone interrupts
them . . . or happens to disagree.

—Jean Laterguy

1

Major Dave Ames, operations officer of the Delta Force, stood at the podium of the situation room in the old post stockade at Fort Bragg, while Major Jim Greer, the Delta Intelligence Officer, tacked several maps and photographs onto the cork wall behind him. Ames watched the others who were to attend the meeting file in and take their seats.

Lieutenant Colonel Jerry Schumann, commander of Delta's Operational Detachment E-1, the ground operations element of the force, stood at a chair near the center of the front row and stared at the map of El Salvador which Greer was pinning to the wall. He glanced at Ames, smiled and sat down.

"Good one?" he asked Ames, as he took a can of Copenhagen snuff from his shirt pocket and shoved a pinch of it into his cheek.

"Good one," Ames answered simply.

Matt Jensen, the sergeant major of Detachment E-1, sat down beside his boss, looked at the map, then at the eight-by-ten photograph of a man tacked next to it. His eyebrows raised slightly, and he rose and walked to the wall for a closer look. He stared at the photo for a moment, then looked at Ames, and retook his seat without speaking.

Colonel Wilton Garrett, the Delta commander, entered the room followed by his Command Sergeant Major, Dick Salem. Salem took a seat, as did Jim Greer, the intelligence officer, and Garrett removed the omnipresent cigar butt from his mouth.

"Men, this is a live one. At this stage, it's highly compartmented. Nobody outside this room—nobody—is to be given access to this information yet.

"Major Ames has just returned from the White House, where he was given this mission by the National Security Advisor. Nobody in the Pentagon has been briefed on it yet—in fact, as I understand it, only a couple of people in CIA and a couple on the NSC staff know about it—right, Major Ames?"

"Yes, sir."

"All right. Our mission right now is to develop a plan, using as few people as possible, for a clandestine operation to snatch a terrorist—an American defector—out of El Salvador. We have to send Major Ames back to the White House tomorrow morning for approval of the plan. If it's approved, we'll alert the necessary people immediately, put them into isolation, and launch as soon after as feasible. So let's get on with it."

He shoved the cigar butt into the corner of his mouth, and took his seat in the center of his subordinates. Ames picked up a pointer from the podium and began.

"This operation—code-named Arctic Falcon—is classified Top Secret and is compartmented on a strict need-to-know basis.

"The mission is for elements of Delta, on order, to conduct a quick reaction, clandestine operation into Morazan Province, El Salvador, to capture one Emilio Ramirez—also known as Raul Valenzuela—and return him to U.S. government control."

"Valenzuela. Yeah, I *thought* it looked like him." It was Sergeant Major Jensen.

"You know him?" Garrett asked.

"Yeah. We were in SOG together in Vietnam, running recon. He went in on a recovery mission for some sensitive item, and ended up missing in action. I remember, because my team was alerted as the backup team. He reported contact, and we tried to get in to them, but never found a trace of 'em. I figured he was long since dead. . . . Go ahead with the briefing, sir, and I'll see if there's anything I can add at the end."

As the intelligence officer briefed on the general communist guerrilla insurgency situation in El Salvador, Matt Jensen recalled the mission Valenzuela had conducted back in 1968.

Shortly after the Tet Offensive, they had gotten word to alert two recon teams to go "across the fence" into Laos to recover a small canister of plutonium. After Hue had been cleared of NVA, the plutonium which had been in the Hue University reactor had been reported missing, and there was an intelligence report stating that it was in a cache in Laos, waiting for a North Vietnamese helicopter to pick it up. It had sounded like a wild-goose chase at the time, but Valenzuela had taken his team in to try to locate the cache and reconnoiter the security around it, so that a reaction force could come in and pick it up.

Matt Jensen again concentrated on the intelligence officer's briefing.

"Now, the target is suspected to be located here, in this little village near the disputed Honduran border, just a couple of kilometers from the regional guerrilla headquarters where Ramirez has been conducting demolition training for their troops. He's reported to have his girlfriend with him, and after training at the guerrilla base all day, goes home to her for the night. According to the source—one of the guerrillas who normally lives in the headquarters area— the security in the target village is almost nonexistent. It's mostly old *campesinos* who support the communists with a share of their crops. There are a couple of young guerrilla troops from the village, and a few visitors from the headquarters who go there on occasion to see girlfriends, but that's about all. However, most of the guerrillas with any horsepower in the area have little AM radios, so it's a good bet our target does, too."

Greer pointed to an enlarged overhead photograph of the area. "Now, you can see by this photo that the surrounding vegetation—not really jungle, but well-wooded and thick, except for the *campesinos'* fields and coffee plantations—should be thick enough to provide concealed approaches to the edge of the village. There aren't many good infiltration landing zones or drop zones in the area. Most are right next to occupied villages, but there are a couple of small ones here . . . and here." He pointed to two small cleared areas a kilometer or two from the nearest villages.

"Now," Major Greer continued, pointing to the eight-by-ten photograph of Ramirez, "the target. Emilio Ramirez, whose real name is Raul Valenzuela, was born in Miami in 1946, finished high school there, and enlisted in the Army in 'sixty-four. He was trained as a combat engineer at Fort Belvoir, joined the 82nd Airborne Division after jump school, and stayed there until 'sixty-six, when he volunteered for Special Forces. He graduated as a 12 Bravo—SF demolitionist—second in his class, and volunteered for immediate assignment to Vietnam. He further volunteered for SOG—Studies and Observation Group, which as you all know, was the long-range reconnaissance element composed mostly of Special Forces soldiers, which ran cross-border missions into Laos, Cambodia, and up into North Vietnam. As Matt mentioned earlier, Valenzuela was assigned as an assistant team leader on one of the recon teams in CCN—Command and Control Detachment North. After just two missions, he did so well that they gave him his own RT, where he served as a one-zero—recon team leader—for nine more missions, during which time he won a Distinguished Service Cross. It's interesting to note that on eleven missions, he did well enough that he was able to earn himself a DSC and four bronze stars for getting into enemy base areas, reporting on them, and getting out without being discovered, except for the time he won his DSC. And even on that mission, he managed to get his whole team out. That's pretty skillful reconnaissance."

Greer turned to the next page of his briefing notes, and Colonel Garrett looked over at Sergeant Major Jensen. "Was he really that good, Sergeant Major?"

"Yes, sir, he was—when he wanted to be," Jensen answered.

Major Greer resumed his briefing. "On his last mission, on 24 May 1968, Valenzuela and his team were launched into Laos to a point along the Ho Chi Minh Trail at which it had been reported that a cache containing sensitive equipment was located. On the second day of the mission, Valenzuela radioed that he was nearing his objective, and shortly after that, that he was in contact with the NVA. The Hatchet Force and tactical air support were sent in to extract him, but no trace was found of any member of the team."

Matt Jensen started to mention that the "sensitive equipment" was a container of plutonium, but decided to wait to see if it had any bearing on the mission.

"He was carried as MIA until 1973, when it was reported by one of the pilots among our prisoners who were released then, that he had encountered Valenzuela in a temporary POW holding camp near the Ho Chi Minh Trail. Valenzuela was able to pass on to the pilot that he was pretending to be a turncoat, but that he intended to escape after collecting all the intel he could on enemy locations along the trail. We don't know whether or not those were actually his intentions at the time, but he never came back, and never showed up on the POW lists. At any rate, he next turned up in Cuba, spouting revolutionary rhetoric and vowing to free his Latin brothers all over the Americas from the oppressive grip of Yankee imperialism."

"You sure this Ramirez and Valenzuela are the same guy?" Colonel Garrett asked.

"Well," Dave Ames said, "the Agency rep at the White House briefing told me, when I asked him the same question, that they had gotten his fingerprints out of Cuba somehow, and, yes, they're absolutely sure it's the same guy."

"That was in 'eighty-one," Jim Greer continued. "Since that time, he's been back in the States. The FBI was put on his trail for a while a year or so ago, but couldn't catch up with him before he hightailed it back to Cuba. But most frequently, he's been reported to be in Cuba and Nicaragua. Now, earlier this year, according to the reports, he was seen in Managua in the company of one Hakim Nidal—usually to be found in Beirut or Tripoli, but occasionally found in Rome or Vienna, murdering innocent civilians."

Everyone in the room was familiar with the name of Hakim Nidal; they had spent many days chasing across the world in reaction to one terrorist event after the other which he had masterminded. But so far, they had always arrived too late.

As Major Greer continued his intelligence brief, Command Sergeant Major Dick Salem's mind flashed back to his near encounter with Nidal two years earlier, when intelligence had indicated that Nidal would be transiting Athens en route to Europe to create another terrorist incident. Salem had taken his team there with the intention of trailing Nidal to Frankfurt, where another team was waiting to make the arrest. They spotted Nidal coming off a Mideast Airlines 707, and all looked good. They drifted into the waiting area after him, but as the flight was called for boarding, two men entered, went to Nidal, and he immediately left the terminal with them. Salem waited until they were out of sight, and grabbed a taxi in an attempt to follow the car in which Nidal and the two men sped away, but they quickly evaded Salem's attempts to follow them. He *had* been able to get the license number of the car, however, and British intelligence later reported that it was a KGB vehicle.

But Nidal had gotten away; someone had blown it— probably some Pentagon staff officer at a Washington cocktail party, Salem had always suspected. Well, at least a couple of good things had come out of the incident, he recalled now; the compartmentation of that sort of operation had been greatly increased, and Nidal had apparently gone back to Lebanon without pulling off whatever incident he was planning. Maybe this operation would somehow lead him back into a situation in which he could be dealt with;

although it was doubtful that Salem would be directly involved, since he had now moved into the Headquarters Detachment as Delta's senior enlisted man.

Major Greer finished his intelligence briefing and asked Jensen if he cared to add any more about Ramirez. The youthful-looking sergeant major stood and faced Colonel Garrett, shoving his hands into the back pockets of the jeans which served as Delta's normal work uniform.

"I'll just say this—he's one fearless and ruthless son of a bitch. A couple of examples—once, out near the Ho Chi Minh Trail, his team captured three NVA. He didn't feel like he could risk taking all three to his pickup zone, so he took the sergeant and killed the other two—tied them up, slit their throats, and left them. Another time, he found a cache of mortar rounds, booby-trapped it with a claymore mine, then stood back in the jungle and yelled at the top of his lungs until a group of NVA showed up. Then he blew up the cache in their faces. He got his DSC on that one, but he was lucky to make it back. Brave, but stupid." He looked at Garrett.

"You know the type, sir, the kind we try to screen out of Delta with our psych tests during selection, the ones with blood lust, the ones who act like the rules were all made for somebody else."

Garrett nodded. "You surprised he's turned terrorist, Sergeant Major?"

"Well, yes and no. He *did* have a chip on his shoulder about being a Latino. The Black Panthers and the Weather Underground were bombing places and raising hell in those days, and he used to admire them—even talked about starting a Latino underground to raise hell when he got back from the war. We just kind of dismissed it as booze talking. Looks like we may have been wrong. . . . One more thing, sir. I'd like to lead the mission to snatch him."

Garrett shifted the cigar butt to the other corner of his mouth and contemplated Jensen's request. Matt Jensen was an experienced recon man. He knew Valenzuela, and it would probably take more than one of Delta's four-man teams to conduct the mission. They would need someone to be overall in charge on the ground—normally an officer's responsibility. But the noncommissioned officers of Delta were more capable than most officers in the Army anyway. He turned to his Command Sergeant Major, Dick Salem, for his valued opinion. "Sergeant Major?"

Salem smiled. "If you're sure you can take the heat from the generals for not having an officer along if it goes wrong, I say let him have it."

Garrett looked back at Jensen. "It's all yours, Sergeant Major," he said, grinning. "Don't screw it up, or I'll *never* make general. Let me know when you're ready to brief me on what—and who—you need. The staff's yours." The lanky colonel stood, adding, "Remember, this is to remain strictly compartmented for now. If there's anybody else we absolutely need to read in on it, let me know, and I'll give you a decision."

Garrett and his Command Sergeant Major walked out of the room, leaving the others behind to assist Sergeant Major Jensen in developing his plan. To more conventional officers, leaving a noncommissioned officer to plan an operation of national importance would have been unthinkable. But in the Delta Force, it was a tradition, and a sensible one, which the officers who founded the unit had started. As much as possible, the planning was pushed down to the lowest level feasible—to the level of those whose responsibility it would be to execute the plan. They were, after all, the ones who knew their true capabilities and limitations, and the ones who would live or die by the plan. Those facts always injected a sense of reality which staff officers' plans sometimes seemed to lack.

Three hours later, as Garrett was ending a tactful argument over the secure telephone with the commanding general of his higher headquarters, who was insisting on having another of the incessant demonstrations the "rubberneckers" from Washington wanted, Ames knocked on his office door, and entered.

"Jensen's ready to brief you, sir," the operations officer said.

Garrett took a fresh cigar from the box of Honduran Don Melos on his desk and followed Ames to the briefing room. The photograph of Ramirez and the map of El Salvador had been supplemented with operational diagrams and several sheets of butcher paper on which the advantages and disadvantages of several courses of action were compared. Garrett took his seat, and Sergeant Major Jensen began his briefing.

"Sir, the purpose of this briefing is to show you the courses of action we considered, and to recommend the one we feel—I feel—offers the greatest chance of success."

In the professional manner Wilton Garrett had come to expect from his subordinates, Matt Jensen outlined the possible courses of action for getting to Ramirez's location undetected, capturing him, and getting out. They had looked at infiltration by foot, by helicopter, and by parachute—including a low-level drop, and both techniques of high-altitude drop: HALO, or high-altitude, low-opening, whereby the team would free-fall to about two thousand feet above the ground before deploying their parachutes; and HAHO, or high-altitude, high-opening, whereby they would deploy their gliding-airfoil parachutes at high altitude and guide them to the selected landing zone several miles away.

"HAHO is the recommended course of action, sir," Jensen explained, "because it's the most difficult to detect from the ground. In fact, we can exit from a helicopter at ten thousand feet, along the normal flight corridor from San Salvador to Tegucigalpa. The chopper shouldn't draw any attention, but even if it does, it'll be well into Honduras before we land on the drop zone around ten minutes later. Also, we can make either the primary or alternate DZ on a HAHO drop. The only real disadvantage is that it's more weather-dependent than some of the other options, but we can use a combination helicopter and foot movement as the alternate means of infil, if the weather's bad."

9

He moved to the next chart, a rough drawing of the little settlement in which Ramirez was believed to be located, and its immediate surroundings.

"At the objective, I figure the number of men I will need to be eight, including me. Four—Dan Holton's team—will recon the objective to ensure that Valenzuela, or Ramirez, is there. They will then block the trail leading into the village as the other four of us—me, Olivera, Maxton, and Lawrence—move in and make the snatch. The primary pickup zone will be just outside the village, here." He indicated a level field just outside the collection of huts. Then he pointed out another small field just across a low ridge on the opposite side of the hamlet. "If there's any reason we can't use the primary, the alternate PZ will be here, just behind this little ridge. If that doesn't work, we'll evade back here to the alternate drop zone."

He laid aside the pointer he had been using, then continued. "For the pickup, I'd like to have a Blackhawk—two of them, actually; a primary, and a flying spare, which would carry a small reaction force. There are Blackhawks in Honduras now, on an exercise, and we can use them with our Nighthawk crews. There shouldn't be much problem in filtering in half a dozen crewmen and a six or eight man reaction force over the next few days."

Garrett interrupted Jensen's briefing to ask Jim Greer, his intelligence officer, "Do you see any problem covering them, Jim?"

"Not if we're smart about it, sir. Jerry Wells happens to be in Hondo at the moment. We can task him to set it up. He has a secure voice satellite radio with him, so we can pass him whatever instructions we want, whenever we need to."

"We'll have to look closely at how we do that one," Garrett remarked, then, to Matt Jensen, "Sorry to interrupt, Sergeant Major Jensen. Go on."

Jensen continued with the details of the plan, including a tentative timetable. Garrett was impressed with its simplicity, and the easily workable alternatives built into the plan. That was another advantage he had found in the plans devised by his subordinates. They were simple yet thorough, with flexibility as the means of dealing with the unexpected events which always occur on combat operations, instead of the innumerable and complex contingency plans which so many staff officers preferred.

Garrett said, "You realize, don't you, Ser'n Major, that if this was planned by JCS, there would be at least one Ranger battalion, two SEAL teams, and half the U.S. Air Force involved?"

"Yes, sir," Jensen replied with a grin. "That's why you asked me to plan it, isn't it, boss?"

For the rest of the evening, the handful of men worked on refinements to the plan. Their cloistering in the locked planning room didn't go unnoticed by the other members of the Delta Force, but those who had been assigned there any length of time were used to it. Strict compartmentation and the restraint of curiosity and rumor were, they knew, one of the reasons that most of their operations went unnoticed by the public, the press, and their adversaries. Still, an unusual number of them hung around the old stockade well after normal duty hours, cleaning their weapons and rechecking their gear, as they always did when their leaders were sequestered behind locked doors. All, of course, were hoping to be given some hint of a pending operation. But the only one who got such a hint that evening was Master Sergeant Dan Holton, when Matt Jensen, standing at the urinal next to him said, out of the earshot of the others, "Make sure your team has their shit together, Danny."

"Wilco, Matt," was Holton's reply.

2

Rachel Brown glanced at the dimly lit face of the alarm clock beside her bed before reaching for the telephone which had awakened her from a deep sleep. It was just after 1:00 A.M.

"Hello?"

"Hello, Rachel? Sorry to wake you."

"Don't be," the young woman answered, recognizing the voice of Major Greer, the intelligence officer of the Delta Force.

"You need to come on in. We need you to look at some records in D.C. tomorrow."

Look at some records, she thought. That meant a surveillance mission, in the open code Delta officers used when alerting members of the Administrative Detachment—the cover name for the small, highly selective team of women the unit maintained for certain operations.

"How long will I be gone?" she asked, wondering whether the suitcase she kept packed for such alerts contained enough of the right kinds of clothes.

"Just for the day," Major Greer answered. "All you'll need is a handbag. You'll be back tomorrow night—or tonight, actually."

"OK. I'll be there in about half an hour."

She hung up the telephone, switched on the light on her bedside table, and swung her shapely legs out from under the covers and onto the floor.

Damn. One o'clock in the morning. An all-day surveillance mission in Washington on two hours sleep would be tough. "But nobody said it would be easy," she muttered, echoing the phrase Delta Force members frequently used when faced with difficult tasks.

After two years in the elite force, Captain Rachel Brown was convinced that her assignment with Delta was the best thing that could ever have happened to her. It was exciting, satisfying work, and the men in the unit—most of them— had become like brothers to her. A few of them seemed unable to get over the fact that she was an attractive young woman and not one of their sisters, true. And she had wanted, several times, to forget not only that one or the other of them wasn't her brother, but wasn't an enlisted soldier, either. She had been getting romantically involved with one of them a few months after her arrival, when one of the female NCOs with whom she had become friends, had noticed.

"Ma'am," the other woman had said to her, "you and that hard-dicked sergeant are about to get each other into a situation where one, or both, of you is going to have to choose between love and duty."

Rachel had broken off the romance then, and the man had since been transferred, and she now confined her social affairs to dates and occasional romantic interludes with other officers from Fort Bragg, or civilian men she met at the clubhouse of Woodlake Country Club, the golf and boating resort just north of Fort Bragg where the small condominium she rented was located.

She walked out of the condominium and got into her Fiero for the twenty-minute drive to the old post stockade on Fort Bragg which Delta used as its headquarters.

When she arrived, Major Greer, tired and unshaven, explained to Rachel the mission she would have for about the next twenty hours.

"It's a simple countersurveillance job, Rachel, to make sure Major Ames isn't being tailed. You'll both be leaving on the seven o'clock Piedmont flight to Charlotte, where you'll change to the eight-ten flight to D.C., arriving around nine-fifteen. From there, you'll take the Metro to the White House. Dave'll be there, oh, probably about an hour or so.

After that, he should be coming back here. He's at home cleaning up and trying to get a little rest right now. He'll be back here about five, and you can get with him then on signals and all that."

"Is there any intel that makes you think he might be tailed?" she asked.

"No. We just want to be certain nobody's following him," Major Greer answered. He hesitated, then added, "We may have to send you overseas with him for a few days, Rachel."

It had been months since she had been given an overseas mission, and then it had been a simple courier mission to Britain. "Where will we be going?" she asked.

Greer smiled. "Afraid I can't say, right now, Rachel. And keep that under your hat. What he finds out at the White House will let us know whether or not you'll be going overseas. If so, though, it may be as early as tomorrow. Now, I'm going to grab a little sleep, unless you have any more questions."

"Just a couple," she said. "Do I need a weapon?"

"No, not for today."

"Cash advance?"

"Oh, sorry," the intelligence officer answered. "Pick it up from finance at five-thirty. We've already made your plane reservations. Buy your ticket at the counter. You're scheduled to come back on the flight that leaves D.C. about three-thirty this afternoon."

"OK, sir. That's all I need right now, I guess," she said, standing to leave his office. As she did, she noticed the map lying atop his desk. It was a map of El Salvador.

Eight hours later, she broke off her countersurveillance of Dave Ames at the southwest gate of the White House grounds. There had been no surveillance of him that she could detect, and even if there had, they would have lost anyone trying to follow him when he got off the Metro at Arlington Cemetery, as they had planned before leaving Fort Bragg. He was the only passenger who got off there. She had gotten off at Rosslyn, waited for the next blue line train, and boarded the second car. He scratched his right ear when he saw her, the signal for "no surveillance detected." She returned his signal.

Now, she had at least an hour to kill before he would be leaving the White House, so she walked down to Constitution Avenue and turned right toward the Vietnam Veterans Memorial. She went straight to the row of names that included her brother's and stared at it for several minutes. *Hello, Ted,* she said in her mind. He had been killed in Vietnam in 1970, when she was only twelve years old, and whenever she was in Washington, she made it a point to visit the memorial. She felt, each time that she stood there, that somehow she was in contact with him— that his spirit could somehow read her thoughts as she stared at his name. She had noticed other people seeming to do the same thing every time she visited the place. And each time, when she left that haunting monument, it was with a renewed sense of duty as an American soldier. She reached into her purse, pulled out a small American flag, and stuck the staff into the ground beneath her brother's name.

In the little briefing room in the west wing of the White House, Dave Ames was explaining to John Carruthers, the newly elevated National Security Advisor, the plan Delta had devised for capturing Emilio Ramirez from northern Morazan Province in El Salvador. The only other people in the room were the same National Security Council staffer and the same CIA representative who had been there when Ames received the initial mission. When Dave got to the exfiltration part of the plan—two Blackhawk helicopters flying from Honduras to pick up the Delta team and Ramirez—Carruthers squirmed in his chair and made a note on his pad. When the briefing was finished, the National Security Advisor looked at Major Ames.

"All right. I only see one major problem—the Blackhawks you want to bring out of Honduras. In the first place, Blackhawks in El Salvador would raise too many eyebrows. Anyway, we're not going to use Honduras to launch an operation into El Salvador. It would be a violation of their sovereignty, and there'd be hell to pay if they ever found out.

And there's no way we could ever risk getting their permission—the whole thing might be blown."

"Couldn't you use the same chopper for the pickup that drops the team in by parachute?" It was the CIA man, Harry Lawson.

"Well, Mr. Lawson," Dave Ames answered, "there are a couple of problems with that. First of all, the Huey helicopter's normal load is only eight people. The team, plus Ramirez, would make nine. And it would be awfully crowded, especially if we had anybody wounded. Then, there's the problem of a spare aircraft and the reaction force."

"Do you really need a reaction force?" Carruthers asked. "I mean, we really do need to keep this thing as small as possible. If your recon team finds out that there's too much security around Ramirez, we may decide to just abort the mission and try to pick him up later, somewhere else."

"Well, sir," Ames argued, "it would be awfully risky not to have some sort of reaction force available. I mean, the whole purpose of having the reaction force is to respond to the unexpected, and as soon as you think you can do without it, something will get fouled up, and you'll wish you had it."

"If I may, sir," interjected the Marine Corps lieutenant colonel from Carruthers's staff, "I'd like to say that I agree with Major Ames on the need for *some* sort of reaction capability, at least a spare aircraft. Don't forget what happened to Delta in the Iranian desert in 'eighty."

"Oh, don't get me wrong, Colonel Brewer. I wouldn't have any heartburn with an extra helicopter, as long as it came from El Salvador. But I want it limited to that. Can you live with that, Major Ames?"

"If Honduras is out, I don't suppose we have much choice," the Delta operations officer answered. "We can make do with using our own guys as door gunners on the choppers, I guess. At least that'll give us *some* reaction capability."

The four men continued to discuss details of the plan for another hour, determining what support would be required to get the operation underway. At five minutes to twelve, the NSC staff officer, Lieutenant Colonel Brewer, interrupted the conversation. "Mr. Carruthers, it's almost twelve o'clock."

The National Security Advisor looked at his watch, then stood. "Right. I'll be back in a few minutes, gents. Wait here for me."

Ten minutes later, he was back. Ames and Brewer stood when he entered, and Carruthers left them standing. Turning to Ames, he said, "All right. The operation is approved. But there are some things the President wants me to emphasize. First, we have to inform the chairmen and minority leaders of the Congressional Armed Services and Intelligence Committees." Ames and Brewer grimaced visibly, and Carruthers noticed. "Let me remind you of something, gentlemen! This Iran-contra thing isn't settled yet, and we're not going to give the administration's detractors another opportunity to run that sort of political circus again because they weren't informed of our activities. Now, you set it up for this afternoon, Colonel Brewer, and take Major Ames with you. Also, I want to be certain that we have secure communications open between here and your headquarters, Major, from the time you're ready to leave Fort Bragg until the operation is over. And I want to emphasize that this thing is to be kept as closely held as possible. I'll take care of informing the Sec Def and Chairman, JCS. And Harry, you go straight to the Director. Tell him that he's to inform only those people in the Agency who have a necessary part in the operation."

"When do you want us to execute, Mr. Carruthers?" Ames asked.

"As soon as you're ready."

"May I use a secure phone to let my boss know that, and tell him about the change in chopper support?"

"Certainly," Carruthers answered as he walked toward his office, adding, "And, Colonel Brewer, let me know right away what reaction you get from the people on the Hill."

While Brewer set up the meetings with the four senators and four congressmen who would have to be briefed, Ames got through to Colonel Garrett at Fort Bragg. As he passed his commander the information, he knew that within half an hour Matt Jensen would have the other eleven men who would take part in the mission with him in the isolation facilities of the Delta headquarters complex.

Brewer informed Dave Ames that their meetings on Capitol Hill to brief the necessary members of Congress were all between one-thirty and four, and asked him if he'd like to have lunch in the NSC mess. Ames declined, explaining that he was supposed to meet someone at the southwest gate. He would meet Brewer at the Horseshoe entrance of the Rayburn House Office Building at one-twenty, if that was all right. Brewer's secretary escorted him to the gate, and he spotted Rachel strolling along the street to the south. He walked toward her, scratching first his right ear, then his upper lip, which meant, "No surveillance detected. I need to talk to you."

He reached her and said, as they walked toward Constitution Avenue, "Change of plans. You go on back to the Ranch and tell Greer to brief you in. . . . How much do you know about this little op, Rachel?"

"Not much. Just that I'm supposed to cover your tail today, and that you and I may be going overseas for a while. . . . Are we?"

"Looks like it." He smiled. "It's going to be pretty quickly, too, so you need to get briefed in and start making the arrangements for us . . . wifey, dear."

" 'Wifey, dear?' Oh, shit!" she muttered. Recalling the map she had seen on Major Greer's desk that morning, she couldn't resist asking, "El Salvador?"

"That's it, sweetheart," he answered as he flagged down an approaching taxi for her. "Don't forget to pack a bikini to wear while we're lounging around the pool."

She flushed slightly, then, as the taxi stopped beside them, said to him, "Don't screw it up, Dave. This is serious business."

"You're right," he answered, opening the door of the taxi for her. "See you tonight. National Airport, please, driver."

A mission to El Salvador, posing as Dave Ames's wife, she thought, as the taxi pulled away. She contemplated it with a mixture of excitement and trepidation. Surely, it was something important—obviously a mission from the White House. And with Dave Ames, of all people—and posing as man and wife . . .

Dave Ames was one of the few Delta officers who was a bachelor—a handsome, athletic man who had a double reputation: in the Special Operations community, he was known as a capable, dedicated professional; in the social community, he was known as a "love 'em and leave 'em" ladies' man.

Rachel suddenly wished the mission called for her to work with someone else—someone married, or someone less, well, less *attractive.* Damn! For two years, she had watched him, noticing every time they were at a party or ran into each other in a bar, that he had a different woman with him, all of them gorgeous. And each time, she had felt a twinge of jealousy. They hadn't really had much work-related contact. He had been the commander of one of the teams in Detachment E-1, the ground operations element, while her work had been with the intelligence section, of which her cover unit, the Admin Detachment, was a part. Then he had gone off to the Armed Forces Staff College, until his return two months ago, when he had taken over the job of operations officer.

And now she was going off to El Salvador with him, posing as his wife. And sharing a hotel room.

"Don't forget to pack a bikini . . ." Why did he have to be so frivolous about it? Well, Major Dave Ames, you're going to find out what kind of professional Army officer *I* am, now.

At four-fifteen, Ames and Brewer shook hands with Representative Wesley Bolton, Chairman of the House Select Committee on Intelligence, the last of the members of Congress they had to brief on Operation Arctic Falcon. "Good luck," he wished Ames, as the two officers walked out of his office. Sticking his head into the office across the anteroom from his own, Bolton said to one of his staff members, "Charlotte, will you come in and take a memo, please?"

"Yes, sir," a dark-haired woman of about thirty answered, pushing herself away from her desk and picking up a steno pad. He was sitting behind his desk when she walked in.

"Close the door, please," he said. She did so, then turned and smiled at him. He stood and looked her slowly up and down. She reached down and grasped the hem of her floral-print silk dress, raising it up her legs, past the tops of her dark hose, held up by black lace garters, until he could see her bikini panties. He walked to her, and they embraced.

They kissed passionately, then she whispered into his ear, "Will I see you tonight, darling?"

"God, yes!" the congressman answered, squeezing her buttocks. "Do you think I could see *that*, and not have you tonight?"

She had learned several years earlier, when they had first become lovers, that he had a thing about garter belts and hose and lacy lingerie. He had bought such things for her frequently since then, and she wore them for him when he came to her Georgetown apartment to see her once or twice a week. They had managed, so far, to keep their clandestine affair a secret, although the members of his staff suspected there was more to their relationship than that of just a congressman and his Staff Assistant for Intelligence Matters. And some of his fellow lawmakers were aware, of course, that he, like a considerable number of them, had more-than-business relationships with members of their personal or committee staffs. But few of them had lovers as beautiful or as passionate as Charlotte Black.

"Eight o'clock?" she asked, humping herself gently against him and feeling his growing erection.

He kissed her on the cheek and released her. "A little later, I have to go to dinner at the Old Ebbitt with a constituent, first. Now, the business of the nation . . ."

He went to his chair, and she sat down on the sofa against the wall.

"Memorandum for the record," he began dictating. "Top secret."

A couple of minutes later, he had finished outlining the operation the two officers had described to him, concluding, "One copy only, in my personal safe when you've finished it."

She stood, walked to the door, then faced him and once more raised her dress so he could see her panties. "Nine-ish," she said as he stared at her crotch, then licked his lips and smiled broadly. She dropped her dress, opened the door, and walked out.

He was gone when she went in to lock the completed memo inside the safe in his office closet. She stayed at her desk until the other staff members left for the day, saying she would lock up once she finished the paper she was typing. When she was by herself, she took the ribbon cartridge from her typewriter and replaced it with a new one from her desk drawer. Then Charlotte Black dropped the other cartridge into her purse, locked the office door, and left.

3

Rachel picked up Dave Ames at the Fayetteville airport in her Fiero when he arrived from Washington just after 8:00 P.M. and drove him the fifteen miles to their headquarters on Fort Bragg. On the way there, she explained the arrangements she had made since she got back about five hours earlier.

"Major Greer gave me the full brief on Arctic Falcon," she said as she pulled away from the airport. "We leave tomorrow for New Orleans on different flights. We'll link up there, stay overnight, and fly direct to El Salvador on Taca early the next morning. The chopper pilots are leaving for Miami tomorrow, and on to El Sal the next morning, all except one of them, who's already there."

"Yeah," Ames interrupted, "John Rayburn. He's been down there a couple of weeks, training some Salvadoran pilots in night flying. He'll be a big help. . . . What else?"

"Jerry Wells is in Tegucigalpa. We got ahold of him and told him to leave Honduras for San Salvador right away to make arrangements for quarters, rental cars, and that sort of thing. He'll pick the pilots up and take care of them."

"What kind of cover are they going in under?"

"They're going as a helicopter maintenance team, on a no-notice maintenance inspection. Rayburn will arrange for them to inspect the choppers that are there to support the Milgroup and the embassy. They'll be taking the choppers out on test flights."

"What about Jensen's team?"

"Well, they haven't decided yet whether to infiltrate them in on commercial flights, or bring them in on the same aircraft that's going to take 'em all out, including Ramirez."

Ames was weighing the merits of having the eight men of Jensen's capture team filter in through the airport, versus landing them together in a single aircraft on some remote airstrip, when Rachel spoke again.

"Wouldn't it be better to bring them in together on the exfil airplane, sir?" she asked him. "I mean, we have to sneak their equipment in, anyway."

He looked at her. "Yeah. Good point. Anyway, that would be quicker, and they'd all be together to hash over the plan on the way in. And if we're going to be covered as man and wife, you might as well knock off the 'sir' bit now."

She glanced over at him and smiled. "Oh, there's one other change. We're going as brother and sister. David and Frances Ames. They want you to use your true name in case you run into someone you know, and since you have a sister named Frances, and no wife, it'll be a more plausible cover."

"Sister? Hell, you don't look anything *like* Fran. I mean, we don't look like brother and sister. We don't even *talk* alike."

"Well, David, I guess you'll just have to try talking like a Southerner. I mean, there's no way I could ever fake that Yankee accent of yours."

He scowled at her, and she added, "Anyway, if we were going as a married couple, we'd have to share one hotel room. This way, we can use two rooms. More space to plan, have meetings, and so forth."

"Yeah, well . . . what about comms?"

"Jerry Wells is hauling a satellite radio from Honduras, and Jensen's team will bring us a spare. I'll have a KL-43 encryption device for a backup."

"What about the team?"

"They'll be using PRC-117s both for ground-to-air and within the team. We'll have one also, of course."

For the remainder of the trip to the stockade, she gave him additional details which had been worked out in his absence. Just before they pulled in through the gate, she said, "Oh, there's one thing I said that isn't really true. We *are* going in as a married couple. I was just kidding with the brother and sister bit."

At the same time Dave Ames and Rachel Brown were pulling into the Delta compound, Congressman Wes Bolton was ringing the doorbell of Charlotte Black's Georgetown apartment. She came to the door wearing a long, dark blue robe, and let him in.

She kissed him lightly, then helped him out of his trench coat.

"I didn't expect you this early," she said, hanging his coat on a hook behind the door.

He held her by the shoulders, kissed her on the neck, and whispered, "I couldn't wait any longer. Told the guy I had another appointment. Now, how 'bout a drink?"

She walked to her side bar and poured him a large shot of Chivas Regal scotch and an equal amount of club soda, dropped in two ice cubes, and handed it to him. He loosened his tie and sat on the couch, motioning Charlotte to sit down beside him.

He took a long drink of the scotch and soda. "Ahhh. Good stuff. I need that after fighting those bastards from the Senate all day."

She stroked the back of his neck with the fingers of one hand after pulling her legs up under her and leaning against him. "On the Iran arms sales hearings?" she asked.

"Yeah. The joint committee rules. They're trying to limit our questioning time to almost nothing." He took another long drink and rested his hand on her stockinged thigh. "Do you realize how much exposure those hearings are going to get? I mean, the whole damn *country* will be watching us fry those White House bastards."

"Do you really think there's that much to it all?" she asked with interest.

"Well, it sure looks like it. It doesn't really matter what their *intentions* were. The fact is that they got caught. Now, the whole question is, 'How much political mileage can we get out of it?'"

"Wouldn't it be better to try to delay it a while longer? If you've really got something on the Republicans, it would make sense to wait until as close to next year's elections as possible to make a fuss about it."

"Oh, I don't know. If we wait too long, they'll find some way to defuse it. Anyway, we may be able to make something as big as Watergate out of it. I mean, if we can catch the President with his pants down—especially if we can catch him in a lie—then we have a whole year to make hay out of it. No Republican would have a chance at winning the presidency for at least eight years."

He drained his glass and put it down. "But enough of politics," he said, pulling her against his chest and reaching inside her robe. "Let's concentrate on that lovely thing you flashed at me in my office this afternoon."

The telephone rang, and she broke away from him, got up, walked across the room, and answered it.

"Hello? . . . Thank you, but I'm not really interested. Good-bye."

She hung up the phone and turned back to him. "Salesmen!" she said. "You should pass a law making them illegal."

"Isn't your number unlisted?" he asked.

"Well, yes. I guess they just dial numbers randomly, or something." She let her gown fall open at the front, revealing a flimsy, white bra encasing her ample breasts, and a matching garter belt holding up flesh-colored stockings. She was wearing no panties. She let one hand fall to her pubic hair and stroked herself gently as he watched her. She crooked the index finger of her other hand and beckoned him to follow as she disappeared into the bedroom.

He followed her, undressed quickly, and got onto the bed where she lay waiting. But she was unresponsive as he kissed and fondled her. "What's wrong?"

"Oh, I don't know," she said, sitting up and leaning against the headboard. "I guess I'm just a little concerned about that last memo you had me type today."

"Why?"

"Oh, never mind. It's really none of my business, anyway."

"Of course it is, sweetheart. Hell, you're my Intelligence Committee staffer. But I don't understand what's bothering you."

"I'm just concerned about *you*. I mean, you've been informed that they're going to go into El Salvador and capture some guy. Suppose something happens and it gets all fouled up. Won't you get blamed for it, too?"

He laughed. "Of course not, honey. Don't you remember, the last line of the memo said something about me expressing my opinion that I thought it was ill-advised, and a possible violation of El Salvadoran sovereignty?"

"Well, yes, but . . ."

"But what? Look, if it goes wrong, I can use the memo to prove that I was against it in the first place. Don't forget, the administration isn't asking our *permission* when they inform us of these covert operations. They're just *informing* us. Now, stop worrying about it. My ass is covered."

He pulled her toward him, but she resisted.

"Well, who's this guy they're going after, anyway? All you said was 'a fugitive American,' in the memo."

He chuckled and tugged at one of her nipples. "Why? Are you writing an exposé on covert operations or something?"

"Ow! That hurts, Wes. . . . No, I was just curious, that's all. After all, aren't women supposed to be curious?"

"If I tell you, will you sit on my face?" he asked jokingly.

She laughed and grabbed his ears. "I'll sit on your face anyway. But if you tell me, I'll sit on it *longer!*"

"And harder?"

She yanked his ears. "Silly boy."

"OK. He's some guy named Ramirez who defected to the communists in Vietnam. *Now* will you?"

"Vietnam? Then what's he doing in El Salvador?"

"Oh, he went to Cuba after Vietnam. Since then, he's been helping Latin American revolutionaries. . . . *Now* will you?" the congressman pleaded.

"Now!" She smiled, pushing him onto his back and straddling him.

Colonel Wilton Garrett stood watching Sergeant Major Matt Jensen and the seven men who were going after Ramirez with him, carefully packing their MT-1X airfoil parachutes. They had already tested their weapons and communications equipment and were nearly ready for the rehearsal they would conduct that night in the Uwharrie National Forest some fifty miles west of Fort Bragg. Rigging the big, camouflage-colored 'chutes under which they would glide the eight or ten miles from their exit point ten thousand feet above the forest, to their intended landing site, was the last thing they had to do before boarding the helicopter for the rehearsal jump.

Watching them, Garrett wished he was one of their small team. He and Jensen were about the same age, but in his position as the commander of the Delta Force, his responsibilities kept him from taking part in small unit operations such as the one for which his men were now preparing. It wasn't that he thought he could do a better job than they, or that he lacked confidence in their ability. It was just that he hated to miss the excitement of it—the thrill of going on a combat operation again, his senses all alert and concentrated on the undescribably satisfying task of pitting all of one's skills and training against an armed enemy, and the elements, in a strange and distant place. He hadn't experienced that feeling since he had led a Provincial Reconnaissance Unit in Vietnam nearly two decades earlier. His mission had been to eliminate the Vietcong leadership in villages where the control was disputed. He winced at the thought of the last time he had done so, when he burst into the communist cadre chief's house in a village in the Mekong Delta, killing the startled enemy leader with a pistol from five feet away as the VC made a desperate attempt to reach his own weapon. The killing was the only part he hated, the only negative part of his profession. The rest of it—the physical and mental challenges, the danger, the risking of one's life for the high principle of fighting an armed enemy whose goals were evil—that was the satisfying part. But the killing. It always left a festering scar of doubt. He hoped Jensen and his team would be able to pull off Ramirez's capture without anyone dying.

Garrett's intel officer, Jim Greer, hurried up to him. "Dave's back, sir. And we've decided, if you and Sergeant Major Jensen agree, to infil the team into El Salvador on the same Twin Otter that's going to bring them out."

Jensen, overhearing Greer, stopped stowing the suspension lines of his parachute. "Where's the Twin Otter coming from, sir?" he asked.

"We're contracting for it out of Miami. Munson will be flying it, with Jorge as his copilot."

"Sounds good to me," the team leader said, and returned to finish the parachute packing task he had nearly completed.

Bud Munson was an aging, highly experienced pilot who had retired from the Army several years earlier, and was ostensibly employed part-time as a flying instructor at the

Fort Bragg flying club. In actuality, he was on Delta's payroll, flying missions for them in a variety of aircraft he was able to lease all over the world. Jorge Peña, whose normal duty was an intelligence analyst in Major Greer's section, had civilian pilot's licenses for a variety of aircraft. Munson had been training him in night flying, expedient airstrip landings, and other special operations flying techniques for nearly a year now.

"Have they selected an airstrip yet, sir?" Jensen asked as he inserted the ripcord pins to close his parachute container.

"Tentatively. I'll show you on the map when you've got time. Jerry Wells will check them out when he gets there, and let us know if they're suitable for the Twin Otter. Dave and Rachel will light them for the infil and meet you there when you land."

Garrett looked at his intel section chief and gave him a mischievous grin. "You sure those two won't forget they're on an operation, and end up seasoning their cover in a hotel bed instead of supporting Jensen and his guys? You know how Ames is. . . ."

Greer laughed. "Yes, sir, but I know Rachel, too. Her biggest problem will probably be keeping him from running off with one of those Salvadoran señoritas."

Jensen laid his packed parachute aside and called to the other members of his team who were still packing theirs, "All right, men, let's get 'em finished up. Load time in twenty minutes." Turning to Greer, he asked, "Is the rehearsal site all set up in Uwharrie, sir?"

"All set, Matt. Captain Brown will play the in-country base radio station from here, so be sure to pass your reports through her. Now, let's go look at those proposed LZs."

As Greer and Jensen examined the map of El Salvador, Charlotte Black, three hundred miles away in Washington, D.C., was kissing Representative Wesley Bolton good night. As soon as he left, she went to the telephone, dialed a number, and when she got an answer, said, "How 'bout some seafood?"

The voice on the other end said, "Bouillabaisse sounds good to me."

"Fine," Charlotte replied. "In half an hour." Then she hung up the telephone and walked back into her bedroom, where she knelt beside her bed. Reaching beneath it, she pulled out a small tape recorder, turned it off, and removed the tape cassette. She placed it in her purse with the typewriter ribbon she had removed from her office that afternoon. Then she showered quickly, dressed, and left her apartment to rendezvous with her case officer.

Jensen's team's rehearsal of their mission went very well that night—too well, he felt. He knew from experience that something unexpected always seemed to crop up on actual operations, and he was worried that they might have missed some potential weakness in the plan. He wished he had more time, so that they could conduct additional rehearsals and insert problems into the mission which might expose any weaknesses in their plan. But there wasn't time. They were leaving in less than twelve hours for Boca Chica Naval Air Station, near Key West, to meet Munson and Peña, who would fly the chartered Twin Otter there to pick them up for the flight into El Salvador.

4

Rachel was waiting at the airport in New Orleans when Dave Ames arrived early the next afternoon. She had already confirmed the reservations with Taca Airlines for their flight the next morning to Comayagua, El Salvador's international airport. While Dave picked up his checked luggage, she went to a telephone and dialed the number of a telephone in Columbia, South Carolina. It was automatically forwarded to the open line in Delta's situation room, where Jim Greer answered it with an innocuous, "Good afternoon. What can I do for you?"

"This is Loretta," Rachel replied. "Any messages for me?"

"No, but why don't you call back this evening?" Greer said, letting her know that all was on schedule, and she could wait until she and Ames had checked into their motel room before making radio contact with Delta's base radio station.

"OK. Thanks," she said, and hung up the telephone.

After Dave claimed his luggage, they took a courtesy van to their motel and checked in as Mr. and Mrs. Dave Ames. As soon as they were in the room, Dave kicked off his shoes and flopped down on one of the twin beds.

"I'm beat," he said. "If you don't mind, I'm going to try to get a couple of hours sleep. If I'm not up by six o'clock, give me a shout, will you?"

"Sure," Rachel replied. Lifting what looked like a lap-top personal computer out of its case and laying it on the other bed, she added, "I'll see if I can get this radio up with the base station, then I'm going to take a nap, too." She plugged the power cord into a wall socket, then laid a Walkman cassette player next to it, and ran a short piece of wire from it to the computer. Next, she opened a small, collapsible umbrella and connected a wire from its tip to another socket in the computer. The umbrella was actually a satellite antenna, and referring to the button compass on her charm bracelet, she oriented it toward the communications satellite twenty-two thousand miles above. Placing the Walkman earphones on her head, she spoke into the tiny hole on the bottom of the cassette player while depressing the back space key on the computer keyboard. She heard the beep of the built-in encryption device, then said, "Juliet Three Three, this is Juliet Five Four, over."

Almost immediately, she heard another beep and a reply

in her earphones, "Juliet Five Four, this is Juliet Three Three, loud and clear."

"This is Five Four. Any traffic for me?"

"Three Three. Wait, out."

Ames was watching her. "Damn thing actually works, huh?"

She smiled. "So far, anyway. I just hope I don't lose this umbrella, like I usually do."

Leaning up on one elbow, Ames asked, "Can you actually *use* it like a real umbrella?"

"Sure," she said, then heard her callsign over the earphones and replied, "This is Five Four. Go ahead."

"This is Three Three,"—it was Jim Greer's voice—"everything's on schedule. The team's on the way to link up with the infil bird, and Wells is in place. He'll pick you up at the airport and take you to the El Presidente Hotel, after he gets the pilots squared away. I've got the LZ coordinates and times for the Twin Otter, if you're ready to copy."

She pulled a notebook and felt tip pen from the computer carrying case, and replied, "This is Five Four, ready to copy."

Greer passed her the map coordinates of the primary and alternate landing zones which Wells had examined and confirmed as the best of those the Twin Otter pilot, Bud Munson, had selected from available maps and overhead photographs. He gave her the landing direction and times for each, and she read the numbers back to Greer to confirm them. Then she passed him the telephone number and extension of their motel room, so that he could call her from Fort Bragg and get her up on the radio if any more information she and Ames needed came in that night. That done, she disassembled the cleverly disguised radio, while Ames located the coordinates of the landing zones on his map.

"The primary is on the highway between the airport and San Salvador," he remarked. "And the alternate's on this secondary road a few miles from there."

Rachel took the map from him and examined the two

locations. Each was on a straight stretch of road just a few hundred meters long—but long enough for the skillful Munson to land the twin-engined, sixteen-passenger infiltration aircraft.

"What about surveillance on them?" she asked. It was standard procedure, she had learned, to place such landing zones and drop zones under surveillance for a full day before bringing an aircraft in, if at all possible.

"Well, we talked about it before I left. We won't be able to watch them for a full twenty-four hours, but since we can't travel the roads at night anyway, we'll have to get into position before dark. That'll give us a few hours to watch the LZs before the Otter shows up, at least. We can keep an eye on the primary, and let Wells man the alternate."

She handed him the map back. "It's awfully rushed, isn't it?"

"Yeah, it is. But we've got to get to Ramirez while we know he's still there. And the less time we have people in El Sal, the better. Now, I'm going to get a little sleep."

"Here," she said, taking a small envelope from her purse and removing two gold wedding bands. "Put this on first." She tossed the larger ring to him, and slipped the other onto her ring finger.

There was no new information for her when she radioed the base station after waking Ames at six o'clock. They had supper in the motel restaurant, then returned to their room to go over their part of the plan once more.

Meanwhile, Jensen and the members of his team were doing the same thing in one of their rooms at the Quality Inn in Key West. And in San Salvador, Jerry Wells and Chief Warrant Officer John Rayburn, the helicopter pilot who, on another mission had gone to El Salvador two weeks earlier, were receiving the details of the operation from the "maintenance inspection team" they had picked up from the airport earlier in the day.

"Won't it be unusual for you guys to be out doing test flights at night?" Jerry Wells asked the elite team of helicopter pilots.

"Oh, no. Not at all," Rayburn answered with confidence.

"That's about the only time the Milgroup choppers are available, anyway. And the Salvadoran Air Force guys are used to me flying at night by now. In fact, almost all of my flying has been at night since I got here."

At the Soviet Embassy in Managua, Nicaragua, the head of the KGB section there finished reading a lengthy cable from Moscow, which he had been called back to his office to read. He read it once more, then reached for his telephone and, from memory, dialed the number of his counterpart at the Cuban Embassy.

Raul Valenzuela was tired of his current assignment as a demolitions instructor for the Salvadoran communist rebels in northern Morazan Province. They were generally an illiterate bunch of disgruntled peasants whose main motivation seemed to be less one of revolutionary fervor than of avoiding the difficult work of cultivating coffee and vegetables from their meager plots of land. Well, in two more days, he could head back to Nicaragua for his meeting with Hakim Nidal. He looked at the dial of his day/date wristwatch to confirm the date, as he found himself doing frequently, of late. Yes. Fourteen days. Two short weeks, and he would make history. All around the world, he would be famous—and not just among the oppressed peoples of Latin America and the Middle East and the ghettos of American cities—but everywhere. *Everywhere!*

A thrill coursed through him as he imagined the results of his brilliant scheme. The awe and respect he would command in the following months and years—indeed, for the rest of his *life*—would be assured, as would his place in the history of revolutionary movements. There was still some work to be done, some last minute preparations and communiqués which would ensure that the credit for his monumental deed would be his, and his alone. Nidal would see to that. Nidal, whose contacts with revolutionaries all over the world would be energized to make the name of Emilio Ramirez one of the best known and most feared of all time, was to meet him in Managua in one week. From there, they would fly to Libya to await the earthshaking effect of his bold, unprecedented act. He tried to imagine the coming moment of his triumph, the awe that the likes of Qaddafi and Arafat, and even Gorbachev and Reagan would hold him in. He laughed aloud at the thought of the American President realizing what had happened—at his helplessness and panic and confusion.

The young Salvadoran revolutionary who was driving Ramirez to the village where he stayed at night looked at him with a mixture of curiosity and fear when he laughed. Ramirez clapped the young man's shoulder and said, "Hey, amigo. I was just thinking about the coming birth of my son. What should I name him? Eh? How about Sandino Salvatore Fidel Yassir Lenin-Marx? A bit too long, eh? Then, how about *Bol del Fuego*—Fireball, as they say in English. Fireball Ramirez. I like that." Again, he laughed aloud at his private joke, as the driver pulled the battered Jeep Wagoneer off the bumpy dirt road and stopped at the small, concrete block house where Ramirez's pregnant Nicaraguan girlfriend, Nadia, waited in the doorway.

The driver told Ramirez that he would pick him up at sunrise the next morning for the trip back to the training site. If Ramirez needed him, he would be at his cousin's house—the next to last one at the far end of the little village. Then he drove away.

Ramirez hugged his woman gently, then patted her belly. "How has the little one behaved today?" he asked. "Has he been kicking away at you again?"

"Yes, he has," she said. "I hope he can wait until we get home to Managua. But come in and sit down, my love. You look very tired." She led him into the house, and he sat at the rough wooden table of the one-room adobe dwelling. She poured him a shot of rum from the large bottle he had brought with him from Nicaragua, then sat down across from him. He took a swallow of it and looked around the room.

"Just two more days of this, my heart, and I'll take you back home. To running water and electricity and our big, soft bed." He had wanted to leave her in Managua when he came to El Salvador two weeks earlier to teach the demolitions course for which he was now well known throughout the revolutionary movements of Latin America, but she had insisted on coming along to care for him. It was not, he knew, that she feared he might take up with some other woman in her absence. But she worshipped him, and had shown many times that she would rather put up with the hardships of primitive life in the guerrilla camps and backcountry hamlets than be away from him. Even during the last five months, since she was certain that she was bearing his child, she had been with him whenever she could. He took her hand in his and caressed it softly.

"Soon, my precious woman, we'll be able to stop this running here and there. We can settle down in a comfortable house, and you can raise our son knowing that he and you will always have whatever you need."

He had been making such remarks ever since they had returned from their clandestine trip to the United States several months earlier. She still hadn't been able to figure out what he had done there that made him speak of the future in such optimistic terms, and she would never ask. But it must have been some important mission for which he felt the Sandinistas or the Cubans were going to reward him richly in the near future. Or perhaps it was something he had done for the Arabs; something for which Nidal was going to pay him when he came back to Nicaragua in the near future, as Emilio had mentioned he would.

The child in her belly stirred, and she placed her hand against her abdomen, then went to the side table to prepare her man the meager meal they would share before going to their narrow, hard bed. She would be happy to be back in Managua in just a few more days.

Jerry Wells was waiting for Dave and Rachel when they cleared customs in Comayagua Airport at noon the next day. As they left the parking lot in the car he had rented for them, he handed Dave a sports bag which contained two Heckler & Koch P-13, 9mm automatic pistols and accessories. Dave took them out, cleared them and tested their actions, then handed one of the weapons and two loaded, 13-round magazines to Rachel. She loaded the weapon with easy familiarity, then placed it and the spare magazine in her purse. Dave strapped on the ankle holster Wells had included and inserted the pistol. There was a small, hand-held radio in the bag as well, and a spare battery for it.

"It's already encoded for the operation. I have one, Rayburn has one, and Jensen and the Twin Otter pilot will have ones on the same code and frequency, too," Wells said.

Ames handed the radio to Rachel, who asked, "What's the alternate frequency?"

"Channel Bravo," Wells replied.

He drove them quickly away from the airport near the coast and up the road toward the city of San Salvador, thirty-five miles away. Just before they began the long climb up the hills toward the capital, they hit a long, broad stretch of road. As he was about to speak, Rachel said, "This is the primary landing zone, isn't it, Jerry?"

"Yes," he replied, slowing the rented Volkswagen van. "And this road just up here is the one to the alternate." He turned off on a road to the east which led away at a right angle from the main road they had traveled since leaving the airport. "It isn't nearly as good a landing zone as the primary, but at least it's a little more isolated." About two miles down the winding side road, they entered a straight stretch which ran for several hundred meters, with a grass-covered field on one side.

"This is it, isn't it?" Ames asked. He had been following their progress on the map stretched out on his knees in the back seat.

"Yes, sir," Wells replied, driving to the end of the straight stretch and turning around. "Do you need to stop and have a look?" he asked.

"No, but you're going to man this one, Jerry," Ames replied. "Rachel and I will man the primary. If something gets fouled up there, they'll come in here instead, forty minutes later. Unless there's something to prevent us from doing so—if we get spotted, for example—that'll give us plenty of time to get from the primary to here. But you need to be here, in case we can't make it."

"Anyway, it'll be good to have somebody here keeping surveillance on the place as long as possible," Rachel added.

"That reminds me," Dave said, reaching into the back of the van and pulling out a cigarette carton from the side pocket of his suitcase. He showed it to Wells, then laid it on the seat beside him. "There are some infrared lights and a pocketscope in here for you to use when you get back here tonight."

"Right," Wells said, then speeded up. "We need to get going, get you guys checked in to the El Presidente, and see if there's anything more from headquarters. I have to get out to Ilopango Air Base and make sure the chopper crews are all set to go tonight, then get back out here before dark. I'll leave this VW for you. I've got a Datsun at the hotel that I'll take tonight."

As they turned right back onto the main road to San Salvador, Ames noticed several places where he and Rachel could pull the van off the road and out of sight until they were ready to mark the landing zone for the Twin Otter to land later that night. He checked his watch. They would be landing, if all went as planned, in less than twelve hours. The chopper would land fifty minutes after that, and head for northern Morazan, climbing as it went. It should reach the release point about fifty minutes later, where Jensen would exit with his team right behind him, then open and steer their parachutes the eight miles or so to their intended landing point. They would move into position around the little mountain hamlet, observe it during the day, then move in to snatch Ramirez in the middle of the night, once they knew the choppers were on the way in to pick them up. Damn, he hoped there wouldn't be any problems they hadn't foreseen.

At Boca Chica Naval Air Station, Matt Jensen's men were loading their parachutes, weapons, and other equipment into the Twin Otter, as Bud Munson went over the details of the route and timings with Matt. "We won't have quite as much fuel as I'd like to have, if we go to the alternate," Munson was saying, "but if worst comes to worst, I'll just drop down to Comayagua straight from the LZ, instead of flying out to sea first and coming in on my filed flight plan. The air traffic controllers there probably wouldn't notice where I came from. Anyway, it won't effect you guys, unless we have to abort at both LZs." He looked at Jensen's face and smiled. "And in that case, we'll just have to let our charm and bullshit carry the day."

Jensen grinned at his pilot friend. "My charm, your bullshit."

"OK," Munson said. "Let's get this thing cranked up and head for Fame and Glory."

Jensen checked his watch as he and several others relieved their bladders before the long, slow flight. It was 2110 zulu time; 4:10 P.M. Eastern Standard—eight hours before their scheduled landing in El Salvador.

Chief Warrant Officer John Rayburn, the Huey helicopter pilot, walked into the little office of Lieutenant Colonel Billy Baer, U.S. Air Force, at the home of the El Salvadoran Air Force, Ilopango Air Base. There was an American Army captain with Rayburn, and he introduced the two men. "Sir, he said to Baer, "this here is Captain Doug Flannery." Then, as Flannery held out his hand to the Air Force officer, Rayburn added, "Colonel Baer is the air attaché."

The two men shook hands, as Rayburn continued, "Captain Flannery is the head of that mean ol' maintenance team I told you was coming from Southcom to inspect our choppers, sir."

"We'll try not to interrupt anything, Colonel," Flannery said. "We just want to make a few test flights in the Milgroup Hueys. In fact, since they're so busy doing the embassy's work, we thought we'd try to get the flights in at night. That way, we won't interfere with their regular flights."

"Yeah, that'll help keep the Milgroup commander off my ass," the Air Force lieutenant colonel said. "But I'll have to clear it with the Salvadorans. They're not likely to have any objection to it, though. Most of 'em don't like to fly at night, themselves, but they won't mind if you do, as long as it doesn't mean a lot of them have to hang around here while you're out flying."

"That's no problem, sir," Rayburn interjected. "I've already checked with Captain Alvarez, and all we'll need is one guy in the tower, and a fuel handler—and they were scheduled to be here anyway for the night training I was going to give 'em."

The Air Force officer peered up at Rayburn from behind his desk. "What do you mean, 'was going to give them'?"

"Oh, I thought it would be best if I flew with Captain Flannery and his people, sir. You know, to avoid any navigation problems and that sort of thing."

"What about the night training?"

"Alvarez and his guys are glad to have a break, sir. I've been pushing them pretty hard, and they're not real happy about all this night flying, anyhow."

"Well, all right," the air attaché agreed. "But get this inspection done and get back to training these guys, whether they like it or not, Mister Rayburn."

"Oh, one other thing, Colonel," Flannery added. "We're going to add a hoist to one of the Hueys while we're here, for an emergency medevac capability."

"OK. Just make sure the Milgroup crews know how to *use* the damn thing, before you leave. Anything else?"

"No, sir. Thanks for your help, Colonel. We'll try to be as little bother as possible, and get out of your hair in a couple of days."

"That was easy," Flannery said to Rayburn as they left the air attaché's office. "Now, let's get that hoist installed and get some chow."

Dave Ames ordered an early dinner from room service for Rachel and himself, while she set up the radio for one last contact with Fort Bragg before they left for the landing zone. The message was the same as it had been during her last contact with the base station. "Constantinople"—all elements of the plan were proceeding on schedule. "Roger," she replied to the operator on the other end, then added the code word which indicated that everything there was on schedule, as well. "Chinatown, Chinatown, over."

"Roger, out."

While Rachel disassembled the satellite-link radio, Dave went to the television set which had been blaring in the background as a security measure in the event their room was bugged for sound. There was a knock on the door, and Rachel went to the peephole and looked out. It was the room service waiter with their meal. Behind him, she noticed another man walking slowly past, glancing toward the door.

"I'll get it," Dave said, and opened the door as Rachel stood back. The waiter wheeled in the dinner cart, and through the open door, Rachel noticed the man she had seen through the peephole walk past again, glancing into the room as he did so.

As Dave signed the check, the waiter opened the bottle of wine he had ordered with their dinner. Then Dave handed him the check and a generous tip, and the waiter left. Rachel went back to the television and turned it on, as Dave poured a swallow of wine into each of their glasses.

"What a waste," he commented, as he took the bottle into the bathroom. He poured the remaining wine into the toilet and flushed it down, wondering if Rachel would be willing to share a bottle with him *after* the mission. He had ordered the wine to avoid any suspicion about a newlywed couple having a dinner without wine. But they wouldn't drink it. They would have a swallow, and that was all. When he came out of the bathroom, he found Rachel looking into the hall through the peephole.

"Problem?" he asked.

She moved close to him and whispered, "Maybe. There was a guy out there peering in when the waiter came in, but I don't see him now."

"Maybe just hotel security," Dave said.

"Maybe," she replied. "But we'd better pull a surveillance detection act after we have dinner, just to be sure."

Dave picked up the wineglasses and handed one to his

fellow Army officer. Holding the glass up, he smiled and said, "You do good work, Mrs. Ames."

She returned his smile, clinked her wineglass to his, and said, "We'll see. *Salud.*"

5

Emilio Ramirez surveyed the young revolutionaries seated before him under the low coffee bushes which shaded them from the hot afternoon sun. They had been fairly good students during the two-week demolitions course he had just finished teaching them, especially with the emplacement of booby traps and the construction of homemade antipersonnel mines. Their only weak area had been in the calculation of charges—the determination of the amount of explosives necessary to cut steel girders, wood bridge supports, and the like. But that was no surprise, as only about half of them were literate. So he had told them to do one of two things when preparing their charges; either leave the calculations to one of their comrades who was good at mathematics, or use the same method he had learned as a Green Beret demolitionist at Fort Bragg nearly two decades earlier—the "P for plenty" method.

It was all very basic stuff, actually—nothing like the course reserved for the more talented, well-educated students he taught in Managua and occasionally in Havana. There, he went into the employment of radio-controlled bombs, long-term digital timers, barometrically actuated firing devices and other such sophisticated techniques. He was a master of innovation in the field of demolitions, and his expertise was being sought with increasing frequency by Libyans, Lebanese, Iranians, and even the IRA and KGB.

He looked at his watch, and thought, *But, in less than two weeks, they will learn what a master I really am!* Then he turned his attention to the group before him, and began his final lecture to them.

"Congratulations, comrades. You have completed the training in a skill which, if applied with courage, persistence, and aggressiveness, can lead to the fall of the Yanqui imperialist puppet Duarte, and his oppressive military henchmen, and the return of El Salvador to her rightful stewards, the people."

It didn't take Rachel and Dave long to discover that the middle-aged man she had seen in the hallway was, in fact, tailing them. After they finished their dinner, they strolled into the lobby and out past the swimming pool to the gardens beyond it. They held hands as they walked, and once, as they wandered among the tropical vines and banana trees, Dave turned, took her in his arms, and kissed her on the neck as he used the opportunity to look over his shoulder toward the corner they had just turned. She knew that it was just a technique to enable him to look behind them, but found a sensual thrill run through her as they embraced.

"Yep," he whispered in her ear as he saw the man turn the corner and pretend to take an interest in the flowers blooming beside the path. "There the bastard is." He kissed her then, pretending not to notice the man who now turned away and took another path.

Dave led her back into the hotel, through the lobby, and out to the front door. Then he stopped, smiled at her, and said, "Excuse me a moment, darling. I'll be right back." He turned and went back to the men's room, noticing with his peripheral vision that the man was standing across the lobby now, looking at a painting on the wall. Dave tried to notice if he had an accomplice, but saw none. Rachel, however, spotted the other man almost immediately—a younger man, who sauntered diagonally to a chair behind her and sat down, studiously avoiding looking at her as he passed. To confirm her suspicion, she stood and walked over to the huge windows which faced out toward the entrance of the hotel. In their reflection, she could see the man looking at her, then glancing back toward the older man she had seen earlier. She turned and walked past him, sliding her fingers into the top of her blouse as if gently scratching the sloping curve of her breast, and swaying her hips seductively. The young man pretended not to notice her, and she thought, *Sure, you Latin spook. I'm supposed to believe you're the only son of a bitch south of San Francisco who wouldn't notice a sexy broad strutting past.*

Dave came out of the men's room and joined her, and they walked out of the front doors of the hotel and turned left toward the entrance road which led up to the hotel from the city below. They walked across the parking lot toward the huge sculpture at the entrance to the hotel driveway, noticing in the reflection of the car windows they passed that the older man was behind them. Without looking at Dave, Rachel muttered, "There's another one with him. Tall, with jeans and a flowered shirt on."

Dave pulled a coin from his pocket and dropped it on the ground, then turned and stooped to pick it up. He saw the second man standing at a car with the door open, apparently waiting to get in and follow them in the event they had a car in the parking lot. "Got 'im."

They walked on toward the sculpture, and Rachel said, "You think they might try to hit us?"

"Nah," Major Ames answered. "Just a third-rate surveillance team. May even just be Salvadoran government . . . OK, here's what we'll do. Walk to the sculpture, admire it for a while, then embrace like we're horny and can't wait to get back to our room. Then we'll give Jerry a call and see if he can help us shake 'em. Got it?"

"Right," Captain Brown answered.

In their hotel room, Dave went straight to the television and turned it on, then took the little radio Wells had given him earlier.

"Wait a second," Rachel said. She went to the closet and pulled out the computer case which held the satellite radio, noticing before she moved it that the strand of hair she had laid across the top of the case was still there, indicating that it had not been disturbed. From it she pulled out the small cassette player, and placed a tape cassette in it. Placing it on a chair near the door, she turned to Dave and said, "Check *this* out," then turned it on. In a few seconds, it began to emanate the sounds of a couple loudly and uninhibitedly making love.

"I won't ask where you got *that,*" Ames muttered.

She grinned. "Nothing to it. We just bugged your bedroom," she joked.

He raised Wells on the radio and told him about the men tailing them.

"No sweat," the counterintelligence officer answered. "I have a contingency plan that'll cover it. You can get to the Sheraton, can't you?"

"Roger," Ames answered into the radio, "that's where I stayed last time I was down here."

"OK," Wells said, "here's the plan. . . ."

"Got it," Ames transmitted when Wells had finished. "See you shortly."

Rachel walked to the recorder, turned it off, and placed it back into the case with the radio, then shoved a pair of jeans, a sweatshirt, and running shoes into the athletic bag which contained the similar clothes that Dave had placed in it.

"Ready?" he asked, placing the hand-held radio on top of the clothes and zipping the bag up.

"Ready."

They walked down to the lobby, where Dave left their room key at the desk, noticing the younger of the two men seated at the far side of the room. Then they walked down to the guarded garage, got into the Volkswagen van, and drove down the hill and into the city, to the Sheraton Hotel. The two men followed them, as expected. Rachel could detect no other vehicle which might also be following them.

They parked outside the lobby of the Sheraton in the walled parking lot, and went straight to the elevator, noticing the surveillance car pull into the parking lot behind them. They took the elevator straight to the sixth floor, then got off, walked quickly to the stairwell, and hurried down to the fourth floor, where Jerry Wells's room was located. The door was slightly ajar, and they walked straight in.

"They follow you here?" Wells asked as he closed the door behind them after glancing into the hallway.

Ames nodded. "By now, they're probably in the lobby waiting for us to show again."

Wells held a set of car keys out to him. "These fit a dark green Toyota Corolla with tinted glass that's parked on the street right out back. There's a VIP entrance there, for the people who live in the top-floor suites. The only elevator there goes straight from the top floor to the back entrance, with no stops, but there's a stairwell you can walk down from here. Just go to the exit sign at the end of the hall."

"Right," Dave said, kicking off his shoes and unbuttoning his shirt to change into the ones he would wear out to the landing zone.

"All right," Wells continued, "I'll go on down to the lobby and see if your tail's still hanging around waiting for you there. What do they look like?"

Rachel described the two men and their car to him.

"If they're there, I'll call up here on the house phone in five minutes. Let it ring. Twice means they're there, and you can scoot out the back. Three times will mean there's some problem. I'll hang up and call straight back. Answer it the second time. If I don't call in five minutes, it means you're on your own, and you'll have to be ready to mark both the primary and the alternate landing zones. If all goes well, I'll leave here in about twenty minutes. I'll be on the radio from that point on. See you later."

"OK," Ames said. "When you get to the turnoff to the alternate, drive on by it a mile or so. I'll call you on the radio to let you know if you're being followed. If so, just take them on a wild-goose chase, and we'll take care of the infil."

"Right," Wells replied. "Good luck."

"Be careful, Jerry," Rachel added as he left. She stepped into the bathroom to change while Dave finished undressing and put on the dark clothing he had taken from the athletic bag. She pinned up her hair and took a short, black wig from her purse, and put it on, then produced a big pair of eyeglasses which she also put on. She looked at herself in the mirror. Her appearance bore little resemblance to the woman who had walked into the room a few minutes before.

The phone rang, and rang again, then went silent.

"Good," Ames said. "All set?"

"Just about." She took the pistol and spare magazine from her purse, and slid them into a side pocket of the computer case which housed her cleverly disguised satellite radio set, while Dave collected their clothes and hung them in Well's closet.

He picked up the athletic bag which contained six cubic-inch-size infrared lights and batteries, the hand-held radio with its spare battery, and a pocketscope—a small, tubular, image-intensification device which enabled the user to see in all but total darkness. Rachel had the computer case. They left the room, hurried down the stairs to the back entrance, and out to the street, where they found the Toyota waiting as Wells had promised. No one followed them as they made their way out of the city and headed toward the coast as the sun set behind the hills to their west.

In the growing darkness, Bud Munson put his Twin Otter into a slow descent from 10,000 feet, fifty miles off the coast of Belize, checking his inertial navigation system against the VOR beacon at Belize City as he did so. From here, he would descend to low level and turn southwest, coming ashore at the mouth of the Motagua River on the border between Guatemala and Honduras. He would follow the river inland for about a hundred miles, then turn due south for eighty miles until he hit Lake Guija. From there, he would skirt the west El Salvadoran city of Santa Ana, turning to the southeast over the lake at the base of the twin volcanoes of Santa Ana and Izalco, for the final leg to the landing zone.

Beside Munson, his copilot, Jorge Peña, was double-checking the progress of the flight. Over the headset, he told Munson, "Looks like we're about eight minutes ahead of schedule."

"Rog," Munson acknowledged, and throttled back slightly. "From the mouth of the Motagua on, I want to try to hit all the checkpoints within a half minute of schedule. Hope we don't run into some damned dope runner on the same flight path."

"Shouldn't be a problem," Peña commented. "Down here, they don't bother much with trying to hide down low. Don't need to."

Matt Jensen stuck his head into the cockpit. He, too, wore a headset so that the pilots could keep him informed of the flight's progress. "How 'bout some coffee, guys?" he asked.

Munson shook his head, and Peña replied, "No, gracias, Matt."

Munson looked around at the youthful-looking sergeant major. "So, when you gonna knock off this shit and get a real job, Matt?" he asked.

"When you refuse to fly me around the world anymore," Jensen answered.

"How much time you got in now, anyway?" the aging pilot inquired.

"Twenty-four years, next month. Time flies." It had been a good twenty-four years for Sergeant Major Matt Jensen. He had enlisted for duty as an infantryman at his local recruiting station in Illinois the week after he graduated from high school. Three years later he was accepted for Special Forces training, and had worn the green beret ever since—for the last six years, as a member of the Delta Force. But he still felt as if he were a product of Vietnam, even though he had completed the last of his two-and-a-half years there some sixteen years ago. But that was where he had grown up, where he had been transformed from a rowdy kid bent on hell-raising and commie-killing, into a quiet, steady professional.

Running reconnaissance patrols deep into enemy-held territory in Laos and North Vietnam had transformed him. A few week-long patrols where every move could mean life or death—where only skill, and a little luck, mattered, were enough to mature any man, if he lived through the maturation process. He had learned to attune all his senses to the environment around him, there in the enemy-infested jungles of Southeast Asia. He had learned to be bold without being reckless, careful without being overcautious. He had learned to rely on his instincts, and those of his tightly knit team of four Montagnard tribesmen and two Americans. The jungle had become his home. A part of him would always be there, and a part of it, in him.

The target of his coming mission was a product of that same environment, and he found himself wondering what had really happened to his former comrade-in-arms, Raul Valenzuela—now Emilio Ramirez. Well, perhaps he'd soon know. By the time the sun rose a second time, his former comrade-in-arms should be here in this same aircraft with Jensen and his team, but headed in the opposite direction.

"Ninety minutes to the coast, Matt," he heard over the headset.

"Roger." He turned back to the cargo compartment of the aircraft, where most of the members of his team were stretched out with their equipment. He would have them all don their parachutes and strap on their equipment before they hit the turbulent, low-level air above the hills and valleys of Central America. Then they would be prepared to bail out if there was trouble en route, or prepared to load the chopper in good order soon after their landing in El Salvador.

Master Sergeant Dan Holton, the leader of the four man reconnaissance and blocking element, and Jensen's second-in-command for the mission, nodded when Jensen told him, "Ninety minutes from the coast." He checked his watch, noting that they were a few minutes ahead of schedule. In the dim, red glow of the cabin lights, he unfolded his map for another of the scores of times he had studied the location of the landing zone, the estimated HAHO release point, the landmarks to their intended drop zone, and the area around the little hamlet where Ramirez was reported to be located. Holton didn't really care for the high-altitude, high-opening parachute infiltration technique. It was too iffy, he felt—too many chances of someone having a main parachute malfunction, and getting separated from the others while he released his main and deployed his reserve. And it was too dependent upon the high-altitude winds being as predicted, and too difficult to navigate above dark hills and valleys. But he knew that, if anyone could do it right, it was Matt Jensen.

Colonel Wilton Garrett parked his car in the reserved parking space near the entrance to his security-fenced headquarters after a light supper at the Fort Bragg Officers Club. He would be spending the time from now until his team returned from El Salvador, here in the headquarters, the old post stockade referred to by Delta's members as "the Ranch." He took a change of clothes and his shaving kit from the car and walked in, noticing by the clock above the duty officer's desk that it was about the time that the Twin Otter would be reaching the coast of Central America near the Guatemalan-Honduran border.

The duty officer stood when he entered and said, "Sir, Major Greer wanted to see you as soon as you got back. He's in the sit room."

"Thanks, Captain Martin." Garrett dropped the clothes off in his office, went to the situation room, and pressed the buzzer. It seemed that every time he learned the cipher numbers to let himself into the classified areas of the old stockade, the security people changed them.

Greer opened the door a crack, saw that it was his commander, and let him in. "Sorry, boss. I thought it would be a good idea to change the cipher lock, with this compartmented exercise going on. Want me to show you the new one?"

"Don't bother, Major." Garrett grinned as he pulled a cigar from his shirt pocket and unwrapped it. "You'll just change it again as soon as I get it memorized. Now, what's up?"

"Everything's on schedule so far," the Delta Intelligence Officer answered. "The Twin Otter left Grenada on schedule, and Ames, Brown, and Wells are at the LZs. Rayburn says his choppers and crews are all set for tonight. Wells reported that Rachel and Dave were under surveillance by a couple of pretty unprofessional Latins—probably Salvadoran government types. Anyway, they lost 'em easily, and just reported that they're in place at the landing zones. This is a little disturbing, though."

He handed Garrett a page of teletype paper with code words at the top and bottom indicating that it contained intelligence derived from intercepted radio transmissions.

"Harry Lawson, up at the Agency, is going to stay there and monitor it closely for us," Greer added, then let his commander read the document.

It was the English translation of the text of a message from the Cuban Embassy in Managua to Cuban Military Headquarters in Havana. It made reference to a message of the day before from the Soviet Embassy, and an earlier message from the Havana headquarters to Managua, then continued as follows:

Two Mi-24 helicopters on standby with all-Cuban crews for mission. Will get crews together with commando team when they arrive this afternoon. Pilot recommends flight over Choluteca and Valle provinces instead of Gulf of Fonseca to reach target, because of enemy radars on Tigre Island. Please advise if approved.

Garrett walked to the map of Central America pinned to the wall. Major Greer pointed out the areas referred to in the intercepted message.

"As you can see, sir, the Gulf of Fonseca is the bay that separates the westernmost tip of Nicaragua from the southeast corner of El Salvador, about twenty-five miles away. Choluteca and Valle provinces are the two provinces of Honduras just north of the Gulf of Fonseca. And Tigre Island is this small island in the Gulf where the Salvadorans have the air defense radar the message refers to. Apparently, the Cubans are planning to fly two Hind helicopters from Nicaragua to either eastern El Salvador or the Valle Province of Honduras for some sort of mission. They've flown a few strike missions against the contra rebels in Choluteca

Province before, but just inside the Honduran border. I've asked Lawson to let us know if there's any contra activity in Valle Province they might be going after, but I haven't heard back from him, yet. As you can see, the analyst doesn't have any idea what they're up to."

Garrett read the CIA analyst's comments which followed the translated text of the intercepted Cuban message:

Cubans apparently planning a strike mission involving two Mi-24 (HIND) helicopters from Nicaragua into either southern Honduras or eastern El Salvador. Probable attack against contra activities in southern Honduras; however, use of all-Cuban force is unprecedented, indicating either high-priority target or activity such as morale-boosting visit to Salvadoran insurgents by high-ranking Cuban official.

Garrett reread the message and the analyst's comments. "Do you know if Lawson has made the National Security Advisor aware of this, Jim?" he asked his intelligence officer.

"No, sir, I don't. I'll ask him when he calls back to let me know if there's any contra activity in Valle Province that they might be going after."

"Good. Have you passed this on to Major Ames?"

"Yes, sir. I passed it to him when he called from the LZ a while ago."

"All right. Now, how long before Jensen's team lands?"

Greer looked at the "opsked"—operations schedule—in his hand, then at the zulu time zone clock on the wall of the Delta situation room. "One hour and forty-eight minutes, boss," he answered.

The secure telephone rang, and Greer answered it. It was Harry Lawson, calling from CIA headquarters in Langley.

"Jim," he reported, "it looks as if they *may* be going after the contras. There's a transload airstrip in Valle Province where we're scheduled to land a load of weapons for the contras tonight. I've got the guys at NSA concentrating on intercepts between Managua and Havana, and our station in

Managua is trying to find out whatever else they can. Of course, they're looking at it from the standpoint of contra operations only, since they don't know anything about your Arctic Falcon operation. I'll tell you one thing, though; if those Hinds show up at that transload airstrip tonight, they'll be in for the surprise of their lives—the *last* surprise of their lives!"

"I've got the picture," Greer replied into the secure telephone. "Let's hope that's where they *are* going. Have you let the National Security Advisor know about the intercept, Harry?"

"I let Brewer know, and he'll pass it on to Mr. Carruthers. Everything on schedule down south?"

"Roger that. The infil bird's over Guatemala now, and Ames is at the landing zone, ready to receive the team. The chopper crews are all set, too."

"All right, buddy. I'll let you know right away if the NSA guys pluck any more information out of the ether."

Greer hung up the telephone, then turned to his boss. "He passed the intercept to Colonel Brewer at the NSC, who'll relay it to Mr. Carruthers. There's a contra resupply airstrip in Valle Province, Honduras, that Lawson thinks the Cubans are going after. I guess they're setting up an ambush for them there. But I don't know, Colonel Garrett. I can't see them using an all-Cuban force to hit a contra resupply site. NSA will concentrate their intercept effort on the area, though, and let Lawson know if they get any more info. . . . I'll tell you, though, I just don't like the smell of it."

Garrett lit the cigar he had been chewing on—a sign, to those who knew him, that he was nervous about something. "Well, Major Greer," he said, "just 'cause we're paranoid doesn't mean they're not out to get us. Keep after Lawson for any new information. I'll be in my office." He walked to the door, then turned back to his intelligence officer. "You don't suppose there's any way they could have gotten wind of Arctic Falcon, do you, Jim?"

"I've been wondering that myself, sir. I don't see how they could have, unless there's some leak from the people in Congress Dave had to brief. But even then, I can't see the

Cubans risking a mission into El Salvador to keep us from getting to some damned disgruntled American turncoat. . . . I just don't know."

Lieutenant Colonel Jerry Schumann, the commander of Delta's ground operations element, Detachment E-1, came into the situation room then. Like Garrett, he would stay in the headquarters until the mission was completed. He had just returned from Camp Mackall, the Special Forces training base thirty miles west of the main Fort Bragg complex. While Camp Mackall was mainly used as a base for training new Green Berets, it was also used, from time to time, as an isolation area for teams from Delta and the other Special Forces units at Fort Bragg preparing to go on training operations or actual missions. In this case, it would be used to debrief Jensen and his team upon their return, and to hold Ramirez in isolation until such time as the CIA transported him to one of their secure bases where he would be interrogated.

"Everything's set at Mackall, boss," he said to Garrett. "As far as the cadre's concerned, they think we have a team coming back from a recon training mission in Panama. Everything on schedule with Matt and the team?"

"One possible glitch, Jerry," Jim Greer said to Schumann, passing him the radio intercept translation.

Schumann read it, then looked at Garrett. "What do you think, sir?"

"Don't know. We'll just have to wait and see."

6

Bud Munson, at the controls of the Twin Otter, pulled back on the control yoke of the droning aircraft to clear the hill rising a mile or so to his front. Just beyond it would be the flat surface of Lake Guija, which he should cross in two more minutes, if he was on schedule. Beside him, Captain Jorge Peña, looking like an alien being with the twin tubes of his night vision goggles protruding from his face, was scanning the horizon for any obstacles Munson might be unable to see. Munson was confident, though, that he could see well enough in the light of the half moon to keep the Twin Otter several hundred feet above the Central American hills. As they crossed the crest of the hill, Munson pushed the yoke slightly forward to follow the contour of the terrain.

"Lake Guija, El Sal," Peña said, noting the time on the chronometer in the middle of the instrument panel. "Right on time." He pressed the location button on the aircraft's inertial navigation system and compared the coordinates displayed there with the actual coordinates of the center of the lake noted on the pad strapped to his thigh. The INS was only two hundred meters off—a very accurate reading, considering that it had not been updated since they overflew the mouth of the Motagua River some 140 miles back. He corrected the instrument to their exact location as they crossed the center of the lake.

On the far side of the lake, Munson could see the moonlight reflecting from the tracks of the railroad which led to the city of Santa Ana, twenty miles to the south. His plan was to follow the track until he saw the lights of the town, then skirt several miles to the east of it. From there, it was just a few miles to the lake at the foot of the twin volcanoes which he should reach twenty minutes prior to his scheduled landing time.

"You up, Matt?" he said to Jensen over the intercom.

"Roger, Bud," the team leader answered from the cargo compartment. "We still on schedule?"

"Affirmative. Fifty-five minutes to the LZ."

At the straight stretch of highway which would serve as the primary landing site, Rachel was watching the lights of two vehicles, traveling together, moving toward them from the south. She could see several miles down the highway which descended straight toward the Pacific coast from her position. Only one other car had passed her location since dark, and Dave had been able to see its lights a minute and a half before it had reached the landing zone from the north—less time than Munson's aircraft would be on the ground. The two cars she was now watching turned off the highway into the Salvadoran Army compound two-and-a-half miles down the road.

Dave was now on the edge of the highway a hundred meters to her north, emplacing the small, infrared lights which would mark the safe touchdown area for the aircraft. Invisible to the naked eye, the lights could be seen through the pilots' night vision goggles.

Ames paced off three hundred meters along the broad, straight road, and placed a fifth infrared light—this one flashing at half-second intervals—at the point to which the aircraft would taxi and turn around, and Jensen and his team would offload. Then he returned to Rachel's location in the thick bushes at the side of the road.

"Two vehicles were coming up the road from the south a few minutes ago," she whispered, "but they turned off into the Army compound."

"Yeah, I saw them," Ames whispered. Then, checking his watch, added, "Just over fifteen minutes."

He lay on his stomach just inside the bushes, peering north through the pocketscope, which would enable him to see the glow of any vehicle lights approaching from the direction of San Salvador long before he would be able to see them with the naked eye.

"Eleven minutes," Rachel said, and he turned on the little secure-voice UHF radio, pressing the push-to-talk button momentarily, hearing the beep and seeing the twinkle of the tiny light which indicated the radio was in working order.

They continued to peer at the approaches to the landing zone, searching for the lights of approaching vehicles. They saw none, and at precisely ten minutes before the scheduled landing time, heard the low, calm voice of Bud Munson from the radio, "Primary, this is Wheels, over."

Dave Ames held the radio to his mouth, pressed the transmit button, and whispered, "Wheels, this is Primary. Alfa Oscar Kilo. Call two minutes."

"Wilco."

A moment later, Jerry Wells's voice came on. "Primary, this is Alternate, radio check."

Ames answered him. "This is Primary. Roger, out."

In the back of the Twin Otter, the eight Delta soldiers of Matt Jensen's team sat facing the cargo door, their MT-1X parachute systems on their backs, and a small rucksack attached to the front of the harness resting on the thighs of each man. Six of the men, including Jensen, had silenced submachine guns slung across their chests, while two others cradled 7.62 millimeter M-21 sniper rifles in their arms. Two of the men with submachine guns also held bulky, Swedish-made AT-4 antitank rockets on their laps. They would jump the powerful AT-4s in, then hand them over to the snipers once they were on the ground. The snipers would use the rockets to destroy any vehicles approaching Ramirez's village during his capture, or to discourage any attempts to follow the team after his capture, until they were safely on the way out by helicopter.

The first and fifth men to exit were wearing AN/PVS-5 night vision goggles which would enable them to scan the area around the landing zone for any intruders.

Over the headset he was still wearing, Jensen heard Bud

Munson call over the radio to Ames, "Primary, this is Wheels; two minutes."

"This is Primary," came Dave's reply. "Two minutes. Alfa Oscar Kilo. Call one minute."

Over the intercom, the pilot said to Jensen, "Get that, Matt?"

"Roger—two minutes, all OK."

He clapped his hands loudly, twice. The others looked at him, and he pointed to his watch, then held up two fingers. The other seven gave him a thumbs-up, and scooted closer to the door, which Dan Holton pulled inward and forward, then locked open, feeling the rush of warm air and seeing the blur of the dark terrain of El Salvador passing by just a hundred feet below.

Munson had donned night vision goggles for the landing. He heard Jorge Pena, his copilot, call, "Ninety seconds," and saw the pinpoints of light of the safe touchdown area a mile or so up the highway, as he brought the aircraft around to his landing heading.

"Looks like we're going to be a few seconds early. Call one minute," he said.

Pena pressed the radio transmit button, and said, "Primary, this is Wheels. One minute."

"One minute. Alfa Oscar Kilo. In sight?"

"Primary in sight," Pena replied.

Dave and Rachel didn't hear the aircraft until Bud reversed the props momentarily as he touched down on the highway.

He taxied quickly to the flashing infrared strobe a short distance in front of him, then swung the airplane around and locked the brakes.

"Thanks, Bud. See you later," Jensen said over the headset before yanking it off and hopping to the ground behind the others.

Munson gunned the engines, released the brakes, and within forty seconds of touching down, was gone, the drone of the Twin Otter's engines disappearing from the earshot of the ten people at the LZ as he throttled back and headed straight toward the coast and out to sea.

Rachel was waiting at the flashing light, which she picked up and turned off as the team unloaded.

"Follow me," she said to the first man off the airplane.

"Yes, ma'am," the man answered.

Rachel led the eight-man team to the brush-shrouded depression twenty meters off the road, which Dave had selected for them to hide in until the choppers arrived. They had cached her satellite radio there earlier, and as Jensen sent security out to the edge of the road, she quickly assembled it. Ames returned to the hide site from the far end of the landing zone, where he had gone to recover the marking lights, just as she raised the base radio station at Fort Bragg.

"This is Juliette Five Four," he heard his female partner whisper into the microphone hidden in the Walkman cassette player she was holding in her hand, "Munich, Munich."

The code word would let Delta headquarters know that the Twin Otter had arrived and departed on schedule, the team was in El Salvador in good order, and everything was going according to plan.

From Fort Bragg, the base radio operator said, "Roger, Five Four. Stand by for traffic from the boss. . . ."

Garrett's voice came over Rachel's earphones. "Five Four, this is Three Three Golf, over."

"This is Five Four, over."

"Roger, Five Four, nice to hear your voice. Let me speak to Dave, will you?"

"Wait one . . ." She pulled the headphones off and handed them to Ames. "It's the colonel. Wants to talk to you. Just push the back space button on the keyboard to transmit."

He put on the headset. Garrett told him about the intercepted radio message from Managua to Havana, adding that they had no further information yet, but they would let him know immediately if they learned anything further. "Be sure to let Jensen know."

"Wilco. Rachel will stay on the net until the choppers

show up and the boys get out of here. Should be in, oh, just over forty minutes."

"OK, Dave. We'll give Rachel a shout if we hear anything else. Tell Matt and his boys 'good luck.' This is Three Three, out."

Ames handed the earphones back to Rachel, then passed the information about the intercepted message on to Jensen.

Jerry Wells called on the small hand-held radio, and Ames answered him.

"Did Wheels get in?" Wells asked.

"Roger, didn't you hear him?"

"Negative. Didn't hear a thing. I'll go pick up my lights, then sit tight here until the other birds come and go."

"Roger," Ames replied. "We'll give you a call when they're gone, then you head on back to your hotel room and wait for us there."

At Ilopango Air Base, just to the west of San Salvador, John Rayburn watched the other pilots from his unit, the 169th Special Operations Aviation Battalion "Nighthawks," lift their Huey helicopter off the runway and climb out to the northwest. They would climb to eight thousand feet, then head for the area of the pickup zone where they would make a wide orbit of the area, scanning the roads below for any traffic, and informing Rayburn when they saw the triangle of infrared lights that Ames was to use to mark the pickup zone. Rayburn would take off in a few minutes, head off to the north at low-level, then turn toward the pickup zone once the other crew reported that the lights were in place and there was no traffic in the area. He would pick up Jensen's team, then head north toward Morazan Province, climbing as he went, until he reached ten thousand feet. He would release the team at the exit point he had calculated based on the reported winds aloft, then head for Tegucigalpa, Honduras, as his flight plan indicated. There, he would refuel, then fly back to Ilopango until the following night, when he was to take another "test flight," during which he would pick up Jensen's team and their prisoner, taking them to the exfiltration airstrip where the Twin Otter would land later to take them home. He turned in his seat and watched as the two Delta men in the door gunners' seats behind him loaded the sinister-looking M-60 machine guns mounted on either side of the Huey.

"All set?" he asked the gunners over the helmet-mounted intercom.

"All set, sir."

Rayburn turned back to the helicopter's controls. "Clear!" he called. "Comin' hot."

In the situation room of Delta's headquarters at Fort Bragg, Colonel Wilton Garrett read the text of the latest message Harry Lawson had transmitted to him from CIA headquarters. Once again, it was the translation of an intercepted Cuban message.

He finished reading the message, then turned to Jerry Schumann, who had been reading the message over his shoulder. "Get Captain Brown on the satcom. Tell her to have Jensen stand by for a message, then get me the National Security Advisor on the secure phone."

Delta's commanding officer read the intercepted message once more:

Must execute mission to pick up or eliminate Ramirez tonight, as an American force will attempt capture tomorrow night. If Ramirez is not in village, leave your team there to capture him upon his arrival. If he fails to show, team should ambush Americans, then force local guerrillas to lead your team to Ramirez. Advise this headquarters immediately of your expected time of departure to target.

"How in the *hell*," Garrett wondered aloud, "did this damned mission get compromised?" Could it possibly have been one of his own men? Had Ames and Brown recklessly discussed the operation in a location bugged by enemy agents? Or could it have been compromised by someone in Washington?

"Jensen's on the radio, boss," Schumann said. Garrett bit the chewed-up end off the cigar in his mouth, spat it into a trashcan, then lit the cigar before picking up the handset to speak to Sergeant Major Jensen.

"Matt, is that you?" he asked, abandoning formal radio procedures over the secure voice satellite communications net.

"This is Five Seven. Roger, over."

"Be advised, your mission is apparently compromised. I say again, your mission has been compromised, over."

"This is Five Seven. Roger, mission compromised. . . . What are your orders? Over."

"Be prepared to abort as soon as I confirm with higher. Do you have contact with the choppers, yet?" Garrett asked, noticing by the clock on the situation room wall that they were scheduled to pick up Jensen's team in less than ten minutes.

"Wait one," he answered, then turned to Ames, who had huddled close to Jensen when he heard him repeat Garrett's "mission compromised." "He wants to know if we have contact with the choppers yet."

Dave spoke into the small UHF radio in his hand, "Pegasus, Pegasus, this is Primary, over."

John Rayburn, in his helicopter flying low behind the hills to northwest of the pickup zone, was unable to receive the transmission, but his wingman, now at eight thousand feet altitude, did, and responded, "This is Pegasus Two. Go ahead."

"Pegasus Two, this is Primary. Wait, out."

Hearing him, Jensen immediately sent out over the satellite radio, "This is Five Seven. Affirmative, we have contact with the choppers on UHF."

"Roger, Five Seven. Advise them to delay pickup until further notice."

"This is Five Seven. Wilco," Garrett heard over the radio.

"Sir," Lieutenant Colonel Schumann called from the table across the room where the secure telephones were located, "Mr. Carruthers is on the line."

Garrett handed the radio handset to Jim Greer and

instructed him to pass the details of the intercepted Cuban message to the team in El Salvador, then walked over to speak to the National Security Advisor.

"Sir, are you aware that the mission has been compromised?" he asked.

"I'm afraid so, Colonel," he heard Carruthers say wearily. "We found out a few minutes ago."

"Very well, sir. I've notified the team. I'll go ahead and have them abort the mission as soon—"

"Just a minute, Colonel," Carruthers interrupted. "We're not ready to have you abort the mission yet. How long would it take your team to get in there?"

Garrett was incredulous. "Mr. Carruthers," he said, "you're not seriously considering going ahead with the mission, are you?"

"Very seriously, Colonel Garrett," Carruthers answered. "Listen, I know it's a little screwed up, but we've *got* to do our best to get Ramirez, especially now that we know the Cubans want him, too."

"Sir, with all due respect, I'll be damned if I can see why you'd want to risk my team getting in a fight with a couple of Hind helicopter-loads of Cubans over some goddamned American *traitor!*"

"I understand why you can't, Colonel. But I'm not going to argue about it. It may be critical to the security of this nation that your team get to Ramirez and bring him back here. Now, we have an agent on the ground in Nicaragua who will advise us when the Hinds take off. As of a few minutes ago, the crews hadn't shown up yet. We figure your men will have at least two hours warning that the Cubans are on the way. Get them moving as soon as possible. I repeat, Colonel Garrett, it's critical that they get Ramirez before the Cubans do."

"All right, sir, we'll do our best. I'll keep you advised. And for God's sake, let us know when the Hinds take off. If you can put someone on the phone, I recommend we keep this line open for the rest of the operation."

He eyed Schumann, who was slowly shaking his head,

then handed his subordinate commander the telephone and went to the radio and called Jensen. He passed the comments of the National Security Advisor to the youthful sergeant major, and was surprised to hear Jensen calmly accept the order to go ahead with a hurried version of the operation.

"I think maybe I've got the reason figured out, boss. Ask Carruthers if it has anything to do with the plutonium from Hue."

"Say again, Matt?" Garrett requested.

"I say again, just ask him if it has anything to do with the plutonium from the reactor at Hue University."

"Wait one. I will," Garrett replied, then had Schumann get Carruthers on the telephone.

When the President's advisor on matters of national security said, "Hello?" Wilton Garrett asked, "Sir, does this mission have anything to do with the plutonium from the reactor at Hue University?"

There was a long pause on the other end of the line, then Carruthers spoke. "I don't know how the hell you learned that, Colonel—but I'll for damned sure find out when I have time. . . . Yes, as a matter of fact it *does* have to do with the material you mentioned."

"Very well, sir," Garrett said. "I'll let you know when I find out myself. Right now, I'd better get my guys moving."

7

Sergeant Major Matt Jensen gathered the other seven members of his team closely around him in the dark. He explained the situation to them as he understood it from Colonel Garrett, emphasizing that it was a matter of national security now, and that speed was essential if they were to ensure they get Ramirez before the Cubans did. "I want to do the hurrying as much as possible *before* we get to the target site, so that, hopefully, we'll be able to slow things down for the actual capture. We should have at least an hour and a half warning time before the Hinds arrive, so if we can get to Ramirez's village before we get word that they're on the way, we should have time to get security into position, then move in slowly with the snatch team, grab him, and get the hell out to the PZ."

He unfolded his map of the area around the target, and the others knelt over it in a tight circle. As he pulled out his penlight, he turned to Ames and said, "Sir, call Rayburn and tell him to pick us up in ten minutes." He scanned the map with the tiny beam of his penlight, bringing the circle of light to rest on a spot which they all recognized as the alternate pickup zone for their extraction from the area, behind a low ridge just to the northeast of the village.

"Change one," he said, "the alternate PZ is now our primary drop zone. Instead of a HAHO, we'll free-fall to five thousand feet. That should be high enough to keep anyone on the ground from hearing our opening. And it'll give us plenty of time to assemble in the air and set up for landing. Now"—he took a blade of grass from the ground and pointed to a sharp bend in the river about a kilometer upwind from the drop zone—"we'll get out here, where the river loops around. The DZ altitude is about, let's see, nine hundred feet. We're at about three hundred and fifty feet now. Three fifty from nine hundred is five fifty, so set your altimeters back five fifty from zero to nineteen thousand, three fifty—right, Dan?"

Dan Holton was double-checking Jensen's calculations on a small note pad. "Correct," he said. "Nineteen thousand, three hundred fifty feet."

Each man adjusted his twenty-thousand-foot scale parachutist's altimeter to the stated figure, so that it would read zero when they touched down on the drop zone at the higher elevation. Jensen checked his watch. "All right," he said. "About seven minutes to pickup. Get those M-21s and AT-4s rigged."

The others helped the two men with the sniper rifles and the two with the bulky antitank rocket launchers secure the weapons along their left sides. Those with submachine guns already had them slung across their chests with the slings around their necks, held in place with Velcro loops around the belly bands of their parachute harnesses. They would stay in place during free-fall, but could easily be brought into action just by ripping apart the Velcro tie-down.

As they worked, Jensen continued to pass instructions. "Now, remember, go where the low man goes, even if he's off the intended drop zone. If anyone is hurt on landing, we'll adjust accordingly, but for Christ's sake, set up good and don't flare too high—the DZ's plenty big. We'll just pile the chutes up on the edge of the DZ and pick 'em up on the way out, if we can. If we can't, we'll just leave them. All right, hustle."

Once the weapons were rigged, the men paired off and made a jumpmaster check of each other by the light of the half moon.

"Two minutes," Jensen said.

In the distance, they could hear the rotor blades of Rayburn's approaching Huey helicopter.

Rachel Brown called Fort Bragg on the satcom radio to see if there was any last minute information for Jensen's team before they loaded the helicopter. The only means she and Dave had of talking to the helicopters was on the little, hand-held UHF radios, and they wouldn't be able to reach them once they were over the horizon. If there was no information before then, Jensen would be completely out of touch until he landed on the drop zone and got his own satellite radio set up.

Delta headquarters had no new information, and Rachel ran to Jensen to tell him that, as the chopper touched down on the highway and the team quickly loaded up. A minute later, the helicopter was gone, climbing off to the north as the sound of its rotor blades faded in Dave and Rachel's ears. He quickly collected the infrared lights with which he had marked the landing zone and put them in the athletic bag. Rachel went back to her satellite radio, and Dave called Jerry Wells to inform him that the helicopter had landed, loaded the team, and departed for the release point.

"Roger," Wells replied. "I heard him. I'll be heading back to the hotel in a few minutes. See you there."

"Negative, negative. There's been a major change in plans," Ames informed him. "Stay where you are, and we'll be there in about a half hour."

He sat down beside Rachel to think his way through the rest of the vastly altered operation. There were less than five hours left until daylight. It would be an hour before Jensen's team got on the ground. If they were on the ground for two hours, and it took another hour for the chopper to return them to the landing zone, he could bring in the Twin Otter and have the team gone before first light. But just barely. If it took longer, they'd just have to make the transfer in daylight on the seldom-traveled road which had been selected as the alternate LZ. Munson should be calling in soon. He was to have flown out over the Pacific, climbed to normal altitude, then made a run in to Comayagua Airport as if he were a regular aircraft in transit from Panama to the States. Prior to calling Comayagua tower for landing instructions, though, he would call Ames on UHF.

Dave made a call to Rayburn, before he got out of range.

"Pegasus, this is Primary. Has Matt informed you of the change?"

"Affirmative, Dave," John Rayburn answered. "Here's what we'll do. After the team gets out, I'll take this bird on to Teguch and refuel as planned. The other bird will orbit just north of the border till I get back, then he'll go refuel. That way, we'll always have a chopper in orbit about ten minutes away, ready to pick 'em up when they call."

"Roger, Pegasus. We'll have satcom contact with Matt once he gets on the ground, but we won't be able to talk to you until you get back in range."

"Roger, Dave. We'll make sure Matt can talk to us on UHF from the orbit point. Understand you want us to bring the team back to the alternate LZ after pickup?"

"Affirmative, Pegasus. Give us a call as soon as you get in range to confirm that."

"Say again, Primary, I'm starting to lose you."

Ames stood up in order to gain a slight increase in range from the little radio, then repeated, "I say again, affirmative, affirmative. Give us a call as soon as you get back within range to confirm."

"This is Pegasus. Wilco, out."

Aboard the helicopter, Jensen was still going over the changes to the plan with the other seven men of his team, who were crowded into the cargo compartment of the Huey with him. He had to yell to make himself heard above the noise of the helicopter.

"We'll keep the snatch team at the LZ until Danny's team clears the top of the ridge for us, then move up there. Dan, you'll have to leave one man on the top of the ridge to monitor the satcom for us when we move in to make the snatch. Got it?"

"Roger. Mike, you'll be the one to stay with the radio," he yelled to Staff Sergeant Mike Haynes, the young ex-Ranger who was the newest member of the team. Haynes gave him a thumbs-up to acknowledge the order.

Jensen crawled over to and knelt between the back of the pilot and copilot's seats and tapped Rayburn on the shoulder. Rayburn turned around, then said something into the intercom. One of the Delta men who was serving as a door gunner pulled off his helmet and handed it to Jensen, who put it on so that he could talk to Rayburn on the intercom.

"Let me see your map," he said to the pilot. He pointed out the new exit point and confirmed with Rayburn the locations of the primary and alternate pickup zones just outside the village. That done, he settled back to think his way through the operation. He was anxious to get out of the helicopter and on the ground—especially since he was now out of radio contact with base, and wouldn't know until he landed and got his radio set up, whether or not the Cubans were on the way to the target, as well.

In Managua, Hector Garza watched through binoculars as the Cuban Hind helicopters taxied into position near the small hangar at the end of the runway. In the light from the lamps atop the building, he counted twelve men leaving the hangar, with six boarding each of the helicopters. As he had several times in the last half hour, Garza crouched and ran across the dirt road to the bushes where his radio was hidden. He picked it up and spoke into it. "Volcan, Volcan, este Tortilla, Tortilla." Again, there was no answer from his CIA contact. He tried several times more, and still got no answer. From the end of the runway, the big Hind-Ds lifted off, heading to the northwest as they disappeared into the night sky. Quickly, Garza stashed the radio behind the seat of his battered Datsun pickup, started it, and drove toward the city, noting the time on his wristwatch as he did so. He needed to get to a telephone and call the emergency number his handler had given him.

As he made his approach toward Comayagua Airport from the Pacific, Bud Munson called Ames on the secure UHF radio of his Twin Otter.

"Roger, Wheels," Ames answered. "Be advised, there's been a major change in the operation. The exfil will be sometime in the next few hours. I say again, sometime within the next few hours, how copy?"

"Just give me the time and place, ol' buddy," Munson replied. "I can be ready to go in about an hour, once I take on fuel at Comayagua, over."

"OK, Bud. It will be the alternate Lima Zulu. We don't know the time yet, but we should have about an hour's notice, once the team lets us know they have their man and are on the way out. My guess is it'll be shortly before daylight."

"Roger that. The primary LZ—correction, correction— the *alternate* LZ, probably just before daylight. We can handle that. Just give me that hour's notice, so I can file my phony flight plan and get there on time. I'll stay up on the radio, once I get refueled. Will call once that's done, over."

"You do good work, Wheels," Ames said to the pilot. "Give me a call once you get refueled, out."

Aboard Rayburn's Huey, the copilot turned around, tapped Matt Jensen on the shoulder, and pointed out the right side of the helicopter to the twinkling lights of a town off to the southeast. "San Francisco Gotera," he yelled. "Six minutes!"

To the other members of his team, Jensen repeated, "Six minutes!" after pointing to his watch and holding up six fingers. The Delta parachutists checked their altimeters, which read just over ten thousand feet, then checked each others' ripcord pins to ensure each was well seated, to avoid an accidental parachute deployment as they prepared to exit. Jensen pulled down his goggles and stuck his head out the door of the helicopter into the blast of warm air rushing past. He still couldn't see the river above which they were to exit. When he pulled his head back inside, he noticed two men from Dan Holton's recon and security element struggling with one of the bulky AT-4 rocket launchers. The carrying strap had torn loose from the weapon, and they couldn't reattach it. Sergeant First Class Santos Baldero, who was to take the weapon in, held up his hands in resignation.

"Damn!" Jensen muttered, then yelled, "Just leave it!"

Quickly, Baldero and one of his teammates derigged the

tube from his parachute harness and secured it to one of the tie-down rings on the floor of the helicopter.

"Two minutes!" the copilot called, and Jensen stuck his head outside the aircraft again. Now, he could see the reflection of the moonlight on the surface of the narrow river a couple of miles ahead and just to the right of the helicopter's direction of flight. He strained to see the omega-shaped bend he had selected as the exit point. Yes, there it was, a short way up the river.

Someone tapped Jensen on the shoulder, and he turned to see the man holding up one finger. "One minute!"

He peered out at the river again, then looked at the copilot, jerking his thumb to the right, and flashing the fingers of his left hand twice to indicate a flight path change of ten degrees to the right. Rayburn quickly brought the helicopter onto the desired heading, and Jensen saw that they were now properly lined up on the exit point. He got himself up into a crouching position, and gave a thumbs-up signal to his teammates. "Standby!"

He could see the four men of Holton's team crowd closer to the door on the far side as they returned his "standby" signal, and the other three men, thumbs raised, crouched in the door on his side. He peered straight down between the edge of the helicopter's floor and the long landing skid which ran the length of the cargo compartment. When the bend of the river was directly beneath him, he pointed to Holton, yelled, "Go!" and dived out into the darkness, nearly two miles above the hilly terrain of El Salvador's Morazan Province, as the others piled out with him. Jensen flipped once, arched his back and relaxed his arms and legs, and as he hurtled toward the earth, fell flat and stable toward the river below. Bending at the waist toward his left, he made a quick, three-hundred-and-sixty degree turn, noticing four of his men falling nearby at about his same altitude. The other three were some distance below, so Jensen pulled his arms in more closely to his body, tucked his knees slightly, and sensed the slight increase in speed as the three men below him appeared to rise slowly toward him. Once he was level with the lowest of his men, he flared out slightly to match the other jumper's rate of descent.

Peering down at the altimeter and swivel-mounted compass attached to the plastic panel on the chest strap of his parachute harness, he noticed that he was now passing seven thousand feet altitude. He made a slight turn to the left until the compass showed that he was facing to the northwest. The exact heading from the bend in the river to the drop zone was three hundred ten degrees. He made one more full turn to check the locations of his teammates. He could see the dim glow of the altimeter lights of five of them. The other two were probably above them. He glanced at his altimeter. Just under six thousand feet. As he watched the needle of the altimeter pass fifty-five hundred, he waved his arms, then grasped the handle of his main parachute ripcord. He unseated it from its elasticized pocket, his left hand now just in front of his helmet to compensate for the change in his body's aerodynamics caused by bringing his right hand in for the ripcord. The needle touched the five-thousand-foot mark, and he jerked the ripcord handle outward, shaking his shoulders as he did so, to ensure that the vacuum on his back was broken momentarily, thus making certain that the spring-loaded pilot chute would catch air and pull the main parachute off his back. He felt the tug as the pilot chute did its job, then, a half second later, the sharp deceleration of his body as his main canopy opened. Instinctively, for Matt Jensen had nearly eight hundred free-fall jumps, he reached up on the risers for the control-line toggles and slipped his hands into their nylon loops, as he looked around to see where the other jumpers were. He could make out the shapes of five parachutes high and to his right. He pumped down on the toggles several times to ensure that his parachute was fully deployed, then checked his heading. He was slightly off course, and corrected his direction of flight, then released the toggles and reached into the neck of his jumpsuit and pulled out the small, light-amplifying pocketscope hanging around his neck. He peered directly ahead and saw the small field, which was his target, about a half mile to his front, behind a long, low ridge. The ridge obscured his sight of the hamlet on the other side, where his prey was supposed to be, but he could see the dirt road leading into it from the west. His altimeter read thirty-eight hundred feet, far more altitude than he needed to easily reach the drop zone with a tail wind predicted to average ten knots.

He pulled down on his toggles to the half-brakes position to slow his forward speed, then transferred the right toggle to his left hand, holding it directly in front of his chest. That would free his right hand to use the pocketscope for the moment. He located the other two parachutes, about fifty feet lower and off to his right rear. Releasing the scope and the toggles, he pulled sharply down on his right front riser, which caused the parachute to dive off to the right in a tight circle. He held it for two revolutions, then grasped the toggles and came back on heading. He was now slightly lower than the two jumpers who had been beneath him before his diving turns. He could see the drop zone—lighter colored in the moonlight than the surrounding trees and bushes—without the pocketscope now. He was at twenty-three hundred feet now, and estimated that the drop zone was five or six hundred feet ahead. He made a wide S-turn, then lined up to the left of the drop zone. He passed fifty meters to the left of it at eight hundred feet, then turned crosswind to the right about fifty meters beyond it. He didn't need to look at his altimeter anymore, as he could judge his approach with the eye of an experienced jumper.

At about one-quarter brakes, he was on a forty-five-degree glide path toward the center of the field. He felt his canopy bounce slightly in the turbulent breeze caused by the ridge and the trees, then was over the edge of the drop zone. Holding the toggles at quarter-brakes until he was ten feet over the center of the drop zone, he brought them smoothly down to waist-level. The big parachute flared, nearly stopped about two feet off the ground, then set him gently down in the ankle-high grass. He dropped one toggle line, pulled the other, and the nylon airfoil collapsed behind him. Quickly, he pulled the parachute off to the side of the drop zone and watched his teammates land. Two of them flared slightly late and fell to their knees, but the other five made near-perfect landings well within the edges of the little field. Quickly, the others dragged their parachutes over to Jensen's position and slipped out of the harnesses.

They cached their parachutes in two piles under low bushes a short distance off the drop zone, then the four men of Master Sergeant Dan Holton's team moved silently off toward the ridge above the little village. Sergeant First Class Mel Lawrence, a member of Jensen's snatch team, unfolded the satellite antenna of the radio in his rucksack, aligned it to the proper deflection and azimuth, and turned the radio on. He handed Jensen the handset.

"Juliet Three Three, Juliet Three Three, this is Juliet Five Seven, Juliet Five Seven, over," Jensen whispered into the handset.

He heard the beep of the voice encryption device almost immediately, followed by the voice of his immediate commander, Lieutenant Colonel Jerry Schumann. "Five Seven, this is Three Three, over."

"This is Five Seven. London, London, over."

Schumann turned to his boss, Wilton Garrett. "London. They're at the drop zone with no problems." Then he called Jensen on the radio again. "Five Seven, this is Three Three, roger. Be advised, there's still no word on the hostile choppers. We'll let you know ASAP, if we hear anything, over."

"Five Seven, roger, out."

Next, Jensen called the helicopter callsign on his UHF radio—the same type that each member carried in a pouch on his harness, along with his ammunition, pistol, and other combat equipment.

"Pegasus, this is Snatcher, over."

"Rog, Snatcher; Pegasus Two here. We're in orbit ten minutes to your north. We'll wait here till Pegasus One relieves us in about, oh, niner-zero minutes. You guys make it in all right?" the pilot asked in the informal manner of aviators.

"Affirm, Pegasus. We'll holler if we need you. Out."

There was nothing to do now until Holton called to tell him the ridge overlooking the hamlet was clear, except monitor the satcom radio for word about the Cuban helicopters. And the later they took off, the better.

Jerry Wells, on the radio to Dave Ames, who was approaching the alternate landing zone with his parking lights on, said, "I've got you in sight. Come on about another hundred meters, and I'll guide you onto this old side road where my car is."

Ames pulled down the straight stretch of road until he saw Wells, then followed him fifty meters up the overgrown side road until Wells halted him. Ames had removed the bulb from the car's interior light, so there was no light when he and Rachel got out, leaving the doors slightly open to avoid the noise of closing them.

"Excuse me, guys," Rachel whispered, then walked farther up the road to relieve herself.

"How's she doing, sir?" the counterintelligence warrant officer asked Ames as Rachel disappeared into the darkness.

"Cool as a cucumber, Jerry. I wonder if she realized she'd be pissing on a dirt road in the boondocks of El Salvador in the middle of the night, when she signed on with this outfit?"

Wells chuckled. "I don't know. I sure didn't. Now, how 'bout filling me in on what the hell's going on with this operation?"

Leon Marcos—believed by the Sandinista government to be an expatriate Nicaraguan now with Canadian citizenship, and an exporter of cotton goods—dozed in his easy chair in his Managua home. The radio with which he was supposed to be in contact with his most reliable agent, Hector Garza, sat silent on the table beside him. He was startled awake by the ring of the telephone across the room from him, then jumped up and answered it.

"Ola?"

"Ola, señor." It was the nervous voice of Hector Garza. In Spanish, the agent told his CIA-employed handler, "The items you wanted were sent about twenty minutes ago, just before two o'clock."

"I understand, amigo. Why didn't you let me know earlier?"

"My apologies, señor. My other 'telephone' apparently doesn't work."

"OK, amigo. Thank you."

Jesus! His earlier conversation with the Chief of Station, Managua, had made it plain that the departure of two Hind helicopters from the air base was an urgent matter, and that he needed to know immediately when the crews boarded them, and when they took off. Marcos hurried into his bathroom, lifted the top from the toilet tank, and detached the radio fastened beneath it. He switched it on and called the CIA station chief in his home a half-mile away.

8

"I got it, boss!" Major Jim Greer said. He had been poring over the information they had about Jensen's target, Raul Valenzuela, now known as Emilio Ramirez.

Garrett looked at his intelligence officer.

Greer continued, "The last mission Ramirez ran in Vietnam—the one when he was captured or went over to the commies—was to locate some kind of 'sensitive equipment.' It must have been the plutonium from the nuclear reactor at Hue University, which I guess the NVA took while they had control of the city during the Tet Offensive in 'sixty-eight. Apparently, Sergeant Major Jensen knew that's what Ramirez's mission was."

"Yeah, good logic, Jim," Garrett said. "But why now? I mean, hell, that was nearly twenty years ago. Surely, he hasn't been dragging a bunch of nuclear material around with him for eighteen or twenty years."

"Well, sir, it does sound kind of farfetched, doesn't it? But the National Security Advisor obviously thinks there's some connection."

"You're right. Get him on the phone again, will you, Jerry?" he asked Schumann, who was sitting with the secure telephone receiver to his ear, but listening attentively to the conversation between Colonel Garrett and Major Greer.

"Still no word on the Cuban helicopters, sir?" Garrett asked when Carruthers came on the telephone.

"No, not yet, but we've just queried the station chief in Managua to double-check."

"All right, sir. Mr. Carruthers, let me tell you what we *think* we know about the connection between Ramirez and the plutonium from Vietnam."

"Please do, Colonel," Carruthers said.

"Well, sir, Sergeant Major Jensen, the man who's leading the team in to capture Ramirez, was in the same recon outfit as Ramirez in Vietnam. Jensen's the one who asked whether there was any connection between the plutonium and this mission. Apparently, he was aware that the last recon mission Ramirez ran in Vietnam had something to do with the stuff."

"I see," Carruthers replied curtly.

"Sir, is there anything else we should know about this? I mean, do you suspect that Ramirez still has the stuff? Should Jensen try to find it when he picks up Ramirez?"

For a moment, the National Security Advisor was silent. "No," Carruthers finally answered. "We don't believe he has it with him. I might as well tell you, since you already know this has something to do with weapons-grade plutonium. But first, Colonel Garrett, I want to strongly emphasize that this is *extremely* sensitive information."

He waited for Garrett to acknowledge that fact, then continued. "We know that Ramirez visited Vietnam last year. One of those international gatherings of communist revolutionaries they're so fond of holding. That was a few months before he turned up in the States, when the FBI almost picked him up, but lost him. On a hunch, because of his connection with the plutonium and some stuff the FBI found in the place he stayed in Arlington, the Agency had a guy from NEST—the Nuclear Emergency Search Team that the Department of Energy maintains—you know, they're the ones who went to Canada to recover the radioactive stuff from the Russian satellite that broke up over Canada a few years back?"

"Yes, sir. I know who you're talking about."

"Well," Carruthers continued, "the NEST guy found some evidence that there *had* been some nuclear material there. It's all magic to me how they could tell, but they're convinced he had the plutonium with him at the time."

"Jesus," Garrett muttered, then asked, "What's the best guess about what he did with the stuff?"

"That's what we don't know—the reason that it's so critical we get our hands on Ramirez. We haven't been able to figure out why the Cubans want him badly enough to risk sending a team into El Salvador after him, either, unless it has something to do with this plutonium business."

"Sir, how the hell did the Cubans learn about our operation?" Garrett asked.

"I was going to ask you the same question, Colonel," the National Security Advisor replied coldly.

"I can assure you, Mr. Carruthers, that the leak didn't come from my people," Garrett stated with equal coolness, then added, "Not intentionally, anyway. The only way that any of my people could possibly have let it get out would either be because the Soviets or the Cubans have the key tapes to our satellite radios, which sure as hell wouldn't be our fault, or the people in El Sal were discussing it someplace that the bad guys had bugged. And that's highly unlikely."

"Yes, well, I hope you're right, Colonel. We don't *think* your people could be involved. But just in case, I want you to inventory the cipher tapes to your satellite radios. We're not really concerned that your people in El Salvador spilled the beans. We know the bad guys were aware of the operation before they even got there. Anyway, unless we're wrong, the leak must have occurred here in Washington—as they usually do."

"Sir, I'll have the inventory done right away. And I'll confirm that my people down south didn't discuss the operation anywhere that might have been bugged. But, quite frankly, sir, I tend to agree with your assessment that, as usual, the beans were spilled by someone up there in the D.C. area. I'll get back to you shortly, Mr. Carruthers."

He handed the telephone back to Schumann, then paced back and forth across the situation room. He pulled a fresh cigar from his shirt pocket, paused to light it, then puffed furiously on it as he continued pacing. It angered and frustrated him when these leaks occurred, but nothing made him angrier than when outsiders insinuated that his own people might be guilty of giving secrets away, whether intentionally or inadvertently. Time after time, he had picked up a newspaper or news magazine to see that some "official source" or other had leaked information about Delta or about some operation in which they had been involved. And time after time, his superiors had called for an investigation to determine if someone in Delta had leaked the information. Each time, he had dutifully conducted his inquiry, but he had yet to find any reason to suspect any member of his unit of leaking secrets. It was ridiculous, not only because of Delta's habit of routinely compartmenting their operations so that only those with a valid need-to-know had access to the activity, but because of the fact that each member knew that even the slightest security violation would lead to immediate dismissal from the unit. And, since each man was subjected to periodic polygraph testing, they knew that they would be found out in the end, if they did let classified information out. No, the leaks, on the rare occasions when they were finally discovered, had always ended up coming from the Washington community. He was certain that such was the case, now.

"Jerry," he said, stopping to look at Schumann, who was

nodding sleepily with the phone to his ear as he monitored the open line to the White House office of the National Security Council staff. "Jerry, I want you to inventory the code tapes to the secure devices that we're using for this operation. Captain Brown, Sergeant Major Jensen, Mr. Wells, and the base station should be the only ones who have them. The other two should be in the Comsec custodian's safe."

"All right, sir," Schumann said, motioning for Major Greer to take over the monitoring of the secure phone. "So, Carruthers thinks we've raffled one to the commies for the All Ranks Club, or something?"

Garrett scowled at him for a moment, then broke into a smile. "Now *there's* an idea!" Then he walked to the satcom radio handset which was remoted from the receiver-transmitter in the nearby base radio station and called Ames, who firmly assured him that he and Rachel had not discussed any aspect of the operation without taking all possible precautions to ensure that their conversation couldn't be bugged. Schumann, accompanied by Delta's Command Sergeant Major Dick Salem, returned to the situation room a moment later to assure Garrett that the code tapes were all properly accounted for.

He passed the information on to Carruthers's assistant, Lieutenant Colonel Brewer.

"I'll pass it on to Mr. Carruthers, Colonel," Brewer said, then, "Hang on a minute, Colonel Garrett, we've got a 'flash' precedence cable coming in from Managua."

"Flash" was the most urgent of priorities assigned to U.S. government message traffic, and meant that actions hostile to the United States were underway or imminent.

From the ridge above the hamlet where Emilio Ramirez lay sleeping, Matt Jensen scanned the area with his pocketscope. The little village consisted of eight adobe dwellings along the dirt road which ran parallel to the ridge—five on the near side, and three on the far side. The team had designated each building with a letter from the phonetic alphabet, and memorized the designations from the aerial photograph of the settlement before they left Fort Bragg.

Behind several of the buildings were small outhouses. As far as they could tell, only one of the houses had any activity in it—building Foxtrot—the largest of the eight, located in the middle of the three across the road from the ridge. There were a couple of lamps burning inside, and the sounds of a guitar playing, and occasional laughter. Dan Holton had gone down to check it out with one of his men about ten minutes earlier, just after he had called Jensen and his assault team forward to the top of the low ridge.

Near him, the other three members of Jensen's team lay quietly, trying to rest before going in after Ramirez. Sitting up beside Jensen, with the headset of the satellite radio on his head, was Mike Haynes, whom Holton had detailed to operate the radio.

In the earphone which was wired to his ear from the little UHF radio on his belt, Jensen heard John Rayburn calling from his helicopter.

"Snatcher, this is Pegasus One. I'll be in orbit ten minutes to your north, while Peg Two goes for fuel, over."

"Roger, roger," Jensen replied, whispering into the tiny microphone attached to the lapel of his camouflaged uniform.

A moment later, Holton called from the far side of the hamlet, his whispered report barely audible in Jensen's earpiece.

"One, this is Five. House Foxtrot has three males, one female. One AK-47 and one pistol seen. May be more. Quarry not in house Foxtrot. I say again, Quarry *not* in house Foxtrot, over."

"Roger, copy. Can you see any activity in house Bravo?" Jensen asked.

"Negative," came Holton's reply. "As soon as Six and Seven get to their security positions, I'll move over there and see if I can confirm Quarry's presence. All I can tell from here is that the door is partially open."

* * *

A MISSION FOR DELTA

At his headquarters in Fort Bragg, Wilton Garrett listened incredulously to the report from the CIA station chief in Managua. The two Cuban helicopters had taken off from Managua, presumably en route to the settlement in El Salvador where Ramirez was located, nearly an hour ago— meaning that they could arrive at the hamlet in another thirty minutes or so, depending upon the skill of the pilots at night flying. "Apparently," Carruthers was saying over the secure telephone from his White House office, "the agent wasn't able to get through on the radio, and had to call the report in by telephone, well after the Hinds were gone."

"Sir, that means they could show up there, where our team is, within a half hour. Can't you get some fighters in to intercept them, or alert the Salvadorans to do so?"

"We've already thought of that, Will. There's not nearly enough time. You've got to get your guys to go in there and get him *now!*"

"I'll get back to you," Garrett said, laying the telephone receiver on the table and moving quickly over to the remoted satellite radio handset. He picked it up and called to the team in El Salvador, "Five Seven, this is Three Three. Put Jensen on!"

Sergeant Major Jensen answered after a brief pause, "This is Five Seven, over."

"Matt, this is Garrett. The two Cuban Hinds left Managua about an hour ago. They could be at your location as soon as thirty minutes from now, copy?"

"Roger. Three zero minutes."

"Affirmative. Are you in position to move in and get Ramirez now?"

"Well, shit!" Jensen exclaimed hoarsely. Thirty god-damned minutes. Why were they just now reporting it? Well, there was certainly no time to bother asking. He quickly ran through his mind what had to be done, then answered, "This is Five Seven. I think we can make it. Will advise, out."

He called softly to the other three men in his assault team to huddle around him, then spoke into the microphone on his lapel, loudly enough for the men around him to hear.

81

"Recon, this is One," he called, so that Holton and the two men down near the village would know that the call was for all of them. They acknowledged his call in turn:

"Five."

"This is Six."

"Seven, here."

"Roger, wait," Jensen ordered, then called, "Pegasus, this is Snatcher."

Rayburn answered with, "Snatcher, Pegasus One, go."

"All right," Jensen continued. "Listen close, then acknowledge in turn. The Cubans are on the way here, estimated arrival in three zero minutes or less. Now, we're going to move straight down to house Bravo ASAP. When we're in position for the hit, I'll let everyone know. Five, you and one of your men will have to hit the people in house Foxtrot at the same time we go in after Quarry. Kill anyone with a weapon. Handle the others at your discretion, but do it quickly, and make sure no one gets a radio call off. How copy so far?"

"Five, roger."

"Six, roger."

"Seven, rog."

"Pegasus, roger."

The men surrounding him each gave a thumbs-up in acknowledgment, and Jensen continued, "If Quarry isn't in house Bravo, my team will split up, with me and Two hitting house Charlie, then house Delta. My other guys—that's Three and Four—will hit house Alfa, then move across the road and hit house Echo. Five, if we haven't found our man by then, you move from Foxtrot over to Golf and see if he's there. If not, we're shit out of luck. Once someone calls to say they've got Quarry, we'll break off and rally behind house Alfa, as previously planned. Acknowledge."

Again, the men around him gave him thumbs-up, and Holton answered first over the radio.

"One, this is Five. Six and I will stay together, and I'll send Seven on down the road with the rocket to secure the road against any bad guys coming from the west. Is Eight going to stay there with the radio?"

"Affirmative, Five," Jensen answered, looking over at the man with the satellite radio. "Everyone else roger?"

"Six, roger."

"Seven, roger."

"This is Pegasus One. When do you want me to come in for the pickup, Matt?"

"As soon as you hear someone say they've got Quarry, Pegasus, head inbound, then call when you're one minute out. If we're not ready, we'll let you know then."

"Wilco, Matt."

"All right," the Delta team leader said. "We're moving. Keep the boss informed, Eight."

"Wilco," Sergeant Haynes, with the satcom radio, answered, as Jensen led the assault team down the ridge toward house Bravo.

Dave Ames, Rachel Brown, and Jerry Wells, two-thirds of the way across El Salvador to the west, had monitored the call from Colonel Garrett to Sergeant Major Jensen informing the latter that the Cuban helicopters were headed for the target. Now, the two men huddled around Rachel as she monitored her satellite radio for further news.

"Five Seven just reported that they've moved out toward the target," she whispered.

Ames gave Bud Munson a call on the brick-size UHF radio to inform him that the team should be arriving by helicopter at the dirt road landing strip sometime between about an hour and a half, and two hours.

"Roger, Dave. I'll go ahead and file, then. Jorge will stay on the airplane and monitor the radio. We'll be set to go anytime after I get back."

Rayburn, orbiting fifteen miles north of Jensen, suddenly turned his helicopter to the southeast.

"Where are you going?" his copilot asked.

"To try to put us between Jensen and those Cuban bastards," Rayburn said over the intercom. "Maybe we can spot them on the way in to the target."

To the two Delta men behind him, in the door gunners'

seats of the chopper, Rayburn added, "You guys in back keep an eye out for those assholes."

"You got it, Chief!" one of them answered with enthusiasm.

Dan Holton and his teammate, Santos Baldero—callsigns Five and Six—reported to Jensen that they were now in position behind house Foxtrot, the center house of the three on the far side of the dirt road from Jensen's target. They could see through the single window in the back of the building that there were still lamps burning in the house and they were able to hear the sound of voices from inside.

From his location beside the dirt road a short distance outside the village, where he was prepared to engage anyone approaching the village from the guerrilla base a mile or so to the west, one of Jensen's snipers, Dezi Danio, set his M-21 sniper rifle down on its bipod, prepared his 84mm AT-4 rocket launcher for action, then made a radio call to Jensen and Holton.

"One and Five, this is Seven. I'm in position, ready for action. Nothing in sight, over." Jensen and Holton acknowledged his call.

Matt Jensen pulled back the sleeve of his uniform and glanced at the luminous dial of his watch. It had been just over fifteen minutes since Garrett had called to inform him that the Cuban helicopters were estimated to be a half-hour away. The four man assault team was now in the treeline just to the rear of the house in which Ramirez was thought to be with his girlfriend. Jensen thought, *I hope to hell that agent knew what he was talking about, because here we go,* then he turned to look back at the other three men who would burst into the house with him. He gave the thumbs-up signal, which the other three men returned, then whispered over the radio, "Thirty seconds."

"Five, roger," came Holton's barely audible reply.

Rayburn and the other members of the Huey helicopter crew, now in orbit fifteen miles to the east at three thousand feet above the ground, heard Jensen's "Thirty seconds" over their headsets.

"Thirty seconds! Anybody see any signs of the commie choppers?" the pilot asked over the intercom.

The other three crewmen all replied, "Negative."

"Best I can figure, they'd pass near here if they were headed for Matt's location," Rayburn stated. "Looks like maybe we'll be out of here before they show up. Keep your eyes peeled and your fingers crossed, gang."

On the ridge above the village, Mike Haynes strained to see if he could pick out any movement from the settlement below, but he could not. He pressed the transmit button of the satcom radio, and in the Delta Force situation room at Fort Bragg and at the landing strip far across El Salvador, seven anxious members of his unit heard him say, "This is Five Seven. About fifteen seconds to the hit, over."

Callsigns Three and Four—Sergeants Joe Olivera and Mel Lawrence—who would lead the way into the house where Quarry was assumed to be sleeping, were at the corner of the house now, with Jensen right behind them. For the moment, "Boo" Maxton, behind Jensen, faced to the rear, covering the area at the back of the house. Olivera was now just around the corner and only four steps from the door of the adobe dwelling, which Holton had reported earlier to be partially open. On signal, Olivera would lead the team's dash to the door and kick it the rest of the way open. Immediately after, Lawrence would enter, searching the room for any threatening targets with the bright beam of the magnesium light attached to his silenced submachine gun. Jensen and Maxton would rush past him to clear the rest of the house, while the other two covered them. If "Quarry"—Ramirez—was not found, the team would split, and rush immediately to the neighboring houses in search of him.

Across the road and one house down, Dan Holton and his teammate crouched low and made their way slowly and quietly along the side of house Foxtrot, their target. For a second, Holton wondered if the man just behind him would have what it takes to pull the trigger, for unlike Holton, Santos Baldero had never been faced with the awful responsibility of taking the life of another human being. As quickly as the thought had entered Holton's mind, he dismissed it. Baldero was a product of the extensive psychological testing and conditioning, and the intense reflexive training which all of Delta's operators underwent. He would, as if by instinct, do what had to be done. Now at the corner of the building around from the open front door, from which the glow of a lamp and the sound of people at play emanated, Holton blew three times into the microphone of his radio, to signal Jensen that he was ready.

"Roger," came Jensen's whispered acknowledgment, then, "Standby . . . ready . . . move, move, *move!*"

In a split-second, the two men in front of Jensen moved around the corner to the door of the small dwelling. Olivero kicked the rickety wooden door open. Lawrence dashed past him into the room, depressing the thumb switch on the bright light atop his weapon as he entered, and making a quick sweep of the room as he sidestepped to let Jensen and Maxton follow him in. The light flashed over two startled figures in a bed in the left rear corner of the room, their hands flying up in front of their faces. After a quick sweep to assure himself that there was no one else in the room, Lawrence immediately brought the light to rest on the faces of the man and woman in the bed, as Matt Jensen raced past him toward them. Covering them with the submachine gun now at his shoulder, two feet from the frightened couple, he said, "Hello, Raul. Long time no see . . ."

Across the dirt street, Dan Holton had appeared in the doorway of house Foxtrot at the same time Lawrence had entered his target. His eyes took in everything before him as he moved straight toward the far right corner of the room, and the muzzle of his weapon followed his eyes. He saw a man, standing, a holstered pistol on his belt. Holton's eyes paused a moment on the man's chest and—his trigger finger reacting instinctively from years of training for such situations—two 9mm rounds slammed into the man's chest within a half second. Another man sat in a chair with a guitar on his lap, his mouth and eyes opened wide with surprise. Behind him, a third man dived for an AK-47 assault rifle leaning against the wall. Holton's silenced submachine gun spat twice, and the man fell with two rounds in his side just below the armpit.

Moving into the room a half step behind him, Holton's teammate, Santos Baldero, swept the area for which he was initially responsible—the left half of the room—with his eyes and his weapon. He saw a chubby man, a bottle in his hand and a pistol shoved into the waistband of his trousers. Baldero felt his weapon kick twice in rapid succession, and the man crumpled to the floor, mortally wounded. A woman sitting in a chair against the back wall screamed and clasped her head in her hands. There was no one else on his side of the room, and Baldero screamed, in Spanish, "Silence! Lie down! Lie down on the floor!" His eyes moved to Holton's side of the room, and he saw one man lying still on the floor, another one prone and writhing in the far corner, and a third one sitting with a guitar in his lap, his hands high above his head.

"Cover!" he heard Holton cry, and replied, "Go!" Holton disappeared into the back room of the building, and as Baldero watched the woman and the man with the guitar drop to the floor in obedience to his command to lie down, he heard his teammate in the back room call, "Clear! Comin' out!"

A second later, all seven of the Delta Force troops under Jensen's command, and the crew of John Rayburn's Huey orbiting fifteen miles away, heard the call they had hoped for: "This is One. We've got Quarry. I say again, we've got Quarry. Moving out now!"

After a long moment, Jensen heard the others reply.

"Five, roger," Holton responded. "See you at the rally point in one minute."

"This is Seven," Dezi Danio called from his lone security position just to the west, "I'm on the way back in."

As he banked his helicopter toward the village, ten minutes flying time away, Rayburn radioed, "Pegasus rogers. Will call one minute out."

Jensen and Lawrence had Emilio Ramirez facedown on the bed, binding his wrists behind him with nylon quickties, while the other two of the four-man assault team guarded the trembling Nicaraguan woman and the door of the house.

"Don't touch the woman! Don't touch the woman, or I'll kill you, Jensen!" Ramirez yelled, his voice muffled by the pillow into which Lawrence had his face pushed.

"Just take it easy, Valenzuela. It's you we want, not your girl," Jensen said as he bound the man's ankles with a chain of three quick-ties. One of the nylon loops was around each ankle, and the third joined the two, so that Ramirez would be able to walk with short steps but unable to run.

Lawrence pulled a strip of two-inch tape from off the stock of his weapon, yanked Ramirez's head back by the hair, and slapped the tape across the prisoner's mouth. Jensen pulled him to his feet, and he and Lawrence grabbed him by each elbow and started toward the door.

"Lie the girl on the bed and quick-tie her hands to it, Joe," he said to Sergeant Olivera as he passed, "then meet us at the RP."

Atop the ridge, Mike Haynes relayed the message of Emilio Ramirez's capture to the people waiting anxiously at the Twin Otter landing zone and in their headquarters in the old stockade at Fort Bragg. "This is Five Seven. They've got Quarry and are headed back. The chopper's inbound, ten minutes out, over."

"Roger, roger, Five Seven, this is Three Three. No sign of the Hinds?"

"This is Five Seven. That's a hard negative."

Rachel added, "Five Four copies," then turned to the two men with her and said, "They've *got* the son of a bitch."

Dave Ames grinned at her, then called Bud Munson to advise him that the snatch had been made.

"All right, pardner," Munson replied from the pilot's seat

of his twin-engine airplane. "I'll take off shortly and head out to sea, then come on in when you call for me."

The seven Delta men rallied with their captive at the bottom of the ridge, where Jensen asked Holton, "What happened in Foxtrot?"

"Three dead. We quick-tied and gagged the other two." He held up the AK-47 rifle which had cost one of the Salvadoran rebels his life. "This and two pistols for the stockade walls," he added.

They hurried to the top of the ridge and linked up with Mike Haynes, who was manning the satcom radio. They heard the approaching sound of Rayburn's helicopter just before he called, "Snatcher, this is Pegasus, one minute out."

It would take them a few minutes to get down the ridge to the pickup zone and collect the parachutes, so Jensen answered, "Roger, Pegasus. We're not quite ready here. Make a three-minute orbit, then call again."

"Pegasus, wilco."

Turning to Dan Holton, Jensen said, "You and Six stay here and cover our rear, just in case. When you hear Pegasus call 'one minute' again, hustle on down. If you promise me one of those pistols, we'll wait for you."

Three minutes later, Rayburn's voice came over the radio. "Snatcher, Pegasus is one minute out."

"Roger, Pegasus, come on in. Winds are light and variable. Break. Five and Six, come on down," Jensen radioed.

Turning to Mike Haynes, he said, "Call base, and the Twin Otter LZ. Tell 'em we're on the way out, and break that radio down. We're *out* of here!"

9

As soon as he had transmitted the report that the helicopter was on the way in to pick them up, Mike Haynes turned off the radio, collapsed the satellite antenna, and shoved it in his rucksack. He could hear the change in pitch of the Huey's rotor blades as Rayburn slowed for landing above the trees just short of the landing zone.

Halfway down from the top of the nearby ridge, Dan Holton suddenly halted, and grabbed his companion by the arm.

"Wait!" he called, then cocked his head as if listening to something. For several seconds, he stood still, then lifted the night vision goggles which were hanging at his chest and held them to his eyes, peering through the treetops toward the night sky.

Rayburn was concentrating on landing within the triangle of lights Jensen's team had placed in the landing zone when he heard a frantic voice over the radio say, "Pull up! Pull up! Get out of here!" Quickly, he nosed the chopper forward, increasing power and pulling up on the collective as he did so, then banked right and climbed away from the little landing zone. As he turned, he saw something flash past him, and there were explosions in the treetops to his left.

On the edge of the LZ, Jensen and the others dived to the ground as rockets from a Soviet-built Hind helicopter hissed over their heads and slammed into the trees beyond them, the flash of the exploding warheads momentarily lighting up the sky. As the first Hind roared past, they heard Holton call, "Look out! Here comes another one!"

The rattle of machine gun fire suddenly filled the air, and

the landing zone was raked with green tracer rounds careen-
ing wildly about, some of them in the midst of Jensen's
team. "Up the ridge! Get up the ridge! Move, move!" Matt
yelled to the others as the second Cuban helicopter zoomed
past overhead. He grabbed his pocketscope and surveyed
the edge of the landing zone. One man was lying on his
belly, his hands clawing the ground. "Take Ramirez!" he
said to Mel Lawrence, then ran toward the fallen Delta
soldier.

Lawrence yanked Ramirez by the arm to pull him to his
feet. He got him up, but could hear Ramirez moaning
deeply, and the trussed captive fell forward heavily. Lawrence ripped the tape from the man's mouth, and heard him
moan again loudly. Pulling the penlight from his shoulder
pocket, Lawrence quickly checked Ramirez over. There was
a bullet wound in his upper thigh, and blood was spurting
from it in a heavy stream.

Jensen reached the fallen Delta man, picked him up, and
ran into the woodline with him, then laid him down and
pulled his rucksack off. It was Mike Haynes. The young
sergeant was gasping for breath, and hoarsely crying, "My
back, my back!" Jensen discovered that a bullet had struck
the radio in Haynes's rucksack and passed through it into
his back, taking fragments of the radio with it when it did.
There was a gaping hole in the soldier's back, his shattered
spinal cord showing through. Haynes gurgled deep in his
throat. Then his eyes rolled back in their sockets, and he was
dead.

At five hundred feet, Rayburn banked the helicopter and
turned back toward the landing zone, now a mile behind
him.

"Everybody keep an eye out for those fucking Hinds," he
commanded.

"Pegasus One, this is Pegasus Two. We're refueled, off
Teguch, and headed your way," he heard his wingman call
over the radio. "You still at the orbit point?"

"Negative, Two, we're in the shit. The Hinds showed up
just as I was on final to the LZ. We're headed back to take a

look now. Climb to three thousand and call when you're one minute north."

"Roger, One. Headed your way at max airspeed!"

After the lead Hind made its first pass, Dezi Danio, back in the woodline waiting for Holton, had bolted toward the LZ. Now he was kneeling at the edge of the field, facing in the direction the Cuban helicopters had come from, the big AT-4 antitank rocket on his shoulder. He could hear one of the Hinds boring in, then two rockets roared past and exploded in a flash of light well to his right rear. He saw the dark silhouette of the big aircraft appear above the trees before him, placed the sight of the weapon on its nose, and when the rocket-spewing helicopter was almost directly above him, he fired the 84mm rocket. It exploded into the belly of the Hind almost directly above him, and the aircraft lifted, rolled to its right, then crashed in a giant fireball in the trees beyond the landing zone.

"Jesus! They got one!" Rayburn heard one of his door gunners call and he looked toward the ball of fire which suddenly blossomed to his left front. "And there's the other one, breaking left over the ridge!"

Rayburn could see the second Cuban chopper unleash a stream of machine gun fire and a pair of rockets toward the little hamlet just beyond the ridge, then break off to the left. "Get that right gun off the mount, and lay it out the left door, gunner!" he ordered over the intercom. Swiftly, the right door gunner disconnected his M-60 machine gun from its mount, and dragging the long belt of 7.62mm ammunition with him, lay on the floor of the Huey with the muzzle of the weapon pointing out the left door. Keeping an eye on the circling Hind through his night vision goggles, Rayburn banked sharply left, then circled right, bringing his slower Huey on a parallel course with the Cuban gunship, but well ahead of and above it. The Cuban crew, concentrating on their second gun-run at the village, never saw the American helicopter until it was too late, when two streams of bullets from the Huey's M-60 machine guns ripped into the vulnerable upper half of the Hind, tearing the spinning turbines of its engines apart and causing them to disintegrate. Trailing a stream of burning fuel, the damaged helicopter flared at the far end of the village, stalled fifty feet above the dirt road, then slammed straight down onto it and began burning.

"Yahoo! Did you see that?" Rayburn exclaimed. He circled the blazing wreck, and the door gunners, seeing several figures staggering away from it, opened up with their machine guns once more. They directed the streams of tracers into the fleeing figures until they saw all of them fall, then ceased firing.

"Pegasus One, this is Pegasus Two, about two miles north. What the *hell's* goin' on down there?"

Rayburn's voice returned to a businesslike tone. "This is Pegasus One. Both enemy helicopters are down and burning. Stand by while I find out the situation on the ground."

Mel Lawrence had tied a battle dressing over the wound in Emilio Ramirez's leg, then called Jensen to inform him that their prisoner was badly wounded. Now the two Delta NCOs were kneeling beside Ramirez. Jensen cut the quick-tie loose from the weakening captive's wrists, then injected him with a syrette of morphine, while Lawrence prepared a bag of fluid for intravenous injection to replace Ramirez's lost blood.

"What do you think, Mel?" Jensen asked Lawrence, who had qualified as a Special Forces medic long before coming to the Delta Force.

"I don't think he's gonna make it. The femoral artery's ripped apart, and his femur's smashed," Lawrence muttered.

"All right. Call the others and get a status report. We've got to get out of here." Jensen yanked the earphone from his ear and leaned over Ramirez, whose moaning had subsided as the morphine took effect, and said, "Raul, it's all over. You might as well tell me why they want you so badly."

"Fuck you," came the murmured reply. "You're a little late, aren't you, Jensen?"

"What?"

"I said, you're a little late, aren't you—by about twenty years? You were supposed to be my backup team. Why didn't you come after me?"

"That was a long time ago, Valenzuela. We tried."

The American-born revolutionary sneered. "Bullshit, man! There's guys who *rotted* over there waiting for somebody to come after 'em. Rotted to *death* waiting for their wonderful country to come get them." He laughed mockingly. *"I* waited. And then the truth began to sink in. What the Vietnamese were telling me was *right.* And every time I began to doubt them, all I had to do was look around—look around at guys wastin' away, man." He coughed. "Gimme a smoke."

Lawrence was the only man on the team who smoked. Fortunately, he was nearby, getting a status report from the others over the radio. Matt Jensen called to him and said, "Light him a cigarette, will you, Mel?"

Mel lit a Vantage and passed it to Jensen, who stuck it between his Vietnam teammate's lips.

"We tried, Raul. I swear to you, we tried. But we couldn't. They wouldn't let us go back." He thought of the efforts they had made to get permission to go back for *years* after the war—to try to find the hundreds, the *thousands* of their comrades still listed as "missing-in-action" in Southeast Asia. But not even generals like Mike Healy and Bob Kingston and Dick Scholtes could get the various administrations' permission to go look for them.

The wounded, former Green Beret took a deep draw on the cigarette and exhaled. "Then why aren't you there *now,* hotshot? What are you doin' *here,* after one guy, instead of back over there where you belong, where those poor bastards are still rotting away, if there's any of 'em left?"

The voice of Valenzuela—Ramirez—was getting weaker, his breathing more labored.

Jensen hung his head. "You know why. The plutonium."

The wounded man's eyes opened widely, then closed as he broke into a macabre laugh. "Yeah, the plutonium. Remember what the guys used to say, Jensen? 'Payback's a motherfucker!' "

"Come on, man. What did you do with the plutonium?"

"Fuck you, and fuck all those capitalist pigs in Washington." He managed a weak laugh. "You'll find out soon enough."

"Listen to me, Raul. Think about your girl. She's pregnant. We could tell that when we captured you. Tell me, and I'll see that she's taken care of, I promise."

Ramirez tried to get up on his elbows, but Jensen pushed him down.

"Come on, Raul. Think of the kid. I'll see that your child is taken care of. Just *tell* me."

"Then go get her," Ramirez whispered weakly.

"All right. I'll send somebody after her now." He broke into the status report Lawrence was attempting to get from the other members of the team over the radio. "Break, break . . . This is One. Who's nearest the village?"

Holton answered. "This is Five, One. I'm up here on the ridge with Baldero. We're closest to the village."

"OK, Dan. Get down to house Bravo and get the woman. She's quick-tied to the bed there. Get her out and down here, ASAP."

"Wilco," Holton replied. "If the fuckin' Hinds didn't nail her."

Lawrence returned to Jensen's side. "Danio's on the LZ with Mike's body," he reported. "The satcom's shot. Maxton and Olivera are securing the far side of the LZ, in case anybody survived in the chopper that crashed over there. Both Hueys are standing by to pick us up, as soon as Holton and Baldero get back with the girl."

"OK. Take Danio and move up the ridge a ways in case somebody comes after us from the village. Come back down with Holton and Baldero when they show up with the girl."

Five minutes later, Holton and Baldero had found the girl still secured with nylon quick-ties to the bed of the house, sobbing softly to herself. The rockets and machine gun fire of the Cuban helicopter had missed the adobe building, and she was unhurt. "We're taking you to Emilio," Baldero told her in Spanish as he cut her loose, and she allowed them to lead her quickly away from the house and up onto the ridge.

"We're coming down with the girl now," Holton radioed when he got to the top of the ridge.

"Roger. Hustle," Jensen demanded.

A couple of minutes later, they appeared at Jensen's position, guided there by Lawrence and Danio. The pregnant woman fell to her knees and held the head of the badly weakened Ramirez in her lap, weeping softly.

"Milio, Milio, what have they done to you?" she wept in Spanish.

"It was the Cubans, not us," Baldero replied in her native tongue.

Ramirez coughed. "What day is it, my heart?" he asked her in a whisper.

She looked up at the dark figures of the men above her.

Again, Baldero spoke. "It is Friday, the tenth of the month."

"Thirteen days," Ramirez whispered. "Thirteen days, and I'll be remembered forever."

Baldero leaned close to him. "What will happen in thirteen days, amigo? What do you mean?"

In English, Ramirez said, "Fuck you, Yankee soldier." He laughed aloud, then said in Spanish, "Tell our son, Nadia. Tell our son." Then he collapsed into unconsciousness.

Feeling the pulse in the wounded man's neck, Lawrence said, "His pulse has dropped off to almost nothing."

"All right," Jensen said. "Mel, you and Baldero get him to the LZ and put him on the first chopper. Dan, you and Dezi take the girl out with them. The other three of us will pick up Haynes and take him out on number Two."

John Rayburn called just then. "Snatcher, this is Pegasus One. There's some people on the road just west of the village, moving that way. Should we engage with our door guns?"

"Negative, Pegasus. You're cleared into the LZ *now*. You'll have six pax. Pegasus Two, come on in as soon as he gets out. You'll have one KIA and three walking."

Two minutes later, the second Huey was lifting out of the little landing zone, turning sharply right to avoid flying over the burning wreck of the Hind helicopter Dezi Danio had shot down with his antitank rocket, as ammunition was still exploding in the flames.

10

It had been over forty-five minutes since Mike Haynes had called from the LZ to say that they had captured Ramirez and were about to be extracted, but Dave Ames still was unable to raise the helicopters on the UHF radio.

"Pegasus, Pegasus, this is Alternate, Alternate. How copy, over?"

"Let me try him," Bud Munson radioed from his Twin Otter out over the Pacific off the coast of El Salvador. "Pegasus, Pegasus, this is Wheels, Wheels, over." Again, there was no answer from the helicopters.

From Fort Bragg, Colonel Garrett called Rachel on the satcom, and asked, "Any word yet, Five Four?"

"Negative, sir," she answered.

"Ask him if he wants me to have Munson fly up there in the Twin Otter and have a look," Ames suggested. She did so, and Garrett replied, "Good idea, but let's give them a few more minutes. We're trying to find out if Managua can find out anything about the Hinds."

For several more minutes the other Delta members waited anxiously for word from the helicopters which had gone in to pick up Jensen's eight-man team until, finally within radio range, Rayburn's voice came over the UHF net, "Alternate, Alternate, this is Pegasus One, over."

"Pegasus One, this *is* Alternate," Dave Ames quickly replied. "What's your status, over?"

"This is Peg One. We're inbound, three five minutes out of your location. We have one zero pax, total. Quarry just died on us, and we have one U.S. Kilo India Alfa. Everybody else is OK."

"This is Alternate. I copy three five minutes out with two KIA, including Quarry, and eight OK. Who's the tenth person?"

"Quarry's girlfriend—pregnant girlfriend, I should say, over."

"Roger. Who's the U.S. KIA, over?"

"This is Pegasus One. Initials Mike Hotel," Rayburn answered.

"Damn. Young Mike Haynes," Ames said to Rachel and Jerry Wells, then, over the radio, "What the hell happened, John?"

"The damn Hinds showed up the same time we did. Dezi blew one out of the sky with his AT-4, and your two guys in the back of my bird took out the other one with the door guns. No survivors in either one, far as I could tell."

"Holy shit!" Ames murmured, then said to Rachel, "You get all that?" She nodded, taking notes in her notebook by the glow of a small, plastic tube of chemical-generated light. "Pass it to Bragg, then, while I get the Twin Otter started this way."

Colonel Wilton Garrett listened as Jerry Schumann took Rachel's report. So, Ramirez and one of the Delta men were dead. And the team had destroyed the two Cuban-manned Hind helicopters. He wondered how the National Security Advisor would handle that—what sort of international repercussions there would be when it was learned that American and Cuban forces had engaged in battle in El Salvador. Well, that wasn't for him to decide how to handle. His people had been given a mission, and they had done their best. It had cost one of them his life, and now it was Garrett's responsibility to see that the rest of them returned safely and quickly, without further compromise, if possible.

He got George Carruthers on the secure telephone in the White House.

"Sir, we've just gotten the word that the team is on the way back to the landing zone by helicopter, where they'll be transloaded to the Twin Otter and flown back here."

"Excellent! Do they have Ramirez?"

"Yes, sir. But I'm afraid he's dead."

"Oh, no! How did that happen, Colonel?"

"I don't know, sir. Let me give you the rest of the information I have, though. Apparently, the Cubans showed up just as our helicopter arrived to take my team out. Our people somehow managed to destroy both Cuban helicopters. They think there were no survivors. One of my men was killed on the operation."

"Oh, I am sorry to hear that, Colonel Garrett. Did they recover his body?"

"Yes, sir, a young sergeant named Michael Haynes. For some reason, they're bringing Ramirez's girlfriend out with them."

"Why would they do *that?*" Carruthers asked.

"I don't know, sir. But I'm sure they wouldn't do it without good reason."

There was a long pause from Carruthers, who then said icily, "Do you realize, Colonel, that we have no legal basis for bringing anyone but Ramirez out? Technically, capturing the girl is kidnapping. As I recall from the intelligence reports, the woman is Nicaraguan, isn't she?"

"Mr. Carruthers, as I said, I don't know yet *what* their reasons are for bringing her. I can only rely on their judgment, at this point. But, if she's not an international terrorist, what is she? I mean, she was in El Salvador illegally. She's an accomplice of Ramirez. And with *him* dead, she may be the only link we have with the missing plutonium."

"Well, perhaps you're right. Maybe it's a good thing they've got her. When can you give me some more information, Colonel Garrett? We need details—especially about the Hind helicopters—as soon as possible."

"They'll transfer to the airplane within the half hour, fly straight to Grenada, refuel, and then come directly here. Altogether, that'll take about ten hours. Then, we'll debrief them in detail. We can give you a full report within about twelve hours, sir."

"Twelve hours," Carruthers repeated. "I see. What about the Nicaraguan woman?"

"Well, sir, I don't know. I guess the best thing would be to hand her over to the CIA or the FBI for interrogation."

"I don't know about that," Carruthers replied. "We're trying to keep knowledge of this thing limited to as few people as possible. . . . Well, we have—what—ten hours to decide that. Let me work on that one. Now, what about your sergeant who was killed? How do you handle that? What do you tell his wife?"

"Haynes wasn't married, sir. We'll have to notify his parents that he's been killed."

"You don't have to let them know where and how, do you?"

"Not precisely. But it's only fair to them to let them know that he was killed overseas, in the service of his country," Garrett answered. He firmly believed that. Delta had once been falsely accused by the news media of having people killed in the invasion of Grenada, then claiming they were killed in a helicopter training accident. The parents of one of the men had raised a big stink about it in the press. No, it was best to give them as much of the truth as possible, and appeal to their patriotism to keep the matter quiet, if possible.

"Well," Carruthers said, "I don't know. I'll have to think about that one, too. Don't forget, we're talking about a matter of national security here. I'll let you know. Thank you, Colonel. I'd better go give the President what information we have, then start checking on what repercussions the downing of those two Hinds may have. And for God's sake, Colonel Garrett, make certain your people keep a lid on this thing."

"Yes, sir," Wilton Garrett answered, thinking that Carruthers was the one who needed to be concerned about keeping the lid on it, since, if word got out, it would probably be from someone in Washington, as usual.

He hung up the secure telephone and sat silently for several minutes, then turned to Jim Greer, his intelligence officer. "Jim, we need to figure out how we're going to handle the bodies of Haynes and Ramirez. The White House will let us know what to do with the woman. But we'd better have one of the girls from the Admin Detachment at Mackall when the Twin Otter lands, to baby-sit her."

"Will do, sir," Greer answered. "I'll send Angela Herndon out there to deal with her. She speaks fluent Spanish. The girl's name, by the way—if she's the same one Ramirez had in Managua—is Nadia Cruz. But I guess we'd better give her a code name. . . . How 'bout 'Papoose'?"

"Papoose it is. Now, Jerry, what about bringing the Twin Otter in, out at Mackall?"

"Well, sir," Schumann, the commander of the ground operations element of the Delta Force, answered, "since it'll be midafternoon when they come in, we'd better try to bring them in somewhere other than the airfield at Mackall. I'll get with the operations people when they show up for work and find one of the isolated field landing strips to use. And, Jim, Sergeant Major Salem and I can go get a couple of body boxes from the warehouse and load them into one of the vans before anybody comes into the supply section this morning. We can store them out in the oxygen shed, at least for the weekend, if need be, as long as you give me a new high-security lock to put on it."

Command Sergeant Major Salem looked at Garrett, sitting stoop shouldered in the chair beside the secure telephone. "Boss," he said, "why don't you go on home and get some sleep now? You look worn-out."

"Yeah, I guess you're right. I will, as soon as they report that the Twin Otter's loaded and gone."

The sky was beginning to lighten over the dirt-road landing strip in El Salvador as Bud Munson touched down in the airplane that would bring Matt Jensen's team home. He taxied to a halt and turned around. A minute later, the two Huey helicopters landed in the field beside the road, and immediately, several dark figures hopped out and headed his way. They were followed by two pairs of men bearing poncho-draped bodies between them. Two of the others guided a blindfolded woman by the elbows. Then the helicopters lifted off the field, and were gone. Within two minutes, the seven men, one woman, and two dead bodies were loaded, and the cargo door closed. Munson called Dave Ames on the radio.

"Wheels is ready for takeoff."

"Roger, Wheels, you're cleared to go. And thanks, mate."

Munson pushed the throttles forward and released the brakes. The powerful twin engines pushed the aircraft forward with rapidly increasing speed, until Munson pulled back on the control yoke, lifted off, and turned toward the ocean, several miles to the south. He would be well out over the Pacific, off the coast of Guatemala, by sunrise.

Behind him, Matt Jensen placed the intercom headphones on and asked, "Can you hear me, Bud?"

"Sure can, Matt. Sorry about Haynes."

"Yeah, damned shame, but we're lucky only one of us bought it," Jensen answered, looking to the rear of the aircraft where the two covered bodies lay side-by-side. He couldn't tell which was Ramirez, and which was Haynes.

"When you get your civvies out of the tail well, there's a handful of plastic pallet-covers there, and some duct tape," the pilot said. "You might want to put the bodies in them and seal them up, before the odor gets bad. Also, there's a couple of five-gallon cans of water, so you can clean up, and a bundle of handi-wipes."

"Thanks. Mel's giving the girl some pills to put her to sleep. We'll take care of it as soon as she's down. Where do we go from here, Bud?"

"We'll stay out over the Pacific 'til we get off the coast of Mexico in a couple of hours, then get clearance across to the Caribbean, gas up in Grenada, then head on home."

"What about customs in the States?"

"No problem. We'll just do like the dopers do. Just make

sure you've got your weapons and stuff out of sight when we get to Grenada. I don't expect they'll check us out, but they might get a peek inside while they refuel us."

"OK," Jensen replied. Then, after thinking about it a moment, said, "Tell you what, Bud. Maybe we'd better dump the weapons, ammo, and uniforms in the ocean, just in case. What do you think?"

"Wouldn't hurt," Munson answered, then added, "and you won't have to worry about anybody finding it. We'll be over the Middle America Trench in a while, and it's several miles deep."

By sunrise, Dave Ames and Rachel Brown were following Jerry Wells up the winding highway into the outskirts of the city of San Salvador. They would return to the Sheraton, clean up and change back into their other clothes in Wells's room. Then they would drop off one of the cars at the in-town rental agency, and Dave and Rachel would go back to the El Presidente to check out. From there, they would take the other two cars Wells had rented to Comayagua Airport, then take the next available flight to the States.

When the two Hueys landed at Ilopango Air Base, Lieutenant Colonel Billy Baer, the American air attaché, was waiting for them. "Where the hell have you guys been, Rayburn?" he asked when John and Captain Doug Flannery, the pilot of Pegasus Two, walked into his office in the air base headquarters which had once served as El Salvador's international airport terminal. "I expected you guys back a couple of hours ago."

"Sorry, Colonel," Flannery said. "We figured it would be best if we got both aircraft fully checked out, so we could get out of your hair as soon as possible."

"Well, the Milgroup commander's been on my ass for the last hour. There was some firefight the people at San Francisco Gotera reported going on, up in the northern part of the province. He wants to go up there first thing this morning and have a look."

Rayburn scratched his chin. "Hmmm. I didn't see anything going on around Gotera when we passed there en route to Tegucigalpa to refuel, did you, Captain Flannery?"

"Nothing that looked like a firefight," the captain answered innocently. "The only firing I know about was when we went out over the ocean and test fired the M-60s. Part of the maintenance inspection, you know."

"Out over the ocean? Why, hell! No wonder you guys were gone for so long," the air attaché remarked. "Didn't you guys hear me calling you on UHF?"

"That was the only thing we found wrong with the aircraft, sir," Flannery lied. "Some idiot had the radios hooked into the wrong antennas. They weren't good for more than a few miles that way, but my maintenance men are getting them squared away now. Once that's finished, we'll wrap it up and get out of here."

"Fine," the Air Force officer said. "Rayburn, you'd better get into crew rest. You've got some night training to give to Alvarez and his people tonight."

"Wilco, sir, soon as I get Captain Flannery and his people on their way."

The men who had followed Dave and Rachel from their hotel to the Sheraton the evening before, where they had switched to the car Wells had waiting for them, picked Rachel up again when she got back into the Volkswagen van to follow Dave to the nearby automobile rental agency, where he dropped off the car they had used the night before. He got into the van with her, and they started back to the El Presidente to check out. Rachel spotted the surveillance team almost immediately, following about a half-block behind.

"I wouldn't worry about 'em," Ames remarked. "They probably just figure we've been shacked up at the Sheraton all night, swinging with some other couple."

Rachel laughed. "If they only knew, it was actually a *ménage à trois* out in the bushes with Jerry."

Dave glanced over at her. "Kinky," he muttered.

As they quickly packed their bags in their room at the El

Presidente, Rachel asked, "What should we do with the pistols?"

"Hang on to them, for now. We'll give them to Jerry when we get to the airport. He's traveling on a diplomatic passport, so he can pouch 'em out with his radio."

They checked out, then got into the van and drove away from the hotel. As planned, Wells was waiting for them in the parking lot, and followed them out. By the time they got out onto the highway leading down past their landing zone of the night before, the two men who had been tailing Dave and Rachel got between then and Wells.

Watching them in the rearview mirror as they descended the curvy road toward the coast, Dave said, "Oh, oh. They're moving up on us!"

They were closing fast, and Ames reached down and drew the automatic pistol from his ankle holster. Seeing him do so, Rachel reached into her purse for her own, turning to see the other car at their left rear, the man on the passenger side raising a submachine gun to the open window. She dived between the bucket seats, yanked the side window open, and fired four shots at the man just as he got the submachine gun out of the window. The car swerved wildly, then straightened out and went past as Ames locked the brakes. Wells shot past in the Datsun he was driving, pulling to the left of the gunman's car as they entered a left-hand curve, the right shoulder of the road dropping steeply away toward a streambed forty feet below. Wells yanked the steering wheel of his car sharply to the right, and it smashed into the side of the other vehicle, which shot off the side of the road and over the steep bank, smashing nose-first into the streambed, parts of it flying into the air.

Wells gave a thumbs-up out the window, then sped on toward the airport. Ames accelerated and followed him down the highway, noticing that there were no other cars in sight.

"You all right, Rachel?" he called, looking around to see her lying on the back seat of the van with her pistol still in her hand.

"I think I killed him," she muttered.

Dave reached back with his right hand and patted her hip. "It's a damn good thing you did, Rache. He probably would have killed me—killed us both—if you hadn't."

"My God, I killed him!"

"It's all right, sweetheart. You did what you had to, that's all. It's OK. You saved my life."

The attractive, young Army captain lay there a while longer, then sat up, cleared the pistol of its magazine and ammunition, and disassembled it, throwing each part out the right rear window as she did so. Then she climbed into the front passenger seat, took the spare magazine of ammunition from her purse, and threw it out of the car, as well. Dave took her hand in his, pulled it to his lips, and kissed it. "Thank you," he said. "You're a brave woman, Rachel. And a good Delta officer."

Two hours later, they were aboard a Taca Airlines flight to Miami, by way of Belize. Dave had upgraded their tickets to first class, paying the difference out of his pocket. Jerry Wells was somewhere back in the coach section.

The stewardess had served them champagne just after takeoff, and Dave had raised his glass to Rachel, and said, "To Mike, and the others."

Rachel, who had barely spoken a word since firing at the gunman on the way out of El Salvador, said, "Yes. And to us." Then she laid her weary head on Dave's shoulder, and fell asleep.

11

Matt Jensen awoke with a start to the sound of Bud Munson's voice in his earphones. "Twenty minutes to Mackall, Matt."

He sat up and looked at the back of the Twin Otter, to the tail well where the bodies of Raul Valenzuela and Mike Haynes lay wrapped in plastic, hidden by water cans and the kit bags which contained his team's radios and combat boots and the disassembled weapons they had used—and the ones they had captured—in El Salvador, now two thousand miles or so to their south. Dan Holton had convinced him not to throw the weapons out with the other gear they had ditched in the Pacific hours earlier.

Jensen had been dreaming, he now realized. He was in Vietnam, a prisoner wasting away in a bamboo cage, where he had been for years. Suddenly, there had been firing, and the Vietnamese guards had fallen dead all around his cage. Valenzuela and Mike Haynes appeared from the edge of the jungle, and tore open the prison cages of the hundreds of Americans imprisoned all around him. Haynes was about to open Jensen's bamboo door, when Valenzuela grabbed the young soldier and said, "No! Not him! Fuck him!" And Haynes had disappeared back into the jungle, leading the mass of Americans he had just helped rescue from captivity. Raul Valenzuela stood in front of Jensen's cage, laughing madly, then turned and ran after the others, his insane laugh echoing through the jungle as Jensen screamed, "Don't leave me! Please, don't leave me!"

Beside him, Mel Lawrence was now asking, "You all right, Matt? You were moaning and mumbling something."

"Yeah. Yeah, Mel, I'm all right. Just dreaming, that's all. Get everybody up. We're landing in twenty minutes."

Wilton Garrett watched as the Twin Otter lumbered over the end of the dirt airstrip on Rhine-Luzon drop zone, the isolated field in the pine woods just northeast of Camp Mackall, then saw it touch down and slow to a halt. Beside him, Dick Salem, his command sergeant major, said, "Sir, we'll let Doc and Angela pick up the girl first, then we'll load the team in here, and you and Major Greer can take 'em over to the isolation area and start the debriefing. I'll help Colonel Schumann get the bodies into the boxes, then we'll come over to the isolation area. We'll have to leave the bodies in the van until after dark, before we can put them in the oxygen building."

Salem put the transmission lever in drive, and pulled onto the airstrip beside the aircraft, its engines now stopped. They watched as Angela Herndon and Doc Reed, the Delta Force physician, assisted the pregnant Nicaraguan woman into the rear of the first van. Then Reed closed the back doors of the van, got into the driver's seat, and drove away. He would take them to the safehouse at Woodlake, the golf and boating community on a man-made lake just north of the Fort Bragg reservation—the same resort where Rachel Brown lived in her condominium. Delta maintained a safehouse there, on a wooded lot on the far side of the lake. Garrett had decided to have his unit physician and Angela Herndon take her there, after the National Security Advisor had informed him that it had been decided to have Delta interrogate the woman, instead of turning her over to the CIA or the FBI—at least for the time being.

When the first van was gone, Garrett got out and went to Matt Jensen, who was watching the others unload the kit bags of weapons.

Jensen came to attention and saluted, and Garrett held out his hand to him. Jensen shook it firmly.

"Well done, Sergeant Major," the Delta commander said. "You and your men did one hell of a good job. I'm sorry about Sergeant Haynes."

"The troops did well, sir, considering everything. All of them did. Did you know that Danio took down a Hind with an AT-4?"

"We heard. Apparently our guys on the choppers got the other one."

"Yeah, they did. . . . Sir, what are they going to do with Valenzuela's body?"

"Valenzuela? Oh, Ramirez. I don't know. Why?" Garrett wondered, looking over as the two bodies were being taken off the aircraft and carried to the airtight aluminum body boxes in the back of the van.

"He was a good soldier, once," Jensen answered. "As good as any of us. He might still be, if we'd gone back after him."

"Yes, he won a DSC in Vietnam, before he was captured, didn't he?"

"Yes, sir, he did. And I'm not sure any of us wouldn't have gone bad, under the same circumstances."

Garrett looked quizzically at his troubled subordinate. *"You* wouldn't have, Sergeant Major."

Jensen looked into his commander's eyes. "I'm not so sure, sir."

For the next several hours, Greer went over every detail of the mission with the seven survivors of the operation, until he had a complete picture of almost every move each of them had made. Several times, he went over what each had heard Ramirez say, in an effort to get every possible clue about what might have happened to the missing plutonium. Finally, he released them to get some food and sleep. He would quiz them again in the morning in an effort to find any of the missing pieces to the puzzle. Then he left for Woodlake, to see what Angela had been able to get from Nadia Cruz, and to question her himself. Several miles from Camp Mackall, he turned around and went back to get Santos Baldero. Baldero had been there and, because he spoke Spanish as his native tongue, he might be able to glean more information from the Nicaraguan woman.

"Sorry to keep you from getting any sleep, Sergeant

Baldero, but I think, when we question the woman, it would be best to have someone along who was there."

"No sweat, Major Greer. I don't think I could sleep, anyway. I keep seeing the man I killed, over and over in my mind. And Lawrence taping Mike Haynes up in plastic."

"It's a tough business, sometimes, I know. At least, I imagine it is," the military intelligence officer said. "I imagine Captain Brown is going through the same sort of feelings you are, about now."

"Rachel Brown?"

"Yeah."

"What do you mean?"

"Major Ames called from Miami a while ago to say that he, Mister Wells, and Captain Brown would get to Fayette-ville later this evening. It seems that on the way to the airport, a couple of bad guys tried to take Ames and her out. Dave said he saw her put two or three rounds in the face of one of them."

"Jesus," Baldero muttered. "Hell of a thing for a woman to have to do."

Baldero slept the rest of the way to the safehouse, where Greer learned from Doc Reed and Angela Herndon that Nadia Cruz was depressed, but physically unharmed. Angela had avoided asking her any questions, and was concentrating on trying to win the Nicaraguan woman's confidence and put her at ease. Nadia was sitting on the couch in the living room, slowly sipping a cup of hot soup, when Doc Reed let Greer and Baldero in.

"So far, all she seems concerned about is what happens to Emilio's body," Angela said. "All I could tell her was that I didn't know, but I'd try to find out."

"Let me have some time with her, will you?" Santos Baldero asked. "Alone."

Angela and Doc looked at Greer, who said, "Sure. That's why I brought you along. We'll be down in the basement rec room."

Baldero sat down in a chair opposite the Nicaraguan woman. He spoke softly to her in her native tongue. "Señora Valenzuela, my name is Santos. I was there when your husband was shot by the Sandinista helicopters. Do you remember me?"

She stared at him a moment, then asked, "Where is he now? What will you do with him?"

"His body is not far away. We will bury him with dignity. Did you know that he was once a hero in this country?"

"He told me he won some medals in Vietnam. Why did you kill him?"

"We didn't kill him, señora. If we had wanted to kill him, we would have killed him and left. We were trying to get him before the Cubans did."

"The Cubans? What Cubans?"

"Cubans were flying the Sandinista helicopters, señora. They came to kill him."

"But why? He worked for the Cubans, taught courses for them in Havana. Why would they want to kill him?"

"Señora Valenzuela . . ."

"We weren't married," Nadia Cruz interrupted. "And his name is Ramirez—Emilio Ramirez."

"You are carrying his child; you were his wife. And we both know his name was Raul Valenzuela. That was his name when he fought heroically for this country. We aren't certain why the Cubans wanted him dead, Señora Valenzuela. That's what we want you to help us find out."

For nearly two hours he spoke softly to the woman, asking her about her family, her life with Ramirez, earlier known as Valenzuela. She told him of her hopes for her unborn child; how under the Sandinista government, he might be able to go to college, even though she herself had been born a peasant.

"If so," Baldero commented, "it would be only because he is the son of 'Emilio Ramirez.' They used him, señora. And then they killed him. Why?"

Angela came in to check on them, getting Nadia a soft drink, and Baldero a cup of coffee.

When she was gone, Baldero continued his conversation with Nadia Cruz. He avoided pressing her for information that might lead to the missing plutonium, concentrating instead on trying to win her confidence, and sowing seeds of doubt in her mind about her dead mate's relationship with the communist regimes who had exploited him since his capture in Vietnam many years earlier.

"You need to get some rest now, señora," he said finally, "for your son as well as yourself. Angela will look after you, as will the physician, if you need him. I will be back tomorrow to see you. And, as I promised, I will find out about your husband's funeral, and do all I can to see that you are allowed to be there."

Baldero drove from the safehouse at Woodlake to the Delta headquarters on Fort Bragg, while Jim Greer debriefed him on his conversation with the woman, recording it all on a small cassette recorder.

"Damn good job, Sergeant Baldero," the intelligence officer commented. "You seem to have really won her over. Of course, we'll need you to go back tomorrow, maybe longer, and continue working on her."

"Well, the whole key now will be to have a funeral service for Ramirez. I think if we can do that, she'll really be ready to open up for us."

"That'll be tough to arrange, I might as well tell you, Sergeant Baldero."

"Well, arrange it, sir. Hell, if you can't pull *that* off, you don't deserve to be the Delta intelligence officer."

A few minutes later, they were in the headquarters, where Dave Ames, Rachel Brown, and Jerry Wells had arrived a short time earlier. Their boss, Colonel Garrett, had returned from Camp Mackall after seeing that Jensen and his men were fed and bedded down for the night. He sat in the situation room while Greer debriefed the three who had just returned from El Salvador by commercial airlines. Then he said, "All right, you've all done an outstanding job with this thing, all the way through. Jim, I want you to get a few hours sleep, then put together two or three pages of the key things you've learned from the debriefings. You and I have to go to D.C. tomorrow to see the National Security Advisor."

He looked over his subordinates, then said, "The rest of you, go on home and get a good night's sleep. Dave, you come on back in the morning and stand by here 'til Jim and I get back from Washington. Rachel, you stay out at Woodlake and help Angela baby-sit Ramirez's girlfriend at the safehouse."

"Sir, one thing. What about Haynes, and a funeral for Ramirez?"

"I'll get guidance on what to tell Sergeant Haynes's parents. I'm not too sure about how to handle Ramirez's body, much less having a funeral for him."

Dave Ames thought a moment, then said, "I'll take care of it, boss. Jerry, you can help me."

"How's that?" Garrett asked his operations officer.

"Trust me, boss. I've got a plan."

Dave and Rachel walked together to the parking lot outside the headquarters building.

"Rachel, I . . . well, I just want to say thanks, and . . ."

She took him by the hand. "I'm glad I got the chance to go, Dave. Glad it was with you, glad it was supporting guys like the ones we have here."

"Yeah, well, none of them could have handled that situation with the man in the car any better than you did. He almost had me."

She moved in front of him and put her head on his chest, and he wrapped his arms around her. For a moment they stood there in the dark parking lot, then she whispered, "Dave, come home with me tonight."

In her condominium at Woodlake, they made love tenderly. Her sleep was restless, for the thought of killing the gunman in El Salvador disturbed her deeply. She woke Dave late in the night with her weeping, and he made love to her again, and then they both slept soundly until morning.

Lieutenant Colonel Roland Brewer, the National Security Council staff officer who was one of the handful of people in Washington aware of the operation to capture Emilio Ramirez, picked Wilton Garrett and Jim Greer up from National Airport. He drove them to the White House, got them cleared by the Secret Service guards, and escorted them to the west wing briefing room of the National Security Advisor, George Carruthers. Harry Lawson, the Central Intelligence Agency officer who had been there when Dave Ames first briefed Carruthers on Delta's plan for Operation Arctic Falcon, was there again, and Brewer introduced him to Garrett and Greer. Then Carruthers came in. He shook hands with Garrett, who introduced him to Greer.

"The reason he looks so tired, sir, is that he *is*," Garrett quipped. "I had him up all night, preparing the debriefing reports."

"All right. Have a seat, gentlemen, and let's see where we are with this thing."

They went over the operation in detail. When they got to the downing of the Cuban-crewed Hind helicopters, Carruthers said, "Damn, I wish your guys could have gotten out of there just a few minutes earlier, Colonel."

"Well," Lawson interjected, "at least there are now twenty-two fewer Cubans to stir things up down there."

"Twenty-two?" Jim Greer asked. "I thought the Hind only had a crew of five."

"It does," the CIA officer answered. "But the agent who saw them leave Managua said he saw six more men load into each of them just before they took off."

"The commandos referred to in the intercepted message," Brewer added.

"With the three guerrillas your team shot in the village, plus Ramirez and your sergeant, that makes twenty-seven people killed. Not exactly what we planned when we decided to go after Ramirez."

"Twenty-nine, sir," Lawson corrected. "Don't forget the two who tried to hit Ames and the girl on the way to the airport. But, if Ramirez was planning to do what we think he might have been, that's a small price to pay compared to what *could* have happened."

"What do you mean?" Garrett asked.

Lawson looked at Carruthers, who said, "You might as well tell him, Harry. He already knows about the plutonium. One of his men who was in Vietnam when Ramirez got the stuff, knew about it."

"Sergeant Major Jensen," Garrett added. "The man who led the team in after Ramirez."

"Small world," Lawson commented, then explained to Garrett and Greer that among the things they found in the house in Arlington that Ramirez had used as a safehouse several months earlier was a notebook. "The remaining pages were all blank, but the top one had some impressions on it which we were able to enhance. We gave it to one of our scientists to look at. When he finally bothered to give us a report on it, he said that it had to do with the construction of an improvised nuclear device—one that would probably work. That's why we wanted Ramirez so badly."

"Holy Mother of God!" Jim Greer said. The others looked at him, and Garrett said, "You mean the comments Ramirez made to Matt before he died?"

"Yes, sir."

Carruthers was looking quizzically at the two Delta officers, and Greer said, "Sir, I hadn't gotten to the part of my briefing about what Ramirez said to our people and his girl after he was wounded. I'm afraid I might understand, now, what he meant."

As the others sat in stunned silence, Greer read the debriefing comments about Ramirez's remarks as he lay dying early the morning before. "When Jensen mentioned the plutonium, Ramirez said, 'Yeah, payback is a motherfucker.' Then he said something about 'you'll find out soon.' When they brought his girlfriend to him, he asked her what day it was, then he said, 'Thirteen days and you'll remember me forever.'"

Greer looked up from his debriefing notes.

"Oh, my God," the National Security Advisor said. Then he said, "All right, gentlemen, let's go over everything we know about the possibility of Ramirez having constructed an improvised nuclear device, which may be set to explode in thirteen, no, now it's eleven or twelve days."

12

Half an hour later, the five men had reached their conclusions, which George Carruthers had written on a single sheet of paper. He looked at his watch, and said, "All right, gentlemen, the President is supposed to leave in a little over an hour for a function up in Philadelphia this afternoon. I'd better get this to him right away."

The others stood as he left to see the Chief Executive. He got to the door, then turned to Harry Lawson of the CIA and asked, "Harry, what was the name of that guy from the Nuclear Emergency Search Team you took out to Ramirez's place in Arlington?"

"Wayne, sir. Toby Wayne," Lawson answered.

"Find out where he is, and get him here right away."

While Lawson tried to track the NEST scientist down by telephone, the others went over what would have to be done to try to determine where, if it actually existed, the improvised nuclear device might be.

"At the least," Roland Brewer offered, "I'm sure they'll want to do everything possible to find the plutonium, whether there's a bomb or not."

While Garrett and Brewer went over who should be notified—the FBI, the Secret Service, the Nuclear Emergency Search Team from the Department of Energy, among others—Lawson got Toby Wayne's wife on the telephone at their home in College Park, Maryland. The scientist was out playing a Saturday morning round of golf, but Mrs. Wayne promised to have him call Lawson as soon as he returned home, which she thought would be any minute. Then he sat beside Jim Greer, and they discussed how to best mobilize the intelligence capabilities of the United States and her allies in order to learn all that could be learned about Ramirez and the device he was assumed to have constructed.

"Jesus, I sure hope they're getting something out of Nadia Cruz," Greer remarked. "Santos Baldero, one of our NCOs who was on the mission, talked to her for a long time last night. He seemed to be winning her over. I hope to God she talks to him and gives him whatever she knows."

A few minutes later, the door to the briefing room opened, and Carruthers said, "Gentlemen, the President."

The men stood up, and after the President said, "Hello, Rollie" to Lieutenant Colonel Brewer, Carruthers introduced him to Garrett, who in turn introduced Jim Greer. Carruthers introduced Harry Lawson, and the President said, "Sit down, sit down." He sat at the head of the briefing room conference table, and the others sat along the sides, as the President looked at Garrett, and said, "Well, Colonel, George tells me it looks like we may have a bit of a problem."

"Yes, we may, Mr. President."

The President looked at each of the others, then said, "All right, we can handle this one of two ways. We can get all of our various agencies working on this thing, in which case we may as well issue a press release about the whole operation and the device— 'alleged device,' I guess I should say— since, once we notify everybody, some bastard is sure to leak it anyway. Or we can continue to work on it with the bare minimum number of people possible, at least for a few more days. That's assuming, of course, that we have the eleven or twelve days we *think* we have. If we don't make any progress after a few days, then, of course, we'll have to get the whole thing out into the open, with all the panic and finger pointing and political damage that would create."

He looked at his National Security Advisor who, prior to assuming that position, had been Assistant Secretary of State. "George, what do you think the chances are of keeping a lid on this, what with all the Cubans Colonel Garrett's boys dispatched down in Central America?"

"Well, there's no way to say for certain, Mr. President, but I've been thinking about it. Neither the Cubans, the Nicaraguans, nor the Salvadorans on either side, have said anything about it."

"Sir," Lieutenant Colonel Brewer interrupted, "the U.S. Military Assistance Group Commander in El Salvador has reported flying over the crash sites and seeing the wrecked Hinds, and he's reported that to the Salvadorans. They're assuming the choppers were resupplying the guerrillas, and are speculating that either they had a midair collision, or the guerrillas shot them down, thinking they were ours. They're planning on issuing a protest to the Nicaraguans this afternoon."

"I see," said the President. "Well, that could work *for* us. We can issue a protest ourselves, backing up the Salvadorans. I doubt that the Nicaraguans or the Cubans can prove otherwise, even though *they'll* know that *we* know better. Remember, they have no reason to think that we didn't get the guy we went after—Ramirez, isn't it?—and that we're now picking his brain."

"That's right, Mr. President," Garrett said. "There's no way they'd know the gunfire from their choppers hit him. For all they know, we got him out alive."

"Exactly," the President agreed. "I doubt that they'll say a thing, until after they see whether or not we're going to parade him in front of the TV cameras. I'm not nearly as worried about that as I am about what we're going to tell the people on the Hill Monday morning, when they start demanding to know the results of the mission."

"Mr. President," Harry Lawson of the CIA said, *"they* don't know that we didn't get Ramirez out alive, either. And they weren't told anything about the plutonium. As far as they know, we were after Ramirez because he's an American turncoat and a terrorist. Do we have to tell them any differently?"

"Are you suggesting that we go up and *lie* to the Congress, Mr. Lawson?" the President asked.

"Well, not exactly *lie*, sir."

"No?" the President said. "It sounds like a good idea to me, under the circumstances. I mean, if we can find this thing before it goes off, there's no way they can second guess our decision to withhold the information from that sieve up there, even if they find out later we didn't tell them everything. And if the damn thing goes off—at least if it goes off somewhere in this country—I'll be such a dead horse anyway that a little more beating from them won't hurt me."

The telephone rang just then, and while Lieutenant Colonel Brewer answered it, the President rose and paced around the room, deep in thought.

Brewer said, "It's for you, Harry," and passed the phone to the CIA man. It was Dr. Toby Wayne. Lawson told him to come to the NSC briefing room as soon as possible, then hung up.

"Toby Wayne. He'll be here within the hour," he informed Carruthers.

The President returned to the head of the table. "All right, gentlemen, here's what we're going to do. For the time being, we will limit knowledge of this thing to as few people as we possibly can. I'll rely on your discretion to decide who else must be brought in, in order to try to find out what we can during the next several days. Now, I'm not going to say exactly how long I'll give you to sort this thing out before I bring the whole of the government to bear on the problem. That will depend on how much progress you make over the next couple of days. But I can tell you this," he added as he looked each man in the eye, "it won't be more than four or five days."

He started toward the door, then turned around to face the five men again. "Gentlemen, I'm sure I don't need to remind you what a nuclear weapon could do if it exploded among the unwarned population of a major city somewhere. Don't do something to try to protect my political career out of a sense of misplaced loyalty, if it means increasing the possibility of innocent people being killed. If you're not making any progress, *say* so. In fact, if you feel I'm increasing the likelihood of people being hurt by trying to do this with a few people for the time being, for God's sake, say so *now,* and I'll get every agency in this government at work on it today."

The other men in the room were silent, then Wilton Garrett said, "Mr. President, we'll give it our best shot."

"Give us a couple of days, sir," George Carruthers said, "and we'll let you know whether or not we're getting anywhere."

"Very well, then," the President of the United States said to the five talented men in the room with him. "Good luck. And God bless you."

At Fort Bragg, Dave Ames was putting into action his plan to conduct a funeral for Ramirez in order to further gain the confidence and cooperation of Nadia Cruz, the pregnant Nicaraguan woman. Jensen's team had returned from the isolation area at Camp Mackall, and Ames had briefed them on the plan.

Several miles west of Fort Bragg's main post area, in the pine woods which cover most of the fifteen-by-thirty mile area of the big military reservation, there is an old, wood frame Presbyterian church which was established in the 1750s by the Scots-Irish immigrants who settled the area before the Revolutionary War. Since Fort Bragg was established as a military base during the First World War, the church has been without a congregation, but the building and the cemetery beside it were maintained by the Army, until, in 1974, Longstreet Church was made a national historical site. Since then, once a year, the descendants of the old church's founders have held a memorial service there. Except for that one annual service, the church is unused—usually.

Dave Ames was intent on making use of the old Presbyterian church for the funeral of Emilio Ramirez, and now two of the members of Jensen's team were there preparing a gravesite for the former Special Forces soldier, while another of them guarded the road which led into the churchyard from the paved road nearby, in the unlikely event that someone might wander into the area of the old church. If so, the guard would simply explain that there was a training exercise going on nearby, and send the intruder away.

The site the men chose for Ramirez's grave was in the lowest corner of the half-acre cemetery where some two hundred people had been buried since the mid-eighteenth century. Dan Holton was one of the men digging the grave, and while he took a short break from digging, he paused to read the inscription on the tombstone nearest the new grave.

Here lies Margaret, the inscription read, *the consort of Angus Gilchrist, and the daughter of Catherine and Archibald McKoy. She was born in Charleston, S.C., June 20th, 1782, and died October 9th, 1811, leaving four children: Effy, Mary, Archibald, and John. Reader; did you but know the worth that's buried here, you'd heave a sigh, my friend, you'd drop a tear. Of her deserts, us 'nough this truth to know; she lived a Christian, she died without fear.*

"Hey, Boo," Holton called to Boo Maxton, the other man on the grave-digging detail. "Check this out."

Maxton climbed out of the nearly completed hole and stood beside Holton, reading the epitaph. "Four kids, and died at twenty-nine," he remarked. He looked around at the old tombstones clustered in family groups within the low stone wall. The names were McPhail, McNeill, Duncan, and McLaughlin.

"You know," he said to Holton, "I notice that almost all the names are Scottish. I guess that's because it's a Presbyterian church, huh?"

"Other way around," Holton replied. "The church is Presbyterian, because the people who settled this area were Scots-Irish. Matter of fact, there was a woman, Flora McDonald, who raised a Scottish Loyalist regiment of guys from around here and fought against the Americans during the Revolutionary War."

"Really?" Maxton asked with interest. "Hell, I didn't know this area had so much history to it."

"Sure," Dan Holton, who was a history buff, replied.

"Did you know that Cornwallis camped just a couple of miles down the road, right here on post? Some of the Scots buried here probably fed the Brits."

"I'll be damned," Maxton said. "Did you notice that mass grave up there by the gate?"

"You mean the Confederate soldiers?"

"Yeah," Maxton, a Midwesterner, replied. "So I guess Ramirez won't be the only traitor buried here."

"Why, you goddamn Yankee," Holton said, "get your ass back in that hole and dig, boy!"

It was almost sunset when Rachel Brown and Angela Herndon arrived at Longstreet Church with Nadia Cruz. Ames and the members of Jensen's team had arrived earlier with Ramirez's body, and had placed it in the spacious, wood-framed church. There was no electricity to the old white building, so they had opened all the shutters to allow some of the fading sunlight in. Jensen met the women at the door and escorted Nadia to the front pew. She sat silent and tearless as Jerry Wells, fluent in several languages, including Spanish, read a brief, dignified service for the soul of Raul Valenzuela. Then, with Nadia Cruz on Jensen's arm directly behind them, the other six surviving members of the team carried the airtight aluminum box into the stone-walled cemetery and lowered it into the hole. Nadia Cruz broke down and wept then, but soon regained her composure, and threw a handful of dirt onto the box in the grave. She took Wells's hand, shook it and said, *"Gracias, Señor,"* then looked at the others in the fading light and said, *"Muchas gracias."* Then Rachel and Angela led her away and got into the car to take her back to the safehouse.

As soon as the women had driven away, Dave Ames said to the others, "All right, get that box out of the hole and let's get it filled back in before somebody comes along and catches us here." Garrett had called from Washington earlier and told him not to actually bury Ramirez, as the man from the Nuclear Emergency Search Team might need to have an autopsy done on the body to determine how much residual plutonium there was in it. He felt that might somehow help him in his efforts to figure out where and when Ramirez might have placed the improvised nuclear bomb. The aluminum box the Delta Force men were now removing from the gravesite contained only sandbags.

13

By the time the men got back to Delta headquarters from Longstreet Church, their commander and his intelligence officer had returned from Washington. Garrett called them all into the situation room and told them what had transpired at the White House.

"Our best guess—and it's only a guess—is that there *is* a nuke, and that it's set to go off sometime on the twenty-third. That's a week from Thursday. And we think it's probably somewhere in the Washington metropolitan area. That being the case, we're going to move our operation up there tomorrow. Dr. Wayne, the NEST scientist; and Harry Lawson from the Agency, are now at the house Ramirez used in Arlington, trying to see if they can pick up any more clues there. Now, let's go over everything we know again, in detail, then I want to hear every idea anyone's got about how we might attack this thing."

"Sir," Matt Jensen asked, "what about Mike Haynes?"

"I've already sent Colonel Schumann to Pennsylvania to notify his parents that Sergeant Haynes was killed in a training accident here at Fort Bragg, Sergeant Major. I'm afraid that's all we're going to be allowed to tell them, at least for now."

For more than three hours, the men went over what they

knew about the situation, and what they might do to try to learn about the device they feared Ramirez had constructed and planted somewhere. Early in the conversation, they decided it would be wise to bring in the chief of Delta's Technical Cell, Master Sergeant Lanny Cabe. Cabe was responsible for the design and development of unique items of technical equipment which the Delta Force sometimes required in the performance of its mission. The cleverly designed satellite radio which Rachel Brown had used during the mission to El Salvador was a product of Cabe's imagination and skill. The chubby, balding master sergeant was a genius at constructing such items. He also happened to know more about nuclear weapons and their functioning than anyone else in the Delta Force. Jim Greer got him on the telephone and told him to get in as soon as possible, and be prepared to be away from home for as long as a week. Cabe arrived twenty minutes later, and was there for most of the discussion.

The men concluded that the best immediately available source of information was Nadia Cruz. Rachel and Angela Herndon were with her in the safehouse at the Woodlake resort now, trying to elicit what information they could. Garrett dispatched Santos Baldero to Woodlake to assist them, as he was the one whom Cruz seemed to trust the most.

When they were discussing Ramirez's association with the Arab terrorist Hakim Nidal, Cabe said, "You know, the bombs that bastard has been linked to are the most technically sophisticated ones we know about, with the possible exception of some of the IRA devices. I wouldn't be surprised if he has more to do with this than meets the eye."

"Let me pull all we have on Nidal out of the computer, then," Jim Greer suggested. "Maybe we can find something there that'll help." He left the situation room and went to the bank of computers in the wing of the building which had been turned into the classified storage vault, and coaxed from the memory banks a printout of everything that was known about the infamous Hakim Nidal. The effort paid off. He returned to the situation room to announce what he had found.

"Bingo!" he said as he entered. "Cabe, you're a genius. Listen to this."

He read portions of several of the intelligence reports, which indicated that Nidal had been reported to be looking for someone with the technical expertise to build a nuclear weapon. It was something that western governments had long feared—that some terrorist group would one day gain the knowledge and the materials necessary to build the ultimate terrorist weapon—a workable atomic bomb.

"In fact, Sergeant Major," he said to Dick Salem, "they think that the time you almost nabbed him, when he was on the way to Frankfurt, it was to see some of the Red Army Faction terrorists in West Germany. They've since been thrown into jail, and the documents the BND got from them indicate they had it figured out, or were on the right track, anyway."

"What about his KGB connection?" Salem inquired. "They were the ones who saved his ass from us in Athens. You think the Russians could be in on this thing, too?"

"No," Greer answered, referring to the sheaf of intelligence reports in his hands. "I don't think so. Here. The reason the KGB wanted him was because Hezbollah was holding one of their people in West Beirut, remember? Nidal has strong ties to Hezbollah, and the Soviets grabbed him to trade for *their* man. It apparently worked. Now Nidal says he hates the Russians, too."

"Too bad Ramirez didn't feel that way. Maybe he would have planted the bomb in Moscow," Salem said. "But if Nidal is tied in to this thing, sir," the command sergeant major of the Delta Force said to Colonel Garrett, "why don't you let me have another crack at him?"

Garrett thought a moment, then said, "Yeah! Why not? We could treat it as a whole, separate operation. Nobody but us would have to know it's connected to this thing with Ramirez and the nuke. We can have Carruthers task the other agencies to help us, and have him just say it's because of the Americans Nidal had killed in Rome and Vienna. OK, Sergeant Major, it's yours. Take whoever you want, but for God's sake, don't let anybody else know the connection."

"The problem," Dave Ames interjected, "is that it's gonna be hard getting the other agencies energized in time to get him during the next few days, and that's all the time we have. Somebody's going to have to think of a good reason why we don't have more time to set it up."

"Yeah, that's right," Garrett said. "But we'll think of something. Meanwhile, Dick, go for it."

"Is this one of those things we're going to have to brief the Congressional Intel Committee people on?" Dave Ames asked.

"Normally, we would," Garrett answered. "But I think that because the leak is probably coming from them, we may be able to avoid it."

"Well, when I go up to the Hill on Monday morning to make them think we got Ramirez out alive, I may be able to find out where the leak's coming from—with a little technical help from Cabe, there." Ames grinned, winking at the chubby technical man.

"How's that?" Garrett asked.

"Trust me, boss, like you did with the funeral. I've got a plan."

The meeting broke up soon after Wilton Garrett gave his subordinates the final guidance to get their plan moving. Salem would alert and assemble a fresh team of Delta Force operators to prepare them to go after Hakim Nidal, presently believed to be at his home in West Beirut. Ames would fly to Washington, D.C., as soon as possible, to arrange for a place for the others to stay while they were there, and to rent the cars they might need. Lanny Cabe would load up a van full of technical equipment and make the six-hour drive to the Washington area that night. The others, including Nadia Cruz and those now at the Woodlake safehouse with her, would start for Washington the following morning—Sunday.

Garrett and Greer left for Woodlake to find out what new information Ramirez's Nicaraguan lover may have given Baldero and the two Delta women.

They arrived to discover that Nadia Cruz was beginning to cooperate with Santos Baldero in his efforts to extract information from her. Rachel summarized what they had gleaned from her since the "funeral" Cruz had insisted upon before she would reveal anything.

"She was in the Washington area with Ramirez when he came to the States last fall. They came in with a flight of what she assumes was a load of cocaine, from Colombia. They stayed for about two weeks. He was away most days and evenings for the first week, but she says they spent most of the second week just walking around the city, visiting all of the public buildings they could get into. And listen to *this* bit of irony. Among other places they visited were the Pentagon, the Capitol, and the White House."

"Holy! . . . Any mention of any sort of device that could be the bomb?"

"No," Rachel responded. "We've pretty well avoided any specific questioning about it. Sergeant Baldero is afraid she might catch on and decide to clam up and let him have his revenge, or something. She *did* say she would be willing to show us all the places in Washington they visited, if she could recognize them. I understand we're leaving for there in the morning?"

"Yes, we are, Captain Brown," her commander answered. "Major Ames is there now, setting it up for us."

"Well, Angela's been sleeping while we talked to Nadia, so I think I'll drop by my house and get packed, then come back and let her go get what she needs for the trip. You gents want to stop by for a drink? You've earned it."

"Thanks," Garrett answered. "I think I will, unless Major Greer has any objections."

"Sounds good to me, boss. I'll come back here with Rachel after she gets packed, and help her baby-sit the woman while Baldero and Angela get ready to go to Washington. You got anything to eat there, Rachel? I've hardly had a bite the last couple of days."

"Sure. In fact, I've got a couple of steaks I need to get out of the fridge before we go. You can throw them on the grill for us while I pack."

They drove the short distance to her condominium, where Greer busied himself starting a fire in her grill as she fixed them all a drink.

Wilton Garrett had seldom spoken to his subordinate, Captain Rachel Brown, on anything except official matters. As he sat in her living room now, he thought about that. She was a very attractive young woman, and Garrett—divorced more than ten years earlier—was, he admitted to himself now, a little afraid of her. She was so desirable that he feared he might be attracted to her to the degree that he might do something foolish. And that, he knew, could be disastrous. He had seen his men's reactions when—as happened now and then—one of their peers had become enamored of her and made a pass at her that became known to the others. They had been like brothers protecting a beautiful sister from someone they didn't care for. He wondered what *she* thought about it, whether Rachel resented her fellow Delta soldiers' protectiveness as an infringement upon her right to privacy; whether she might not *want* to become romantically involved with one of the fine young men who filled the ranks of the Delta Force.

She came into the living room and handed him the bourbon and water he had asked for, smiling and saying, "Here you are, sir," as she did so. He couldn't help noticing the shapeliness of her hips as she went to the sliding glass door which opened onto her patio to take Jim Greer his drink.

"I'm going to go ahead and pack," she said when she stepped back in. "Help yourself to another drink, if you like, then we'll throw those steaks on the grill."

"Thanks," Garrett muttered as she disappeared into her bedroom.

He smiled to himself and shook his head, thinking, *Man,*

*if she was in the KGB and offered to trade me a night with her
for telling her some national secrets, I'd tell her everything I
know.* He wondered about her love life, entertained a brief
fantasy about making love to her himself, then sighed
heavily before stepping onto the patio with Jim Greer.

"Ah, Major Greer," he said, "the burden of command!"

Greer looked at him with a serious face and said, "Yeah,
boss. But I wouldn't worry too much. Even if we can't find
the thing in the next few days, I'm sure it'll be found once
they get the FBI and everybody else looking for it."

Garrett smiled at his intelligence officer, realizing that, for
the first time since he had learned about the nuclear device,
the sensuousness of Rachel Brown had caused him, for a few
minutes, at least, to forget it.

"Look," he said to his intelligence officer now that his
mind was back on his duties as the Delta Force commander,
"I need to get on back to the stockade. You and Captain
Brown go ahead and have dinner, then you can get a ride
back in with her or one of the other people in the safehouse,
OK?"

Garrett's deputy commander, Lieutenant Colonel Paul
McCarthy, was due back at Fort Bragg that evening from a
two-week trip to Britain, and Garrett decided that he'd
better fill him in on what was happening, not only so that he
could run things at Delta headquarters for the next few days,
and fend off speculation about what might be going on with
so many key members of the Delta Force gone, but so that he
could support the requests of the teams in Washington as
well as Salem's efforts to get Nidal. As soon as Garrett got
back to the stockade, he telephoned Paul McCarthy at his
home, and asked him to come on in.

He arrived from his on-post quarters ten minutes later.

"How was your trip?" Garrett asked McCarthy as he
entered the situation room and closed the door.

"Great. All the folks in Hereford send their regards.
They're looking forward to a visit from you. So, what's been
going on here?"

Garrett struck a match and lit the cigar in his mouth, then

said, "Oh, the same old shit. We sent a team to El Sal to capture a guy, and they shot down two Hinds and killed a couple of dozen Cubans. The guy we went after was killed, so we kidnapped his pregnant girlfriend. She's going to go with us to D.C. tomorrow and help us try to find the nuclear time bomb he set there, while Sergeant Major Salem takes a team to the Mediterranean to capture Hakim Nidal."

Garrett's deputy grinned at his commander's lighthearted description of events for a moment, then his mouth dropped open. Ever since Garrett's assignment as the commander of the unit, the two men—friends since they had served as captains together many years before—had engaged in this sort of banter whenever one of them learned something of great importance and broke the news of it to the other.

It had started one day when McCarthy was sitting in Garrett's office, and the secure telephone had rung. The deputy answered it while Garrett continued telling a joke to the two sergeants major in the office with them. McCarthy said, "Of course, sir, just a moment," then laid the telephone down and listened to the rest of Garrett's joke. When they had finished laughing, Garrett asked, "Who's on the phone, anyway?"

"Oh, just the Vice President," McCarthy answered. Garrett rolled his eyes, then picked up the telephone to see who it *really* was. It was the Vice President of the United States.

Not long after that, Delta's higher headquarters had called and asked that Garrett come over right away to see the commanding general. Garrett was on the way in from the rifle range at the time, so Paul McCarthy went in his stead. He walked into the mess hall an hour or so later, where Garrett was having lunch. "So, what did the general want?" Garrett inquired after his second-in-command got a cup of coffee and sat down at the table with him.

"Aw, not much. He just wants us to go invade some little island tomorrow."

They had invaded Grenada the next day.

Now, Garrett had finally gotten one up on Paul McCarthy.

The stunned lieutenant colonel stared at him. "You're not kidding, are you, boss?"

Garrett shook his head.

"Fuck me to tears," McCarthy muttered, lowering his head at the realization that Garrett was telling the truth.

14

By Sunday afternoon, Colonel Wilton Garrett and the other Delta Force members who would attempt to solve the mystery of the improvised nuclear weapon, which they were increasingly convinced was in the Washington, D.C. area, had arrived at the safehouses Dave Ames had arranged for them to stay in. One was a furnished apartment in Arlington, near the safehouse that Emilio Ramirez and Nadia Cruz had occupied when they had illegally entered the United States for a two-week stay several months earlier. Angela Herndon, Santos Baldero, and Delta's physician, Doc Reed, would stay there with Nadia Cruz. The others would occupy two suites Ames had reserved in the Crystal City Holiday Inn, just south of the Potomac River from Washington.

Wilton Garrett, Jim Greer, and Rachel Brown went straight to one of the Holiday Inn suites, where they found Harry Lawson of the CIA and Lieutenant Colonel Roland Brewer of the National Security Council staff waiting. Dave Ames would join them there as soon as he got the others settled into the Arlington apartment. Lanny Cabe, Delta's technical genius, had set up a satellite radio in the bedroom of the suite, and had installed a KL-43 encryption device on the telephone beside it. On the bed were two open suitcases full of electronic devices and other tools of Cabe's trade, and four small briefcases. Cabe was slitting open the linings of the briefcases when Garrett looked into the bedroom. "What are you rigging up there, Sergeant Cabe?" Garrett asked him.

"Part of Major Ames's plan, sir. Oh, Dick Salem called a few minutes ago—wanted you to give him a call on the satcom as soon as you got in."

"What callsigns are we using?"

"Sierra One Four is base, you're Sierra Four Two Golf. But the DCO said we ought to just drop all those numbered callsigns and use last names or duty positions, since it's all secure voice and there're only Delta people on the net."

Garrett smiled. Delta's Paul McCarthy never could seem to remember the formal lettered and numbered callsigns they were required to use when communicating with other units, and in this case, he had a point. Garrett picked up the radio handset and said, "Base, Base, this is Garrett, Garrett, over."

A moment later, Dick Salem responded with, "Garrett, this is Salem." The command sergeant major went on to request that the people with Nadia Cruz question her to see if she might be able to give them some information which would be helpful in somehow luring Hakim Nidal out of West Beirut. "We can't come up with any really feasible way of getting in there to get him, boss. Maybe she'll come up with something that'll at least give us some ideas."

"Okay, Sergeant Major. I'll have them start working on that angle. Stand by while I find out from the Agency man here what they've come up with since the Director was tasked last night to help get him. Wait, out."

The night before, Garrett had called the National Security Advisor about the need to try to capture the Lebanese terrorist to see if he could help solve the mystery of the nuclear device. Carruthers had assured him that the Director of Central Intelligence would be tasked immediately to offer all possible assistance. Garrett went to Harry Lawson and asked him what had been done so far.

"The Director called in the Mideast desk and Terrorist Branch people last night," Lawson responded. "Of course, he didn't tell them why we want Nidal so badly—just that we were to assist your people fully in trying to grab him as quickly as possible. They've been working on it all morning. Would it be possible for you to put a liaison team out at Langley, to pass on to your people what they come up with, Colonel?"

"Of course. I'll call my deputy, and tell him to bring in a few people strictly for the Nidal operation. We can run it as a separate, compartmented activity." Turning to his intelligence officer, he said, "Jim, get one of our secure key tapes from Sergeant Cabe and go on out there, so you can talk directly to Salem from the Agency on one of their satcoms. I'll get the DCO to send someone up here to relieve you right away."

Shortly after Garrett called Fort Bragg to get a liaison team dispatched to CIA headquarters in Langley, Dave Ames called from the apartment in Arlington to say that the people there were all settled in, and he would be coming to the Holiday Inn in Crystal City shortly. Garrett passed him Salem's request to question Nadia Cruz about Nidal.

By the time Ames arrived at the suite, Angela Herndon called Garrett on the satellite radio with some good news. Nadia Cruz *did* have some information about Nidal; he was supposed to have met Ramirez in Managua about a week after Ramirez and she returned there from El Salvador. She wasn't certain about the exact date, but it would be sometime during the coming week.

"That means he would have to leave Beirut sometime during the next few days, if he was going to travel by normal, commercial means," Angela speculated.

In the situation room of Delta's Fort Bragg headquarters, Dick Salem monitored Angela's news over the radio net. He broke into the conversation and said, "This is Salem. I monitored that. If he does go commercial, then that means he has to go through Cyprus. I think Beirut Airport is still closed, but even if it isn't, Mideast Airlines is the only airline operating through there, and they make all their transatlantic connections in Larnaca. And if it *is* still closed, then he'll have to either travel up to Damascus by road, or take a boat to Cyprus to get out. Of course, all that's assuming he hasn't heard about Ramirez, and changed whatever plans he has."

"Roger that," Garrett said. "But right now, it's all we've got to go on. I think we'd be well advised to have you head that way as soon as possible, Sergeant Major. I'll get the Agency people started on seeing what they can find out. You decide who you want to go where, and I'll get you the clearances you need."

"This is Salem. Roger, sir. We'll let you know shortly what we think makes the most sense. You might as well warn the Agency that we may be needing weapons and communications support at both locations. And transportation, safehouses, and that sort of thing, too. Anyway, I'll get back to you shortly. Out here."

When Rachel Brown heard her commanding officer discussing the matter with the CIA man, Harry Lawson, she said, "Sir, why don't I get over to Cyprus right away? I can take the concealed satcom radio in, and help the people from the embassy in Nicosia get what they need for Salem's team."

Garrett thought about it a moment. Rachel had spent several weeks in the eastern Mediterranean about a year earlier during an area orientation visit. The whole purpose of those visits was to enable the women from the Admin Detachment to become familiar with the area, the transportation systems, the security situation, the local customs, and so forth, so that they could better support Delta's operations there, if there was ever a requirement to do so. And there was certainly a requirement for such support now.

"Yes," he said. "Good idea, Captain Brown. Get started right away. I'll let Salem know, so he can task you with getting whatever he thinks he'll need there."

The following morning—Monday—Captain Rachel Brown found herself aboard the Air France Concorde from Washington's Dulles Airport, flying toward Paris at twice the speed of sound. With her she had the cleverly disguised satellite radio she had used in El Salvador a few days before, one suitcase of clothing, and ten thousand dollars in cash from the operational fund the CIA man had given her. When she got there that evening, she was to buy the appropriate clothing she would need to support her cover as a vacationing photographer on a busman's holiday in sunny Cyprus.

Meanwhile, Dave Ames and the NSC staff officer, Roland Brewer, were on Capitol Hill, where they had gone to brief the two senators and two representatives who were the senior members from each party of the Senate and House Intelligence Committees, on the untrue story of the successful capture of Emilio Ramirez. Elsewhere in Washington, Sergeants Angela Herndon and Santos Baldero were escorting Nadia Cruz, who was trying to retrace the movements of Ramirez when she had been there with him several months earlier. The efforts of the Delta Force members to win her over with kindness, reinforced by the promise of a new life in the United States for her and her unborn child, had won the Nicaraguan woman's cooperation.

In the office of Senator Daniel Cronan, the Democratic Chairman of the Senate Select Committee on Intelligence, Ames was completing the false tale of Delta's successful capture of the turncoat, Emilio Ramirez.

"Right now, Senator," he lied, "he's under interrogation up at Fort Meade. We should be finished with him in about a week, at which time the White House will probably release a statement. Meanwhile, sir, I remind you that all aspects of the operation are still classified Top Secret."

When they left Senator Cronan's office, Ames said to Brewer, "One down, three to go. Give me the briefcase."

They briefed the Republican senator who was his party's senior member of the Intelligence Committee, whom Ames told that Ramirez was currently under interrogation at Fort Belvoir. Then they left the Hart Senate Office Building and went to the Rayburn Building to brief the two congressmen in their offices there. First, though, they went to Brewer's car, where Ames took two briefcases from the back seat, and handed one to Brewer.

After they had briefed Representative Wes Bolton—informing him that Ramirez was being interrogated at MacDill Air Force Base—they went to the office of Bolton's Republican counterpart, where Ames explained that Ramirez was currently under questioning at nearby Andrews Air Force Base.

As they were leaving the building, the Republican congressman's receptionist caught up with them, and called, "Colonel Brewer."

The two men stopped and turned around. She held out a briefcase and said, "One of you left this in the congressman's office."

"Oh," Dave Ames said, "That's mine. Thank you. If my head wasn't attached, I'd probably lose it, too."

He took the briefcase, and as he and Brewer walked out of the building, said, "Well, three out of four ain't bad."

Dr. Toby Wayne followed Nadia Cruz and her two escorts everywhere they went. After the Pentagon tour with a group of other "tourists," they took the Metro train from Virginia into the District of Columbia, getting off at the Smithsonian station, where Nadia took them first to the Air and Space Museum. As he had done in the Pentagon, Wayne avoided having his briefcase inspected by showing the guard the FBI credentials which the National Security Advisor had arranged to be issued to him. His briefcase contained delicate sensors which could detect even the most minute traces of radioactive material, so that he would know if they happened to pass anywhere near a concentration of such material. When he walked past the Apollo capsule which had returned the first men from the surface of the moon, the sensors detected enough radiation to trigger the vibrating alarm in the handle of Wayne's briefcase. He gave Angela the prearranged signal to indicate that the alarm had been activated, and while she and Baldero steered the Nicaraguan woman to a bench to sit and wait for him, Wayne went into a stall in the men's room, where he opened the briefcase and examined the sensors' digital readout of the radiation they had detected. As he had suspected, the Apollo capsule had triggered the alarm from the small amount of residual radiation it had absorbed during its flight through outer space years earlier—not enough to be harmful, and with no indication that it was emitting the telltale subatomic particles which were characteristic of plutonium. He closed the briefcase, walked out of the men's room, and scratched the back of his neck when he saw Angela looking at him—the signal they had arranged to denote "false alarm."

They went to the Capitol next, and took the guided tour. When they had completed it, and learned that the next place Nadia had visited with Ramirez was the National Art Museum, Angela said, "Let's get some lunch in the cafeteria there, before we trace their route, then."

"Good idea," Santos Baldero responded. "I'm starved."

In Paris, Rachel Brown checked the additional suitcase she had bought at Charles de Gaulle Airport for her flight on to Larnaca, Cyprus. It was filled with the fashionable clothes she had bought in the smart shops at the airport—the kinds of outfits she would need as a vacationer to Cyprus, including two bathing suits. As she boarded her flight, she couldn't help wondering how many women could only dream of such a life; of boarding a jet in Paris with a suitcase of the latest in French fashions, en route to a Mediterranean island with a purse full of money to help her government capture an international terrorist. What a life! And then she thought of the man with the submachine gun in the car in El Salvador, and recalled, in slow motion, raising her pistol toward his face, and pulling the trigger again and again. She shuddered, and prayed that she would never have to do such a thing again. And she wished that Dave Ames was there with her, in case she did, remembering the way his lovemaking had chased the image of the incident from her mind that night in her condominium—at least for a while.

In Washington, as he rode with Brewer back toward Crystal City, Dave Ames had Rachel on his mind, too. In spite of the obvious need for her to do so, he was deeply disappointed when it was decided to send her to Cyprus to support Salem. She had completely changed his mind about the need for women in the Delta Force. Until their trip to El Salvador—in fact, until the moment she killed the gunman who was about to fire his submachine gun at them—he'd felt that the women of Delta's so-called Admin Detachment were little more than a frivolous effort to placate the women's rights advocates in the Army. He enjoyed having them around, as he enjoyed the company of any attractive woman. But he really hadn't seen them as being worth the effort. Rachel's actions in El Salvador had changed his mind about their professional ability and value. And the night in her condominium had changed his mind about her, personally.

Before that night, he had sometimes entertained the idea of trying to seduce her—to make her another of his sexual conquests. Even while he had followed her car in his on the way to her place at Woodlake that night, he had found himself issuing self-congratulations for another amorous victory. But when they got there, and she had wept in his arms, and he had comforted her, it all seemed to change. For the first time, he felt needed by a woman in more than just a physical sense. And when he took her to her bed, he found for the first time that he wanted to *give* to a lover, instead of just taking from her. And he had done so. But Rachel had been so giving in return, that he felt a sense of sharing he had never really known before. Yes, sharing, that was it. The more he felt he was giving, the more it seemed that he was receiving. He had never known anything like it, and now he wondered if he was, for the first time in a long while, falling in love. Now, he laughed at himself. For without informing Garrett or the others, he had rented a motel room in the Twin Bridges Marriott, not far from Crystal City, so that he would have a place to take Rachel if they found themselves with some time to be alone during the operation in Washington. And now she was thousands of miles away, and there was no one else he wanted to go there with.

He laughed at himself again, and Brewer said, "What are you chuckling about, Dave?"

"Oh, just thinking about that secretary running after us

with the briefcase. He's probably the guy we want to catch, since he's the only one who found the briefcase."

"You should have shoved it farther up under the sofa," Brewer remarked.

"Yeah, I guess. Anyway, after we check in at the safehouse and get some lunch, we can go back over and pick up the other three. The tape recorders only have ninety-minute tapes in them." He peeled back the lining inside the briefcase the secretary had run to give them, and retrieved the microcassette from the tiny recorder Cabe had concealed there. Picking up a cassette player from the seat of the car, he inserted the tape, rewound it partway, then played it back. The sound of them telling the congressman good-bye came on, followed a few moments later by his voice saying, "Miss Jacobs, take this briefcase and run catch those two guys who were just in here. One of 'em left it on the floor."

That was followed by the sound of her saying, "Yes, sir," then running down the hall and the steps to catch them. When he heard the girl's voice call, "Colonel Brewer!" Ames turned the cassette player off.

"Ah, well," he mumbled. "Maybe we'll get something worthwhile off the other ones."

15

It was well after midnight, Cyprus time, when Rachel cleared customs at Larnaca International Airport. An aging gentleman from the CIA station in Nicosia met her to drive her to the Palm Beach Hotel, on the beach just north of Larnaca, where he had reserved a room for her. As they left the airport, he told her that the station in Beirut had reported that they had learned that a man they believed was actually Hakim Nidal was already on Cyprus, traveling on a Libyan passport under the name of Salim Nir. He was thought to be in Limassol, the resort town some thirty miles down the coast, where so many Palestinians and other Arabs spent their vacations and conducted business while enjoying the western liquor and the European women who frequented the resort hotels there.

Rachel convinced the man to take her to Limassol to get a hotel room instead of staying in Larnaca. He argued that she should go to the Palm Beach, as arranged, but she insisted. "I've got to go where I can do the most good," she said. "And if Nidal is in Limassol, that's where I should be. Aren't your orders to support us fully?"

"Well, yes," the CIA bureaucrat said. "You just make sure you amateur spies don't get in over your heads, and count on us to bail you out."

You son of a bitch, Rachel thought to herself. *You're a goddamn admin officer, and I know it, or you wouldn't be pulling that "amateur" crap. If it was up to people like you, Nidal would die of old age before he was caught.*

Instead of expressing her thoughts, though, she handed the man a thousand dollars and said, "Here. When we get there, get me a room for a week. Pay cash, like you're a dirty old man and I'm your whore, and you don't want to pay with a credit card, in case your wife finds out. That shouldn't be hard for an old pro of a spy like you to carry off."

The man glared at her, then took the money and, when they got to Limassol, did as Rachel had said, while she hung on his arm like a prostitute anxious to get her share of the hundred dollar bills he forked over to the hotel clerk. He was shaking like a leaf, and when Rachel leaned over and kissed him on the cheek, the man dropped the handful of money onto the floor, his face ablaze as he reached down to retrieve it. Then he escorted her to her room, and tipped the bellman who had carried her bags up.

"Here's a card with the numbers of our embassy office," he said when the bellman was gone, holding a small card out to her. "Someone from the station calling himself Smith will call you in the morning to arrange to meet you and see how we can help."

She took the card. "Smith. Sneaky, but I think I can remember that," she said.

The man turned toward the door to leave, and Rachel said, "Wait. You can't leave yet. You've at least got to wait long enough to pretend you've had a quickie, before you go. If you don't, you'll blow my cover. Just wait 'til I get my radio set up and call back to the States to see if they've got anything for me," she said as she laid the computer case onto the bed and opened it. "And turn the shower on, and the television, to give me some background noise, please."

She set up the radio quickly and called the Crystal City safehouse to give her initial entry report. Dave answered, and she explained that she had gone to Limassol, where Hakim was reported to be. "The admin officer from the station here is with me. Pass me Salem's requirements, and I'll give them to him now, so he can start working on them."

After she got the list of weapons, radios, and automobiles that Salem and his team would need, she tore the page out of her notebook and handed them to the CIA man. He took the list, and asked, "What makes you think I'm the admin officer?" he asked.

"Just a guess. OK, it's been long enough for a quickie. You can leave now," she said.

The man stared at her for a moment, then said, "I'm sorry about that remark I made about you being an amateur, Miss Brown. It looks like you know your business."

She held out her hand, which the man shook, then she said, "No problem. And you gave a great performance as a nervous, dirty old man registering his concubine, down there a little while ago."

The man flushed, looked at the floor, and said, "Who was acting? I was nervous as hell."

As soon as he had left, she called Ames on the radio again to say that she was going to put the radio away, then go down to the hotel cabaret and check the place out.

"What time is it there?" he asked.

"Almost two A.M., but they were still going strong a few

minutes ago when I checked in. I'll set up and call again when I get back to my room, then I'm going to need to get some sleep before Salem and his people get here tomorrow afternoon."

"Roger," Ames replied, then added, "For God's sake, Rachel, be careful."

"Wilco. Out," she answered, then broke the radio down.

By the time Rachel had showered, put on the new cocktail dress she had bought at Charles de Gaulle Airport, and gone down to the hotel lobby, Dave was back on Capitol Hill. He went to each of the first three offices he and Brewer had visited that morning, explaining at each that he had forgotten his briefcase when he had been there earlier. He collected all three, and while Brewer drove him back to Crystal City, he listened to portions of the tape from Senator Cronan's office. There was nothing on it which aroused his suspicion.

When they got back to the safehouse, Sergeant Cabe listened to the tape from Congressman Wesley Bolton's office, while Ames played the one from the office of the other senator they had briefed. Again, Ames heard nothing on the tape which would lead him to believe that the senator whose voice he heard, or the people he spoke to during the ninety minutes that the tape recorder had been running, had said anything to lead him to believe anyone from the senator's office might be guilty of leaking information.

But a few minutes after starting the tape from Congressman Bolton's office, Sergeant Cabe called Ames from the other room. "Sir, come here and listen to this!"

He backed the tape all the way up to the point at which Ames and Brewer were saying good-bye, and leaving the office. After a few moments, they heard a voice on Bolton's intercom say, "Yes, Congressman?"

"Ask Miss Black to come see me for a moment, please, Mary," they heard Bolton say.

A minute later, they heard a door close and a woman's voice say, "You wanted to see me, darling?"

"I *always* want to see you, Charlotte. You remember that

memo on the covert operation to El Salvador you did for me last week?"

"Yes?"

Ames looked at Cabe, who was grinning, as they heard Bolton continue, "Get it out of the safe, will you, sweetheart? I want to change it from sounding like I objected to the operation, and make it read as if I insisted on it. It looks like they actually managed to capture the guy."

"Stop it right there, and back it up, Lanny. Let me get the others in here to hear this!" Ames said with excitement.

A few minutes later, the others were gathered around the cassette player, listening to the recording. They let it run on past the part Ames had heard, and heard the woman say, "Really?"

"Yep," Bolton answered. "But before you get it, come here and let me smell your perfume."

For the next few moments, the men heard a "Mmmm," then a deep sigh, and Bolton said, "My God, Charlotte, you turn me on. Can I come by tonight?"

"Oh, I guess so, you horny man," the woman whispered, then, "but let me get that memo out." There were a few more moments of silence, then the woman said, "So, what are they doing with the guy they captured, Wes?"

"Huh? Oh, they're interrogating him at some Air Force base in Florida. Can you go ahead and change that, while I run over to the floor and vote on the homeless persons issue? I'll sign it when I get back."

"Sure. But what Air Force base are they holding him at?"

"What difference does it make?" the congressman asked, then added, "MacDill, if you must know, you nosy sexpot. I'll see you in a few minutes."

They heard a door close, and Garrett asked Ames, "What's the bit about Ramirez being at MacDill? I thought we were going to say he was being interrogated at Bragg."

"Last minute addition to the plan," his operations officer replied. "I told each of them Ramirez was being held at a different place. That way, if it leaked out, we'd know who the loose-lipped bastard was who leaked it."

"Shhh!" Sergeant Cabe said, his ear next to the speaker of

the little tape player. He could hear the faint sounds of telephone tones as someone dialed a number. Then they all heard Charlotte Black say, "It's Charlotte. The package is at MacDill Air Force Base, Florida. I'll see what else I can find out tonight."

They heard her hang up the telephone and walk across the room, then heard the door close.

"Bingo!" Ames shouted, as he reached over and rubbed the bald head of Delta's technical expert, Lanny Cabe.

"Major Ames, you never cease to amaze me," Garrett declared. "You guys are fuckin' geniuses!"

Lanny Cabe scowled and said, "All right, gents, if you'll get the hell out of the room and give me some quiet, I'll figure out what phone number the broad was dialing."

"You can do *that?*" the amazed Roland Brewer asked.

"Maybe, sir. But not if you guys don't get out of here and give me some quiet," Cabe grunted.

They left the tech alone to try to figure out the number Charlotte Black had dialed, and when they were all in the other room, Garrett said, "All right, it looks as if we've found the leak. Now, what do we do about it?"

The CIA man, Harry Lawson, said, "We can bring the FBI in and put a tail on her, tap her phone, and all of that."

"I don't know," Roland Brewer commented. "The President said to keep it to as few people as possible. We'd better ask Mr. Carruthers about it. And the FBI would have to get a court order before they could bug her, anyway. That would take some time to get done, even if Carruthers buys it."

"Yeah," Dave Ames offered, "and time is our most precious resource right now." He rubbed his chin a moment, then said, "Tell you what, boss. You guys go ahead and decide what you want Carruthers to get the FBI to do. Right now, I'm gonna jump on it." He grabbed his trench coat, went to the coffee table of the hotel suite's sitting room and picked up a set of keys to one of the cars he had rented, and headed for the door.

"Wait a minute, Major Ames. Where the hell are you going?" Garrett asked him.

Ames stopped, turned around for a moment and said, "Trust me, Colonel, I've got a plan. I'll be in touch." Then he was out of the door and gone.

Rachel had showered, changed, and gone down to the lobby of her resort hotel in Limassol, Cyprus. The revealing cocktail dress she was wearing drew approving stares from the Greek Cypriot, Lebanese, and European men she passed as she walked into the hotel nightclub and took a seat at the bar. She ordered a Campari and soda, and when the bartender returned with it, he said, "Compliments of the gentleman in the white jacket at the end of the bar," as he nodded to her left.

She looked in that direction and saw a middle-aged man in a white jacket smiling at her. He looked German, or perhaps Scandinavian, and without returning his smile, she turned back to the bartender and said, "Thank the gentleman for me, but I would prefer to pay for the drink myself." She took a one hundred dollar bill from her sequined handbag and handed it to the barman.

He smiled and said, "Yes, mademoiselle. I understand." He shook his head slightly at the man in the white jacket as he walked to the cash register, then brought Rachel ninety-five dollars in change. She picked up ninety of it and put it in her handbag.

The next man who tried to hit on her was a young, Greek Cypriot—probably a gigolo, she quickly decided—who came up to the bar and bumped against her. The bartender noticed, and she gave him the slightest shake of her head. A moment later, the bartender mumbled something to the man in Greek, and after leering at her for a moment, the gigolo disappeared. No one else made a pass at her for a while, and she finished the Campari and soda, then ordered another from the bartender, once again tipping him five dollars when he brought it. A short time later, she noticed one of the floor waiters whisper something to the bartender and glance at her a moment. The waiter came to her and said, "Ma'moiselle, the gentlemen at the table behind you—the Lebanese gentlemen—wonder if you might like to join them at their table?"

Rachel looked at the mirror behind the bar. At the table behind her, she saw three men who looked to be in their thirties. They appeared to be well-dressed and self-assured. She smiled at the bartender and asked, "What is your name, garçon?"

"Dimitri, ma'm'selle," the Cypriot barman answered.

"Please tell the gentlemen, Dimitri, that I must meet a friend in a little while. But if they wish, I would be pleased to join them at their table for a few minutes." She waited until Dimitri had time to pass her answer through the floor waiter to the men at the table, then return to her and say, "Ma'm'selle?"

She stood and stepped toward the men at the table, only one of whom rose to greet her. Good, she thought to herself, that probably means they're Muslim Lebanese, not Christians. The fact that none of the three was wearing a wedding band on his right hand further reinforced her suspicion that they were Muslim. Maybe, just maybe, they might provide her with a link to Hakim Nidal.

Dave Ames got back to the Rayburn House Office Building at about three-thirty in the afternoon, Washington time. He waited around the corner of the hallway from Congressman Wes Bolton's office until he saw Bolton appear and go to the "members only" elevator with his trench coat over his arm and a briefcase in his hand. Then Ames walked to the congressman's office and went in.

"Hi," he said to Bolton's receptionist. "I'm Major Dave Ames. I was in here this morning to brief Mr. Bolton on something."

The receptionist smiled. "I remember, Major Ames. You're the one who forgot his briefcase."

"Yes, ma'am," he answered, looking as sheepish as he could. "I'm afraid I also forgot to mention a key point to Mr. Bolton while I was briefing him. Is he available for just a few seconds?"

"I'm afraid he just left for home, Major. Is it something important?"

"Well," Ames answered, "I'm not sure whether he'd think so, but I *was* supposed to mention it. Is there someone who handles his Intelligence Committee matters I could pass it on to? I'm sure that would be just as good."

"Sure," the receptionist said, then pressed a button on the office intercom set. "Charlotte, could you come out here and speak to a Major Ames about some Intelligence Committee matter he briefed Mr. Bolton on this morning?"

Rachel sat in the chair which the man who had introduced himself as Rashad held out for her. "You said your name is Rose?" he asked.

"Yes, Rose Brown."

"And you are English?" another of them inquired.

"No, I'm an American," Rachel answered.

"In Cyprus on holiday?"

"Yes. Well, part holiday, part work. I have a photography assignment to do for an American travel magazine, but it's more fun than work, really."

Two of the three men at the table discussed with her places she should go in Cyprus to get appealing photographs of the type suitable for a travel magazine. Occasionally, they would converse with the third man in Arabic, who she quickly ascertained did not speak English.

"Are you gentlemen all Lebanese?" she asked.

"Yes."

"Such a shame that I can't visit your beautiful country," Rachel remarked. "I would love to be able to photograph Beirut, and the other ancient port cities."

"But, of course you can!" Rashad exclaimed. "What is to prevent you from doing so?"

"Why, all the kidnappings of Westerners, the car bombs, and the fighting. Our State Department forbids Americans to travel there."

"Oh, pay no attention to that," Rashad said. "Except for the Israelis and their bombs, there is no danger. Only along the Green Line in Beirut is there any fighting, and that is only the militias taking target practice. A block from there, there is no danger. There are nightclubs and restaurants, and beautiful beaches. If you would like to go and see for yourself, it can easily be arranged. In fact, you *should* go, and help us rid the West of this silly notion about Lebanon being dangerous."

"Is it that easy, really?" she asked.

"But of course! I mean, except for the Palestinian camps and the southern suburbs which those fanatics from Hezbollah control—which you wouldn't wish to see, anyway—it is a very safe and, as you said, very lovely place to visit."

"Hezbollah . . . now, they're one of the militia groups fighting the Druze militia, who are also fighting the Christian militia, and Nabi Berri's Amal, right? It's all very confusing to an outsider," she said.

"Yes," he said. "That's why I've moved to Cyprus."

Well, Rachel thought to herself, *if he lives here now, he probably won't be of much use in finding Nidal. Time to break contact. But maybe one more stab at it, first.*

'Well, there's still one thing I'm confused about. If all these militias fight each other in Lebanon, then what do they do when they come to, for example, Limassol? I mean, so many Lebanese come here for vacation. Is there trouble among the various militias when they see each other here?"

The man laughed. "No, no, of course not. They have certain hotels where each group normally goes. My friend Ahmed here," he said as he gestured to the one who spoke no English, "is in the Amal, as are many of the others here. The Lebanese Front, as the Christians call themselves, stay mostly up in Larnaca. And the Hezbollah—the few who come to Cyprus—usually stay down the beach at the Grand Hotel. But there's no trouble here. The fighting is all for control of territory in Lebanon. Away from there, we're all one big, happy family."

"I see," Rachel said, then yawned. "Excuse me, gentlemen, but my jet lag seems to have caught up with me. My editor is probably here by now, and I have to see him about our schedule for tomorrow. Thank you very much." She stood, and only Rashad stood with her. "It's nice to have met you all. Perhaps Paul, my editor, and I will see you here again sometime during our stay. Good night."

She stopped at the desk before going up to her room and asked the clerk, "Pardon me, but where is the Grand Hotel? I'm supposed to meet a friend there tomorrow."

The clerk leered at her a moment, then pointed and said, "That way. Two hotels down."

Charlotte Black came out of her office cubicle, and Congressman Bolton's receptionist introduced her to Dave Ames. "Nice to meet you, Ms. Black," Ames said with a warm smile, then looked her over briefly. "What a nice-looking dress," he said.

"Why, thank you," she said, and returned his smile warmly. "What can I do for you, Major?"

"I gave Mr. Bolton a briefing this morning on a certain activity. Is there someplace we can speak in private?"

"Yes, of course. Mr. Bolton's gone. We can use his office."

He held the door of the congressman's private office open for her, and she swished past. *OK, Ames,* said to himself, *turn on your best charm. This broad can be had, especially if you make her think she can screw secrets out of you, like she does her boss.*

He closed the door, and she sat down on the couch against the wall. He sat down beside her.

"Well, at the briefing this morning, I'm afraid I gave Mr. Bolton some incorrect information."

"Yes?" Charlotte Black asked with genuine interest. "What sort of incorrect information?"

"Well, I really don't know how much of this I'm allowed to mention to you, Ms. Black."

"Please, call me Charlotte. Is it about the Ramirez thing?"

"You *know* about it, Charlotte?"

"Yes. I mean, after all, I *am* Mr. Bolton's assistant for intelligence matters, Major Ames."

"Dave," he said. "If I'm going to call you Charlotte, please call me Dave. Anyway, Charlotte, are you aware of where Ramirez is being held?"

"Yes, I am."

He looked surprised, and she placed her hand on his arm a moment, smiled and said, "I have all the clearances, you know. Why do you Pentagon officers always act so secretive?"

"Well, we have to be, when we're dealing with the activities of the Delta Force." He lowered his voice and leaned toward her when he said it.

"Yes, of course," she said.

"That certainly is nice perfume you're wearing. What is it?" he asked.

"Thank you. It's called Charlie. Now, what's this misinformation you gave my congressman this morning, Dave?"

"Oh, yes." He leaned still closer to her and whispered, "I told him Ramirez was being held in the wrong place. I said he was at MacDill. I meant to say Eglin."

"I see," she said. "I'll be certain to tell him that first thing in the morning."

"Yes, please do."

He stood, and she thought, *I wonder how much more I can get from this guy? He probably knows all about the Ramirez operation, and who knows how much else.*

"Mr. Bolton was very much interested in this operation," she said. "He's very supportive of these activities, you know—except when they're done without the committee's knowledge, like these arms sales to the Iranians."

"Yes. Well, I'll try to keep him as up-to-date as possible. But I've been given strict limits on how much I'm allowed to say."

"Of course. Are they getting much information from Ramirez?" Charlotte asked.

He leaned down and said softly, "You'd be *shocked* to learn what we're hearing from him, Charlotte. But I'm afraid that's all I can say, for now. I really like those printed stockings. They go very well with the dress."

She smiled at him and raised her skirt above her knees to

look at the patterned hose he referred to, saying, "Thank you. You're very complimentary, Dave."

"Oh. Well, it's just that you're a very attractive woman," he said.

God, she thought, *is this guy ever horny!* "Well, thank you *again,* sir," she said to him. "And you're a very handsome man." She meant it, for she did find the finely chiseled features of his face handsome, and the body beneath the pin-striped blue suit he was wearing was obviously well-muscled and trim at the waist. She supposed he was probably as clumsy a lover as he was at making passes, though. But he'd be an easy target, and perhaps as good a source of information as Wes Bolton. And that could mean a much larger payoff from her secret employers.

Dave looked at his watch and said, "Well, no sense in going back to the Pentagon now. What time do you get off work, Charlotte?"

"Oh, in a few minutes."

"Well, would you like to go for a drink with me while the traffic dies down? I *detest* D.C. rush hour traffic. Do you have to drive in it?"

"Oh, no. I take a bus to Georgetown, usually. Yes, thank you, I'd be happy to go for a drink. Would you be able to drop me off at my apartment, afterward?"

"Sure," he replied.

She stood. "Do you know where Bullfeathers Pub is?"

"Yeah, up a block, and right a block, just past the South Capitol Metro stop, right?"

"Right. Why don't you go and get us a table, before the after-work crowd swamps the place? I'll be along as soon as I tidy up a couple of things here."

Sure, he thought. *As soon as you tell your handler Ramirez is at Eglin, not MacDill.* He smiled at her and said, "Sure. See you in a few minutes, then."

On the way out of the building, he stopped at a pay phone and called the Crystal City safehouse. Garrett answered.

"Boss, I've made contact with the secretary who's been spilling the beans—*close* contact. She's ready to screw me out of every secret I know," Ames reported. "I'm not sure how that can help us find the item we want, but if you guys think of something, I'll try to work it. At least we can feed disinformation through her, and maybe roll up the people she's working for."

"Yeah, well, just remember—as soon as she passes your name on, they're going to try to find out all they can about you," Garrett warned.

"As if they didn't already know, thanks to that asshole, Martin," Ames replied, referring to the reporter who had exposed his name a year earlier, in a half-accurate news magazine article about the Delta Force.

"I'm afraid the walk-around with the girl today didn't do us much good," Garrett said. "But Rachel may be on to something. Get back over here when you finish your plumbing chores—no pun intended. And don't come back with a case of AIDS."

"Hey, this is serious business, boss."

"You're right about that," Garrett said in a serious tone. "Don't fuck it up."

16

In one of the two suites of the Crystal City Holiday Inn that were being used as safehouses, Dr. Toby Wayne was studiously reexamining the documents and material which had been recovered from the apartment Emilio Ramirez had occupied several months earlier. When he first saw the enhanced impression of the drawing of the device, which Harry Lawson had given to him when he got to the White House two days ago, he had said, "This is a diagram of a crude, but workable, nuclear weapon. But drawings like these are easily attainable in any library. Any nuclear physics student could make drawings like this, these days. That's why the safeguarding of weapons-grade nuclear material is of such critical importance." He wasn't aware that there was any connection between the drawing and the traces of plutonium he had discovered in a house in Arlington months earlier, when the CIA man took him there to survey it with his sensors.

Now he was acutely aware of the connection, and it was frightening. The drawing was of a device which was particularly well suited for the detonation of a small amount of plutonium. It would be a relatively small explosion, compared to that of one of the thousands of huge warheads the Americans and Soviets had aimed at each other. But even so, it would be equivalent to hundreds of tons of dynamite going off at once.

He examined the drawings again, then looked at the other documents Lawson had given him. One was an inventory of everything that had been in the house, and he concentrated on that for the time being, trying to see if there was anything on it that might give him a clue how to better go about conducting a search for the weapon.

In the suite next door, Lawson had just returned to tell the others that he had discovered whose telephone Charlotte Black had called during the time she was being taped on the recorder hidden in the briefcase Ames had "accidentally" left in Congressman Bolton's office.

"It was another woman, Marlene Graf, a secretary at the West German Embassy," he announced. "The question now is whether Charlotte Black is working for our enemies, or our so-called friends from Bonn. Anyway, Sergeant Cabe, you've managed to help us break into an espionage net we had no idea existed. Well done. Mr. Carruthers has decided to go ahead and put the FBI on Graf's tail, without telling them the connection between her and Black."

Across the Potomac in the District of Columbia, Dave Ames was driving Charlotte Black to her Georgetown apartment. They had stayed at Bullfeathers long enough to have two drinks, and for Charlotte to decide that she would begin that evening to try to wrest secrets from Ames in exchange for sexual favors. But first, she would have to see Wes Bolton, who had asked to come over tonight at seven. She didn't want to do anything to spoil her relationship with the valuable source of secrets she already had.

"Listen, Dave," she said as he stopped his rented car in front of her apartment, "this meeting I have this evening doesn't include dinner. Why don't we go out for a bite to eat later—say, nine o'clock?"

"Well," he answered, "I'd sure like to." He didn't know whether Garrett had anything else for him to do, so he didn't want to make a commitment. "But I don't know whether they have anything at work that might prevent it. Can I go find out, then call you?"

She didn't want to risk having him call while Bolton was there, so she said, "Why don't you come in and call from here?"

"OK," he said. "I need to use your bathroom for a minute, anyway, if I may."

Inside her stylish apartment, a refinished, two-story "shotgun," as the narrow old houses of Georgetown were known, she said, "The phone's in the back there, and the bathroom's at the head of the stairs. I'm going to go on up and start changing."

He went to the telephone, found the safehouse phone number in his wallet, and dialed the number. Lanny Cabe answered, and he said, "Let me talk to the boss, please."

Garrett came on. "Where are you?" he asked.

"It's Major Ames, Colonel. Do you need me back at the Pentagon for anything?"

It was obvious that Ames couldn't speak openly, so Garrett said, "Did you pick up the thing you went after?"

"Yes, sir. I'll work on it tonight and give you a report in the morning, unless you need me to come in now."

"No. But we found part two of the thing you went after. It's just like the one you picked up, but it's in German."

What the hell does that mean? Dave wondered. Well, he could find out later at the safehouse.

"Very well, Colonel. I should be at my place around midnight, if you need me for anything. Good-bye."

He hung up, then went upstairs to the bathroom. The room to the right at the top of the stairs was Charlotte's bedroom, and she had left the door partially open to enable him to see inside. There was a large mirror in front of a dressing table, where Charlotte was sitting, wearing only lacy, black underwear as she applied lipstick to her mouth. He went into the bathroom. When he came out, she was standing at the bedroom door, a red silk robe pulled around her. "Did you make your phone call?" she asked. Behind her, he could see—through the door she had intentionally opened fully—a big canopy bed with shiny silk or satin sheets on it, and a mirrored headboard.

"Yes," he answered. "By the way, the light on your answering machine is blinking."

"I'll go check it," she said, brushing past him and starting downstairs. "Will you be able to come back later?"

He followed her down the stairs, thinking, *Boy, she's really trying to show me what I'm in store for, if I do come back.* "Yes," he called after her, "I certainly will."

She was listening to the message on her answering machine, and he heard a man's voice say, "Charlotte, it's Wes. I'm afraid the meeting's off for this evening. See you tomorrow."

"Well," she said, turning to Dave and smiling. "Looks like we don't need to wait to go out to dinner after all." She let go of the robe she had been holding closed at the waist, and it fell open revealing the lacy underwear and her trim, lithe body. "Or should we just stay here and have something?"

It was Tuesday morning in Cyprus by then, and Rachel awoke to her travel alarm. She hadn't really had enough sleep, but she needed to get up and see if she could find out anything that would be helpful to Sergeant Major Salem and his team when they arrived that afternoon to try to nab Hakim Nidal. She turned the shower on to create background noise, then took the satellite radio from the computer case in her closet, set the umbrella antenna up at the correct angle, and called back to the States. Jim Greer answered her call first. "I'm out at Langley," Delta's intelligence officer said. "We've got a report here that says there's a reservation for Thursday for a Mr. S. Nir in Air France's computers for flight AF 1201 from Larnaca to Paris."

Salim Nir was the name the CIA station in Beirut had reported that Hakim Nidal was using in the Libyan passport on which he was traveling.

"Got it," Rachel answered. "What time does the flight leave on Thursday?"

"Wait one," Greer said, then, "Here. It leaves at 0835, and arrives at CDG at 1040 Paris time. There's also a phone number in the reservation printout where he can be reached. We'll get Nicosia to run it down, and let you know where it is."

"Let me have it," Rachel said, and reached for the telephone directory. "Hang on a minute," she said after Greer gave her the number. On a hunch, she turned to "hotels" in the directory. It was the telephone number of the Grand Hotel, just down the beach from her own.

She called Greer on the radio again, and said, "It's the number of the Grand Hotel, just down the street from where I am."

"Super! Have you made all the arrangements for Salem and his guys?"

"I'll go case the place, and see where the best places are to get them some rooms. I'll at least get one or two in the Grand, if I can. The station in Nicosia is supposed to contact me this morning to confirm the weapons and cars and stuff. What are our guys going to do with Nidal after they grab him?"

"We're still working on that. Either we'll have the helicopter that supports the embassy between Larnaca and Beirut take him somewhere, or maybe a chopper off one of our carriers, if one's close enough. Salem was also talking about maybe renting a boat, and meeting either a chopper or a ship offshore somewhere. We'll have to let you know what looks like it's going to work best."

"OK," Rachel replied, brushing out her hair as she talked on the radio. "Do you have anything else for me?"

"Not from here," Greer answered. "We're trying to find out what airline connections Nidal has out of Paris, but no luck, so far. It may be an Aeroflot flight to Havana or Managua, but we can't get into their computers. We'll be monitoring, if you get anything for us, though."

"Brown, this is Cabe," the Delta technician called on the Crystal City safehouse radio. "The boss is out right now, getting something to eat, but he said to tell you that Salem called from London to say they were still on schedule en route to your location."

"Roger, Lanny," Rachel answered, then asked, "Have Angela and the others made any headway in finding the item?"

"Negative," Cabe said, "but it looks like we've found the leak up on Capitol Hill. A secretary for one of our illustrious members of Congress. Ames is with her now, trying to— how shall I put it?—seduce her out of any information she may have."

From the other of the four radios on the net, at Delta headquarters in Fort Bragg, Paul McCarthy, Delta's deputy, broke in and said, "All right, Cabe, knock it off. This is a family radio net. You got anything for us here, Rachel?"

"Negative, sir. I'll call back once the Agency people confirm the support for Salem. Out."

She found herself feeling hurt by Cabe's remark about Dave's being with a congressional secretary, trying to "seduce" her for information. Was it true? She recalled her night of lovemaking with him, and imagined some young, blond Washington secretary surrendering herself to his tender advances. "Oh, come on, Rachel," she muttered to herself, "he isn't really . . ." Or was he? If one of the men at the table with her last night had been Hakim Nidal, would she have slept with him? If that's what it took, would she allow a man to make love to her, in order to get information from him? She had thought about it before, when she had read about an American agent in the Second World War, who traded sex for secrets. The woman seduced a Vichy

French naval attaché expressly for the purpose of getting some secret codebooks from him, and he had given them to her without hesitation. She always doubted that she would be able to do such a thing herself. But what if it meant the difference between life and death? What if it meant finding a nuclear time bomb in time to prevent its killing thousands of people?

The telephone in her hotel room rang, startling her. She answered, and a man's voice said, "Miss Brown?"

"This is she."

"My name is Smith, Miss Brown. The man who met you at the airport last night will meet you there again, a half hour before your friends arrive. He'll have the things you wanted. Is there anything else we can do for you?"

"Thank you, Mr. Smith. No, that's all I can think of, for the moment. If there's anything else, I'll call you at the number I was given."

She hung up, called back to the States on the radio to tell them the support Salem needed had been confirmed, and that she would call back in about three hours. Then she put the radio away, showered, and donned the bikini swimsuit she had bought in Paris. She looked at herself in the mirror. It was an awfully small bikini—really just two strings which were threaded through small triangles of material that could be adjusted to whatever size the wearer dared to wear. But it wasn't too scant for wear at a beach or pool in Limassol, Cyprus, where most vacationing European women wore no top, and very little bottom. She put on a wraparound white dress, pinned her hair up on top of her head, slipped into a pair of sandals, then picked up her straw handbag and left her hotel for the Grand Hotel a short way down the street.

In his suite on the sixth floor of the Grand, the terrorist Hakim Nidal hung up the telephone. As had been the case each time he had tried since he arrived in Cyprus, Emilio Ramirez had failed to answer the call Nidal put through to Managua. Only, this time, someone else had answered— someone who refused to say who he was, or when Ramirez was expected to be there. When the man in Managua asked who was trying to reach Señor Ramirez, Nidal said, "Just tell him to call Nir at the Grand Hotel in Limassol, Cyprus, when he returns." Now, he wondered if something was wrong. Well, he would wait until Thursday to see if Ramirez returned his call. If not, he would go on to Paris and use his contacts there to find out what had happened.

He called to one of his bodyguards in the next room, and told the man to get ready to go down to the swimming pool with him.

17

Charlotte Black lay on her silk sheets looking up at her reflection and that of the sleeping Dave Ames, in the mirrored canopy of her bed. She was drained, yet still excited by the wild experience she had just shared with him. It had been an almost endless succession of whirling, erotic acts, playing out with him every fantasy she was able to imagine. It had been as if he could read her mind, could sense what she wanted to further heighten the pleasure of every move they made. And, dear God, he was so very strong.

She was no stranger to sex, but she had only imagined that it could ever be like this. Only with Marlene had she ever even come close to such erotic enjoyment. Marlene. Sweet, demanding, but ever-giving Marlene, who had turned her life from one of the boredom of just another minor civil servant, to one of excitement and wealth and sex, and international espionage. As she had often wondered before, Charlotte now wondered how much of Marlene's motivation was collecting the bits of information Charlotte passed to her, and how much was just enjoyment of the power she held over her American agent. She loved giving Charlotte orders, whether it was how to dress seductively when Wes Bolton was coming to see her, how to tease him to get the information she wanted, or when she and Marlene were making love.

Charlotte had met Marlene Graf three years earlier, at a reception at the West German Embassy, where Marlene was a secretary. Wes Bolton had taken her there because she was fluent in German, and she had quickly become friends with the seductive woman. Their relationship had soon become one of lesbian love, and not long after, Marlene had convinced her bisexual lover to provide her with secrets garnered from Congressman Bolton. Charlotte had protested initially, crying, "But that would be spying on my own country!"

"Don't be silly, pet," Marlene Graf had responded. "Your country and mine share all our secrets anyway. All you would be doing would be to serve as—as a check, of sorts, to ensure they don't forget something. Besides, if you aren't on my payroll, darling, I don't see how I could afford for us to spend time together any longer."

The naive congressional secretary had acceded to her lover's argument, and now, three years later, was still on Marlene's payroll, and at a salary which had increased with the value of the information she got from her job and her trysts with Wes Bolton.

She looked at the reflection of the muscular Dave Ames in the mirror above her. She had gotten no secrets from him yet, other than the location at which the turncoat Ramirez was being interrogated. But she was certain that she could. And she had found a lover who thrilled her even more than Marlene. Ames stirred, and she reached to arouse him, thinking that she could hardly wait to excite Marlene with descriptions of the wild and exotic ways that she and her new source of secrets made love.

Once again, Dr. Toby Wayne searched through the list of items in the Arlington house where Emilio Ramirez was suspected of having built his plutonium bomb. There *must* be something there which would give him a clue about the device. During his earlier perusal of the list, he had been struck by the fact that there was no sign of the heavy steel case in which the device would have to be enclosed to contain the detonation of the conventional explosives long enough to enable its force to trigger the plutonium. But Ramirez would have *had* to have such a case, if the bomb was to function. It was, after all, included in the sketch from the notebook. Wayne had mentioned that fact to Harry Lawson, and the CIA officer was now away trying to get information about where Ramirez might have had such a device manufactured.

Now, something caught Toby Wayne's attention. He compared the inventory of items found in the garage with one of the items from the living room, where the notebook had been found. There were three fire extinguishers on the garage list with the notation, "two usable, one broken." Included on the long, detailed list of things from the living room was, "pkt. of fire ext. insp. tags." Fire extinguisher inspection tags. Why would they be needed in a private home? And why would someone have three fire extinguishers, and keep them all in the garage? He turned back to the enhanced sketch of the device and looked at the measurements on the drawing. "Yes," he thought aloud, "it would fit in one of those standard fire extinguishers." Was it possible that it might be in one of the fire extinguishers still at the house in Arlington? When he and Harry Lawson had gone out there two days earlier, they found a Pakistani family living in the house. Lawson flashed some credentials at the woman, claiming they were health inspectors. It had been completely rearranged since their visit of several months earlier, when Wayne had discovered the traces of plutonium radiation, and they found nothing that would give them any further clues to the device. He dialed the telephone number which would initiate the beeping pager in Lawson's pocket, and when Lawson phoned the safehouse, Wayne told him to go back to the house where the Pakistanis now lived and recover the fire extinguishers from the garage. If they weren't there, he recommended that Lawson try to find out where they were now.

He went next door to the suite where Cabe and Garrett were monitoring the radios, and told them what he had found. Garrett passed the word to Angela Herndon and Santos Baldero, so that they could use the information in their questioning of Nadia Cruz.

"We'll see what we can find out along those lines, then," she said. "We're planning on trying to retrace their steps some more tomorrow, but I'll tell you, sir, we're going to have to walk less and ride more. Because she's pregnant, she gets worn out pretty quickly."

"OK," Garrett said. "We're getting in a time crunch, anyway. Call us back when you find out what she knows about the fire extinguishers."

The commander of the Delta Force sat staring at the floor, thinking. What had begun as a fairly simple operation to capture one man from a rural Central American hamlet a few days earlier had turned into a confusing, worldwide search for clues to the location of a nuclear device they weren't even certain actually existed. His people had killed two helicopter loads of Cubans and a handful of Salvadoran guerrillas. The man they had gone after was dead, and they had abducted his pregnant Nicaraguan girlfriend. Then they had gone to Congress and lied about the results of the operation—only to discover that it was a good thing they had. Now one of his officers was trying to seduce a spy posing as a congressman's secretary and lover, and another was all the way out in Cyprus, trying to locate an international terrorist, whom his command sergeant major would attempt to capture. It had become too tangled, too loosely connected. And it didn't seem to be leading anywhere quickly enough.

He sighed deeply, unwrapped a long cigar, and shoved it into the corner of his mouth. Well, if there was no real progress made by noon tomorrow—Tuesday, the 16th— when he was next scheduled to meet with the National

Security Advisor, George Carruthers, he would recommend to Carruthers that they bring in the FBI and the Secret Service and everyone else they might need, get the problem out in the open, and solve it.

He stood and lit his cigar, wondering if the President was having second thoughts yet about leaving the Delta Force, with so little outside help, to try to solve a problem with such potentially disastrous ramifications.

Harry Lawson returned to the safehouse a short time later. After checking with several machine milling plants that afternoon, he had found none which had manufactured a steel container of the type in the sketch Toby Wayne had made for him. But he had gotten leads on two more such milling companies in the area, which he would check out in the morning. When he went to the Pakistani family now living in the house that Ramirez had used, he learned that they had sold the three fire extinguishers—all of which were empty—to a local junk dealer.

Then Angela Herndon called on the radio. Nadia Cruz remembered a fire extinguisher. The day before she and Ramirez had left the States to return to Nicaragua, she had seen him putting one into the trunk of his rented car in the garage. She remembered, because he had carried it from the spare bedroom, which he kept locked the whole time they were there, and because he struggled with it, as it was very heavy.

"Does she have any idea where he took it?" Garrett asked. "Or how long he was gone, what he said before he left, and after he got back?"

"She said he was gone for several hours," Angela replied. "We'll try to find out if she can remember anything he said at the time, and get back to you."

"All right, Sergeant Herndon. Good job. Also, try to find out the last places they visited before he took the extinguisher, and if she remembers seeing any fire extinguishers at the places they went."

"Wilco, sir. I'll call you back, out."

He went next door to the suite where Toby Wayne was,

and gave him the new information. Wayne was elated. Convinced that they now knew the type of container the improvised nuclear bomb was in, he felt that they would now have a much better chance of finding it—especially if he could get permission to bring in more Nuclear Emergency Search Team scientists to help. Garrett promised to try to get permission to do so from the National Security Advisor when he saw him at noon the next day.

Several miles away in Georgetown, Charlotte Black heard the doorbell of her apartment ring, as she watched Dave Ames getting dressed to leave. The bell rang again, and she hopped off the bed, wondering who it could be. She had disconnected her telephone earlier, so that its ringing wouldn't interrupt them. Probably Wes Bolton, she thought. Damn! Well, she would have to send him away. She could tell him that a girlfriend from out of town was coming to spend the night, or something. "I'll be right back," she whispered to Dave as she pulled on a robe and went downstairs to the door.

She cracked it open. "Marlene!" She held a finger to her lips and pointed upstairs, then opened the door and led the German woman to the back of the apartment.

"I tried to telephone you," Marlene said, "but there was no answer, so I drove by and when I saw the lights on, decided to come in."

"I'm sorry, darling," Charlotte whispered, drawing Marlene to her in an embrace. "I disconnected the telephone earlier, because I was seducing a new lover."

Marlene drew back from her, her eyebrows arched as if saying, "Really?"

"God, Marlene, he's *such* a lover!" she told the woman who had taught her about espionage and sex. "And listen to this. He's an officer in the Pentagon who knows all about the Delta Force!"

Marlene looked surprised. How could it be possible? The very reason she needed to see Charlotte so badly was because she had been tasked to find out all she could about the man the Delta Force had captured in El Salvador, and what sort of information he was giving under interrogation.

"How did you find him?" Marlene asked suspiciously.

"He's one of the men who has been coming to Wes's office to brief him on the operation in El Salvador I told you about." Charlotte smiled and added, "He came by to see Wes this afternoon, and seemed attracted to me, so I let him take me out for a drink, then brought him here and got him into my bed."

"I see." Marlene said. "And has he told you anything, yet?"

"Yes. Well, only that the man you wanted to know about is being held at Eglin Air Force Base, not MacDill. But, my God, darling, it's only my first time with him."

"Yes, yes," the German girl muttered, trying to think of how to best capitalize on the stroke of luck. "Is he planning to stay all night?"

"No, he's just getting ready to leave, in fact."

Marlene thought for a moment. She didn't know why her case officer was putting so much pressure on her—more pressure on her than at anytime since she had been recruited as an agent during her days as a student at Mainz University in Germany. She had to do something to get the information from the man Charlotte had so fortuitously seduced.

"Can you convince him to stay, Charlotte?"

"Oh, I don't know. And now that you're here," Charlotte answered as she stroked her lesbian lover's cheek, "I'd rather be with you, anyway. I've learned a few things from him that I can't wait to tell you, to show you, lover."

Marlene had an idea. "Charlotte, there's something we *must* find out from this man. Bring him down here to meet me."

She looked at Marlene quizzically.

"Do as I say, Charlotte, and I'll open up another delightful world to you."

Charlotte stared at her with uncertainty for a moment, then walked to the foot of the stairs and called, "Dave, can you come down here? I want you to meet a friend of mine."

He was fully dressed by then, wondering whom she had let in while entertaining someone from whom she was trying to elicit information.

He walked downstairs, and saw Charlotte standing beside a sultry blond woman.

"Dave, I'd like you to meet a friend of mine, Marlene Graf."

The woman came to him and held out her hand, and he said, "Hi, Marlene. Nice to meet you."

She held onto his hand, and looked him up and down, then said, "Charlotte *said* you are a handsome man. It was an understatement. I'm happy to meet you, Dave."

Dave Ames noticed the woman's German accent, and an alarm went off in his mind. What was it that Garrett had said on the telephone earlier?

"Danke schoen, Fraulein Graf," he said. "That *is* a German accent, isn't it?"

"Verstimmt," she answered, "indeed. I work at the German Embassy. Charlotte and I are friends and, as you are now, lovers. She tells me that you are the best lover she has ever known, and now I want to find out for myself."

Marlene reached back, unfastened her dress, and dropped it from her shoulders. It fell to her ankles, and less than a minute after he had met the beautiful German woman, she stood there before him in nothing but a low-cut, red lace bra, tiny lace bikini panties, and a garter belt holding up dark stockings.

He looked at Charlotte, who appeared to be as shocked as he was.

"Was ist los, Liebchen?" Marlene asked him. "Can't you believe that you are about to make love to two sexy women at once?"

Charlotte suddenly caught on to what Marlene had in mind. If one woman could get secrets from a man through sex, two should be able to get even more. A thrill coursed through her as she realized she was about to share a *ménage à trois* with the two best lovers she had known.

Just as suddenly, Dave recalled what Garrett had said on the telephone a couple of hours earlier— *We found part two of the thing you went after. It's just like the one you picked up, but it's in German.* The woman who stood there offering herself to him was Charlotte's contact—her partner in espionage. *Oh, shit,* he thought to himself. *What have I gotten myself into?*

18

Rachel Brown looked like anything but a United States Army captain as she walked through the lobby of the Grand Hotel in Limassol, Cyprus, and out to the swimming pool beyond the lobby. The pool was large and oval shaped, surrounded by a wide, marble-tiled patio. There were a dozen or so tables with big umbrellas in them, each surrounded by lawn chairs, and about thirty lounge chairs set up around the pool. The L-shaped hotel rose above the patio on two sides, and off to one side was a long outdoor bar set beneath palm trees. The other side of the patio led past a row of low, flowering bushes, to the beach. There, she could see a number of beach umbrellas and more lounge chairs sitting on the sand above the flat, clear water of the Mediterranean.

She skirted the pool, passing several young couples sunning themselves, and a group of men at one of the tables who were having a discussion in low tones and studying the architectural drawings on the table in front of them. There were several single young European women lounging on the chairs beside the pool, and two paddling in the water. All but two of the women were bare-breasted.

Rachel chose a lounge chair on the beach side of the patio, from which she could see people entering the patio from the lobby, those at the bar, and people on the beach as well.

She kicked off her sandals, spread the towel from her straw bag on one of the lounge chairs, and took out a bottle of suntan oil. Feeling somewhat self-conscious, she untied the wraparound cotton dress and took it off, then lay down on the chair.

She spread suntain oil on her legs and shoulders, then on her flat stomach and arms, wondering as she did so what Dave would say when he saw her suntan.

As she lay back, feeling the warm Cyprus sun beginning to soak into her, she saw three swarthy men enter the pool area from the hotel. Behind her sunglasses, Rachel's eyes opened wide in startled recognition. Although she couldn't be absolutely certain, the middle of the three men looked very much like the photographs she had studied many times of Hakim Nidal, the elusive international terrorist. He was wearing sunglasses, but they were of the same style as those he had on in one of the photographs they had of him. And, judging by his height in comparison to the men on either side of him, he was short enough to be Nidal, who stood just five feet four. She watched as the three men surveyed the people around the pool, then moved to a table on the side of the patio nearest the bar. The two men flanking Nidal were carrying athletic bags. No doubt they were Nidal's bodyguards, with their weapons stashed in the bags. The two taller men sat at the table, and the short one took off his shirt, laid it on the back of the nearest lounge chair, which he then adjusted to a sitting position, and sat down. He said something to one of the men at the table, who took a newspaper out of his bag, handed it to the short, dark man, then went to the bar and returned with a glass of orange juice, which he also handed to the man.

Rachel watched them for a while. One of the man's bodyguards kept an eye on people coming onto the patio from the lobby, while the other looked back and forth over the rest of the area, his glances lingering on the women lounging around the pool. He stared particularly long at Rachel, who had her head turned somewhat away from the three men, but whose eyes, behind the dark glasses, were studying them. She stood, walked to the ladder of the pool, and lowered herself into the cool water. Then, using a breaststroke, she swam slowly around for a while, pausing to rest, now and then, at the edge of the pool. The man she suspected of being Nidal took off his glasses to clean them on his shirt, and seeing him from close range without them, all doubt left her mind. The man beside the pool, not twenty feet from her, was the man Dick Salem and his team were on the way to Cyprus to capture, the infamous Hakim Nidal.

It was nearly midnight when Dave Ames walked back into the suite where Colonel Wilton Garrett and Master Sergeant Lanny Cabe were monitoring the satellite radio.

"Boss," he said to Garrett, "you ain't gonna believe this shit." For the next few minutes, he related to Garrett how he had ended up in Charlotte Black's Georgetown apartment. "I couldn't figure out, at first, what you meant on the telephone, when you were talking about 'part two of the thing I went after,' and about it 'being just like the one I had, but in German.'"

"Yeah, well, what I was trying to tell you," Garrett said, "was that her contact is another woman, a West German named, let's see . . ."

"Marlene Graf," Ames interrupted.

"Yeah, that's right, Marlene Graf. . . . How the hell did you know that?" Garrett asked in astonishment.

"I was just going to get to that," Ames said. "Just as I was getting ready to leave, in walks this other gorgeous broad, tells me *she's* Charlotte's lover, too, then hops out of her dress and tells me I'm about to get laid by *both* of them."

"The German girl, Graf?" Garrett asked, as he switched the omnipresent cigar to the other side of his mouth.

Ames grinned and nodded, and Garrett exclaimed, "Holy! . . . What the hell did you *do?*"

"What would *any* red-blooded Delta officer do, Colonel?"

"I shudder to think, Major Ames," Garrett mumbled.

"What I *did,*" the handsome operations officer replied, "was get the hell *out* of there."

Garrett looked at him skeptically, but Ames continued, "No, seriously, boss. I did. I said, 'Miss, I've never had an offer like this in my life. But Charlotte here has worn me out, my wife's at home, wondering where the hell I am, and anyway, I'm afraid to death of AIDS!' Then I walked out the damn door, with her hollering, 'No, no, come back!' " He chuckled, then added, "If she hadn't been almost naked, she would probably have followed me outside. Never had a day like today in my whole life. So, what's been going on back here?"

Garrett lit his cigar, stood, and said, "Come in the other room, Major Ames."

Ames followed him into the sitting room of the suite and closed the door, so that Lanny Cabe would be unable to hear their conversation.

"Sit down, Major Ames," Garrett directed, remaining standing himself.

Ames did so, now well aware that he was about to receive an ass-chewing.

"I'm afraid you've gotten a bit carried away, this time. Or we've gotten carried away. I should have ordered you back here when you first phoned about being with the Black woman. And I *damned* sure should have done so when we learned who her contact was. But I didn't, so I guess I'm as much, or more, to blame than you are."

He sat down opposite Ames, who remained silent.

"Now, let me tell you what's probably happened, Dave. When Carruthers found out who Charlotte Black's contact is—the German woman—he had the FBI put a tail on her, right away. They did, and Harry Lawson called from Carruthers's office a while ago, not long after you called from the woman's place. No sooner had she been put under surveillance, than she made a meeting with *her* handler, who happens to be known to the FBI as a *big* officer in the KGB."

The point was not lost on Ames, who said, "Jesus. That means the FBI would have followed her to Charlotte's apartment, and they would have seen *me* leaving . . ."

Garrett sighed. "I'm afraid so. And *that* means they may

have followed you here, or even if they didn't, they would have taken down the license number of your rental car. So, if they don't know who you are by now, they will soon."

"Oh, shit," Ames mumbled.

Colonel Garrett stood again, and said, "So now, the FBI has made a connection that runs from the KGB to the Delta Force. It'll be the talk of the Bureau by tomorrow. But the worst thing is, they'll be asking so many questions that they may figure out we're up here playing spook and infringing on their turf."

"Boy, I've really blown it this time, haven't I, Colonel?"

Garrett bit the soggy end off his cigar, spat it into a trash can, then shoved the remainder back in his mouth and lit it. "Well, maybe, maybe not. If they haven't followed you here, maybe we can get you out of here and back to Bragg before they find out the rest of us are up here. If so, then we can just say that you happened to pick up this sexpot from Bolton's office while you were there briefing him on something."

"Yeah," Ames said, standing up. "But they'll still probably have me picked up. And polygraphed, too." He stood up, and paced the room with his commanding officer. "Sir, maybe I'll just have to say I knew the broad is a spy, and that I let her seduce me. I can resign my commission, and if they nail me with some espionage charge, I'll just bite the bullet and go to jail. Hell, I mean, this nuclear bomb thing is too important to blow, just because I've been running around here looking at the world through the head of my dick."

Garrett stopped, looked at his aggressive, young subordinate, and said, "That's noble of you, Major. But I'm afraid it won't do much to salvage the reputation of the unit, if this gets out."

The telephone rang in the bedroom where Cabe was monitoring the radio. He answered it, then knocked on the door and said, "It's Lawson, Colonel. Wants to talk to you."

When he picked up the telephone, Harry Lawson said, "Is Dave back yet?"

"Yeah, he is," Garrett replied. "And as you've probably been made aware by now, we've got a real problem."

"Well, that's not the way we see it, Will," Harry Lawson said. "Can you and Dave get over here to the NSC office right away?"

"I was about to send him back home. You know, to minimize the damage."

"Oh, don't do that, Will. As he said to you earlier, 'we've got a plan.' Get him and come on over here. My boss is waiting to meet him."

Convinced that she had found the elusive Hakim Nidal there beside the swimming pool of the Grand Hotel in Limassol, Rachel Brown got out of the water and returned to her lounge chair to decide what to do next. He had taken little notice of her while she swam in the pool, although he did look up from his newspaper when one of his bodyguards apparently called his attention to her as she backstroked across the pool.

One of the bodyguards continued to look over at her frequently, and she debated whether or not to try to capitalize on the man's obvious interest in her. "One step at a time, Brown," she said to herself. She now knew that Nidal was staying at the Grand Hotel, and that he had at least two bodyguards with him—although, if they always carried their weapons in athletic bags as they were doing now, they would find themselves at a severe disadvantage when Dick Salem and his men made their move against them.

The next thing she needed to try to find out, she decided, was what room or rooms of the hotel Nidal and his men were occupying. She took some money from her straw bag, stood, and walked to the bar. She ordered a soft drink, then strolled around near the bar sipping it and examining the flowers in the pots which lined that side of the patio. When she was at a point where Nidal's table was on the direct route back to her chair, she walked past the table, passing within a few feet of it. The bodyguard who had been paying so much attention to her was smoking a cigarette. On the table were his cigarettes, his lighter, and a room key. She was unable to see the number on the key tag, but the cigarettes gave her an idea. She went back to her chair, took some more money from her bag, and went back to the bar, where she bought a pack of Dunhill cigarettes. As she approached the table where Nidal's cigarette-smoking bodyguard sat with his back to her, she took out one of the Dunhills, and when she was beside the man, stopped, turned toward him, and said in French, "Pardon, monsieur. May I bother you for a light?"

He looked up at her, said, *"Certainement!"* and reached for his lighter. She leaned forward and let him light the cigarette, noting that the key on the table was for room 611.

"Merci," she said, smiling and nearly choking on the smoke to which she was unaccustomed, then walked back to her chair.

After she finished the cigarette, she took her camera out of the straw bag and set it down on the patio beside her chair. Ensuring that it was pointed toward Nidal, she reached down and pressed the shutter. The automatic advance whirred three times.

A short time later, she wrapped the dress around her, took her bag, and went into the hotel. She took the elevator to the sixth floor, where she found that room 611 was to the right, at the end of the hall on the wing of the hotel which faced the beach. There was no way for her to tell whether 611 was the only room the men were using, but judging from the distance between the doors on either side, she assumed that 611 was a single room, not a suite.

She went back down to the lobby, and went to the reception desk. There, she explained to the young, female clerk that she had received a telephone call from some friends staying in Larnaca. They wanted to stay in Limassol, and had asked if she could reserve them two double rooms for the next few nights.

"Of course," the desk clerk said.

As the girl made out the reservations, Rachel said, "May I ask what rooms they will have?"

"Yes, of course. They will have adjoining rooms on the fourth floor."

"And are they on the beach side of the hotel?"

The girl checked, then said, "No, they're on the land side. But they're the only adjoining rooms we have available at the moment."

"Oh, well. It's not important that they be adjoining," Rachel said. "Would it be possible to get two rooms on the beach side, and perhaps a bit higher up?"

Again, the girl checked the available rooms, then said, "Well, I can give you one room on the beach side on the eighth floor, and—let me see—yes, and one on the beach side of the sixth floor."

"That will be fine, I'm sure. And may I register for them now?"

"Oh, I'm afraid not, miss," the girl replied. "They will be required to register for themselves. We must check their passports, you see."

"Yes, of course," Rachel said. "Thank you very much for your help."

She walked past the doors which led out to the poolside patio. Nidal and the two other men were still there. There was a small hotel across the street from the Grand. If she could get rooms there on the side which faced the entrance to the Grand, Salem's men would be able to establish an observation post there, so that they could monitor the comings and goings of the terrorist and his bodyguards.

She went across the street and gave the clerk there the same story about some friends who wanted to leave Larnaca and stay in Limassol. When she asked about the location of the rooms, she was informed that one of them faced the Grand Hotel across the street.

She went back to the Grand and discovered that Nidal and his men were no longer at the table. She went into the hotel coffee shop and took a seat from which she could see back into the lobby, then ordered a light lunch. For more than an hour, she sat there nibbling at her food and reading a magazine she had taken from her Air France flight and brought with her in the straw bag. She was about to give up, and go back to her hotel to make a radio call about what she had learned, before getting ready to go up to Larnaca to meet Salem. She saw Nidal and the two bodyguards come into the lobby and turn toward the front entrance. Leaving enough money on the table to cover her bill and a generous tip, she hurried out to the hotel entrance. One of the men let Nidal into the back seat of a tan Mercedes sedan, then went around and got in back on the other side. The one who had given her a light for her cigarette got into the driver's seat.

She asked the doorman to get her a taxi, but by the time one pulled up, the tan Mercedes had pulled out of sight. She took the taxi two doors down to her own hotel, where she gave the astonished driver a nice tip and a smile.

Then she went up to her room, and after showering and changing into a light, yellow jumpsuit, she set up her radio and called back to the States. Cabe answered her call, and said, "I'm the only one here right now, Captain Brown."

"Understand. I have a long message," she reported. "Are you prepared to copy?"

"Roger, send it."

After she had passed the report on what she had learned about Delta's latest quarry, Hakim Nidal, she added, "If I'd thought about it, I could have snitched the glass he used on the patio, after he left. That way, I could have sent you a report on the fingerprints. But I didn't. I got some photos, though, which I'll pass on to the local Agency guy when I see him up at Larnaca. That's all I have, Lanny. Anything for me?"

"Negative, ma'am," Cabe replied. "Like I said, everyone else is away right now, and they left no messages for you."

She looked at her watch. It would be way after midnight on the East Coast of the U.S. She couldn't help asking, "Is the ops officer still out trying to seduce that loose-tongued secretary from the Hill?"

"Oh, no, ma'am. I'm afraid he got in a bit over his head on that one. The Old Man said a while ago that he's probably going to send him back to Bragg," Cabe informed her.

Oh, hell, Dave Ames, she thought. *What in God's name have you done?* If it was bad enough to get him sent back to Bragg, then it was probably the end of his assignment to Delta. The Delta commander's requirement to maintain the reputation of the unit left him little choice when someone did something too reckless. If it was bad enough to require a member to be sent back to the unit, reassignment usually followed.

"Roger," she said. "I'm heading for Larnaca. I'll report Salem's status when I get back."

Delta's deputy, Paul McCarthy, broke into the net from the Fort Bragg headquarters, and said, "That's damned fine work on tracking down the Quarry, Rachel. I'm sure Salem and his boys have enough to nail him now, so don't get yourself blown like Dave did—no pun intended. You're too damned valuable, and we'll need you again, no doubt."

"Roger, copy. Is Dave really in hot water, sir?"

"Oh, I wouldn't worry about it, kid," the deputy answered. "You know how the guy is. Even *hot* water runs off his back like it does off a duck's. I'm sure he'll be OK."

He wasn't surprised by Rachel's interest in Dave Ames. He had gone out to Delta's Woodlake Resort safehouse early the morning after the couple had returned from El Salvador. And he had noticed Ames's car parked at Rachel's condominium. Their personal lives were their own business, as long as they were discreet. But he hoped their romance wouldn't have an adverse effect on the operation.

Rachel put her radio away, praying as she did so that Dave wouldn't have to leave Fort Bragg. Not now, not after she had come to realize that she was falling in love with him.

She tried to dismiss him from her mind during the taxi ride to Larnaca Airport, but couldn't. When she saw her CIA contact there, though, her mind returned to her profession, and she followed him to the parking lot. He handed her the keys to a Mitsubishi van and a white Mercedes sedan, then said, "The gear you ordered is all inside the van. Call us if you need us. And good luck, Miss Brown." Then he turned and walked away.

19

It was well after midnight when Colonel Wilton Garrett, the Delta Force commander, and his operations officer, Major Dave Ames, were ushered into the National Security Advisor's briefing room in the west wing of the White House. Harry Lawson led them to where George Carruthers was sitting, talking to an elderly, silver-haired man whom Garrett and Ames recognized immediately. It was Jason Moore, the Director of Central Intelligence. Carruthers introduced him to Garrett, and he shook his hand, then turned to Ames and said, "And this must be your infamous Major David Ames."

Being called infamous by the unsmiling chief of the Central Intelligence Agency was not something Ames expected, but he held out his hand, and Moore shook it briefly, then said, "Sit down please, gentlemen." They all sat around the conference table, Dave sitting stiffly, aware that Director Moore was studying him.

"Well, Major," the DCI finally said, "it's been quite a busy day for you, hasn't it?"

Dave shifted uncomfortably in his chair, not knowing how to answer the legendary head of the Free World's premiere intelligence gathering organization. "Yes, sir," he mumbled.

"Yes, I'd say so," Moore commented, still gazing steadily at Dave from beneath his bushy, gray eyebrows. "First, you bug four members of the United States Congress. Then, you take it upon yourself to escort the agent of a foreign government to her home, where you spend several hours, until her handler arrives and sees you. And finally, you get yourself reported by the Federal Bureau of Investigation for having been seen with the handler, who happens to be a West German seductress apparently working for the highest-ranking KGB officer in Washington. And all of that on your own authority, with no assistance."

"I'm afraid you're correct, Director Moore," Ames replied. He would have to resign his commission immediately, the dedicated officer thought. What the hell would he do afterward? He had never considered being anything but a soldier. He would never be able to get a security clearance again, so there went the chance to ever work for the government. *What the hell,* he thought; *I'll probably end up in the federal penitentiary at Fort Leavenworth, anyway, for fifteen or twenty years. Jesus, what embarrassment this will cause my family. And Delta.*

"Director Moore," he said, "I'd like to reinforce one point here." Moore's bushy eyebrows arched, and Dave continued, "What I did *was* strictly on my own, without direction or consent from Colonel Garrett, or anyone else—strictly my own initiative. I hope you realize that, and that members of the Delta Force have it hammered into them *never* to take illegal actions. My screw-up shouldn't reflect on Colonel Garrett's unit, sir. That's all I'm trying to say."

"That isn't quite true, I'm afraid, Mr. Moore," Garrett interjected. "I was aware of what Major Ames was up to from the beginning, and I failed to call him off. I'm as much to blame as he is. More, in fact, because I'm his commander, and responsible for both his actions and my own."

"Yes," Moore said, sitting back in his chair. "I understand—and appreciate—what you're both saying. And I assure you, I have as high a regard for the laws of this land as you do, even though I disagree with a hell of a lot of them, especially the ones that hamper my agency's ability to do its job."

He allowed that comment to sink in a moment, then continued, "But some son of a bitch is about to blow up this town with a nuclear weapon—which is somewhat illegal in itself, I must say. And for the last couple of years, someone has been passing our secrets to the Soviets, while our *legal*

efforts to discover who the hell it was have proved fruitless."
He leaned his elbows on the table, then looked at Ames. "So
thank God, Major, that you didn't ask for authority to do
what you did, because it would have been denied, and we
wouldn't have found the leak. And we wouldn't have been
led to an agent of the KGB, who is not only giving the
Soviets *our* secrets, apparently, but those of her native West
Germany, as well. No, gentlemen, the good gods have been
with us on this one, and, by God, we're going to do our best
to capitalize on it." Finally, the old professional intelligence
officer smiled and said, "So get that damned hangdog look
off your face, Major—you, too, Colonel—and let me tell
you how we're going to use one of the biggest breaks we've
had in the counterespionage trade in years. Oh, and one
other thing, Colonel. From here on out, the responsibility
for Major Ames's actions are mine. By verbal executive
order, he is now a member of the CIA, not the Army, until I
decide to give him back. So if you have any questions about
whether what you have to do is legal, Major, you come ask
me. And I'll damn well tell you it is."

"You understand that Mr. Moore is right when he says
that Major Ames works for him, for the time being, don't
you, Colonel Garrett?" George Carruthers asked.

"Yes, sir," Garrett answered. "I was sheep-dipped like
that once, myself."

"All right, now," Director Moore began, "this is how
we're going to do this. First of all, Major, tell me all you
know about Charlotte Black and Marlene Graf, and what
they know about you."

Ames did so, and with some embarrassment, explained
what had happened when Marlene Graf arrived at Charlotte's apartment.

"And you just walked away?" Moore asked. "My God,
Colonel, you Delta troops *do* have self-discipline, don't
you?"

His mood now buoyant with relief, Dave said, "Well, with
all this AIDS scare, sir, I just chickened out."

"Yes," Moore said seriously. "Well, Major, I hope your
fears are unfounded, because if it becomes necessary, you

may be the first to die of it in the service of your country." Then he got back to his plan for using his newest Agency employee. "The first thing you have to do is get back in the good graces of the Black woman, which, eventually, will also mean getting back with the German girl."

"But, what about the FBI surveillance, sir?" Garrett asked.

"We've already called them off," Moore stated. "Told them it was an operation of ours, and that they were about to blow it. Now, once you get that done, Major, you'll convince the Black woman that we know all about her, about the wonderful Mr. Bolton—the loose-lipped son of a bitch—and the Graf woman. You simply explain to her that her choice is to either spend the rest of her life in prison as a traitor, or cooperate with us and spend her life quietly somewhere at the taxpayers' expense. Then—and this could be tricky, especially if she's in the game for ideology instead of only money—we'll try to turn the German woman. By the way, Major, do you know whether or not she carries a weapon?"

Picturing Marlene Graf standing there in nothing but her sexy red lingerie when he last saw her, Ames grinned and said, "Not unless she was planning on using her brassiere as a slingshot, Mr. Director!"

They all laughed, then Moore explained that Ames should simply confront her with the facts—that they knew she was guilty of espionage against both the United States and the Federal Republic of Germany, that they knew who her KGB contact is—"and you can give her his name, the time and place of her meeting with him, and even the FBI photos of the meeting, if you need to. If she decides she doesn't want to be turned, then she can spend her life in a German prison, since she has no diplomatic immunity with them."

"What if she just decides to get asylum from the Russians?" Garrett asked.

"Well, if she *is* a zealot of communist ideology, she just might. But, from the way it sounds, she doesn't seem like the kind of young woman who would want to forsake the freedom of Western lifestyle for the drab existence of a concubine to some old fart counterpart of mine from the KGB. And if we *can* turn her, she can serve as a double agent for us until they either catch on to her, or until she retires to the quiet life with her lover, Charlotte Black—also at the taxpayers' expense."

"One problem, though, sir," Dave offered. "I may not be the man to do it. I told them I worked in the Pentagon, that I was married, and all of that. When she passes my name to the KGB, they'll make me as a Delta officer, thanks to some damned reporter who blew my name in his news magazine a while back."

"So?" the CIA chief asked. "What would they expect a Delta guy to admit to? That he's in some secret outfit, and trying to burn them as spies? No, Major. Right now, there's no reason for them to think you're anything but a horny soldier who wants to get in their knickers. And if Graf *does* pass your name to the Sovs, they'll think they've stumbled into a major bonanza. You see, *we* know that *they* know Delta is not allowed, by law, to be in the espionage business. And as I did, until tonight, they think you guys are too law-abiding to do something illegal—like spy on congressional secretaries, for example. No, Major Ames, as I said, the gods are with us on this one. Now, let's see if we can figure out how to use this windfall to try to find that damned atomic bomb."

He went on to say that his agency was aware of quite a bit of the information their adversaries in Soviet and Cuban intelligence had about the Ramirez affair. "And don't bother to ask how we know all of this," he interjected, "just make certain you all protect the knowledge," then he winked at Dave Ames and added, "We've got *our* share of Marlene Grafs, too."

The cagey old Director of Central Intelligence went on to explain what his agency had discovered through the myriad technical and human sources at his disposal as chief of the Free World's intelligence effort.

The Soviets had ascertained, too late, that Ramirez had cached the container of nuclear material in Vietnam nearly two decades earlier, as he was about to be captured by the

North Vietnamese. He had then smuggled it out of Vietnam when he had attended a seminar for Marxist revolutionaries there the previous year. They knew that Ramirez was allegedly going to pass the material, perhaps even an improvised weapon constructed from it, to Hakim Nidal, in exchange for a huge amount of money. Their fear, in the hierarchy of the KGB, was that Nidal would use it to fulfill the threat he had made to get even with them, after their agents had picked Nidal up and exchanged him for the Soviet diplomat who was taken hostage in Beirut. "Nidal had been on their payroll, you see," Moore added, "and took issue with the fact that one of the KGB boys pulled his genitals out in front of everybody and rested them on a knife. At first, it seems, the plan was to send Nidal's balls to Hezbollah and tell them that, unless they got their comrade hostage back straight away, his dick would be next, then his head. Anyway, the exchange was made, but our boy Nidal has been sorely angry with the Russians ever since."

As the other four men in the National Security Council briefing room listened, Director Moore went on to explain what his communist counterparts knew about the Delta operation into El Salvador. "Apparently, they think we only wanted Ramirez because he was an American citizen turned revolutionary, and that we wanted to bring him back and put him on trial. They don't think we knew about his plutonium before we got him, but they figure we've probably gotten that information out of him, by now. In fact, I personally think that they've let us find out *on purpose* that they're aware he may have built a bomb. That way, if Nidal has it, as they suspect, then they think we'll help them try to find out where it is, before he sets it off under some Soviet Embassy, somewhere."

Garrett broke in to say, "Sir, if that's the case, then the KGB will be after Nidal by now, won't they? What if my team in Cyprus bumps into them, and we end up with another mess like we had with the Hinds in El Salvador?"

"No, they think he's still holed up somewhere in Beirut— waiting for his bomb to go off, perhaps. I figure they'll use the old hostage technique to try to get him. You know, they'll take a few of his Hezbollah buddies hostage, and try to trade them for Nidal. Anyway, they know that the Brits and the Izzies have such good intel nets in Cyprus, that a KGB snatch there would be far too risky. The only thing you need to be worried about there, is that, if the Israelis know he's in Cyprus, they might make a stab at getting him before *your* guys do."

George Carruthers asked, "If we manage to double the Graf woman, do you think she might be able to find out what else the Soviets know about Ramirez's bomb?"

"That's the only reason I want to try to double her to our side, George. If it wasn't for that, then we would just feed her disinformation as an unwitting agent. If Ames here is able to bring her over to *our* payroll, then she might just be able to get some critical piece of the puzzle for us."

"I see," the National Security Advisor said. "Is there anything else? I'm afraid if we don't get out of here soon, we'll still be here when the morning staff meeting starts."

"No, I think that's about it, unless anyone else has something."

"Just one thing, sir," his CIA subordinate Harry Lawson said. "You didn't mention that the Cubans and Sovs think we have Nadia Cruz, as well as Ramirez."

"Right," Moore said. "Apparently, they looked all over the area for her after your raid, Colonel. And they ransacked every place Ramirez had ever been, trying to find the bomb, or some clues to its location, or something. As far as we know, though, they're still even more confused than we are. . . . Now, Major Ames, make sure you break contact with these other Delta people right away. Harry here will set up whatever dead drops and other means of clandestine communications you'll need. Then you'd better get your beauty sleep, so you can handle these two Mata Haris you've stumbled on to. . . . I don't need to tell you that it's important to get this done, and done right, do I?"

"No, sir. I'll do my best."

As he walked out of the briefing room, the old, gray

veteran of forty years of intelligence operations mumbled to himself, "Oh, to be young again."

Dave Ames took his clothes from the Crystal City Holiday Inn and moved into the Twin Bridges Marriott—to the extra room that he had gotten there in case he and Rachel found an opportunity to be alone during the time they were in Washington together. But now she was away in Cyprus, assisting Sergeant Major Salem and his team in their efforts to capture Hakim Nidal. He was glad she was gone, so that she wouldn't know he had gotten himself hooked up with Charlotte Black, and had spent an evening in her bed. At the time, he had excused it as dutifully seizing an opportunity to help his country. But now, even though he had to admit to himself that he had enjoyed the erotic evening with her, he felt dirty for having used sex as a trap.

I'm as much a whore as she and Marlene Graf, he thought as he unpacked his suitcase. *But at least I'm on the right side.* Well, he had his orders now. He only hoped that he could complete the shady mission the CIA chief had given him, and get back into the operations of the Delta Force, where he belonged. And he hoped Rachel Brown would never learn of his involvement with the two women he had been charged to convert to agents under CIA control.

He was wondering what would be the best way to reestablish contact with Charlotte Black—whether to call her at her apartment, at her office in the Rayburn Building the next morning, or to send her flowers. Suddenly, something he had seen in the lobby of the motel when he was moving in gave him an idea. He walked back into the lobby and saw that the bunch of helium-filled balloons he had seen tied to one of the tables in the waiting area was still there. He went to the desk clerk and said, "Hi. I was wondering if there's anywhere I could get a bouquet of balloons like those over there?"

"Sure," the clerk answered, "just look in the Yellow Pages under 'balloons.' There's quite a few shops that sell them around here. Call one of them in the morning, and they'll deliver them here, or wherever you want."

"I know," Dave replied, "but I was wondering if there's somewhere I could get some tonight."

The clerk looked at the clock on the wall behind him and said, "At after two in the morning? I doubt it, sir."

"Well, whose are those over there?"

"Oh, some guy gave them to a girl who was staying here, but she's gone now. Had a flight to catch, or something. Why don't you take them, if you want?"

"Thanks," Dave said. "I think I will."

He took them to his room, then sat down and wrote a note, which he sealed in an envelope and tied to the strings of the multicolored bunch of balloons. Then he went to his rented car, put the balloons in the back seat, and drove to Georgetown. He tied them to the railing on the porch of Charlotte's apartment, then drove back to his motel and went to bed.

20

Rachel Brown was sitting in the small, rectangular waiting lounge of Larnaca Airport reading a day-old London *Times* when the passengers of Dick Salem's British Airways flight from London began filing out of the customs area with their luggage. There were six Delta Force NCOs in all, and they came out of the customs area in pairs. Moon Morton and Birdie Sadler appeared first, and when Rachel caught Sadler's eye, she scratched her ear to signal that she had detected no one she suspected of having her under surveillance. Sadler returned the signal to let Rachel know that they, too, were "clean." She then heard him tell Moon to wait while he went to the men's room, and Morton sat in one of the chairs opposite her. He pulled out a science fiction paperback and began to read it, and Rachel turned her head away and smiled to herself, remembering how Morton had acquired his nickname. Because Morton was always reading science fiction, Charlie Beckwith, Delta's first commander, had introduced him to a high government official once as "Sergeant Morton, who always has his nose buried in one of them space stories. In fact," Beckwith said, "we're thinking about running him for Secretary of Space in the next elections." Ever since then, as "Secretary of Space" was too long to be used as a nickname, Morton had been known simply as Moon. Like his teammate Birdie Sadler, he was one of Delta's most capable snipers, and Rachel was not at all surprised that Salem had selected him for the important mission. While she waited for the other members of Salem's team to appear, she wondered why it was that Delta's snipers all seemed to have some nickname. "Birdie" Sadler's real first name was Durwood, but someone had decided that he looked like Big Bird on the Sesame Street children's show, and he had been called "Birdie" ever since.

The youngest members of Salem's team, Staff Sergeant Pat Howson and Sergeant Jay Pollock, were the next to appear from the customs area. They were two of the best handgunners the Delta Force had ever had. Pollock saw Rachel sitting there, and scratched his right ear in the "no surveillance detected" sign. She returned it, and the two mid-twenties-aged men sauntered past, then stopped at the far end of the waiting lounge while Howson pretended to search for something in his suitcase.

Dick Salem and his Vietnam-era teammate, Master Sergeant Robert Small, were the last to clear the customs area. The clever Rob Small was a good devil's advocate for any plan, and although he and Sergeant Major Salem bickered like enemies over meaningless things, Salem knew he could turn to his longtime friend for sage and timely advice and unquestioning obedience when it came to an important matter such as the capture of Hakim Nidal.

Rachel scratched her ear once more, saw Salem's return signal, then folded her paper and walked out to the parking lot. In pairs, the others drifted out behind her. She walked to the Mitsubishi van which held the CIA-supplied equipment, and handed the keys to Birdie Sadler. "Take Moon and two more, and follow me," she said. He gestured with his eyes for the two young sergeants to put their bags in and ride with Moon and him, as Rachel walked to the white Mercedes Benz sedan and opened the trunk for Salem and Small to put their suitcases inside. They got into the sedan with her, and she drove away from the airport, with the others following in the dark blue van.

"Nice to see you guys," she said, and Salem replied, "Thanks for meeting us, Captain Brown. What's the latest?"

"It's 'Rachel' here, Dick," she corrected him. "The equipment's in the van with Birdie and the others, but I haven't checked it out yet. We're going to Limassol, by the way."

Salem was familiar with Cyprus, and he said, "Why? Do they think the Quarry is there."

"I *know* he's there. I saw him this morning. In fact, I've got rooms for four of you in the same hotel he's in, the Grand Hotel. The snipers can stay in the rooms I reserved in the hotel across from it. They can watch the entrance of the Grand from one of them."

"Damn, Capt—I mean, Rachel," Small stammered from the back seat of the sedan, "you've done all that? You're gonna change my mind about having women in the unit, yet."

Small was well known for his skepticism about the need for the female operators who had been in Delta for the last two years or so, and Rachel was pleased that the stubborn master sergeant was beginning to appreciate their value on such operations as the one they were now conducting.

She filled the two men in on all the information she had garnered since her arrival in Cyprus only eighteen hours or so earlier, and Sergeant Major Salem said, "That's a lot more than I expected to have to work with, Rachel. Good job."

"Hell, Rachel," Rob Small added from the back seat, "why didn't you just bring him to the airport for us? We could have just hopped back on the airplane with him, and headed for Fort Bragg!"

"I would have, but I didn't have a weapon," she joked.

After she led the van through a route which doubled back toward the airport for a distance—a surveillance detection route, as she had learned it was called during her training—she pulled off the main road and drove up a rocky track to an unpopulated stretch which was masked from the highway by a grassy knoll. Quickly, Salem briefed the others on what he had learned from Rachel. "Moon, you and Birdie get your bags and go with Rachel, and she'll drop you off at the hotel across the street. Get an OP set up and start watching the entrance to Quarry's hotel as soon as you can. The rest of us will go on in the van, and check the gear to make sure it all works. We'll check into our rooms in the Grand, then bring you guys your gear."

"Let me have a radio to take with me now, will you?" Rachel asked.

"Sure," Salem answered, then directed, "Hop in there and get her one, Rob."

As Small crawled into the back of the van, he called, "You want a weapon, too, Rachel?"

"Yes, I'll take a pistol and a spare magazine, thanks."

Rachel's spirits were high because she had done so well at tracking Hakim Nidal down, and because the men seemed to be accepting her as one of their own—a full-fledged Delta operator.

Dick Salem had even more respect for her than the men of his team, for unlike them, he was aware that she had proved her mettle in El Salvador, when she had killed an armed enemy in close combat. Of the six men in his team, only he and Small had had that soul-wrenching experience. He wondered which two would be the ones to have to kill Hakim's bodyguards.

Small came out of the van with a small, short-range, secure voice radio and a pistol, and handed them to Rachel. "All right," Salem ordered, "let's move."

On the road from Larnaca to Limassol, Salem slowed down at several spots which looked as if they might be suitable for the ambush of a vehicle coming from the other direction. Rob Small took a number of Polaroid photographs of each location, so they could be used later when they made specific plans for the ambush of Nidal and his bodyguards.

To the three men riding in the van with him, Salem said, "Our best chance will probably be on Thursday morning, the day after tomorrow, when we can assume he'll be going from his hotel to the airport for his flight to Paris. Even if it isn't our *best* chance, it'll be our *last* chance, so Howson, you and Pollock concentrate on a plan to hit him then at one of these sites."

"What time did Rachel say his flight was on Thursday morning?" Small asked.

"Eight thirty-five," Salem responded. "That means he'll have to be there no later than, say, seven forty-five, which means departure from Limassol by no later than seven o'clock. Of course, it could be as much as an hour or so earlier, so we'll need to be in position by six."

From the rear of the van where he and Pat Howson were checking out the weapons and equipment the CIA had provided for them, Jay Pollock said, "Pat and I can come up here early tomorrow morning to recon the ambush site and see what the traffic's like from around six o'clock to seven."

"Good, Jay," Sergeant Major Salem said. He recalled that, from the time he had first met Pollock, when Jay was undergoing his rapid-fire interview by the Delta leaders as the final part of the selection process, Jay Pollock had developed a reputation for thinking ahead. That, and his proven skill as a first-class handgunner, were the reasons that Salem had selected him for the mission.

Within two hours of their arrival in Limassol, the team was settled into their hotel rooms and prepared to begin the execution phase of their mission to capture Hakim Nidal. While Moon Morton observed the entrance of their quarry's hotel from his room across the street, Rob Small sat in his room on the same floor of the Grand Hotel that Rachel had determined Nidal's room was on. With the door to his room cracked open, Small was able to observe the doors of the elevators, and he sat in a chair watching them, his little team radio at his side.

The other four members of the team had drifted one-by-one up the street to Rachel's hotel, and were now gathered in her room to get their orders from Command Sergeant Major Dick Salem.

Pat Howson was the last to arrive, after returning from renting an additional car from a local rental agency, to give the team some additional mobility.

"Did you get some more wheels?" Birdie Sadler asked him as he sat down on the bed.

"Yeah," Howson replied, "another Mercedes sedan—tan, like the Quarry's."

Salem was talking on Rachel's satellite radio, exchanging information with Delta's Intelligence Officer, Jim Greer. Greer had been replaced at the CIA's Langley headquarters by a liaison team of two of his Intelligence section subordinates, and he was now on radio watch at Delta's Washington area safehouse in the Crystal City Holiday Inn.

Salem had just asked Greer if they had been able to arrange a way for Nidal and the team to be exfiltrated from Cyprus, when and if they were able to capture the terrorist.

"The only thing we've got so far," Greer answered, "is a Bell Jet Ranger the Agency has in Athens—you know, the same type of helicopter the Army calls an OH-58."

Salem realized that only two passengers would fit into the rear of the small helicopter—which meant Nidal and one member of the team were the only two he would be able to exfiltrate by that means.

"They'll reposition it to Larnaca first thing in the morning," Greer continued. "As soon as the pilots get into Larnaca—around nine-thirty your time—they'll give Rachel a call in her hotel room, and you can send somebody up to coordinate the exfil with them then, unless you want to send someone up to Larnaca in the morning to meet them when they come in."

Salem glanced at Howson as he told Greer, "Howson and Pollock are going up that way in the morning, anyway, so I'll have them meet the chopper pilots and coordinate with them then."

Pat Howson gave him a thumbs-up in acknowledgment,

then Salem asked Greer over the radio, "Where are they going to take the Quarry after we get him?"

"There's a cruiser in the eastern Med, the *Yorktown*, that we're sending a message to through JCS tonight," Greer answered. "All they'll know is that if a Bell Jet Ranger with the right callsign calls them to say that he's got an in-flight emergency, the *Yorktown* is to allow them to land on her chopper deck, and then offer all possible assistance to the crew. Once you get him to the *Yorktown*, we'll send a Navy helicopter to pick him and your guy up, and take them somewhere to link up with an airplane for the flight back here to the States."

"Roger that," Salem acknowledged, and Greer said, "One more thing, Dick. The boss wanted me to pass on to you that, since only one of your people can go out with the chopper, getting the rest of the team out could get hairy, especially if there's any shooting, and the local authorities get after you. He said to tell you that if—God forbid—you lose somebody, to just cache the body and get the hell out. We'll let the embassy in Nicosia recover them."

"I understand," Salem answered. "But tell the Old Man that we're not going to lose anybody, and even if we did, we'd figure a way to bring them out. There'll be no Delta soldier left behind, not on *my* watch, anyway." In his mind, he saw again the vision which had been burned there years earlier, after Delta's ill-fated attempt to rescue the hostages from the American Embassy in Iran. A few days after the mission ended in a fiery collision in the desert between a helicopter and a C-130 transport, he had watched in horror as an Iranian official picked with his pocketknife at the charred body of one of the men they had had to leave behind in the blazing wreck. "Never again," Dick Salem had vowed when he saw the disgusting desecration on a television newscast. He intended to keep that vow.

Just then, the small radio Rachel had been given to keep her in touch with the rest of the team emitted the faint voice of Rob Small. "Rachel, this is Small, over."

Salem picked up her radio from the bedside table and answered, "Small, this is Salem."

"This is Small. One of Quarry's boys just entered the elevator by himself and went down, over."

"Roger, Rob. We're all here at Rachel's place, now. Keep us informed, over."

Then Sergeant Morton, from his observation post in the hotel across the street, came on with, "This is Moon. I think the man Rob just reported is coming out now. He's a medium-size Arab wearing white pants and a striped shirt with rolled up sleeves, and carrying a faggot-looking hand-bag."

"That's him, Moon," Small confirmed over the radio net.

"Roger, Rob. From now on, we'll call him Number One. . . . He's going to a tan Mercedes sedan and getting in . . . backing out . . . now he's pulling out onto the street and turning right, going north."

"This is Salem, roger that. Keep us informed."

He set the radio down, and young Jay Pollock said, "Why don't we get a blowout device or two on there as soon as we can, just in case?"

"Yeah, good idea, Jay," Salem agreed. "Why don't you and Pat see if you can get a couple of them on the front tires tonight, after Number One gets back?"

Rachel had never heard of a "blowout device," and asked Pollock what it was.

"It's something Lanny Cabe just came up with a week or so ago," Pollock explained. "It's just a little disc not much bigger than a checker, that you can superglue onto the side of a tire, with a little bit of C-4 explosive mixed with magnesium powder. It has an itty-bitty transistor receiver in it, and a wristwatch battery hooked up to a squib. When it gets the right frequency signal, the squib lights the C-4 and magnesium, which burns a hole in the rubber in about two seconds, causing a blowout. The blowout knocks the checker off, so when you look at the tire, you can't even tell what caused the hole."

"Pretty clever," Rachel commented.

"Yeah," Birdie Sadler added, "and unlike about half the shit Cabe comes up with, it actually works."

Salem went over the various assignments for the next day's activities of the team, interrupted twice by reports from Morton and Small that Number One had returned to the Grand Hotel in the Mercedes, and had gone back up to his room. When he finished his instructions to the team, he said, "Let's get on back. Rob and I will take turns watching the hallway. Birdie, you and Moon spell each other at the OP. And Pat, as soon as you and Jay get the blowout devices on the car, if you can do it without getting caught, go on up and get some sleep. In fact, everybody get as much sleep as you can tonight. But keep your team radio next to your ear, in case something comes up."

When the others had left, Rachel called Jim Greer on the satcom radio to ask how the operation in Washington was going. Since only Sergeant Major Salem and she, of those in Cyprus, were aware of the details of the compartmented effort going on in Washington, she had to wait until the others were gone before she could ask. What she really wanted to know was if Dave Ames had been fired, as she feared from Cabe's earlier report.

"No real break, yet," Greer reported from the Crystal City safehouse.

"Cabe said earlier that Dave was going back to Bragg," she said, hoping for some response that would indicate otherwise.

"May be. All I know is, he and the Old Man went off to some meeting, then Dave came back, packed up his gear, and left."

"Roger, sir," she answered. "I'll be sleeping with the headphones on, so if you have anything for me, just keep calling. Out."

She stripped to her panties and crawled into bed, the Walkman headset which was hooked into the satellite radio and the small team radio which connected her to Salem and the others, on the pillow beside her.

So, Dave had left. Then the report that Lanny Cabe had given her earlier, about Ames having gotten in "over his head" somehow with the congressional secretary he found out was leaking classified information, was apparently true. And now he's packed up and left. As she drifted off to sleep, it was with the hope that she would at least get back to Fort Bragg before he left there. She was unaware that he was still in Washington, implementing the plan of the Director of Central Intelligence to double Charlotte Black and Marlene Graf, and change their involvement in the shadowy business of espionage to the benefit of the United States.

21

Charlotte Black awoke in her Georgetown apartment on that Tuesday morning, Washington time, and lay in bed for a while looking at her reflection in the mirror above her. When Dave Ames had abruptly walked out the night before, Marlene had suddenly become very angry with her, cursing her in German and asking Charlotte why she hadn't called her earlier to tell her that she had the Army major there.

"Don't you see how valuable he could be?" Marlene had screamed at her.

"Yes, Marlene. But if you hadn't run him off with your overaggressive come-on, he probably would still be here!" she had replied.

Marlene softened then and said, "Yes, perhaps you're right. It's just that, if we could have gotten certain information from him about the man they captured in El Salvador . . . well, it would make my superiors very happy. And it would mean more money in the bank for both of us."

"Don't worry, sweetheart," Charlotte said. "I can get ahold of him in the Pentagon as soon as I get to work in the morning. As much as he seemed to enjoy me earlier, I'm sure I can convince him to come see me again. I'll just tell him that Wes wanted me to be sure to get all the information I could about Ramirez—you know, so he could stay up-to-date on what they're learning from him. I'm pretty sure he'll tell me. I mean, after all, he came over yesterday and told me the guy was at Eglin Air Force Base, and I'd never even *met* him before. Now that he's my lover, it shouldn't be too hard to get whatever else you need to know out of him."

"Yes," Marlene said. "Yes, I guess you're right. Sit down, *liebchen,* and let me tell you the exact things I need to know."

After she had repeated the questions Marlene wanted her to ask Dave, Charlotte tried to get Marlene to go to bed with her, but the German girl said, "No, I must go. Save your energy for him. You *must* get this information from him for me, Charlotte."

Now, the morning after, Charlotte opened the front door to find that the unseasonable warm spell Washington had enjoyed for the past week had passed. Pulling her robe tightly around her, she stepped out onto her front stoop to get her newspaper and discovered the bunch of balloons Dave Ames had left tied there. She took the balloons and the paper inside and opened the envelope. A smile lit up her face as she read Dave's note.

Dear Charlotte,

Sorry to run off so suddenly last night, but I was a little shocked by what your friend said and did. But, I just want to say how much I enjoyed being with you, and I hope I can see you again very soon. And forgive me for being such a prude. I guess I was a little jealous or something at first, because I've never been with two women at once before. One other thing—I'm afraid I wasn't totally honest with you. I'm just here on temporary duty from Fort Bragg for a few days.

Anyway, Charlotte, I'd love to see you again. If I can see you for lunch, or after you get off work, please give me a call at my motel. I'm at the Twin Bridges Marriott, room 1021. Call anytime today—I've got the day off.

Hope you enjoy the balloons. Please call,

Dave

Charlotte telephoned Marlene and told her about the balloons. "Listen to this," she said.

After she read the letter over the telephone, Marlene said, "That's wonderful, *liebchen*. Wonderful. Call your office and tell them that you're ill today, and won't be in. Then call the major, tell him you have the day off, too, and invite him over."

Charlotte said, "Can you come over, too, darling? He sounds like he'd enjoy it, and God knows, *I* would."

"I'll be there early this afternoon, *liebchen*. Meanwhile, use what I've taught you."

"I will, darling. See you later, then."

Charlotte called the Twin Bridges Marriott and asked for room 1021. Dave answered sleepily.

"I got the pretty balloons, Dave, and your note. Thank you very much."

"Can I see you for lunch then?" he asked. "Or after work?"

"Why not for breakfast, lover?" she said. "I have the day off, too."

"Oh, Charlotte, honey, that's great! I'll be there in an hour. Shall I pick up something for breakfast?"

"If you like," she said. "But make sure it doesn't have crumbs."

"Crumbs?"

"Yes. They'd fall on my silk sheets. I want *my* breakfast in bed, don't you?"

"Wow, don't I ever! See you in a little bit," he said, then hung up the phone and added, "you horny traitor bitch."

Rachel Brown awoke to the sound of Dick Salem's voice from the intrateam radio on the pillow beside her.

He was talking to Birdie Sadler, who was manning the

observation post in the hotel across the street from the Grand Hotel.

"They're entering the elevator now."

"Roger," Birdie answered.

Rachel looked at the digital alarm clock on her bedside table. It was just after nine P.M. She had only been asleep about half an hour. She lay there in the dark, until she heard Moon Morton, also in the OP, call, "OK. Number One and Quarry and one other dude are coming out of the entrance now. One has on the same clothes as earlier. Quarry has on dark pants and a white jacket, and the other guy has white pants and a blue shirt on. Let's call him Number Two."

"Roger," Salem replied.

Moon went on, "One and Two are carrying athletic bags. . . . They're at the car, and getting in."

Salem said, "One of you hop in the van and follow them, if you can."

"Birdie's already headed down to do that," Moon reported.

"Roger, break. Pat, you guys up?"

"Roger that. You want us to hustle down and follow 'em, too?" Howson asked.

"Negative. Let Bird see where they're headed, first."

Moon continued to report on Nidal and his bodyguards as their tan sedan pulled out of the Grand Hotel parking lot and turned north. "There goes Birdie. Shouldn't have any problem catching up with them," Moon added.

Still lying in her bed in the darkness of her hotel room, Rachel picked up her radio and said, "Salem, this is Rachel. I'm up, too, if you need me."

"Roger," Salem acknowledged, then said, "Did you guys get the blowout discs on their tires, Pat?"

"That's most affirmative," Pat Howson answered from his room two floors above Salem. "We got one on the inside of both right-side tires. We couldn't get any on the left side without risking being seen from the entrance of the hotel. Jay has the transmitter, if we need it."

"Good job. OK, everybody sit tight until we hear from Birdie."

"I've got 'em in sight now, about a half-mile north," Birdie Sadler reported from the van.

A few minutes later, he came back on to say, "All right, they're pulling off to the left. It's a restaurant. It's about—let's see—two point eight klicks north of the hotel."

Sadler's radio signal was weak, and Salem said, "You're kinda weak, Bird. Understand they've pulled into a restaurant eight kilometers north?"

"Negative, negative," came Sadler's reply, "two decimal eight kilometers. I say again, two decimal eight klicks north. . . . I'll call back in a minute."

Rachel tried to recall if she had noticed a restaurant about two miles north of the hotel on the road to Larnaca. That would be a little way outside of Limassol. Yes, she did remember a Greek restaurant, set back off the road about thirty meters. She picked up her radio and said, "Salem, if that's the one I'm thinking of, we might be able to hit them on their way out."

"Roger, ma'am. Everybody hear what Rachel said?"

"Pat and Jay, roger."

"This is Moon, roger that."

Rachel turned on the light beside her bed and got up. She pulled on a pair of Levi's and a Mickey Mouse T-shirt, then heard Sadler call Salem from the van and say, "They're in a Greek restaurant back off the highway twenty meters or so. Traffic's pretty light up here, and their car's at the side of the place, pretty much in the shadows. If we can get set up in time, Dick, we might just be able to have a go at 'em when they come out. You want to come up here and have a look?"

"That's a hard roger, Bird. We'll be there shortly. Meet us somewhere between here and there."

"Wilco," Sadler said. "I'm at a closed-up gas station on the east side of the road about a quarter of a mile short of the restaurant. I'll make another run past there, then meet you back here."

"Roger, Birdie. Everybody got that?"

The others acknowledged, then Salem said, "Here's how we'll work it. Pat, you and Jay get your gear and meet me and Small out in the parking lot. We'll take your car. Rachel, you pick up Moon from his hotel, then come on up to the service station. We'll all meet up there."

"Shall I call the States and tell them what we're up to?" Rachel asked after the others had acknowledged Salem's instructions.

"Negative. Not enough time, right now. Let's move."

Rachel shoved the satellite radio under her bed and put her team radio into her straw bag with the silenced .380 caliber Beretta pistol that Rob Small had given her earlier. Then she left to pick up Moon Morton.

When she got to the service station, Salem and his passengers had already left to drive by the restaurant on a reconnaissance. She and Moon Morton got into the van with Birdie Sadler to await the others' return. "I think we can take him tonight," Sadler said to the others. "It looks a hell of a lot easier to me than trying to hit them on the way up to Larnaca in broad daylight."

Salem and the other three Delta Force soldiers pulled into the closed service station just then, got out of their car, and climbed into the van. Sergeant Major Salem agreed with Birdie Sadler's assessment—the current situation offered a better opportunity to capture Nidal than they would probably have again.

"Pat," he said to Sergeant Howson, "I want you and Jay to go on in there and get a beer or something. Scope the place out, see what they're doing, and whether they're with anybody else. You both got your heat?"

Howson patted his side beneath his left arm to show that he was wearing his pistol in a shoulder holster under his black nylon windbreaker. "With silencer," he said.

Jay Pollock pulled up his trouser leg to reveal a Beretta .380 in an ankle holster.

"All right," Dick Salem continued, "when it looks like they're getting up to leave, you two go out just in front of them. I want you to park your car beside theirs—not too close, but between them and the road. Fumble with the keys or something, Jay, so that they get to their car before you guys get in yours."

"That won't work," Rob Small interjected. Salem looked

at him, irritated momentarily, then realizing that Small was only doing his part as the devil's advocate of the plan. "Why won't it, Rob?" he asked.

"If they're worth a damn as bodyguards, they won't go near Pat and Jay until they get in the car and leave," Small explained. "I mean, here these two Americans are, who just *happen* to show up at a restaurant where a guy is who knows he's wanted by the U.S., who just *happen* to leave at the same time he and his thugs do, and who just *happen* to be parked next to him, in a car that's exactly like his. Hell, Ray Charles could see through *that!*"

"Yeah. Yeah, you're right, Rob."

"May I make a suggestion, Sergeant Major?" Rachel asked.

"Yes, ma'am," he replied. "Of course."

"If the guys inside could signal us on the radio as Nidal leaves the restaurant, the two of us could pull into the parking lot and park near them, then get out of our car just as they're about to get in theirs. I mean, a man and a woman just showing up, should be a lot less suspicious looking. We could hit the bodyguards, grab Nidal, throw him in our car, and be gone."

Salem thought about it, then said, "No, it's too messy, and we're not making use of all of our assets . . . even though you're right about a man and woman being less suspicious looking than two men."

Birdie Sadler said, "You know, the row of bushes there that runs along the edge of the parking lot, looks thick enough to hide a couple of guys in. Why don't Moon and I hide in there, just in front of the car? You and Captain Brown could pull up like she said, and be getting out while they're getting in. Then Moon and I can do in the body-guards, drag them into the bushes, and you two can grab Nidal, throw him into your car, and go."

"Yeah," Salem said, "that does sound better. And Rob, you can be in the van. We'll throw the bodies in there, and you, Birdie, and Moon can take them somewhere and dump them."

Jay Pollock spoke up. "We need to get rid of their car,

though. We can't just leave it in the parking lot, especially with those blowout discs on it."

"Good point," Salem said. He thought for a minute, then said, "OK, ma'am, you and Moon haven't had a chance to see the place yet, have you?"

"No," they both answered, and Salem said, "OK, let's make one more drive by. We'll take your car, Rachel. Let's go, Moon."

Across the Potomac River from Washington, D.C., Colonel Wilton Garrett was holding a meeting in one of the hotel suites which he was using as a safehouse and headquarters. He and Sergeant Cabe had moved several chairs from the suite next door, where Cabe was now monitoring the secure voice satellite radio. Now, seated around the sitting room of the suite were most of the other key players of the team which had been assembled to try to find the improvised nuclear bomb that Ramirez was believed to have planted somewhere in the Washington area. Angela Herndon, the tall, blond sergeant who had been with Ramirez's pregnant consort, Nadia Cruz, was there, while the two Delta men who had been helping her escort and question Cruz—Doc Reed and Sergeant Baldero—remained with the woman in nearby Arlington.

Seated on either side of Angela were Dr. Toby Wayne, the Nuclear Emergency Search Team scientist, and Harry Lawson, the Central Intelligence Agency officer who had been in on the operation since the beginning.

Sitting beside Colonel Garrett was Lieutenant Colonel Jerry Schumann, the commander of Delta's Detachment E-1, which was the ground operations element of the team, to which most of the Delta men involved in the El Salvador phase of the operation and those now in Cyprus, were assigned.

Garrett introduced Schumann to Wayne and Lawson, adding, "He would have been here all along, but as you know, we had a man killed in El Salvador on Friday. Colonel Schumann has been in Pennsylvania with the man's parents, and taking care of his funeral."

"Dr. Wayne," Garrett said to the scientist, "Colonel Schumann will be one of the men giving you additional help in looking for the bomb with your sensing devices." They had learned earlier that the White House decision was to not bring any more NEST scientists in to help with the search, yet. Instead, they would have to use other Delta men who were already involved in the operation.

"I hope those things are easy to operate, Dr. Wayne," Jerry Schumann said.

"Don't worry, Colonel," Wayne answered. "I've already got them set up, so that all you have to do is turn them on and walk around. If you feel the handle start to vibrate, you're probably near the bomb. All you have to do is stay there and send for me."

"Good," Schumann said. "Matt Jensen, who's my sergeant major, and five more of our guys—the ones who were in El Sal with him—will be here shortly. They're on the way here from Sergeant Haynes's funeral. Once Mr. Lawson gets us fixed up with our phony FBI credentials, we'll be ready to go."

"Now," Colonel Garrett said, "the reason I called this meeting is to see where we stand with this thing—to see if we think we're really making any progress, or if we feel we should advise the President to go ahead and call in everybody in the government to work on it. Sergeant Herndon?"

"Well, sir," the attractive blonde said, "Nadia's being as cooperative with us as she can, I think. She's taken quite a liking to Sergeant Baldero, and vice versa, I might add. But I'm not sure she's given us much that's been helpful, except to verify that the thing is probably in one of those big chrome fire extinguishers. But she can't remember seeing any of them anywhere that he took her in Washington."

"Would it be possible to check with the D.C. fire department, to see if they might know where all—or at least some—of that kind of fire extinguishers are?" Jerry Schumann asked.

"Good idea, Jerry. Can you handle that, Harry?" Garrett inquired.

Lawson nodded, and made a note on the pad in his lap.

Angela Herndon went on, "We're going to go back again today to all the places she and Ramirez went, to see if anything sparks her memory."

"All right," the Delta Force commander said. "Harry, what have you got?"

"Well, I wasn't able to find out where he had the case for the thing made, or the vessel, or whatever you call it. But I did find out that it's a fairly simple thing to get built. There must be a dozen places around here that could have done it. Would the people who machined it have known what they were making, Toby?" Lawson asked the NEST scientist.

"I wouldn't think so," Wayne replied. "He could have said it was something for a boat, or an engine he was experimenting with, or anything like that. In fact, as far as we know, he might have even brought it here from Managua with him. I think we can just go on the assumption he *did* get it made somewhere, and quit wasting our effort on that aspect."

"Suits me," Lawson said, then to Garrett, "As far as whether or not we ought to advise the White House to go public with this thing, Will, I say let's give it another twenty-four or thirty-six hours. Maybe your people in Cyprus will have Nidal by then, and can get something out of him, or maybe the Cruz girl will remember something. And it's possible that the little project Major Ames is working on might even yield a clue."

"What project is that?" Toby Wayne asked.

"Oh, it's another activity we had to put him on," Garrett said, "not really related to this."

"Well, for my money," Wayne said, "I have to agree with Harry. Let's give ourselves another day or two, especially now that I'll have Colonel Schumann and his men to help. Even if we don't find the thing, once the rest of the NEST people are brought in, we'll either be able to find it within a few days, or we probably won't find it at all . . . until it goes off, that is—God forbid."

"All right, then," Garrett said. "I won't keep you people any longer. I know you need to get on with looking for the damned thing. Thanks for coming. Let's get together back here at, say, nine o'clock tonight, to see where we stand. I'll see Mr. Carruthers at noon, and recommend that we keep trying for another day or so. Except for the meeting with him, I'll be next door on the radio all day. Let me know if anybody thinks they've got *anything,* and I'll do the same."

The meeting broke up then, and Garrett went next door to relieve Lanny Cabe on radio watch, so the Delta technician could get some well-deserved sleep.

22

Dick Salem returned to the darkened service station lot with Rachel and Moon Morton, and the three climbed back into the van with the others. After taking another look at the restaurant where Nidal and his bodyguards were having dinner, he had decided on a plan for the terrorist's capture. He took a notepad from the little knapsack in which he had his silenced pistol and his team radio, and told the others to gather around him in the back of the darkened van. All of them knelt around the notepad except Birdie Sadler, in the driver's seat, who shifted around so that he could see, as well. Rob Small held a penlight for Salem, as he sketched out his plan on the sheet of paper.

First, he drew a large square, then a smaller one in the top of the first. Pointing to the small box, he said, "This is the restaurant, where Howson and Pollock will be," and placing the point of his pencil in the middle of the larger square, said, "This is the parking lot." At the bottom of it, he drew two parallel lines, and said, "And the road."

On the left side of the parking lot, he drew a row of bushes, and just left of the bushes, a small rectangle. "These are the bushes, where Moon and Birdie will be hidden, and

behind them, facing the road, the van, with Rob driving."
He looked at Small and said, "Make sure you open the back
doors after you park it. These bushes are tall enough to hide
the van, and it's in the shadows."

He drew two more small rectangles in the parking lot, one
on the right edge, just below the restaurant, about which he
said, "This is the only car there now, besides the bad guys'
Mercedes, which is here." He pointed to the rectangle he
had drawn on the left side of the parking lot, next to the
bushes and about halfway between the restaurant and the
road.

On the right side of the parking lot, he drew another car,
and said, "Pat, you and Jay park over here when you get
there."

"Got it," Pat Howson said.

Salem next drew a car on the edge of the road at the right
side of the paper, and said, "Rachel and I will be here in her
car, just to the north of the restaurant, with the engine
running." He pointed to the restaurant, and said, "Now,
you two guys on the inside . . ."

"Oh, shit!" Birdie Sadler exclaimed from the front seat of
the van. He had been glancing back and forth from Salem's
drawing to the roadside edge of the restaurant parking lot,
which was visible to him on the left side of the road several
hundred meters distant, and now he saw the lights of a car as
it pulled up to the edge of the parking lot and stopped.

"I think he's leaving now!" Sadler said.

After only a split-second's hesitation, Dick Salem began
barking orders, sliding open the door on the right side of the
van as he did so. "Get your guns and get down! Bird, stay
where you are. You got the blowout transmitter, Jay?"

Jay Pollock snatched the transmitter, which was nothing
but an electronic garage door opener, from his pocket.
"Right here!" he said.

"OK, get ready to blow 'em as soon as I say to—just
before they reach here. This is the only place they have to
pull off the road."

"He's pulling out now," Sadler said.

"How long we got?"

"Ten or fifteen seconds!"

"Moon and Rob, go behind the van and take the far side of 'em! Rachel, me an' you got the near side. Follow me around the front. Ready, Jay?"

"Rog!" Pollock said, his head just to the left of Birdie's as he pointed the transmitter out of the open left door window at the approaching car, now only a hundred meters or so away. Moon Morton and Rob Small had jumped out and run to the back of the van, and were now crouched there, weapons at the ready, waiting for Salem's command. Salem jumped from the van, squatted beside the right front tire, and peered around the corner of the van toward the target vehicle. Crouched behind him was Rachel Brown. Her heart was racing, but the hand which held her silenced Beretta, she noticed, was strangely steady.

"Freeze, freeze, freeze!" Salem cried suddenly. "Wrong car!"

The vehicle flashed past, as they all noticed that it was not Nidal's tan Mercedes Benz sedan, but a blue Honda—the other car which had been at the restaurant.

The Delta soldiers relaxed, and Birdie Sadler said, "Oh, fuck me! Sorry about that, gang."

"No sweat, Bird," Salem replied. "It *could* have been them. All right, everybody get inside and let's go over this once more. If we don't get moving, they *will* be gone."

They climbed back into the van, and he quickly went over the rest of the plan. He and Rachel would pull into the parking lot when Moon and Birdie, from their hiding place in the bushes, saw Nidal and his men at the door of the restaurant, preparing to leave. Inside, Jay and Pat would do something a moment later to distract anyone in the restaurant from noticing the commotion which would occur in the parking lot outside.

On his sketch, Salem drew the spot at which Rachel was to park—about two car-widths from Nidal's car, between it and the road. She would get out a second or so before Salem and walk toward the restaurant in an effort to distract the men. Salem would hop out and take the man nearest him. Birdie and Moon were to kill the bodyguard nearest them, then snatch Nidal, drag him through the bushes, and throw him into the back of the van. They would pull out immediately and drive north. Salem and Rachel would then put the bodyguards into one of the cars, and head north, also, taking both her car and Nidal's.

"If I can find their keys, that is."

"If not," Pollock said, "just leave it. When Pat and I come out of the restaurant a few minutes later, if it's still there, I'll just hot-wire it and bring it with me."

"Good," Salem replied. "All right, let's go. Pat, you and Jay first. If something's changed, and it doesn't look like the plan will work when you get there—you know, a bunch of cars pulling in or something—just drive on past. The rest of us will meet you a klick or so up the road, and I'll either change the plan, or call it quits. We've still got the plan for Thursday morning, if we need it. Any questions? All right, let's go."

There was only one car in the parking lot when Pollock and Howson pulled in—Nidal's. Rachel drove the white Mercedes past there, turned around up the road, then pulled off onto the shoulder just north of the restaurant. She turned off the lights, but left the motor running. She could see the van stop short of the other side of the parking lot, turn off its lights, and back into position behind the row of tall bushes. A moment later, Birdie called on the radio and said, "We're ready, here, boss man."

"Roger," Salem, sitting beside Rachel, answered. Now there was nothing to do except wait.

Dave Ames walked up to the door of Charlotte Black's apartment with a grocery bag in one hand and a Nike athletic bag in the other. He set the Nike bag down, hearing a *thump* as the .45 caliber Colt automatic pistol in the bottom of it hit the brick floor of the stoop. Beneath the towel and shaving kit which he had placed on top of it were also two pairs of handcuffs and a photograph of Marlene Graf, meeting with her KGB contact. Harry Lawson had given it to him—along with a photo of Ames taken on the very spot on which he now stood. An FBI surveillance team had taken both photographs the day before, while they were tailing the German agent as a result of Dave's own discovery that her lover, Charlotte Black, was passing American secrets to her.

"What goes around, comes around," Lawson had said, chuckling as he handed Dave the photos in the White House the night before.

"Or how about, 'Oh, what a tangled web we weave, when first we practice to deceive'?" Dave had answered as he looked at the photos. He had torn the photograph of himself to shreds, but kept the one of Marlene and her KGB contact to use in his efforts to "double" the two women.

He rang the doorbell, then picked up the Nike bag and waited for Charlotte to come to the door, thinking, *If I ever get out of this shit, I'm never coming to this goddamned town again.*

Charlotte opened the door, and he spoke the words that he had rehearsed: "Hi, gorgeous. If wine and fruit and cheese don't make crumbs, we've got it made."

She opened the door for him, and he stepped inside, thinking how much he wished that she really was just a sexy Washington secretary who wanted to share a day off with him, making love on the silk sheets of her big bed.

"Oh, Dave," she said, smiling. "You really are a remarkable man. Here, let me take that." She reached for the grocery bag, and he let her take it, then watched as she walked back through the well-appointed living room of her apartment, her hips swaying beneath the deep-pink robe which was tied closely around her slender waist.

He followed her in, wondering why he didn't just say, "Charlotte, let's just knock off the bullshit. I know you're a spy, and I'm here to make you an offer to either cooperate or spend the rest of your life in prison." But he didn't.

She thanked him for the bouquet of balloons. "I was so *surprised!* And your note—well, it was perfect, Dave." She stepped to him and kissed him lightly, then said, "Let's sit down and talk a minute." She walked to the couch in the little alcove at the back of the narrow house and sat down. As she crossed her legs, her lace-trimmed robe parted, revealing her long, well-shaped legs and the pink silk pants she wore. She patted the seat of the couch beside her and he joined her there.

"Well," she said, "I know you were a little shocked at Marlene last night. And I just want you to understand that, well, she's . . . she's . . ."

He wanted to say, "A fucking KGB spy!" but instead, he said, "Hey, I understand, Charlotte. But don't you think maybe she's . . . well . . . *using* you?" Good, he thought, here's the opening I was waiting for.

Charlotte said, "Oh, Dave, don't you see? She's in *love* with me. Look, if you couldn't tell last night, I'm—how should I say this?—I'm a very sexual woman."

He looked at her, thinking, *God damn, you're just a poor, stupid pawn in all of this.*

"Well," she continued, "Marlene is a very sexual person, too. She's, well, she's been good to me. And I'm afraid that, when she came over last night, while you were upstairs getting dressed, I just couldn't help telling her that I'd found somebody as sexual, or sex hungry, or whatever, as she is. And I am. All she wanted to do was share her own sexuality with you—with us. See what I mean?"

Charlotte untied her robe and straddled Dave, facing him. She put her hands on his shoulders and said, "Anyway, Major Dave Ames, you mysterious, sexy man, what was that in your note about you just being here temporarily from Fort Bragg?"

OK, he thought, *here comes her pitch for information. Time to give her the hard truth about why you're here, Ames.*

The telephone on the end table of the sofa rang, startling him as he was about to speak.

"Oh, hell," Charlotte said, leaning to the side and picking up the receiver. "Hello?"

"Oh, hi!" she said to the caller. "Yes . . . Oh, goody . . . but, just a second." She put the mouthpiece of the telephone against her shoulder and said, "It's Marlene. You're not going to run away this time, if she comes over, are you?"

Damn! He needed some time with Charlotte, first. Time for her to get over the shock of what he was about to tell her, to turn her first, and get her on his side so he could use her to help double Marlene. But if he *did* run out again, how suspicious would that make them? Hadn't he hinted in his note that he had thought it over, and *wanted* to be with both women?

Ames faked a smile and said, "No, of course not," and Charlotte put the telephone back to her ear and said, "How soon will you be here? . . . Yes! . . . Yes, and he even brought wine and fruit and cheese, so we won't get crumbs in the bed." She laughed at whatever Marlene said, then replied, "Yes, crumbs. I'll explain it when you get here. See you in about ten minutes, then."

She hung up the phone, as Dave thought, *Shit! Ten minutes.*

Charlotte took one of his hands and slid it up into the loose-fitting leg of her pink silk pants, whispering, "Oh, god, Dave, I can hardly wait."

He let her guide his hand to toy with her, and thought, *Ames, you're a whore—a whore!"* Then he closed his eyes and tried to pretend that she was Rachel.

Birdie Sadler's voice broke the silence in the car where Captain Rachel Brown and Command Sergeant Major Dick Salem waited for word that Hakim Nidal and his two bodyguards were coming out of the restaurant. "Salem, this is Birdie. They're at the door, coming out. Move out now."

"Salem, roger," he replied calmly as Rachel pulled the automatic transmission into gear and turned on the headlights simultaneously. As she pulled into the parking lot just seconds later, she and Salem could see the three Lebanese men about halfway between the nearly deserted restaurant and their tan Mercedes Benz sedan. "Easy, easy," Salem muttered from beside her. She slowed down, glancing over at Salem. He was looking at the men from the corner of his eye, his silenced pistol resting on his right thigh, against the door.

As she pulled to a halt parallel to their tan sedan and fifteen feet to its left, she noticed that the shortest of the three—Nidal—and one of the others were going to the far side of the tan Mercedes. The man from whom she had gotten a light at the swimming pool was preparing to unlock the driver's door. All three of them were glancing toward her car, and Salem was looking away from them, at her. Quickly, she put the car in park, turned it off, and opened her door, taking the straw handbag from the seat beside her as she got out. She sensed the men all looking at her as she walked past the rear of the car toward the restaurant. She could see no one who could observe them from inside.

She heard the spitting sound of a silenced pistol, and turned in time to see Birdie Sadler emerging from the bushes behind the men. Three puffs of smoke came from his pistol in rapid succession, and the man beside Nidal crumpled to the ground. She drew her own weapon from her handbag as she glanced toward Dick Salem. He was looking down at his pistol and pulling the slide to the rear as the driver, now facing Salem, yanked a gun from the athletic bag in his left hand. "Malfunction!" she thought aloud. Her hand flew up and her pistol kicked three times in half a second, the bullets striking where her wide eyes were fixed—in the middle of the man's back. In her peripheral vision, she saw figures to her right, running, as Hakim Nidal made a dash for the restaurant. Two steps behind, diving after him, was Moon Morton. Moon's hands grasped Nidal's ankles, his face plowing into the gravel of the parking lot as he tackled the squat terrorist. Nidal fell forward heavily, just to Rachel's right, his face turned toward her, mouth agape and eyes clenched shut. Two quick steps and she was at his head. She grasped his hair with her left hand as she shoved the silencer of her pistol into his mouth. "One sound, Nidal," she whispered hoarsely, "and I'll blow your fucking brains out!"

Birdie was suddenly above Nidal, yanking his arms behind his back and slapping handcuffs on his wrists, then pulling him to his feet. Rachel rose with him, her pistol still shoved into Nidal's mouth. Nearby, Moon was on his hands and knees, blood dripping from his face onto the ground. Birdie shoved the gun in his right hand under Nidal's chin, turned him, and with his left hand grasping the chain between the handcuffs, pushed Nidal toward the bushes. Rachel ran to Moon and helped him to his feet as he wiped the blood which streamed from cuts on his nose and forehead.

"I'm all right," he muttered, and trotted off after Birdie, stopping to pick up his pistol from the ground beside Nidal's car. Rachel ran to her handbag, picked it up, and dropped her gun in it, then ran to help Salem. He had dragged one of the bodyguards into the back seat of the tan Mercedes and was now coming to the right side of the car to get the other one. The man was on his back, groaning loudly as he lay atop the athletic bag from which he'd had no chance to draw his weapon.

She glanced toward the road as the van pulled from around the far side of the bushes and accelerated away to the north. Rob Small was at the wheel, looking straight ahead.

Salem dragged the groaning man by the shoulders, then shoved him into the floor of the front seat as Rachel picked up the athletic bag and threw it into the back.

"Give me your gun," Salem said to her. She pulled it from her handbag and Salem snatched it from her, then turned, placed it at the groaning man's temple, and fired twice.

Rachel vomited, as Salem leaned over the back of the seat and she heard the silencer cough twice more.

"Move!" he ordered, guiding her around the back of the car as she wiped the vomit from her lips with the back of her hand. They saw the lights of a car approaching from the north, and ducked down between the two Mercedes Benz sedans until it had sped on past. Then Salem handed her the pistol back and asked, "You all right, ma'am?"

"Yeah, fine."

"Let's go, then. Lead me to that dirt road where we stopped on the way down from Larnaca."

He hopped into the seat of the tan Mercedes, took from his pocket the keys he had grabbed from the man Rachel shot, and started the engine.

Rachel ran to the driver's side of her white sedan and got in. Less than two minutes after she had turned into the restaurant parking lot, she pulled back onto the highway and headed north. Salem pulled out right behind her, the two dead bodyguards crumpled on the floor of the sedan.

Pat Howson and Jay Pollock left the restaurant five minutes later, and walked out into the parking lot where only their car remained. They had heard nothing from inside the restaurant except two cars leaving, because just after Jay Pollock saw Nidal and his men walk out of the door, he knocked a full glass of beer into Howson's lap. Howson jumped up, cursing Pollock in a good-natured manner, then picked up the other glass of beer and acted as if he were going to throw it on his friend. Pollock ran to the back of the restaurant with Howson chasing him in order to draw the attention of the owner and his waiter away from the parking lot. The owner saw that it was only a playful fight and stood there laughing as Howson chased Pollock around and around the back area of the restaurant. Finally, they stopped the charade, and Howson got a towel from the waiter and mopped his beer-soaked clothing with it. After they heard the two cars leave, they had another beer, then left. As the others had done, they pulled out of the restaurant parking lot and turned north to rendezvous with the rest of the team.

23

Dr. Toby Wayne had four Trace Radiation Detection Devices, "tracers," as they were called by the Nuclear Emergency Search Team scientists who normally employed them. He had just finished instructing the Delta Force members who were going to assist him in the search for the improvised nuclear bomb, in how to use them.

"Time is our most precious commodity at the moment, gentlemen," he said. "If we don't make some progress toward finding this thing today, then it's likely that the President will go public with the fact that there's probably a nuclear time bomb planted somewhere in this town."

Lieutenant Colonel Jerry Schumann, Delta's ground element commander, reinforced Wayne's statement of the urgency of their mission. "And just think for a moment about what that would mean, guys," he said as he looked his subordinates in the eyes. Schumann's detachment sergeant major, Matt Jensen; Mel Lawrence; and Boo Maxton were all members of the team which had gone into El Salvador in the attempt to capture Emilio Ramirez. Schumann added, "Even if it turned out to be a false alarm, or if we found the thing shortly after the announcement, just think what it would do to this administration—this President."

Matt Jensen spoke up. "What can we do *now* to find the damn thing before the public has to be told about it?"

"Yes," Toby Wayne agreed, *"tempus fugit,* as they say. Now, all we have to go on is what the Cruz girl has told us about where she and Ramirez went while they were in Washington. There's no sense in going anywhere else until we've thoroughly swept those particular buildings."

"Angela and Baldero are going to go with Nadia Cruz again today," Schumann said. "The hope is that she'll remember *some* little thing Ramirez said or did that'll be an indication of where he might have planted the nuke. Matt, you and Boo will be following them. What you need to do is each sweep one flank of their route, looking for one of those big chrome fire extinguishers. Dr. Wayne has already gone along the direct route they took, so concentrate on the surrounding terrain, you know, hallways and rest rooms you pass, and that sort of thing."

"Exactly," Dr. Wayne said. "And remember, if you go back to the Air and Space Museum, you'll get a false reading near the Apollo capsule, so don't waste time there thinking you've found it. By the way, I'll be at the White House, making a routine sweep, as far as the Secret Service is concerned, so there's no use in retracing the tour they took through there."

"Jesus," Maxton said, "you don't think the bastard could have gotten a bomb in there, do you?"

"Probably not," Schumann replied, "but we can't take the chance that he might somehow have figured out a way to."

"Don't forget, Boo," Matt Jensen said. "He was one bold and clever son of a bitch."

"Let's get going," Lieutenant Colonel Schumann ordered. "You two have to link up with Nadia Cruz and the others at the Smithsonian Metro station in twenty minutes."

"Where are you going to be, boss?" Jensen asked.

"I'll be in the Pentagon, sweeping the flanks of the route tourists take through there. Everybody have a pager with him, in case somebody finds something?"

They all replied affirmatively, so he said, "Well, let's get on with it. A case of beer to whoever finds the thing."

"Make it a case of Irish whiskey," Boo joked, "then bring the deputy up here from Bragg and give him one of these tracers. For a case of Bushmills, McCarthy would have the damn thing found by lunchtime!"

By the time Marlene Graf arrived at Charlotte Black's Georgetown apartment, Dave Ames had gone over several plans in his mind for how he could confront them with the evidence that they were both Soviet agents. He had to ensure that he was in a position to prevent them—especially Marlene—from escaping, until he could convince them that he was deadly serious about the fact that they would either have to cooperate—and cooperate convincingly—or face life-long jail sentences. His pistol was in the athletic bag he had left in the kitchen. He would surely need to cover them with it while he made his pitch, but suppose one of them actually made a run for it? Would he shoot her? That would blow the whole thing. Maybe he should wait until they were undressed, to ensure that they would be unable to just run outside and get away. But suppose one of them did so anyway? Suppose one of them just ran outside naked and claimed that he was trying to rape them at gunpoint or something? He wouldn't put it past Marlene to do such a thing, if she felt cornered before the full explanation of their options had a chance to sink into her mind.

He still had not made up his mind how to handle the situation, when the doorbell rang. He went to the door and opened it for Marlene. She smiled at him, stepped into the apartment, and said, "Hello. I'm glad you decided to come back."

"Me, too," he said, helping her out of her coat. Noticing her large purse, he said, "Do you want me to take your purse?"

"Uh, no. No, thank you. I'll just keep it, for now."

So, he thought, she's probably got a gun in it. I hope that doesn't mean she's onto me.

Beneath her coat she wore a well-tailored gray suit with a white blouse, dark hose, and high-heeled black shoes. Her blond hair was curly and fashionably wild-looking, and the only makeup she wore—or needed—was shiny red lip gloss.

"You look very nice, Marlene," he said sincerely.

"Thank you," she said as she went to greet Charlotte. Dave followed her.

The two women embraced and kissed a bit more warmly than mere friends would do. "I'm so glad you were able to make it, darling," Charlotte said. "It's such a nice day for staying inside to play."

Marlene opened Charlotte's robe to look at the lithe body in the pink silk nightie. "Yes, especially with such nice toys to play with. Wouldn't you agree, Dave?"

"Hell, yes!" he said.

"Well, let Dave see the nice toys *you* have." Charlotte giggled as she began unbuttoning the white blouse Marlene wore beneath the open jacket of her suit. Dave watched as Charlotte pulled the blouse from the waist of the skirt, and unbuttoned it to reveal a black lace bra nearly brimming over with the unblemished white flesh of the German woman's breasts. She then pulled Marlene to her, reached around and unfastened the skirt so that it fell to the floor, then pulled her black half-slip down.

Charlotte set Marlene's purse down, then pulled the suit jacket and blouse off her lover's shoulders and arms, and dropped them onto the floor. Marlene looked at Dave and smiled, once more standing before him in only her lingerie —this time all of black lace. She wore no panties with her black garter belt and stockings.

"Now, let's see what toys *Dave* has brought along," she said with a giggle as she reached for the waistband of his corduroy trousers.

"Uh, why don't we go up to the bedroom?" he suggested as he stopped her from unbuckling his belt.

"Ah, yes," Marlene agreed, scooping up her clothes and purse.

They went to the stairs, Charlotte holding hands with both her lovers, and Dave said, "Oh, wait. I'll run back and get the wine." He got the wine from the refrigerator and his athletic bag from the kitchen table. He found a corkscrew and three wineglasses, unzipped the bag and placed them on top of the towel, then went upstairs.

About five miles north of Limassol, Dick Salem called Rob Small on the radio to find out where he was with the van that held Nidal, Birdie Sadler, and Moon Morton. They were just to his north, so he asked Small if he could find the dirt road up near Larnaca where Rachel had taken them shortly after they arrived that afternoon.

"Birdie knows where it is," Small replied. "Do you want us to meet you there?"

"Wait 'til I catch up, then lead me to it," Salem replied. He tried to raise Howson and Pollock on the radio, but they were either still in the restaurant or out of radio range, so he called to Rachel in the car just in front of him and said, "You pull off and wait here 'til Pat and Jay show up, Rachel. If they know the way to that dirt road, send them on up here to link up with us. If not, you'll have to guide them there. But I want you to get back to your room and call a report back to the States as soon as possible."

"Wilco," she answered. "I'm pulling off now."

Pollock called on the radio a couple of minutes later. Rachel answered, and asked if they knew the way to the isolated dirt road. They weren't certain that they could find it, so she waited until they caught up with her, then led them on up the road to link up with the others.

In the back of the van, Birdie Sadler was sitting on Hakim Nidal's back, with his pistol to the back of the terrorist's head. He had tied a blindfold over Nidal's eyes, and was now watching Moon Morton dabbing at the cuts on his face with a handkerchief.

"You all right, Moon?" he asked his Delta Force teammate.

"Yeah. This gash on my forehead's still bleeding, but I think it'll be OK."

Finally, the squat terrorist said something. "Who are you people?" he asked in English.

"You'll find out soon enough, asshole!" Sadler replied.

Nidal muttered something in Arabic, then said, "You will never get away with this."

Morton retorted, "Looks to me like we already have, you son of a bitch!"

Then Sadler grabbed his captive by the hair, smacked his face against the floor of the van and added, "You just keep your damned mouth shut, you murdering bastard. When we want you to talk, we'll say so."

"Plug up his ears," Rob Small directed from the driver's seat, "and if he says another word without being told to, take off his filthy socks and shove 'em in his mouth."

Their statements reflected their deep hatred for the man they knew was responsible for the deaths and maiming of so many innocent people. Nidal sensed their inner anger, and lay quietly to preclude their having an excuse to further abuse him.

When Dave Ames got upstairs to Charlotte's erotically furnished bedroom, she was lying on the big bed in her pink nightie, her robe now discarded and lying on the floor. As he took the glasses from his athletic bag and set them on the bedside table, Marlene came out of the bathroom and put her purse on the chair where her suit and blouse lay folded.

She sat on the bed in her black lingerie, and Charlotte stroked her back as they watched Dave open the bottle of wine.

"What do you have in the bag?" Marlene asked as he dropped the corkscrew back on top of the towel.

"Oh, just some more toys," he replied. *Do it now, Ames!* his mind cried, and he reached into the bag and felt the grip of his pistol. Then an idea struck him, and he let go of the pistol. Instead, he pulled out the handcuffs and said, "Toys!" as he held them up for the women to see.

Marlene gave him a startled look, but Charlotte said, "Ah, so you're going to tie us up and tease us first, aren't you?"

Dave pushed Marlene back and pinned her to the bed. "No, you and I are going to tie *Marlene* up!"

He slapped one of the cuffs onto her wrist, as the German woman cried, *"Nein, nein, du schwein!"* Charlotte laughed and helped Dave pin her down as he got one of her wrists shackled to the nearest post of the bed, then helped him cuff Marlene's other wrist to the same post. He got off the bed and stood back, as Charlotte began to rub her body on the other woman's.

Then he pulled his pistol from the athletic bag and said, "Charlotte, I'm not messing around, now! We know that you've been passing secrets to Marlene, and that she's been passing them to the Soviets."

The woman cowered on the far side of the bed, wide-eyed at the sight of the pistol pointed at her face.

In German, Marlene cried, "Don't listen to him! Get my pistol from my purse and kill him!" But Charlotte was too shocked and frightened to do anything but put her hands to her mouth and begin sobbing.

Ames knew enough German to know that Marlene had said something about killing him, so he backed up to the chair where she had placed her purse, and took the 9mm automatic pistol out of it.

"You stupid bitch!" Marlene cursed. "Look what you've gotten us into!"

"You're wrong, Dave. You're wrong!" Charlotte cried. "She's only been telling the West Germans what they already know! Honestly. You've got to believe me!"

"I'm afraid not, Miss Black. She's been passing secrets to the KGB," he replied.

"No, no, no!" Charlotte sobbed into her hands.

Marlene became suddenly calm. "Really, Major, she's telling the truth, you know. There's been no harm done to your country. I only used it as an excuse to be with my beautiful Charlotte." She struggled with the handcuffs which had her shackled to the bed. Her bra had been pulled down during the scuffle, and now she writhed erotically, trying to give credence to the story she quickly decided might divert Ames from the truth. "I just can't help it. I'm obsessed with her—with our lovemaking—and I just pretended to want secrets from her so that I could be with her, so that there would be excitement for us."

Dave reached into the athletic bag and pulled out the photograph of Marlene and her KGB contact.

"And now you have the chance to have us both," the German woman continued. "We can show you pleasures you've never even imagined, fulfill every fantasy you've ever . . ."

She stopped in midsentence as he held out the photograph for her to see.

"Sorry, Marlene Graf," he said. "You can knock off the bullshit and seduction, now. You've been had, lady."

"Scheisse," the woman mumbled. "So, what do you do now, Major? Call in the FBI team that's waiting in the wings?"

"No," he replied, pulling the silk sheet over her lace-clothed body, "now I tell you how you can avoid going to prison for the rest of your life."

Charlotte Black had slowly ceased sobbing, and sat on the bed listening in near shock as he explained to the women how the Central Intelligence Agency intended to employ them.

Once Dick Salem's team had rendezvoused on the isolated dirt road near Larnaca, Cyprus, he quickly gave them his plan for what to do next. "Rachel, you listen to all of this, then go back to your room and report it all to the boss on the satcom. Then just wait there 'til one of us contacts you."

She nodded, then listened as he gave the others their orders.

"Pat, you and Jay are going to have to get rid of the two stiffs in Nidal's car. Make sure you strip them and dump their clothes and wallets and stuff somewhere they won't be found. And leave the car somewhere that it won't be easily discovered—you know, in a busy parking lot somewhere, or something. If you can, steal some license plates and change them for the ones on the car. Once you've got that done, come back to this area and give me a call on the radio. We'll be somewhere near enough to hear you, but if the radios quit or something, we'll meet you right here at first light. By then, we'll know where the pickup zone for the Agency chopper will be. Once we give you the coordinates of the PZ, you'll go to the airport, meet the pilots, and coordinate the pickup with them."

He thought for a minute, then continued. "All right, Birdie, Rob, and I will stay with Quarry until the pickup. I'll go out on the chopper with him, and then Rob, you and Bird go back to Limassol, check out of your rooms, and get the next thing smoking out of Cyprus. Moon, you go on back with Rachel now and get your face unfucked—sorry, ma'am—and be sure you make up some cover story about how your face got messed up."

"When do you want us to pull out, Sergeant Major?" Pat Howson asked.

"As soon as you make coordination with the chopper crew. In fact, if you have time after you get rid of the bodies, go ahead and check out, and just stay at the airport until you can get a flight out of here."

"Got it," Howson replied.

"OK, ma'am, let's see," Salem said, "that would leave you here by yourself. . . . I'm not gonna do that."

"It's all right, Sergeant Major," she said. "I'll be just fine. As soon as everybody else gets out, I'll pack up and leave—and see you at Fort Bragg in a couple of days."

"No, ma'am," he replied, "I'm not going to leave you hanging out like that." Turning to Birdie Sadler, he said, "Bird, you move in with her once you get checked out. You two can just hang around until everybody else is out of here, then coordinate with the Agency people in Nicosia to pick up the cars and radios. Once that's done, make your way on back to the States together."

He looked around at the others in the darkness. "All right, you've all done a great job, so far. Let's not screw it up now. Rachel, you and Moon give your guns to Pat and Jay to get rid of, along with the ones the bodyguards had on them. Any questions?"

A minute later, the team had split up. The van, with Small driving, and Sadler and Salem in the back with Nidal, drove slowly around on the back roads of Cyprus, looking for a suitable pickup zone for the helicopter exfiltration of Nidal and Salem. Pollock and Howson left to get rid of the corpses and weapons, and Rachel drove the injured Moon Morton back to his hotel in Limassol.

As soon as she got to her hotel room, she pulled the satellite radio out from beneath her bed, set it up, and called

Colonel Garrett at the safehouse in the Crystal City Holiday Inn. As she reported the capture of Nidal and the death of his two bodyguards, she interrupted her report with, "Wait, out." She ran into the bathroom and vomited into the toilet, rinsed her mouth out, then returned to the radio and completed her report.

"Outstanding job, Captain Brown," her commanding officer said. "Let me know as soon as the Quarry and Salem get out. And get out as soon after that as you can. We'll be standing by here if you have anything more for us."

"Roger," she said. "How's the other thing going?"

"No luck so far, I'm afraid," he replied. "But Colonel Schumann and some of his men are helping the NEST guy try to find it, so maybe we'll find the thing yet."

"Roger," Rachel said. "Good luck, boss. Out here."

She went to bed then, with the headset of the radio on the pillow beside her head. But the image of the man in the parking lot whom she had shot when Salem's pistol jammed, and the sound of Salem finishing him off with shots to the head, would not leave her mind, and she was unable to sleep. She remembered how Dave Ames had made love to her when she was disturbed by the memory of the man she had killed in El Salvador. Was it only four or five days ago? God, it seemed so long ago.

"Dave," she whispered in the darkness. "Dave, why can't you be here now?"

24

Matt Jensen and Boo Maxton met Angela Herndon, Santos Baldero, and the pregnant Nicaraguan woman, Nadia Cruz, at the Smithsonian station of Washington's Metrorail just after rush hour on the morning of Tuesday, the 14th of January. For the next several hours, they retraced the route that Nadia and her now-deceased lover, Emilio Ramirez, had followed several months prior. It was a cold morning, and Nadia shivered beneath the warm clothing that Angela had bought for her, as she walked between Angela and Santos. Not far behind, Matt and Boo followed the trio first through the Air and Space Museum, then up toward Capitol Hill to the National Arboretum. They would drift off from the others now and then, and search for likely places where a bomb disguised as a fire extinguisher might be found. On a number of occasions, they located fire extinguishers, but when they passed near them, there was no vibration from the handles of the briefcases they carried, which were actually "tracers"—trace radiation detection devices. If a fire extinguisher had actually contained any nuclear material, the small amount of radiation it emitted would have been sensed by the delicate detectors, and the vibrators built into the handles of the tracers would have gone off to alert them to its presence.

They next went to the massive Capitol Building in search of the bomb. Shortly after noon, Jensen came up to Angela and said, "Look, let's take a break and get some lunch."

"Yeah," the tall, blond staff sergeant said, "Nadia needs to get off her feet for a while anyway and get some food into her. Where shall we go?"

"I don't know. Isn't there a cafeteria or something in here?"

"Well, I know there are in the congressional office buildings, but you either have to be a congressional staffer, or be accompanied by one," Angela explained. "I tried to get some lunch over in the Rayburn Building the other day, but they wouldn't let me in because I didn't have a badge. We can go to one of the commercial places up the street, though."

Nadia, who spoke little English, asked Santos Baldero what Jensen and Angela were saying, and he explained it to her in Spanish.

"But that's not true," Nadia replied. "Emilio and I got something to eat here, I remember. He asked someone, and the man directed us to a small restaurant in the basement."

Baldero told the others what Nadia had just said, and Jensen walked over to a nearby guard, who confirmed that they could get lunch in the little Capitol Cafe in the basement. They took the elevator down into the labyrinth of corridors in the basement of the Capitol Building and located the cafe.

"This will do just fine," Angela said, so they hung their coats over the backs of the chairs at one of the wrought iron tables. Jensen and Maxton set their NEST briefcases down on two of the chairs and joined the others in line to get some lunch.

After they finished, Matt Jensen said, "Well, let's get on with it, gang."

"Let me get a refill of coffee," Boo Maxton said, and went to the end of the line where the coffee urns were. He set his briefcase down, filled his cup and added cream and sugar, then picked up the briefcase. He dropped the full cup of coffee, and it splashed on his shoes and the feet of the young woman directly behind him.

The others laughed at his clumsiness as he apologized to the woman, who said, with a deep-South twang, "Oh, don't worry about it. It'll just wash off some of the ankle-deep bullshit from this place."

As he bent to wipe the coffee from the woman's shoes with

his handkerchief, Matt Jensen came over to help him. He picked up Maxton's briefcase and discovered what had caused Boo to drop the coffee. The handle of the briefcase vibrated in the palm of his hand.

Maxton apologized again to the southern woman, then moved out of her way to let her and the people in line behind her pass. He stepped around the end of the steam cabinets and bent down to wipe off his own shoes with his handkerchief, peering beneath the stainless steel cabinet which held the coffee urns. Shoved far back under the cabinet, he saw a chrome fire extinguisher.

Standing and looking into the wide eyes of Matt Jensen, who held the vibrating handle of the briefcase in his hand, Boo Maxton smiled and said, "There *is* a God, after all."

In the White House office of George Carruthers, the Delta Force commander, Colonel Wilton Garrett, was informing Carruthers of the capture of Hakim Nidal. "Of course, the problem right now is getting him out of Cyprus and out to the *Yorktown*. They've still got something like six hours before the CIA helicopter shows up from Athens, and that'll be in broad daylight, Cyprus time. I don't know whether they're going to try to exfiltrate him during daylight, or wait until after nightfall."

"Well, with two dead bodies on their hands, I hope they'll elect to get him out of there as soon as they can. I'd hate for them to have to try to explain away a couple of dead Lebanese to the Greek Cypriot police."

The pager in the inside pocket of Garrett's suit coat started beeping, and he took it out to read the phone number from which he was being paged. It was not one he recognized.

"Excuse me, Mr. Carruthers," he said, "but I'd better answer this page."

Carruthers pointed to the telephone on his desk and said, "Punch nine, then the number."

Matt Jensen answered with, "Jensen speaking."

"It's Garrett. What have you got?"

"We've found it, boss. At least, we're pretty sure we have."

"Where are you?"

"In the basement of the United States Capitol Building."

For a moment Garrett said nothing, then asked, "What do you mean, 'pretty sure'?"

"Boss," Matt Jensen said in an almost scolding manner, "if we weren't pretty damned certain, I wouldn't have called you. Boo found it with his tracer, and it's in the type of container we were looking for. I verified the contents with my tracer. Now it *might* not be what we've been looking for, but I'll bet my ass that it is . . . sir."

Garrett smiled. "Of course, Matt. Hang on a minute."

Looking at the National Security Advisor, he said, "Sir, they've found it. It's in the basement of the Capitol."

"My God! Are they sure?"

"Yes, sir. As sure as they can be without actually taking it apart."

"Can they bring it out *now?* What the hell do we do with it, anyway? Where's Dr. Wayne?"

Garrett asked Jensen, "Can you get it out of there?"

"No, sir, not without a bunch of questions being asked, anyway. Sir, I think we'd better meet to talk about this, instead of using the telephone."

"Good point," Garrett said. It was a well-known fact that the Soviets were able to monitor many telephone calls in the United States. "I'll get Dr. Wayne and meet you somewhere up there."

"OK, boss. How 'bout the parking lot right between here and the Library of Congress?"

"Done," Garrett answered. "I'll be there as soon as I can find Wayne and get up there—about fifteen minutes or so."

"Yes, sir. See you then."

He hung up and said to Carruthers, "They can't get it out right now. I'd better find Dr. Wayne and get up there right away to have a look, sir. He's somewhere here in the White House, sweeping the building with his radiation tracer."

He got ahold of Wayne by calling his pager number and having him call Carruthers's office. He instructed the scientist to come there immediately, and Wayne walked in less than two minutes later. When Garrett explained to the

NEST man what Matt Jensen had told him, Wayne took the information calmly, then said, "Every night since we formed NEST, I have prayed to God that we would be allowed to find an improvised nuclear device, if one was ever a threat to this country. Now that we have, I'm scared to death. If there's one, then sooner or later, there'll be others. Eventually, there will be one that goes off before we find it." He looked at the floor, deep in thought, then glanced up at Wilton Garrett with an unmistakable look of sadness and said, "Let's go have a look at this message from hell, Colonel."

Major Dave Ames sat in a chair in Charlotte Black's bedroom, watching the two women get dressed. For some two hours, he had left Marlene Graf handcuffed to the bed while he explained to them that their choice was but one: either doublecross the KGB, or go to jail for the rest of their lives on espionage charges. It had soon become apparent that Marlene was the key to it all. The frightened Charlotte said little, her dark eyes flashing from Dave's to Marlene's as they spoke.

"Of course," he had acknowledged to Marlene shortly after he handcuffed her, "you can always seek asylum with the Russians, and no doubt you'd be granted it and shipped out of the country on a Russian passport. Maybe you'd even be allowed to spend the rest of your youth as a mistress to some KGB bigwig. But is that what you really want? And what will be better when you become an old woman—a retirement flat with a small pension in Moscow, or a retirement home in California, with a bigger pension, and with the one commodity the Russkies could *never* offer you—*freedom* as a way of life?"

Marlene Graf was an intelligent woman, and a selfish one. It didn't take her long to see the truth and merit in his argument. Once she was convinced, Charlotte quickly followed her lead.

As she dressed, Marlene continued to think of questions about how she would be handled. Most of them were to reassure herself that the Soviets wouldn't catch on to the fact that she had been turned.

"You're too smart to allow that to happen to you, Marlene."

She laughed. "Yes, just as I was too smart to allow you to catch me."

"Bad luck, that's all," he replied. "Life is a risky business. There was a higher probability that you'd be run over crossing the street in this city, than be caught spying. We have a hard enough time catching our own spies and those in the Soviet bloc embassies, much less trying to track down spies from the embassies of our *allies.*"

She smoothed her skirt over her buttocks and checked herself in the mirror. Turning to him, she asked, "How *did* you catch me, Major?"

Ames smiled. "We have *our* share of Marlene Grafs, too," he replied, recalling the words of the elderly Director of Central Intelligence, Jason Moore.

She shot a suspicious glance at Charlotte Black, whose back was turned while she brushed her hair.

"Well, Major, what now?" Marlene asked.

"Now," he said, standing, "we find out if I've actually turned you, or if you're still bullshitting me." With that, he handed her the 9mm automatic pistol he had taken from her purse while she was handcuffed to the bed. He placed his own .45 automatic back in the bottom of his athletic bag, then turned to face her.

She raised the pistol, pointed it at him, and said, "You're a brave man, Major."

Charlotte recoiled in horror at the sight of Marlene standing there with her pistol pointed at Dave's face, as he said, "Not really—just extremely self-confident."

Marlene laughed, picked up her purse, and dropped the pistol into it. "You didn't look so self-confident last night, when you ran away after I took my dress off," she said as she got to her knees and reached under Charlotte's bed. She pulled out the small tape recorder hidden there, turned it off, then ejected the tape cassette and handed it to Ames.

"Further proof that I'm not 'bullshitting,'" she said.

She reached to the bedside table and picked up two of the glasses of now-warm wine. She handed one to Charlotte and the other to Dave, then picked up the third and raised it to him. "To my new employers," she said.

"Prosit!" he said, as he pocketed the tape cassette.

The two newly recruited American agents replied, *"Prosit!"*

He looked at his watch. "Now," he lied confidently, "we'd better get the hell out of here before the FBI team waiting around the corner busts in to see if I'm still alive. We've got to meet your new case officer out on Manassas Battlefield in about an hour."

Dr. Wayne and Colonel Garrett were back in the National Security Advisor's briefing room in the west wing of the White House after being gone less than forty-five minutes. They had met Matt Jensen and Boo Maxton in the Capitol Building parking lot, and Wayne had examined the sensor readout their trace radiation detection devices had recorded.

"Exactly the recording I would have expected," he said, shaking his head. Then Maxton had escorted them into the cafe beneath the sprawling building. They didn't see the fire extinguisher, which was pushed well back under the cabinet on which the big coffee urns sat, but they had no doubt that it was there. Silently, they walked back out to the parking lot.

"Well done, men," Garrett said to the two Delta Force NCOs. He smiled and shook their hands.

"Do you realize how many lives your discovery has possibly saved?" Toby Wayne asked.

The Delta Force men were silent until Matt Jensen said, "Yeah, but it ain't over yet. Suppose he has the thing booby-trapped with an antidisturbance device?"

"You're exactly right, Sergeant Jensen," Toby Wayne said. "We still have to get to it, examine it closely, and disarm it."

"All right," Garrett said, "I want you two to case the area down there and come up with some ideas about how we can get in there, examine the bomb, and either disarm it or get it the hell out. And you'd better hang around down there as long as you can—until closing time, if possible. God knows, we wouldn't want somebody to just stumble on it, now that we know where it is. Anyway, the goddamned Soviets are pressing hard on this matter, and even though we're doing our best to keep this thing secret, you never know. . . . I'll page you if I need you. Otherwise, I'll meet you back at the suite in Crystal City."

"Boss," Matt Jensen said, "why don't we bring our EOD guys up here right away?"

"I was going to recommend the same thing," Toby Wayne said. "Your Explosive Ordnance Disposal team is the best I've seen anywhere. Is Ennis Fox still in charge of them?"

"You know Fox?" Garrett asked.

"Sure," Wayne responded, "and his sidekick—the other one who was the first bomb tech to pass your selection course . . ."

"Mark Vinson," Jensen said.

"Yeah, Vinson. They're a damned good team," Wayne said. "And we need the best guys available for this one."

"Whatever you say," Garrett agreed. "I'll call my deputy from the White House as soon as we get back, and have one of our pilots fly them up here this afternoon."

They went straight back to the National Security Advisor's office, and Wilton Garrett got on the secure telephone to his deputy, Paul McCarthy, at their headquarters in Fort Bragg.

"So, what's up, boss man?" McCarthy asked when he got to the telephone in Delta's situation room.

Continuing the understated banter they used when speaking to each other about matters of importance, Garrett said, "Oh, not too much. But do you think you can get Fox and Vinson up here this afternoon?"

"Don't see why not. What's the problem, you find a suspicious-looking package in your fan mail, or something?"

"Well," Garrett replied, then yawned loudly into the secure telephone and said, "Excuse me . . . No, something a little better than a letter bomb. We just found a nuclear bomb in the basement of the Capitol Building."

"Holy Mother of the Pyramids!" Garrett heard his second-in-command mutter, then, "Well, I guess we can spare them for that. I'll get Bud Munson to fly them into National right away. Can you have somebody meet 'em?"

"Yeah," the Delta Force commander replied, "and make sure they bring their best tools."

"Yes, sir, of course. And, boss?"

"Yeah?"

"Good job."

"I'll pass that on to the NCOs who did it. . . . You think we officers are ever going to get a chance to do anything wonderful in this outfit, Colonel?" Garrett asked McCarthy good-naturedly.

"Goddamn, boss, I sure hope so," Lieutenant Colonel McCarthy replied from Fort Bragg. "How else are you ever going to fulfill your blind ambition to be a general?"

The two men laughed, elated by the discovery of the bomb.

"I'll get them up there ASAP, Colonel Garrett," McCarthy said.

"Roger. Just call Cabe at the safehouse when you know their arrival time, and we'll be sure somebody meets them."

Carruthers returned a couple of minutes later from a luncheon meeting he'd had to attend with several NATO dignitaries. When Wayne and Garrett told him that they were convinced the bomb had been located, he said, "Stay right here," then rushed out of the briefing room. A short time later, Carruthers called them and informed them that a Secret Service agent would be there for them in a moment.

A powerfully built man walked into the room a moment later and said, "Colonel Garrett and Dr. Wayne?"

They nodded, and the immaculately groomed agent said, "I'm Tom McEwan, Presidential Protective Detail. Please follow me, gentlemen."

McEwan ushered them into the Oval Office, then closed the door behind them as they left. The President of the United States was standing at the window, looking off into the distance at the dome of the U.S. Capitol. His National Security Advisor, George Carruthers, said, "Mr. President, Dr. Wayne and Colonel Garrett are here."

For another half minute, the President continued to gaze out toward the Capitol, then he turned around, smiled warmly, and said, "I don't know how you did it, but George tells me you've found the bomb."

The three men stood silently, and the President walked over and shook the hands of Garrett and Wayne.

"Thank God," he said to each, then gestured to them to sit down in the chairs in front of his desk. They did so, and Garrett noticed the small sign sitting on the desk which the President had resurrected from the presidential memorabilia of Harry Truman. "The buck stops here," the little sign stated.

"Dr. Wayne," he said, "suppose that bomb went off right now?"

After a moment of thought, Wayne said, "Mr. President, if that device was to detonate, everything within a hundred yards would be vaporized—turned into radioactive dust."

The President sat silently, his gaze fixed steadily on Wayne's.

"The Capitol would lift a few feet, then collapse on itself. Beyond that, the reaction would be channelized by the course of least resistance—some of it upward, but much of it through the tunnels running from beneath the building in all directions—the utilities and air-conditioning shafts, elevator shafts, subways. Within milliseconds, these would all direct a blast of superheated gases toward the basements of all the surrounding buildings. Everything in the paths of those fingers of the explosion would rupture, causing anything combustible to ignite. The blast and heat would collapse the subsurface floors of those buildings, and they'd probably collapse on themselves as well."

He looked out the window toward Capitol Hill before continuing. "The shock wave would shatter windows all the way to here. God only knows how many people would be cut to shreds just by flying glass.

"For a few seconds, the blast wave would move away from

the detonation, but following that, there would be a rush of air back toward the center—an implosion. It would be more violent than the initial blast, sucking air toward the fireball, where that beautiful dome now stands—hurricane force winds."

The President's brow was furrowed deeply, Garrett noticed, as he stared at the top of his desk, listening intently to Toby Wayne.

"And that wouldn't be the end, Mr. President," the scientist continued. "It would be a 'dirty' bomb. It would raise a thick cloud of radioactive dust, blanketing everything for miles downwind with a lethal dose of radioactivity. It would be hell, sir."

The President rose and faced the three men in the Oval Office with him.

"Well, thanks to you and your men, Colonel, and you, Dr. Wayne, that isn't going to happen. And thanks to Almighty God. Now, when can you get that devilish thing out of here?"

His question was directed to Toby Wayne, who replied, "Mr. President, Colonel Garrett has the best bomb disposal people in the business, and they're on the way here now. What we need to be able to do is get in there tonight, make certain it hasn't been booby-trapped, then take it off somewhere and disarm it."

There was a buzz from the intercom on the President's telephone system, and he picked it up and said, "Yes?"

"Good," the President replied to the caller. "Send him straight in." He hung up the handset and said to the others, "Jason Moore."

No one said anything else until there was a knock at the Oval Office door, and Tom McEwan, the Secret Service agent, opened it and said, "Director Moore, Mr. President."

The aging chief of the Central Intelligence Agency walked in. "Jase," the President said, "we've found it!"

He gestured to Moore to sit in the chair Wilton Garrett rose from, and while Garrett got himself another chair from against the wall, the President asked Toby Wayne to explain what had happened.

When Wayne had finished explaining to the smiling intelligence chieftain how and where the Delta men had found the nuclear device, Director Moore looked at Wilton Garrett and said, "Well, Colonel, I'd say this will be a day to remember in the Delta Force. First, your people capture that asshole Nidal in Cyprus. Then your boy Ames manages to turn two Soviet spies into agents of the United States. And now," he said as he slapped Wilton Garrett on the back, "you've managed to find an atomic bomb set to go off in the basement of the Capitol!"

Garrett grinned. "So, that damned Ames actually did it, did he, sir?"

"Sure as hell did," Moore replied, reaching into his suit jacket pocket and producing a fat Cuban cigar. He handed it to Garrett and said, "Chew on that, boy, but don't light it. Unlike you and me, our chief executive doesn't enjoy a good cigar."

The President laughed heartily. "Jason Moore, you old devil, this time I'll make an exception for you nicotine addicts. 'Smoke 'em if you've got 'em,' as they say in the movies, gentlemen."

Moore pulled out an old Zippo lighter, flicked it open, and lit it, then held it out to the Delta Force commander.

Garrett smiled, but mumbled, "No, thank you, Mr. Director. I think this time I'll just say 'No' to nicotine."

The five men laughed together, then George Carruthers, in an attempt to get back to the serious matter of the improvised nuclear device, said, "I think we'd better get back to what we're going to do with Ramirez's bomb."

"Let's just get the hell out of town, Mr. President," Jason Moore said, unwilling to let the elation of the moment pass yet. "Then, after it goes off, we'll send Garrett and his boys up to the Hill, and finally get some decent legislation passed before the next elections!"

Once more, the President gave a hearty laugh, then said soberly, "Well, let's get back to the subject of the bomb up on the Hill there, before it *does* go off."

For several moments, they considered what steps to take next.

"If we just had some plausible reason for going in there tonight," Wilton Garrett said, "we could make certain it isn't rigged to explode if it's moved, then take it out over the ocean or somewhere, and disarm it."

The CIA Director leaned forward in his chair. "That shouldn't be a problem, Mr. President. We can have the Secret Service take them in."

"Wouldn't that raise questions, though, Mr. Director?" Garrett asked, as he chewed on the big cigar Moore had given him.

"It shouldn't," Director Moore responded. "Remember, the President's scheduled to go up there next Thursday to deliver the State of the Union address."

Wayne and Garrett stared at each other with a look of sudden shock. "Don't look so surprised, you youngsters," Moore said to them. "We figured out this morning that the thing is probably set to go off while the President is giving his speech. The reason I came over here was to tell you to concentrate your efforts on the Capitol Building."

"Well, I'll be damned," the President said.

"Who in the Secret Service do you trust the most, Mr. President?" Jason Moore asked, suddenly very serious.

The President walked to the door of the Oval Office, and opened it.

"Tom," the others heard him say, "come in here a minute, will you?"

Special Agent Thomas D. McEwan of the Presidential Protective Detail, United States Secret Service, walked into the Oval Office with a look of curiosity on his face.

"Pull up a chair, Tom," the President said, and when the Secret Service man had done so, he asked, "Have you met Colonel Garrett of the Delta Force, and Dr. Wayne from the Department of Energy?"

McEwan shook hands with the two men, and the President said, "Colonel Garrett—Wilton, isn't it?—why don't you tell Tom what it is we want him to do for us?"

One thing was always foremost in the minds of the capable and dedicated men and women assigned to the Presidential Protective Detail, and that was the safety of the

President of the United States. When Garrett first informed him that there was a nuclear time bomb less than a mile away, McEwan looked with incredulity at the President, who nodded to verify for him that the Delta Force commander was telling the truth.

"Mr. President, I recommend that you move down to the basement bomb shelter immediately, sir."

The chief executive smiled and said, "I appreciate your concern, Tom, but I'm not going to do that."

"Mr. President, with all respect, I'm afraid I must insist that—"

"Tom, listen to me. Other than a few of Wilton's men and a couple of others we've chosen to bring in, we in this room are the only people aware of this thing—"

Putting the safety of the President above his deep respect for the man and the office he held, McEwan interrupted him. "Sir, what about the man who planted it? He might be preparing to remotely fire it this very minute."

"The man who planted it is dead, son," Jason Moore said. "We're quite certain it's not set to go off for another week, yet."

Again, McEwan looked at the only man in the room who could order him to do less than what he felt was necessary to protect the President—the President himself.

"Just let us finish telling you what we plan to do, and why we can't allow anyone else—*anyone* else—to know about this."

"Is the Vice President aware, sir?" McEwan asked, thinking that, if the chief executive was going to refuse to be concerned about his own safety, at least the next in line to assume the duties of running the United States government should be aware of the potential disaster.

"No," the President responded. "In the first place, we'll have the thing disarmed—pray God—before he gets back to Washington. And in the second place, I don't want him to be aware of it, because if it leaks out, ever, I want him to be able to honestly say that he knew nothing about the matter. Otherwise, his chances of being the next man elected to sit at this desk would be ruined."

The aging man behind the big desk exchanged a glance with his Director of Central Intelligence, then continued. "And the country *deserves* to have him as their next president. Now, let's get back to what Colonel Garrett needs you to help him do."

Once the issue had been fully explained to him, Tom McEwan said, "I see no problem with that at all, sir. Our advance team will be sweeping the place a couple of times between now and the State of the Union, anyway. I can take your people in there this evening, Colonel, and the Capitol Police would see nothing unusual in it."

"Good," the President said, standing as he added, "Now I'm afraid you'll have to excuse me, gentlemen."

The others stood, and he shook the hand of each as he said, "I know you'll take care of the rest of this problem as well as you've done with it so far. If I can do my job as well as you are all doing yours, we'll come out of this thing in good shape."

The men started for the door, and the President said, "Let me see you alone for just a minute, Jason."

"Yes, sir," the intelligence chief said, as the other men left for George Carruthers's briefing room.

25

By the time Jason Moore returned to the briefing room from the Oval Office, Colonel Garrett, Dr. Wayne, and Special Agent McEwan had come up with a plan for getting to the fire extinguisher–enclosed bomb, checking it for anti-disturbance devices, and getting it out of the Capitol Building.

"Once the EOD team is sure it's safe to move, we'll replace it with a real fire extinguisher, and take the bomb back out to the van," McEwan was explaining.

Jason Moore sat down with the others, and Carruthers quickly brought him up-to-date on the plan. "What do you plan to do with it then?" Moore asked after he lit the Cuban cigar in his mouth, then held out his lighter for Garrett to light the one he had given him.

Tom McEwan waved the cigar smoke away from his face and said, "Get it the hell out of this town to somewhere unpopulated as quickly as possible, I hope, Mr. Director."

"Dr. Wayne," Garrett said, "would it be feasible to put it on an airplane and fly out over the Atlantic before we open it up so you can examine and disarm it?"

Wayne stroked his goatee and answered, "Yes, as long as there's plenty of room in the plane to work on it. And if it isn't too turbulent."

"Good," Garrett said. "I can keep the airplane here that's bringing Sergeants Fox and Vinson up from Fort Bragg. It's a Twin Otter, so there'll be plenty of room in the back."

"I hope the pilots are discreet, Colonel," Moore said.

"Absolutely, sir. Actually, there's only one man flying it, and he's the same one who took the team into El Salvador."

"Well, once we get it temporarily disarmed, I think it would be in the best interests of the nation if I took it out to the Nevada Test Site and arranged to detonate it underground there," Toby Wayne commented. "I'm afraid this isn't the last improvised nuclear device the world is going to encounter, and we'd be well advised to find out just what sort of yield such a bomb can produce."

"I don't know, Doctor," Jason Moore said. "I think we'd be better off just dumping it in the damned ocean and letting it go at that."

"I disagree, Mr. Director," Wayne said. "We should be able to come up with some plausible story about picking up the thing overseas or something. Anyway, we'll need a decision on that before we take off with it."

"I don't know much about nukes, Dr. Wayne," Wilton

Garrett said, "but if you want to actually blow up a device like that, couldn't you just take the plans and build one like it?"

"Yes, I suppose we could," the nuclear physicist agreed.

"Good," Moore said. "Then it's agreed we'll just dump it in the ocean?"

"Yes," Wayne answered, "as long as we drop it in piece by piece, and it's in extremely deep water."

"Can you come with me to our safehouse in Crystal City?" Garrett asked the Secret Service agent. "We need to meet up with the men who are going to go with you to the Capitol this evening."

McEwan looked at his watch. "I get relieved at two o'clock. I'd better wait until then. Let me know where the safehouse is, and I'll meet you there at about two-thirty."

When he left Charlotte Black's place in Georgetown, Dave Ames took Charlotte with him. Marlene Graf followed him in her car as he led her through a surveillance detection route, then drove out to Dulles Airport. There, he had her park her car in the big parking lot, then get into his car with him. After running through another series of surveillance detection maneuvers and determining that he was still "clean," he drove to Manassas Battlefield and met up with Harry Lawson. The CIA officer led them to an isolated area of the park before speaking.

When he was certain they were out of sight and earshot of anyone else, he turned to the two women and said, "Let me introduce myself. My name is Charlie Powers, and you'll be taking your orders from me, and me only."

The women nodded, then Lawson turned to Dave Ames and said, "OK, Pete. Your part's finished. You'd better reassume your real name, go back to Langley and get to work, before that major at Fort Bragg finds out you've been using his name."

"Yeah," Ames said. "I will." Shaking hands with Marlene and Charlotte, he said, "Ladies, I assure you you're doing the right thing. It's, well, it's been a pleasure. Good luck."

Marlene smiled. "Well," she said, "perhaps we'll meet

again, Dave, or Pete, or whatever your name really is, especially now that we're working for the same employer."

"Perhaps," he replied.

Charlotte stepped to him and kissed him on the cheek, then said, "Maybe one day we can all *three* get together again."

"Yes," Marlene added, "in that retirement house in California you promised us."

He smiled faintly at her, then waved to Harry Lawson and said, "See you back at the office, Charlie," turned and walked away.

As Garrett and the others were leaving the National Security Council offices in the west wing of the White House, Jason Moore said, "Wait just a moment, will you, Colonel? I need to see you alone." When the others were gone, he said, "Sit down, Wilton."

"It's Will, sir," the Delta Force commander replied. "Only my mother calls me Wilton."

Moore smiled, then said, "And the President . . . Will, we need to talk about Hakim Nidal."

"Well, they should have him out of Cyprus and onto the *Yorktown* in a few hours, Mr. Director."

"Yes, well, I wish *you* were there, Will."

"Sergeant Major Salem is at least as capable of handling the situation as I would be, sir, I assure you."

"I've looked at the files on both of you, Colonel, and there's one big difference—you were in a Provincial Reconnaissance Unit in Vietnam, and he wasn't."

Wilton Garrett suddenly knew what the Director of Central Intelligence was going to tell him to do. The mission of the PRUs in Vietnam was to seek out the leadership of the Vietnamese Communist underground and kill them. Sometimes that meant sneaking into their villages in the dead of night and murdering them in their beds. He had done it himself, and although he had been able to justify it as the duty of a soldier at war, it still bothered him.

He looked at Moore steadily and asked, "Do you want me to have Nidal killed, sir?"

"Yes," the elderly intelligence chief answered, then snuffed out his cigar and looked at Garrett. "But you know that I can't order you to, Colonel."

"No, sir. You can't. It's an illegal order, and even if I obeyed it, I couldn't order Sergeant Major Salem to do so."

Garrett weighed the situation in his mind. It was such a fine line, this difference between a legal and an illegal killing. In the shadowy world of espionage and counterterrorism, the line was even more difficult to define. Yes, the men and one of the women under his command had already killed more than two dozen people since the operation began in El Salvador less than a week earlier. But those deaths all fell within the hazy edge of legal killings. Even the deaths of the two bodyguards could be justified. If they had not been quickly eliminated, they would have done their best to kill Garrett's subordinates; they all knew that.

"Difficult arrest" was the term they gave to those situations, where it was implied that the individual to be captured must have the protection around him swiftly and ruthlessly eliminated. And assaults such as those required in hostage rescue situations were best effected by eliminating the hostage-holders before they could make a suicidal attempt to eliminate their captives along with themselves.

But Nidal was now in Salem's custody, and no longer a threat. To order him to kill the terrorist, even though he was wanted for murder in several countries, was illegal. And unlike Major Ames's unauthorized surveillance of Congressman Bolton and his secretary, it could not even be rectified by sheep-dipping Salem—making him temporarily a member of the CIA instead of the Army—because assassination was an illegal practice in the Central Intelligence Agency now, as well.

"Shit!" Garrett exclaimed as he stood and paced the room while Moore watched him. The KGB had no such rules, and the terrorists—*especially* the likes of Hakim Nidal—used the indiscriminate and brutal murder of innocent women and children as a means to their ends. And, according to Moore's sources, Nidal's whole reason for being in Cyprus anyway was to go on to Managua to meet Emilio Ramirez, get his nuclear bomb, and use it to kill or threaten to kill thousands, perhaps even hundreds of thousands, of innocent people.

"Why do we have such damned self-destructive laws in this country, Mr. Moore?" he asked the CIA head.

"Because, Colonel Garrett," Moore replied, "the legislators who make them have never been in our shoes. Because they are genuinely concerned that the United States be a decent and civilized nation. And because," the old veteran of espionage and world war said, "they can't see past their fucking noses!"

He put his arm around the lanky Texan's shoulder. "They can't seem to be made to realize that the survival of the body of this nation sometimes requires that concerned and dedicated men such as you need authority to eliminate cancers like Hakim Nidal."

Garrett looked into the sincere eyes of Jason Moore and said, "Mr. Moore, I can't order Sergeant Major Salem to kill that son of a bitch. But I can guarantee you it will be done."

Twenty minutes later, he walked into the bedroom of the hotel suite where two of his subordinates, Lieutenant Colonel Jerry Schumann and Master Sergeant Lanny Cabe, were monitoring the secure voice satellite radio that linked the Crystal City safehouse with the team in Cyprus and Delta headquarters in Fort Bragg.

The two men stood when he entered, and Schumann smiled and said, "Boss, I could hardly believe it when Dr. Wayne came in here a few minutes ago and said that Matt and the others found the bomb. I was beginning to think we didn't stand a chance in hell of finding it without calling in the whole FBI, NEST, and all the rest."

"Excuse me for a couple of minutes, will you, men?" Garrett said.

They could tell that their commander had something other than the bomb on his mind, so they walked into the adjoining room and closed the door behind them.

The Delta Force commander picked up the handset of the satellite radio and said, "Salem, Salem, this is Garrett, Garrett, over."

There was no response, and before he could call again, Paul McCarthy came on the radio from Fort Bragg and said, "Boss man, this is Deputy Dog. Be advised, Salem is not with the radio. Rachel has it in her room. I called her a while ago, after your secure phone call, to tell her that you'd found the bomb. She wanted to know if she should drive up to where Salem is holding Shithead and tell him about it, but I just told her to wait there 'til she heard from you. Also, the Twin Otter's on the way up to National now with the EOD guys. Cabe said he'd meet them when they get there in about, oh, forty-five minutes from now, over."

"Roger," Garrett replied. "Is anybody else there with you who can hear the radio?"

"Negative, sir. I'm here by my lonesome."

"Good. I don't mind you hearing this, but I don't want anyone else to."

"No problem, boss."

Their chatter in the headset on the pillow beside her woke Rachel up in her hotel room in Limassol, and she said, "Garrett, this is Brown, you have something for me?"

"Roger. Understand Salem is not available, is that correct?"

"Affirmative," she replied. "He's up near Larnaca somewhere. I'll have to copy your message, drive up there, and call him on the team radio."

"I understand," Garrett said to her. "Are you ready to copy?"

"Affirmative, send your message."

Garrett thought again about what he wanted her to tell his command sergeant major, then said slowly, "From Garrett to Salem, break. Device has been located, break. Quarry no longer required for interrogation. He is now a threat to the future disclosure of this highly compartmented matter of national security, break. How copy so far, Captain Brown?"

"This is Brown. Solid copy. Continue."

"This is Garrett. Message continues. If I were there, I would kill Quarry, break. However, it would be illegal for me to order you to do so, break. How copy?"

Rachel answered with, "Good copy. Any further?"

"Message continues," Garrett said. "If you murder him and I learn of it, I will be required to report you. End of message, over."

"Garrett, this is Brown," she replied. "Roger your complete message. I'll leave now and advise Salem as soon as possible, over."

From Fort Bragg, Paul McCarthy broke in and said, "Add the following from me, Rachel. 'Nobody said it was going to be easy,' over."

"Wilco," she acknowledged. "Will advise. Out here."

"Nobody said it was going to be easy" was a phrase heard frequently in the Delta Force. Sometimes they used it as a facetious comment when they found themselves enjoying some unusual benefit, such as traveling on commercial airlines to exotic places in the performance of their duty. Rachel had used the phrase herself, when the decision was made to fly her to Paris on the Concorde. But just as often, it was used in situations such as these, when they found themselves in a situation requiring them to make tough decisions. It had been a part of the Delta Force dialect ever since someone had uttered it years earlier, when they learned that they were going to infiltrate Iran and attempt to rescue the hostages from the American Embassy in Tehran.

Rachel dressed quickly and drove north to make contact with Dick Salem and the other Delta men who were guarding Hakim Nidal until he could be exfiltrated to the USS *Yorktown* by helicopter.

She fully understood what Garrett intended for Salem to do, and she had no doubt that it was necessary. If Nidal was taken to the United States and brought to trial for murder, he would be given the same rights as any other criminal subjected to U.S. judicial proceedings. No matter how secret the trial was, and even if he were sentenced to death—as she believed the terrorist should be—by the time all the appeals were completed, there was bound to be some clever reporter who would tie the inevitable leaks together. Eventually, that would lead to the revelation that there had been a nuclear time bomb discovered in Washington. When that was made public, it would mean a scandal of proportions that would make the Iran-contra affair, and even Watergate, seem like minor incidents.

She knew that Salem would understand that, as well. When he read Colonel Garrett's message, he would kill Hakim Nidal.

The sky was beginning to lighten over the horizon of the eastern Mediterranean as she pulled off the road south of Larnaca and called Salem on the little team radio.

He answered, judging from the strength of his reply, from somewhere nearby.

"I have a hard copy message from the boss," Rachel told him. "Where can I meet you?"

"How about the dirt road where we met earlier?" he asked. "I'm about five minutes from there now."

"Roger," she answered. "See you there in zero-five."

The darkened van was already there when she drove up the dirt road to their rendezvous behind the low hill. In the growing dawn, she saw Rob Small standing outside the van. Birdie Sadler was in the driver's seat, and she said to the two men, "Would you guys mind taking a short walk? I need to talk to Dick in private for a minute."

The two men looked at each other, and obeyed her order without speaking. She opened the side door of the van and saw Salem sitting beside the prone, handcuffed captive.

"Mornin', Rachel," he whispered. "What did the Old Man have for me?"

She reached into the watch pocket of her jeans and pulled out a slip of paper. Holding it out to Salem, she said, "Give me your weapon and hop out here so you can read it." He passed the silenced pistol to her, took the note, and slid out of the van to read it by the tiny beam of his penlight.

As he read it, Rachel Brown placed the muzzle of the pistol against Nidal's temple, squeezed her eyes closed, and pulled the trigger twice in rapid succession.

A short distance away, Small and Sadler heard the muffled sounds of the gunshots, and ran back to the van to find Salem shining the beam of his penlight on the terrorist's head. Brains and blood were oozing out of a hole above his right ear. Beside the van, Rachel Brown was bent over, retching, the pistol still in her hand. Without speaking, Salem handed the note to Small, and held the light on it so that he and Sadler could read it.

To Rachel, he said, "You didn't have to do that, ma'am. The message was from Colonel Garrett to me."

She straightened up and wiped her mouth with her hand, then said softly, "I'm an officer, Sergeant Major, a Delta officer. It was *my* duty, not yours."

"Son of a bitch, Birdie!" Rob Small said to Sadler after he read the note. "Did you see that? The fucker was trying to escape!"

Birdie looked at him and smiled. "Goddamned right he was," he said. "Good thing Rachel got him before he got away!"

Small walked up to her and hugged her. "You're a hell of a soldier, Captain Brown," he muttered.

Birdie Sadler hugged her, too, then Sergeant Major Salem said, "Ma'am, with your permission, Sergeant Small and I will get rid of Nidal's body, then meet you and Bird in your room in Limassol. I'll tell Howson and Pollock to meet the chopper at the airport and tell the pilots we don't need them, then we can all get out of here and go home."

"OK," she said as she passed the pistol back to him. "Let's go, Birdie."

"And you will reply to the message the colonel sent me, won't you, ma'am?" Salem asked. "Tell him the Quarry tried to escape and was killed."

"I can handle it, Dick," she replied. "And it's Rachel, not ma'am. We're still on an operation."

She walked up to him and gave him a hug, and said, "You're one of the two best big brothers I ever had, Sergeant Major. The other one died in Vietnam." Turning to the other two Delta NCOs she added, "And you *kid* brothers ain't bad, either. . . . Let's get going, Birdie."

Before he got into the car with her, Sadler burned to ashes the slip of paper with Garrett's message to Salem on it.

26

When he got to Rosslyn, the northern Virginia business district just across the Potomac from Georgetown, Dave Ames parked at a meter on the street and went into the trendy Pawn Shop bistro. He ordered a Bloody Mary, then went back to the pay phones near the men's room and called the Crystal City safehouse. When Lanny Cabe answered, he said, "Let me talk to the boss, please."

Garrett came on the line a moment later, and Dave said, "Mission accomplished. What next?"

His commander thought a moment, then said, "Go to the place Angela and the others are staying, pick them up, and take them down to the lake. Then go to the Ranch and report to Colonel McCarthy."

"No luck with Angela's friend?" Ames asked, unaware that the improvised nuclear device had been located.

"Luck is right, *good* luck. We found it," he said.

"You're kidding!" Dave exclaimed.

"Not at all," his commander said. "See you at the Ranch in a day or so. Meanwhile, don't let that trouser worm of yours get you into any more trouble."

Ames laughed, then asked, "Rachel and her buddies have any luck?"

"Yeah, they did," Garrett said. "They got what they were after."

"No shit? Everybody OK?"

"Affirmative. Now, go on out and close down Angela's place."

"Wilco," Ames said. "See you later."

An hour later, Angela called from the Arlington safehouse on the satcom radio they had there and said to Garrett, "Major Ames is here, sir, and we're getting ready to leave. We'll call when we get to the Woodlake safehouse."

"OK, Sergeant Herndon. You folks did an outstanding job with the girl. How is she, anyway?"

"Oh, Nadia's fine, sir. She still doesn't really know what's going on. But she sure seems to be taking a liking to Baldero. What's going to happen to her, anyway, sir?"

"I don't know, Angie. I guess they'll give her a new identity, send her to school here, or something. I guess I'd better get a reading from the Agency on that. I'll try to get them to take her off our hands before long, at any rate."

"Suits me," Angela Herndon said. "But I'm not too sure Sergeant Baldero is in any hurry to be rid of her."

"I see," Garrett said. "Well, maybe that's the solution. Anyway, I'll let you know as soon as I find out something."

"How're Captain Brown and Sergeant Major Salem and the guys doing?" she asked.

"They're just fine. You did well when you recommended I bring her in as your boss, Angie."

"Yes, sir. I thought she'd do all right. Well, I'm going to break this thing down now, so we can get out of here. See you back at the Ranch."

When Bud Munson landed the Twin Otter from the Fort Bragg Flying Club at Washington's National Airport, Delta's electronic technician, Lanny Cabe, was there to meet it.

To Bud Munson, the balding technician said, "The Old Man said to tell you to refuel, then wait here in the pilots' lounge, Bud."

"Can do easy," Munson replied.

"He said it would probably be around six tonight when he has another mission for you," Cabe added.

"Roger that. Where are we going?" Munson asked.

"Don't know. He just said to tell you to take your orders from the senior man aboard."

"I can do that. See you later."

Cabe helped the two Delta EOD men, Ennis Fox and Mark Vinson, carry their toolboxes from the airplane to the van, then drove them to the Crystal City Holiday Inn.

Colonel Garrett was waiting for them in the safehouse suite when they walked in.

"Hi, boss," Fox said, "what have you got for us? All your deputy said was for us to grab our best shit and get on up here."

Dr. Toby Wayne walked in from the bathroom of the suite, and Fox said, "Hey, Doc Wayne! What are *you* doing he— Oh, shit!" He quickly surmised that the fact that he and his old acquaintance from the Nuclear Emergency Search Team had been called together could mean only one thing.

His EOD teammate, Mark Vinson, made the same deduction, and said, "Some kook call in a nuke threat again?"

"Not a threat," Toby Wayne replied as he shook the Delta Explosive Ordnance Disposal men's hands. "This time, it's a promise, I'm afraid."

Matt Jensen, Boo Maxton, and the Secret Service agent, Tom McEwan, were there also, and Garrett quickly briefed the newly arrived EOD experts on the situation. McEwan explained how he was going to get them in to the Capitol, then Toby Wayne showed them the technical drawings he had of the device.

He was lying on the floor with Fox and Vinson so that they could all see the drawings, discussing it in technical terms the others barely understood, when there was a knock at the door. They went silent as Garrett walked over and looked through the peephole.

"It's all right," he said as he cracked the door open. "It's Sergeant Cabe. What do you need, Lanny?"

"Rachel's on the horn," Cabe replied.

Garrett went with Cabe to the suite next door and returned her call on the satellite radio.

"Reference your last message to Salem, sir . . ."

"Yes?"

"The Quarry tried to escape. He's dead, over."

"I see. Thank you for the information, Captain Brown. I'll see that it gets passed on to the appropriate people right away."

"Roger," she replied. "We'll start filtering out of here as soon as we can, unless you have anything more for us to do out this way."

"No. You've all done a good job over there. Come on home."

"Wilco, sir . . . Sir, one other thing . . . Do you know when Da— Oh, never mind. I'll call when I know everybody's schedule out of here. Birdie Sadler and I are going to wait until the others are gone, then we'll turn the vehicles and radios back over to the people from the station in Nicosia. We'll see you at the Ranch in a couple of days."

"Roger, Rachel. Anything further?"

"Negative. I'll call from time to time, in case anything comes up. Out for now."

The shift leader of the guards at the United States Capitol Building was waiting for Special Agent Tom McEwan when he drove up to the service entrance in the enclosed Secret Service van. McEwan had coordinated with him earlier to meet him there.

He showed the shift leader his credentials, but the man smiled and said, "Hell, that ain't necessary, sir. I've seen you lots of times with the President, on TV, you know."

"Right," McEwan said. "Well, we're going to sweep the basement area this evening. Just making a routine check before the State of the Union address next week."

The burly Capitol policeman opened the gate to allow McEwan to pull the van in, saying, "Have at it. Ain't gonna find nothin' but cockroaches down there, though!"

"I'm sure you're right," McEwan replied. He turned to the five men in the back of the van and said, "OK, guys, let's get on down there. I've got a hot date tonight with a honey from DEA, so let's get this over with."

"See y'all later," the policeman said as he walked away.

"See ya'," Boo Maxton replied as he got out of the van

wearing a blue windbreaker with USSS in large letters on the back of it. He couldn't resist adding, "Hey, how 'bout them 'Skins, eh?"

The guard turned around and grinned broadly. "Yeah, ain't they somethin'?" he said, then turned and walked away.

Ten minutes later they were in the deserted corridors deep in the bowels of the building. McEwan opened the door to the small cafe with the skeleton keys he had gotten from the office of the Capitol sergeant-at-arms earlier that afternoon. While McEwan and Boo Maxton stood guard in the hallway in case any guards wandered by, the others went inside and locked the doors behind them.

Matt Jensen walked to the back of the serving line, pointed to the space under the cabinet on which the coffee urns sat, and said simply, "It's under there."

Ennis Fox and Mark Vinson, the Delta Force EOD men, got down on their hands and knees and shined their battery-powered lamps on the fire extinguisher which was shoved well up under the cabinet. It would have been out of sight of anyone not specifically looking for something beneath the cabinet.

Carefully, the pair searched the area around the extinguisher for any signs that it was booby-trapped. Finding no such signs, Fox stood and said to Toby Wayne, "Well, it doesn't look like it's wired or anything. But I think we should X-ray it, even though the diagram doesn't indicate any antidisturbance devices."

"Only problem is," Vinson, still on his knees, commented, "we'll have to move it a little to get the plates behind it."

"Well, for Christ's sake, be careful," Wayne said.

"Have no fear of *that*, Doc," Fox said as he got down on his knees beside Vinson with the twenty-inch-square X-ray plate. Carefully, millimeter by millimeter, they slid the fire extinguisher away from the back of the cabinet. When they had it far enough out to slide the plate behind it, Vinson carefully did so, then Fox set up the little X-ray transmitter in front of it.

Two minutes later, the EOD team had developed the plate in the small, flat, dry-system developer. With Wayne, they examined it closely while Jensen held one of their portable lamps behind it.

"Looks clean," Fox commented.

"Yep," Vinson agreed. Pointing to several points on the X-ray, he said, "Unless he's got something inside the vessel, the only thing attached to it is this timer, the battery, and these two blasting caps."

"Well," Fox said, "what do you think, Doc?"

Toby Wayne stroked his graying goatee while he studied the X-ray for another minute. "Let's get the damned thing out of here," he said. "And I'll bet you both a beer that it doesn't go off."

"Some bet," Matt Jensen said.

The two EOD men opened the steel case Jensen and Maxton had carried from McEwan's van for them. It contained a normal fire extinguisher wrapped in sheets of plastic air-bubble cushioning material. They removed the fire extinguisher from the box, then together lifted the one containing the bomb from beneath the cabinet.

"Boy, this sucker is *heavy!*" Vinson said. "Doc, how about helping Ennis hold it a minute, while I take a look underneath."

He examined the bottom of the extinguisher carefully for half a minute, then said, "Yep, here's where he cut the bottom out to put the bomb in. Looks like these two small bolts are all that's holding this steel strap across the bottom. Unscrew one of them, and the damn thing would just fall out on the floor."

"Well," his EOD teammate said, "let's put it in the box before that happens."

Together, the three men carefully placed the nuclear bomb in the box, cushioning it with the plastic-enclosed bubbles of air. They closed the box, clamped it shut, then shoved the extinguisher they had brought with them up under the cabinet.

"You sure you put the right one in the box?" Toby Wayne joked as the two EOD men picked up their lamps and the

X-ray equipment and put them back in their heavy tool-boxes.

Matt Jensen opened the door to the corridor outside the restaurant. "We're all set. Help me carry this thing, Boo," he said. They picked up the box by its carrying handles and started out of the building, with Tom McEwan leading.

"Damned heavy," Boo commented. "How do you suppose he managed to get the thing in here?"

"I guess we'll never know. Do you think he might have had an accomplice?" Jensen wondered aloud.

As they rode the elevator up, McEwan asked the others, "Do you think it's possible he planted more than *one* of those things?"

Toby Wayne said, "I don't think so. The amount of plutonium he had would only have been enough for one—and a low-yield warhead, at that. But we'll know for sure once we open the thing up."

"What about the radiation? I mean, how can you shield yourself from the radiation, riding around in the back of an airplane while you open the thing?" Jensen inquired.

Fox answered the question. "Hell, it's only plutonium. A thin sheet of plastic is all it takes to shield the harmful radiation from plutonium. Right, Doc?"

"That's true," the scientist agreed. "In fact, you could carry a pellet of plutonium around in the picture holder of your wallet, and it probably wouldn't do you any harm."

"Well, it's all magic to me," Boo commented. "I'm sort of glad I *don't* understand too much about this nuclear shit."

Toby Wayne looked at the box containing the bomb and muttered, "Sometimes I wish I didn't, either."

They loaded the toolboxes and the nuclear device into Tom McEwan's Secret Service van, then climbed in. McEwan pulled up to the service entrance gate and tooted the horn. The fat policeman opened the gate, and when Tom pulled out, the policeman said, "That didn't take long."

"That was just the initial check. We'll be back next week," the Secret Service agent said. "By the way, you'd better get hold of the fire department and tell them they'd better damn well get somebody in here to inspect the fire extinguishers in this place. I noticed that the inspection tags on some of them are way out of date."

"Yes sir," the policeman answered. "I'll see they get notified right away. Have a nice evenin', y'all."

As McEwan drove cautiously toward National Airport, keeping his route as far away from the White House as feasible, Ennis Fox called on the radio to Wilton Garrett, who was waiting anxiously for his call in the Crystal City Holiday Inn.

"Boss Man, Boss Man, this is Foxy, over."

"This is Boss Man, go!" they heard Garrett reply.

"This is Foxy. Safety, safety, safety," Fox said. "ETA at Bud's bird in ten or fifteen minutes."

"Roger, roger, roger!" Garrett acknowledged. "Wait for me there, if you get there first."

"Wilco," Fox answered.

They rode along in silence, until Matt Jensen commented on the incredible fact that an armed nuclear time bomb was being transported through the nation's capital. "And without an armed escort at that."

They were crossing over the 14th Street Bridge into Virginia at the time, and Tom McEwan felt a sudden sense of relief. Even if the thing went off now, the President would probably escape harm, he felt. "What do you mean, 'without an armed escort'? I've got my trusty Glock 17 right here," he said, and patted the pistol in his concealed shoulder holster.

Wayne said, "It really is incredible, though, isn't it? I mean, every other nuclear weapon in this country is guarded by about three rings of security forces, even when they're being moved. And of course they aren't armed when they *are* moved. And—"

"Look out!" Ennis Fox yelled from the passenger's seat of the van.

A taxi was pulling from the right lane into the left lane, right at the van's right-front fender. McEwan braked, swerved left slightly, and the taxi scooted in front of the van, missing it by only two feet.

The pale Fox mumbled, "Damn . . . thought he had us."

"Typical D.C. taxi driver," McEwan said. "If we didn't have that bomb back there, I'd pull him over and check his green card."

"Just get this fucking thing to the airport," Boo Maxton pleaded. "I think I just shit my pants."

Colonel Garrett was waiting for them when they pulled into the general aviation terminal of National Airport. He flagged them down, and Fox opened the door for him.

"OK, there's been a change in plans," he said, yanking from his mouth the cigar butt on which he had been chewing furiously. "You're to go on out over the ocean and disarm the device, but don't make it unusable, or dump any of the components or anything. Director Moore's orders. Once you've disarmed it, have Munson fly to Camp Mackall. The deputy will have some people there to secure the area around the airplane."

"Why the change, Colonel?" Dr. Wayne asked.

"Don't know. That's all he told me. Who's going on the airplane, anyway?"

"Me, Mark, the Doc, and the pilot," Ennis Fox replied.

"Good. For Christ's sake, men, be careful. And remember, our security guys at Mackall won't know why they're guarding the airplane. Make sure it stays that way."

Fifteen minutes later, Bud Munson lifted the Twin Otter off the runway of National Airport and headed southeast down the broad Potomac River.

Munson surmised from the fact that Ennis and Fox had been rushed to Washington with their toolboxes, and were now two of the three passengers riding in the cargo compartment behind him, that they were on an explosive ordnance disposal mission. And when Fox told him that he was to fly out over the Atlantic at an altitude where there was no turbulence, he guessed that they were going to disarm a bomb in the back of his airplane. But he had no idea that it was a nuclear bomb, and—being a good special operations pilot—he asked no questions.

McEwan, Garrett, and the two Delta NCOs watched as the lights of the Twin Otter disappeared to the southeast.

"Thank God," McEwan said.

"Amen," Jensen and Maxton muttered simultaneously.

Fifty minutes later, the aircraft was well out over the ocean, and the two EOD men and the nuclear physicist carefully slid the stainless steel vessel out of the fire extinguisher and laid it gently on the packing material in the box. The vessel was a capsule-shaped cylinder about sixteen inches in length. It was joined in the center by eight bolts through the inch-wide lips which surrounded the two halves of the capsule, which was about six inches in diameter. At the top of the bomb was the firing device, wrapped in a sheet of foam rubber padding.

Cautiously, Ennis Fox cut the tape holding the foam rubber padding with a scalpel, then laid the scalpel down and slowly peeled the padding away. Glued to a three-inch-square piece of thin plywood were two small six-volt batteries, and a thin, black rectangle about half the size of a pocket calculator. The rectangle was a digital timer, and two wires ran from each of the batteries into it, and from the timer into tiny holes drilled through the heads of two bolts which were screwed into the top of the bomb.

The numbers on the timer read 008:22:11:04. As the three men watched, the last digits ticked down second by second, until the last three digits all read zero.

"Eight days, twenty-two hours, ten minutes," Mark Vinson said softly. "Not quite as close as they get in the movies."

"Just like I thought, Mark," Ennis Fox said. "It's the same kind of timer the Red Army Faction used in those two bombs we saw in Frankfurt."

"Yep," his teammate agreed, "they can set these damned things from anywhere between one second and a thousand days—well, nine-hundred-ninety-nine days, twenty-three hours, fifty-nine minutes, and fifty-nine seconds, anyway."

"Damned accurate little boogers, too," Fox commented. To Toby Wayne, he said, "We tested one we got from Germany. Over a thirty-day test, it was only one second off."

"Where do they get them?" Wayne asked.

"Libya," Vinson said. "That damned Qaddafi gets them from Japan, and ships 'em to terrorists all over the world."

"Well, at least it's something we've seen before," Fox said. "Unless he modified it, there's no chance it'll go off if we try to disconnect it from the power source."

Vinson examined the timer with a flashlight in one hand and a magnifying glass in the other. "Looks OK to me," he said, then passed the flashlight and magnifying glass to Fox to let him take a look.

After he studied it for a moment, Fox handed them back to Vinson and yelled to Bud Munson in the cockpit, "Hey, Bud!"

"Yeah?" Munson answered.

"Turn all your electronics off for a minute!"

"Wait one!" he replied, then a few seconds later, "OK, everything's off."

Ennis Fox mumbled, "Well, here goes nothing, I hope."

He rubbed his hands together, then disconnected the wires from the digital timer to the bomb, twisting each pair together to shunt them, in the event that the avionics equipment of the Twin Otter caused an electrical charge to pass through the aircraft and into the wires. Such a charge could set off the electrical blasting caps of the bomb, and it would react just as if it had been initiated intentionally.

Once the wires were shunted, Fox moved back. Mark Vinson ensured that his wrench was the correct size for the two bolts in the top of the capsule, then carefully unscrewed one of them. Slowly, he extracted it from the body of the bomb, pulling the electrical blasting cap, whose wires ran through the bolt, out of the threaded hole in the bomb. Fox took the cap from him and held it while he removed the other bolt and the blasting cap wired through it. Vinson handed the second cap to Fox, who held one of them in each hand, pointed away from the bomb.

The little square of plywood to which the timer and batteries were attached was itself glued to the top of the capsule, and Vinson grasped it firmly and twisted it. It came off the stainless steel capsule.

Slowly, Ennis Fox got to his feet and walked to the back of the aircraft with the firing assembly of the device. Vinson followed him with a small steel box, and they placed the mechanism into it, then set it down in the tail compartment of the airplane. Returning to the center of the aircraft where the bomb lay in its padded container, Vinson found two plastic bolts in his toolbox of the same size as the ones he had removed from the capsule. He screwed them into the holes, then the two men replaced the padding atop the disarmed nuclear bomb and fastened the top of the box.

The two longtime friends and bomb-disposal teammates grinned broadly at each other, then hugged.

"Good job, old buddy," Fox said, then yelled, "Turn your electronics on and get this airplane to a bar, Bud! The Doc here owes me a beer!"

As Wayne shook the EOD men's hands, Munson called from the cockpit. "Why wait, Ennis? If you look all the way back in the tail compartment, you'll find a cooler with a six-pack in it."

Fox went to the compartment and pulled two cans of beer out. He handed one of them to Toby Wayne and opened the other for himself, and Mark Vinson said, "Hey, where's mine?"

"Whaddya mean?" Fox replied. "You don't drink."

Mark Vinson grinned. "That was yesterday," he said. "After today, I *do!*"

Taking his watch from his toolbox—for EOD men never wear watches when they are working with explosives—Mark said, "And while you're back there, Ennis, check the readout on the timer. I want to figure out exactly when this thing would have gone off."

Fox opened the box in which they had placed the firing mechanism and said, "Right now, it reads eight days, twenty-two hours, and just over one minute."

After Vinson added that to the time and date on his watch, he said, "Right. That means it was set to blow at about eight-thirty P.M. on January the twenty-third."

Dr. Toby Wayne looked at the two Delta Force men and said, with his voice cracking slightly as he spoke, "That means that it would have killed the President—and all of his Cabinet, and the Congress, and God knows how many hundreds of others—as he was in the middle of his State of the Union address."

27

It was after ten P.M. when Wilton Garrett pulled off the George Washington Parkway above the Great Falls of the Potomac River. He drove up to the gate of the Central Intelligence Agency headquarters, where Harry Lawson stood waiting for him, his overcoat collar turned up to ward off the cold and the light snowfall. Lawson got Garrett through the security checkpoint, then got in and directed him to a parking space in front of the big, spacious headquarters building.

Three minutes later they were seated in the seventh-floor office of the Director of Central Intelligence, Jason Moore.

Moore poured three large shots of Glenlivet scotch into glasses from the dry bar against the side wall of his office, and handed one to Garrett and one to his most trusted subordinate, Harry Lawson.

He raised his glass to them and said, "Cheers."

"Good health," Garrett replied, and drank a large swallow. Moore took a small sip, then sat down in the chair beside Garrett's.

"Tell me, Will," he said, "do you think your people will be able to keep their mouths shut about this thing?"

Garrett looked him steadily in the eyes. "Director Moore," he said, setting his drink down on the table beside his chair, "let me give you the *long* answer to that. The selection course we put people through before they're accepted into the Delta Force is an extremely grueling process. It includes thorough psychological testing—and I mean thorough. By the time Doc Frye, our psychologist, gets through interviewing them, he knows things about them that they don't even know about themselves. Then they get handed over to my senior subordinates and me, and *we* pick their brains for another hour or so."

Moore pulled two Cuban cigars out of his suit pocket and handed one to the Army colonel. Garrett continued speaking without taking time to say, "Thank you."

"Now remember, sir, this is only after they've passed the stress phase of the course, which is a test of pure will, more than anything else."

Moore held out his lighter to Garrett, who puffed the cigar until it was well lit, this time saying, "Thanks.

"For the next six months," he continued, "we continue to look at them. They're exposed daily to fairly low-level classified material, and if they make one small slip that we find out about, they're gone. Keeping secrets becomes a way of life to them—so much so that it ends up costing some of them their marriages, I might add. Now and then, one of them might find that it's too much pressure and ask to be reassigned. But that's rare."

He took a drink of his scotch and a puff of his cigar, then said. "The bottom line, Mr. Moore, is that they're proven, dedicated soldiers who are used to putting not just their trust on the line, but their lives, as well. And the ones who have knowledge of the various parts of this operation are some of the best of the lot. I wouldn't hesitate to trust them with my life or my most intimate personal *and* professional secrets."

Moore smiled. "I wish I could say the same about everybody in *this* outfit—right, Harry?"

"Yes, sir," Lawson replied. "I'm afraid I have to agree."

Garrett took the cigar out of his mouth and said, "Well, I didn't want to say so, sir, but I was thinking the same thing myself."

"Very well, then, Will," Moore said. "Now, let me tell you what I have in mind."

He sipped his scotch, then set it down on the table. "What we have here is an ideal set of circumstances which, if we manipulate things correctly, can lead to a major coup for this country."

He sat back in his chair and stared at the ceiling a moment before continuing. "We have a homemade atom bomb that the Russians know may exist, but they don't know we have it. The bastard who built it is dead, but they don't know that, either. In fact, they think we've captured him, and that we're interrogating the shit out of him right now. They know Nidal is trying to get ahold of it, and they know he's pissed off at them. What they don't know about *Nidal*, is that he no longer even exists."

He looked at Garrett and, with a hint of a smile on his face, added, "Killed by your boys while trying to escape."

"Won't they figure out before long that he's missing, though?" Garrett asked.

"Sure. And we'll let them find out, through the West German tart your boy Ames reeled in, that we were the ones who did him in. We'll also drop the hint that he told us he got the bomb from Ramirez. And that, before he died, he might just have told us what he *did* with it."

Garrett looked at his watch and said, "Just about now, my EOD guys should be disarming it. If they screw it up, the Russians won't have to *wonder* what happened to it."

Moore chuckled and said, "Just keep your eye on that window over there. If you see a bright flash, we can finish off that bottle of Glenlivet, then commit hara-kiri together. . . . Now, back to how we're going to pull the fur over the Soviet bear's eyes."

He continued to outline his clever plan for manipulating the situation to the benefit of the United States, and when he had finished, he walked over to the bottle of scotch and returned to pour each of them another drink.

"All right," he said, "now I want you two bright boys to tell me if there are any holes in the plan."

For another half hour, they discussed the potential difficulties with Jason Moore's plan and arrived at solutions for most of them.

"There are still some risks, sir. But I agree they're worth it," Garrett said after they had covered every eventuality they could think of. "And if anybody can get it done, my people can—with a little help from Harry, here."

"I hope so, Will," Director Moore said, "which brings up one last item we need to discuss. If they get caught, they will have to kill themselves."

He let the CIA chief's comment sink in a moment, then said, "And then we deny that this government knew anything about it, right?"

"That's right," Moore replied. "Before they leave, we'll have a story already prepared, to be released after we've had a reasonable amount of time to have conducted an investigation. We'll make them out to be the most crazed, evil people you could possibly imagine. They'll go down in history as fanatical madmen who deserved to die and go to hell with the likes of Adolf Hitler. We'll deny to our deaths that they were the brave and dedicated soldiers they'll have to be to carry this thing off."

"Plausible denial again, Mr. Director?"

"Yes. Plausible denial."

Wilton Garrett thought about it for a moment, then said, "Sir, once they learn how critical it is to the well-being of this nation and this planet, I have no doubt that they will commit suicide, if they have to."

Ten minutes later, he was driving back down the parkway toward Alexandria. He was going to have to ask two or three of his subordinates to risk their lives again. Only this time, if they failed, they would not only be required to die by their own hands, but their families and their friends and the rest of the nation—the whole world, for that matter—would record them in history as evil villains who tried to provoke a nuclear war.

Four words kept running through his mind; words he had first heard used together years earlier, when he was in the precommand course at Fort Leavenworth. A colonel named Mike Malone had used them in the classes on ethics he presented to the future battalion and brigade commanders in the course.

"Courage, competence, commitment, and candor," he said aloud as he drove toward the safehouse in the Holiday Inn in Crystal City.

They've got the first three, he thought to himself. The "candor" is up to me, when I explain their mission.

It was midmorning in Cyprus by the time Dick Salem got to Rachel's hotel room in Limassol. Birdie Sadler and she were drinking coffee ordered from room service a little earlier.

"Get rid of the stiff OK?" Sadler asked after he had let Salem in and closed the door.

"It's up to the sharks, now," he replied.

"Good riddance," Sadler muttered, then asked, "What now, coach?"

Salem took the cup of coffee that Rachel offered him, then said, "Pollock and Howson are on the way to Athens in the Agency chopper by now. They'll make their way home from there. Rob's down the street at the Grand, packing up our gear and getting us checked out. He'll go get Moon and meet me downstairs in a few minutes."

He took a gulp of coffee, then handed the cup back to Rachel. "We'll leave the van in the airport parking lot, ma'am, with the keys on top of the right front tire. We're on a twelve-ten flight home, by way of London."

"You're a mess, Dick," she commented, looking at his dirty and disheveled clothing.

"Yeah, I know. Let me use your shaving kit, Birdie. I can change clothes in the van on the way up to Larnaca."

Sadler got his toilet kit out of his hang-up bag and handed it to the Delta sergeant major.

"How long do you want us to hang around here before we head west ourselves?" he asked.

"As soon as you can get the stuff handed back over to the Agency. There's a British Airways flight to London a little before five that you should be able to make."

As he walked into the bathroom, Rachel said, "Hey, why don't we meet up in London, then? We can rest up there, and go on to the States tomorrow or Friday."

"That's up to you guys. I'm going to go on home as soon as I can, and Moon will probably want to go on back, too, with his face all cut up like it is. But you two and Rob Small can hang around London for a couple of days, if you want."

He stuck his shaving cream–covered face around the corner of the bathroom door and looked at Rachel. "What am I saying? You're the boss lady, Rachel, do what you want to."

It was standard procedure to allow Delta Force members to stop off somewhere on the way home, after tough missions such as the one they had just completed. They were encouraged to do so by Doc Frye, the Delta psychologist. It gave them a chance to rest and unwind before getting back to Fort Bragg, and to rehearse their stories about where they would claim to have been.

"What do you say, Birdie?" she asked.

"Hell, yes. 'Course, the weather's lousy in England in January, so we'll have to go pub crawling, I guess."

"Pub crawling?" she asked.

"Yeah, you know, going from one pub to another, sucking down pints of that warm piss they call bitter."

She laughed. "Tell you what, Birdie. I'll go pub crawling with you, if you'll go to an art gallery and a play with me."

"Well, I don't know, ma'am. I'm not really into that culture stuff."

"Aw, come on, Bird. It'll do you good to get a little culture. Rob, too."

"The only 'culture' I want, ma'am, is the kind that grows in penicillin dishes. If I find what I'm looking for in London, I'll have to get a few million cc's from Doc Reed as a precautionary measure when I get back home!"

Rachel laughed, as did Salem, who heard the comment as he shaved. Then she pulled her Mickey Mouse T-shirt off one shoulder and thrust her hip out to the side. She put one hand on her hip and with the other, patted her hair.

Imitating a Hollywood vamp with her voice, she said, "Well, why wait for London, big boy?"

"Wow!" Sadler exclaimed. "Hey, Dick, do you do marriages?"

"'Fraid not, Birdie."

"Oh, hell!" Rachel said in mock protest. "Not even for the *weekend?*"

The trio laughed together, then Rachel pulled the satellite radio out from beneath her bed. As she set up the umbrella-shaped antenna, she said, "I'd better call the States and give them a report on who's leaving when."

Lanny Cabe answered, and she passed him the information about the planned times of departure of the team from Cyprus.

"Is the boss around?" she asked. "I want to get his OK for me, Birdie, and Rob to spend a couple of days in London on the way home."

"He's next door discussing something with Matt Jensen," Cabe advised. "I'll ask him to clear it as soon as he gets back over here."

"Roger that," she said. "I'll call back in a little bit. Out."

Salem came out of the bathroom and handed Sadler his toilet kit. "I'd better get going. Robbie and Moon should be waiting for me outside."

He shook hands with Sadler and said, "Good job, Bird Man."

"Thanks, boss. See you at the Ranch Monday morning."

He turned to Rachel. She walked to the tough, capable noncommissioned officer who epitomized the Delta Force soldier, and embraced him. He patted her on the back and said, "You're as good an officer as this outfit has ever seen, ma'am. I'm going to put you in for a medal when I get back."

She smiled warmly and said, "Thanks, but you know I'd never be able to wear it, anyway. Besides, I didn't do anything more than anyone else in this team. I *will* settle for a beer at McKeller's Lodge some day, though."

"Wear that T-shirt," he joked, "and I'll make it a six-pack. Have a nice time in London."

In the safehouse suite next door to the one where Lanny Cabe was on radio watch in Crystal City, Sergeant Major

A MISSION FOR DELTA

Matt Jensen listened intently to his commander. Garrett explained the complex situation that had evolved since Jensen's attempt to capture his former Special Forces teammate, Raul Valenzuela, lately known by the name Emilio Ramirez. Then he explained the CIA chief's plan to capitalize on the bizarre set of circumstances.

"Weird situation, isn't it, Colonel Garrett?" Jensen commented. "I mean, it's been almost twenty years since Valenzuela was captured in Vietnam. For years, he sat there as a POW, while this government refused to let us go back in after him—him, and God only knows how many others. Meanwhile, they work on his mind, turn him into a damned revolutionary, and about fifteen years later, or whatever it's been, he goes back to Vietnam, recovers the stuff *we* sent him after in the first place, and makes a bomb out of it."

He stood up and shoved his hands into the back pockets of his jeans before continuing. "He plants the thing in Washington, escapes back to Central America, and then his old teammie, Matt Jensen, goes down there to get him. But instead, his new comrades, the Cubans, kill him with their Russian gunships.

"Meanwhile, he's been letting that bastard Nidal believe he's willing to sell him the bomb to blow up a bunch of Russians. So we go after Nidal, who gets killed, too, and now we're the only ones who know we have the bomb.

"So what do we decide to do, now that it's been disarmed? We decide to rearm it, let it out of our control again, and hope that, somehow, that will let us get a leg up on the Russians. It's just all too weird, Colonel. Too weird."

Garrett watched the youthful-looking sergeant major pace back and forth across the room, trying to sort it all out. Finally, Jensen stopped, faced Garrett, and said, "All right, sir. I'll give it a try. And if I get caught, I'll commit suicide and let you tell the world that you didn't know anything about it—that I went nuts and tried to set the bomb off on my own, or whatever story you plan to come up with. But I want something in return, Colonel Garrett, whether we manage to pull this thing off or not."

"What's that, Matt?" Garrett asked.

"I want you to promise me that you'll do everything in your power—everything—to see that this government makes a wholehearted effort to go back to Southeast Asia and find out if any of our MIAs are still being held there. And if there *are* any, even just *one,* whether he looks like he's there of his own free will or not—get him out and bring him home."

Garrett sat there and looked at his subordinate for a while. The Missing-in-Action/Prisoner-of-War issue was something that many of the Vietnam veterans in the Delta Force were concerned about. There was a big, black MIA/POW flag hanging in the main corridor of the former post stockade that Delta now used as its headquarters, and he had often seen T-shirts on his men, and bumper stickers on their cars, which served to keep the unresolved issue alive in people's minds. Although he, himself, was nearly convinced that there were no living American prisoners left from the Vietnam War, he had long since concluded why it was such an important issue to so many of his men: to them, the right of Americans to be free was more than just a concept—it was their creed, their bond, and they were willing to die for it.

Wilton Garrett got up from his chair and stood in front of Sergeant Major Jensen. "If we'd gone back after him and the others, as we should have done so many years ago, we wouldn't be in this goddamned mess today, would we, Matt?" he asked rhetorically. "Yes, Sergeant Major, I'll do my best—make every effort I possibly can—to get this government to do whatever's needed to find out if there are any remaining POWs in Vietnam. And if there are, I'll make damned sure you get to go help rescue them."

Jensen held out his hand and Garrett shook it.

"I know you will, boss. And when we pull this thing off, I'm sure the President will give us the chance."

"I am, too. And I hope you know that I'd go do this job myself, if I could," Garrett added sincerely.

"Hell, I know that, sir. But the Russians would be on you

like stink on shit, the minute you hit Europe. Besides, you don't speak German, and you don't know your way around Berlin like I do. Now, let's figure out who I should take with me."

28

"You want to get some sleep, Birdie?" Rachel asked.

"I was thinking about going down to the swimming pool and catching some rays while I took a nap," he said.

"Hey, that's a good idea," she said. "Let me call the embassy first, and arrange for them to pick the cars up from the airport. And I'll call British Airways to confirm that we can get seats on that flight this afternoon. Why don't you get on the satcom and find out if the Colonel's back yet and see if he's got any problem with our staying in London?"

She called the airline first, and got two seats on the 4:55 P.M. flight to London, then called the number in Nicosia that the CIA admin officer had given her two nights earlier.

"Is Mr. Smith there?" she asked the woman who answered. When he came on the line, she said, "Can you pick up the cars at the airport at about four o'clock?"

"Leaving already?" he asked.

"Yes. See you at four?"

"Fine," he answered. "Four o'clock, then. Good-bye."

Birdie Sadler called the safehouse in Washington. Jim Greer, the Delta intelligence officer, answered from the room in the Crystal City safehouse. He had spent most of the time before the bomb was found conducting counter-surveillance for the team who retraced Ramirez's steps through the capital. Since then, he had been assisting Lanny Cabe in monitoring the radio. One of his duties as the Delta

Force intelligence officer included the supervision of Rachel's Administrative Detachment, as the handful of Delta's female operatives was called. As such, he had the authority to grant her request.

"The boss is still next door with Sergeant Major Jensen," he said, "but tell Captain Brown that her request to stop off in London is approved. Just tell her to call the Ranch once or twice a day to see if we've got anything for you guys."

"Roger," Sadler answered. "And be advised, we'll be leaving here for the airport around three o'clock. We'll call before we leave."

"Roger, out," Greer replied.

Rachel and Birdie changed into their bathing suits and went downstairs to the hotel swimming pool.

"Damn," Birdie commented, looking around the pool-side patio at the half-dozen European women wearing topless bikinis, "I *was* gonna take a nap, but the scenery's so good, my eyes won't close."

Rachel laughed, then lay back to enjoy the feel of the warm Mediterranean sun on her body. *A day ago,* she thought, *I wouldn't have felt comfortable about lying around a pool in a skimpy bikini with one of the guys. But somehow, it doesn't bother me at all today. I wonder why? Does killing Nidal and one of his men have something to do with it?*

She looked over at Sadler, whose eyes were closed behind his sunglasses.

Yes, she thought, *that must be it.* She recalled that it was he who had killed the other bodyguard, and thought, *If we can bare our souls to each other like that, if we can share that most intimate of human experiences, then, no wonder that baring mere flesh becomes such a meaningless thing. Maybe that's why Salem felt free to make that comment about my T-shirt earlier. He would never have said something like that before today. And most certainly he would never have said it to a female officer. No, there is nothing more intimate than the taking of human lives together,* her thoughts continued. *Not even sex. Maybe bearing a child is a more emotional, personal experience, I don't know. But taking the life of another human being . . .*

She felt as if she were about to vomit, so she picked up her shirt and held it to her mouth. She heaved once, but nothing came up.

Sadler looked at her and sat up. "You OK, Rachel?" he asked.

"Yeah, I'll be all right. Think I'll hop in the pool for a minute, though."

He watched her as she sat on the edge of the pool, then lowered herself into it and breast-stroked through the cool water.

You're a remarkable woman, Captain Rachel Brown, he thought to himself, then tried to think of the words which best described her. *Beautiful* was certainly the first one. *Tough. Smart. Courageous. Sensitive?* Could a woman who kills someone in cold blood be sensitive? Sure, why not? *He* had done the same thing, when he killed one of Nidal's men. And if Garrett's message suggesting that it would be good if Nidal died had been addressed to him, he would have had no qualms about executing the terrorist. But he didn't feel insensitive about it.

He rolled over and lay on his stomach, his head turned toward the pool so he could continue to watch Rachel.

"The most precious thing on the face of the earth is a human life," he recalled Charlie Beckwith, Delta's founder, saying the first day he met the burly, tough-exteriored colonel. It was during the commander's board, when Sadler was being interviewed by Beckwith and his principal subordinates as the final step in deciding whether or not he was suited for an assignment with the Delta Force.

"What do you consider to be the most precious thing on the face of the earth, Sergeant Saddle?" Beckwith had asked. Beckwith often used incorrect names of the people he was grilling, to add to their sense of discomfort.

"Sad*ler,* sir," Birdie had replied, then thought about the question for a moment before trying to give the response he thought Beckwith and the others wanted to hear.

"The Constitution of the United States," he answered finally.

"Bullshit!" Beckwith shot back. "That's only a handful of

paper. The most precious thing on the face of the earth is a human life."

At the time, Sadler had wondered if the tough, hard-charging Georgian had really meant it. The longer he served under Beckwith, the more he realized the man *did* mean it. And the day he gave Sadler the mission of killing a terrorist they had tracked down in Beirut, he did so with tears in his eyes.

Ever since, Sadler had wondered whether or not he would have been able to pull the trigger that day years earlier, if Beckwith had not made him understand what an awesome responsibility it was to kill someone. If the now-retired colonel had been flippant about it, Sadler would probably have said something like, "Fuck you. Kill him yourself." But, because of the sense of responsibility with which the soldiers of Delta were ingrained by the unit's founding officers, he had said simply, "Yes, sir."

Half an hour later, he had the terrorist in the scope of his Remington sniper rifle, and he blew the man's brains out from four hundred yards away.

Years later, when he read a newspaper article that said Beckwith had a sign on his desk at his Texas-based security company, which read, "Kill 'em all and let God sort 'em out," he had been disappointed in the man he now considered his mentor. He wrote him a scathing letter, and one of the former Delta officers who worked for Beckwith, Wade Ishimoto, told Sadler that when he read the letter, Beckwith replaced the sign.

The most precious thing on the face of the earth is a human life.

Rachel climbed out of the pool and came back to lie on the lounge chair next to Sadler.

"Feeling better?" he asked her.

"Yeah, thanks," she said, patting her shoulders dry.

When she had lain there for a while, she said, "Birdie, does it bother you to have to do things like we did last night?"

He rolled over and looked at her. "Of course it does,

Rachel. It's the most awesome, awful responsibility there is. If it didn't bother me, I'd quit."

"Ever have to do it before?"

"Yes," he replied. "Once. But it was a hell of a lot farther away, and I guess that made it less . . . well, less *personal.* You know what I mean?"

"No, not really," she said after thinking about it a moment.

"Well, now that I think about it," he said, "maybe it *wasn't* less personal. I had a hell of a lot longer to think about it. And the guy wasn't really a threat to me at the time. I mean, he wasn't even armed. He was standing there talking to some other guy, smiling, when I blew him away."

She was staring up at the sky, and a tear fell out of her eye and slid down her cheek. He reached over and squeezed her hand, and she looked at him.

"Let me remind you of something, Rachel," he said, sitting up and taking her hand in both of his. "Picture this. A group of women and children are standing in line at a counter at the airport in Vienna. On Nidal's orders, two men pull out pistols and grenades, and start killing everyone in sight. Did you ever see the picture of that little eleven-year-old girl with her legs blown off? And her parents lying there beside her, bleeding to death themselves while they watched her die?

"And remember the old, crippled guy in the wheelchair on the *Achille Lauro?* Remember how they shot him in the head and dumped him overboard? And that sailor, being dumped out of the airplane onto the tarmac after he was beat nearly to death to intimidate the other passengers, then shot in the head?"

She reached up and wiped the tears from her cheeks, and he continued. "Well, that rotten, no good bastard can't do those things anymore, Rachel."

More tears fell from her eyes as she looked absently up at the sky again.

"But, Bird, he was handcuffed. We could have gotten him out of here and given him a trial, and—"

"Oh, sure," he interrupted in a loud whisper. "So some pinko lawyer could get him off on a technicality, or something. And how many more terrorist acts would have been committed? How many hostages taken by assholes like the two we got rid of at the restaurant, to try to trade for him? No way, Rachel Brown. No way I'm gonna sit here and let you feel like you've done anything wrong. No way. Look at me, Rachel."

She turned her head and looked at his eyes, full of fire and sincerity.

"You're a brave, dedicated American officer, goddamn it, Captain Brown, and what you did this morning and last night—and may have to do again—not only probably saved a hell of a lot of innocent lives, but makes *me* damned proud to be a Delta soldier."

Tears streamed out of her eyes as she lay there looking at the sky again for a while. Then she got up, walked to the pool, and dived in. She swam across the pool and back twice, then got out and came back to where Birdie Sadler sat watching her.

"Let's go get some brunch, Bird Man," she said. "I could eat a horse."

When they got back up to the room to change, she turned the shower on, undressed, and got in. Then she stuck her head out from around the shower curtain and called, "Hey, Birdie?"

"Yo!" he answered from the other room.

"Want to take a shower with me?"

It was after three o'clock when Rachel made her final call from Limassol to Washington. Birdie Sadler had taken their bags and gone down to put them in the Mercedes sedan they would give back to the CIA man when they got to Larnaca Airport.

Major Greer answered her call and said, "Hang on a minute, Rachel. The Old Man wants to talk to you. Let me go next door and get him."

A minute later, Garrett's voice came over the secure voice radio. "Brown, this is Garrett, over."

"Go ahead, sir."

"Do you know where our London safehouse is, Rachel?"

She didn't even know the Delta Force *had* a London safehouse, so she answered, "Negative, sir."

"Roger," Garrett said. "Where are you planning on staying in London?"

"There's a hotel on Basil Street in Knightsbridge where I've stayed before. I was planning on staying there. Shouldn't be a problem getting a room this time of year."

"Understand," he said. "But if you end up somewhere else, be sure to let us know as soon as you get there."

"Will do. Something else going on?" she asked.

"Affirmative," her commanding officer replied. "I'm afraid I'm going to have to ask you to stay overseas for a few more days. Sergeant Major Jensen will link up with you in London and explain the mission."

She sighed heavily, because she really wasn't sure that her emotions could handle another nerve-racking mission of the kind that she had undergone during the previous week. And if Jensen was being sent out again so soon after the Ramirez capture attempt, it must still be something related to the emotion-stretching events which had begun in El Salvador.

"Brown, Garrett. You copy my last?" he asked when she failed to answer him after a few moments.

"Roger, sir. Jensen will meet me in London and explain the mission. When will he get there?"

"Probably sometime Saturday," Garrett explained. "Maybe Sunday, so you'll have some time to rest up before he gets there."

"That's good news," she said. "Is it part of the same situation we've been working on all week?"

"Jensen will explain when he gets there," he replied. "But, listen now, Rachel. After he tells you what the job is, if you feel like you can't handle it . . . scratch that—I know you can handle it. But if you don't want to do it, just say so. I mean that. This one's purely voluntary."

When she heard the encryption device beep as he released the transmitter button of his handset, she asked, "What are you trying to tell me, Colonel?"

Garrett was dead tired, and he wasn't explaining himself very well. "Disregard all that, Captain Brown. After Jensen links up with you in London and explains the job, give me a call. I'll speak to you about it then. Meanwhile, have some fun in London, all right?"

"Sounds like I'd better. OK, sir, I've got to break this thing down and get moving, or we won't make our flight. Anything further?"

"Yeah, just one thing. How did Sergeant Major Salem take my message last night? I mean . . . aw, shit, what *do* I mean? I'm so tired I can't think straight. I guess what I'm asking is whether or not he's pissed off at me. I should've flown over there and taken care of it myself, over."

She sighed deeply again, then said, "Sir, while Salem was reading the message, I was guarding the Quarry. He died before Salem got a chance to finish reading it."

There was a long moment of silence before Garrett came back on and said, "Uh, roger. . . . That wasn't my intent, you know, over."

"It should have been, boss. I'm the officer, remember."

Again, there was a period of silence before Garrett said, "Roger that, Captain Brown. And a damned good one, but—well, hell. Tell me to shut up and get off this damned radio, will you? I'll talk to you when you get to London, and I get some sleep."

"Shut up and get off this damned radio, will you, Colonel? And remember what the guys say, sir, 'Nobody said it was gonna be easy.' Out here."

"Roger, out."

29

Just after five o'clock, the half-empty British Airways flight lifted off the runway of Larnaca Airport and made a long, slow turn to the right over the eastern Mediterranean.

From her window seat on the right side of the aircraft, Rachel looked out and saw Limassol. She was able to make out the road leading north from the resort town, and beside it, the Greek restaurant where they had killed his two bodyguards and captured Hakim Nidal. For a moment, she felt nauseated, then the feeling passed, and she muttered, "So long, Limassol."

"What?" Birdie Sadler asked from the seat beside her, but before Rachel could answer, a stewardess stopped at their seats.

"Would you care for something to drink, miss?" she inquired.

Rachel smiled and said, "Yes, please. I'd like a couple of very large gins and a little bit of tonic."

Birdie looked at her and raised his eyebrows. When the stewardess said, "And you, sir?" he replied, "Scotch and soda, please."

When she had moved on, Birdie looked at Rachel and said, "You plan on getting smashed, Rache?"

"Yep," she answered as she reclined her seat.

By the time the stewardess returned with their drinks, she was asleep. Birdie paid for them and drank all three, and by the time the aircraft passed the heel of Italy's boot, he, too, was sleeping soundly.

* * *

Matt Jensen spent that Wednesday, the fifteenth of January, planning the operation he had been charged with conducting in Berlin. Harry Lawson of the Central Intelligence Agency, who was to assist him, helped him formulate the plan. Other than the two of them, the only people in the world who were aware of what they were planning were Jason Moore, the Director of Central Intelligence, and Colonel Wilton Garrett, commander of the Delta Force.

The only other person who would be told of the plan was Rachel Brown and that was only if she agreed to go on a mission which, if she was caught conducting it, required that she be willing to take her own life before she could be interrogated. Garrett had made it plain to Matt Jensen the night before that he must explain that fact to her and get her consent before telling her exactly what the mission was about. Also, she had to be willing to agree that she would allow the United States government to defame her name in the eyes of her family, her friends, and the world press.

Delta's senior Explosive Ordnance Disposal technician, Master Sergeant Ennis Fox, was going to know that Jensen was to have some connection with the presently harmless plutonium bomb, because he would be instructed to rehearse Jensen on how to reset the timing mechanism and rearm the device. But Fox would do so only after Garrett had explained to him that he was never to discuss having done so with anyone, regardless of what happened in the future.

Delta's deputy, Paul McCarthy, received a strange request from Colonel Garrett that morning, but he had no idea why it was necessary for him to do what his boss ordered. Dutifully, he took a stamp pad and a fingerprint card and went out to the temperature-controlled oxygen storage shed behind the former Fort Bragg stockade. He unlocked the high-security lock, stepped inside, and closed the door behind him before turning on the light. He opened the air valve on the aluminum box which contained the body of Emilio Ramirez.

"God *damn!*" McCarthy muttered as the resulting stench entered his nostrils while he unfastened the latches of the eight-foot-long body box. He lifted the lid and leaned it against the wall, nearly vomiting at the smell of the corpse. Quickly, he pulled the dead man's stiff arms up far enough to allow him to ink the bloated fingers, then pressed each one onto the appropriate place on the fingerprint card. That done, he replaced the top over Ramirez's body, fastened the latches, and closed the air valve.

Before leaving the shed, he placed his mouth over the valve opening of one of the oxygen tanks, opened the valve slightly, and took several deep breaths of the clean, pure gas. Then he took the fingerprint card and returned to his office, placing the card in a manila envelope and sealing it.

He couldn't get the smell out of his nostrils, so he changed into a sweatsuit, ran six miles through the woods behind the stockade, then took a long, hot shower. He thought he could still smell the corpse, even though he had changed the clothes he was wearing while he took the fingerprints, so he went into Garrett's office, took a Honduran cigar from the box on the desk, and smoked it. At last, the smell of Ramirez's body subsided in his nostrils.

Betsy Dennis, the cute little civilian secretary from the intelligence section, came into his office with a video cassette. She waved the cigar smoke away from her face and said, "Hi, Paul. Jerry Wells asked me to bring you this tape. It's something he just taped from Cable News."

"Thanks, kid," he said, taking it from her and watching admiringly as the pretty young woman walked away.

He placed it in the video cassette player on the table beside his desk and turned the monitor on.

"In El Salvador today," the announcer said, "sources from within the antigovernment guerrillas claim that government commandos conducted a raid last Friday into a guerrilla stronghold near the Honduran border. The insurgents claim that the helicopter-borne commandos first raked the sleeping village with gunfire, killing several innocent civilians. Then, they allege, the soldiers abducted an agricultural advisor and his pregnant wife. El Salvadoran officials, however, claim no knowledge of the raid. Amy Settle reports from El Salvador . . ."

A young reporter appeared on the screen, speaking into a microphone above the rotor noise of the helicopter in which she was riding.

"Although guerrilla forces claim that a raid was conducted here in Morazan Province by El Salvadoran troops," she reported, "the evidence below raises serious doubts about what occurred here on Friday night."

The video which followed showed the remains of two crashed helicopters filmed from above. Although the helicopters were mostly burned, it was obvious to the trained eye that they were Soviet-built Hinds.

"The wrecked helicopters you see below are Mi-24 Hind gunships," the reporter continued as footage of the two crash sites was shown. "The only nation in Central America with these Soviet-built aircraft is Nicaragua, so the question is, what were they doing here? And what happened? We asked the American air attaché to El Salvador these questions, and this was his response."

The picture switched to a U.S. Air Force lieutenant colonel standing in front of a row of American-made Hueys at Ilopango Air Base. "Well," the man said, "I've personally flown up there, and I can tell you that the two wrecked choppers I saw are Nicaraguan Hinds. As far as any claims about any Salvadoran Air Force helicopters being involved in a night raid, I can tell you that we're only now training the pilots here in night flying techniques."

The reporter asked from off camera, "Then what do you suppose happened up in northern Morazan last Friday night, Colonel?"

"Probably a resupply flight to the guerrillas that went wrong. I don't know. It's possible that there was a midair collision, or that the choppers were in the wrong location and the guerrillas took them under fire. But I can tell you this—the fact there are Hinds violating Salvadoran airspace is not something that the Air Force here takes lightly."

The camera switched to the reporter again, who said, "So, as you can see, both American and El Salvadoran government officials here make it plain that, in their opinion, the guerrillas' claims of a government raid are unfounded, and probably being used to cover up a resupply operation from Nicaragua that went awry. . . . This is Amy Settle reporting from El Salvador."

After McCarthy turned the VCR off, he walked to the situation room and called his boss on the secure satcom radio.

When Garrett came on, he said, "I got the prints you wanted, sir, and I'll have them up there by courier this afternoon. Have you seen the news reports on the Nicaraguan choppers that went down in El Sal, over?"

"Affirmative, Paul," Garrett replied. "Looks good to us, since everybody seems to agree that it's guerrilla propaganda they're putting out to try to cover up for something that happened during a resupply mission."

"Roger that. Angela and the others are out at Woodlake now, and we've got the schedules of most of the people coming back in from overseas. When do you and the guys with you expect to be leaving D.C., boss?"

"Schumann and most of them are on the way back there now," Garrett answered. "But we've got a little more to do on this thing. I've got a couple of orders for you. You ready to copy?"

McCarthy sat down and picked up a pencil, then said, "Send your traffic."

"Roger. Sometime after dark," Garrett directed, "when everybody clears out of there, I want you to take Ramirez's body out to Camp Mackall and load it up on the Twin Otter. Tell Munson to fly all the cargo to Fort A.P. Hill, Virginia, to arrive at twenty-three hundred hours tonight. I'll meet him there with further instructions. Also, advise Sergeant Fox that he's to go with Munson. How copy so far?"

"Good copy, sir. Continue."

"All right, instead of sending Ramirez's prints up here by courier, take them to Mackall, give them to Fox, and tell him to bring them with him and give them to me."

"Wilco. Anything further?"

"Negative," Colonel Garrett said. "Once you get the Twin

Otter out of Camp Mackall, Paul, you can go ahead and close the radios down for the night. If I need you to do anything else, I'll call the duty officer on the phone and have him get you in to talk on the radio. Out."

When Bud Munson landed his aircraft on the isolated airstrip at Fort A.P. Hill at precisely eleven P.M. that night, he had Ennis Fox, the disarmed nuclear bomb, and the box containing the remains of Emilio Ramirez aboard.

Garrett met him and told him to taxi to the far end of the airstrip, where Sergeant Major Matt Jensen and the CIA's Harry Lawson sat waiting in a van. There, Jensen and Lawson helped Ennis Fox move the box containing the bomb into the van, where they strapped it down.

Fox gave Garrett the envelope with Emilio Ramirez's fingerprints in it and said, "Colonel McCarthy said to be sure to give you this."

"This is for you, Harry," Garrett said, and passed the envelope to Lawson.

After Fox got the small steel box containing the timing device and detonators for the bomb, he got into the van with Jensen and Lawson, and they drove away.

"What about this body box, Colonel?" the pilot asked the Delta Force commander.

"Crank this thing up again, Bud," Garrett answered, "and let's head out over the ocean."

"Again?" Munson asked. "I sure as hell hope this box doesn't contain what the last one did."

"No problem," Wilton Garrett responded. "There's nothing in this one but fish food."

An hour later, well out over the Atlantic, Garrett said, "Slow this thing down, Bud. Time to unload the cargo."

He climbed out of the copilot's seat into the cargo compartment of the Twin Otter, unlatched the back door, and folded it up. Next, he removed the tie-downs from the body box, slid it back to the door, and opened the air valve, then released the latches holding the top. The smell of the putrid corpse whirled around him as he sat on the floor, put his feet against the end of the box, and pushed it out of the door into the night sky above the ocean.

In a Northern Virginia safehouse, Ennis Fox showed Matt Jensen how to set the timing device for the bomb, and explained how to place the detonators into the vessel containing the conventional explosives which would initiate the nuclear reaction. While he did so, Harry Lawson took the fingerprint card to CIA headquarters so a technician could transfer the prints to a pair of rubber gloves. Once they were transferred, the gloves would be treated so that anyone wearing them while handling an object would leave not his own fingerprints on the object, but those of Ramirez.

By noon the next day—Thursday, the sixteenth—Fox had completed his training of Jensen and was on the way back to Fort Bragg by commercial air. Garrett and Munson were already there, having flown directly to Fort Bragg's Simmons Army Airfield after dumping Ramirez's body into the Atlantic.

By evening, the only Delta Force people involved in the operation not back in North Carolina were Matt Jensen, Rachel Brown, and Birdie Sadler. Once he saw what the weather in London was like, Rob Small had decided not to stay there and rendezvous with Rachel and Birdie, but had gone on home with Sergeant Major Salem.

In London, Rachel and Birdie were asleep in their rooms in the Basil Street Hotel, when Rachel was awakened by a nightmare. She couldn't remember what she had been dreaming, but she was soaked in sweat, and couldn't go back to sleep.

She started to pull on a robe and go down the hall to Birdie's room, then decided against it. Instead, she sat on the edge of her bed in the darkness, listening to the rain beat against the window of her chilly room and thinking about the events of the previous week. Finally, when the light of dawn crept into the room, she lay back down and went to sleep.

It was early Friday morning in Washington. In less than a week, most of the leaders of the United States government would gather in the Capitol Building to hear the President deliver his annual State of the Union address.

30

It was nearly noon on Friday when Rachel Brown awoke to the sound of someone knocking on her hotel room door. Through her window, Rachel could see that the weather had changed to bright sunshine.

"Who is it?" she asked.

"It's Birdie. Did I wake you up?"

"Just a second," she said. She hopped out of bed and pulled on a robe, then opened the door to let him in.

"Hi," he said. "Get enough rest?"

"Not really," Rachel replied as she picked up a brush and went to the mirror to brush her hair. "Did you?"

"I slept like a rock." He sat down on her bed. "I phoned the States last night."

"Yeah? What's going on back there?" she asked as she took some clothes out of her suitcase.

"My girlfriend's coming up from Florida to see me this weekend. I'm gonna head on back to Fort Bragg, if it's OK with you."

"Sure," she replied, turning to look at him and smiling. "Is she that pretty little one you brought to the dinner dance in November?"

"Yeah. Becky, the little, rich one," he answered. "You going to come on back home with me?"

She hadn't told him that she had been ordered to stay in London to wait for Matt Jensen, so she said, "No, I'm going to stay here for the rest of the weekend, Birdie. Go to a couple of museums this afternoon, and maybe see a play tonight."

"You sure you don't mind if I take off? I mean, I *did* agree that I'd go to a play and a museum with you, if you went on a pub crawl with me last night."

She laughed. "Bird Man, you just go on home and see that little rich girl. She looks like she'd be a hell of a lot more fun than a museum." Feigning a British accent, she chirped, "I can always go back to Bill Bentley's and pick up that rich Yank soldier who was lusting after me."

"That son of a bitch," he mumbled.

The night before, they had been going from bar to bar, having a drink at each during what was known in Britain as a "pub crawl." At a wine bar not far from the hotel, Bill Bentley's, they had noticed that much of the clientele was American, so they'd decided to pretend to be British, just to see if they could carry it off. One of the American men had taken an immediate liking to Rachel, and had sent her a bottle of good French wine. Then he came and took a seat beside Rachel, ignoring Birdie and making a play for her.

"Hi, my name's Lane Rothberg," he said. "What's yours, beautiful?"

"Helen Shumate," she replied with a voice that sounded like Julia Child's. "Thank you *veddy* much for the wine. Excuse me," she said in her best British accent as the man slid his arm onto the back of her chair and moved closer to her, "but I haven't introduced you to my escort, Major Bird, of the Queen's Own Lowland Fusiliers."

Birdie Sadler pursed his lips as he held out his hand to the man and shook it limply, lisping, "A pleasure to meet you, my good man, I'm veddy sure."

"Major Bird is only just back from Africa today," Rachel squeaked.

"Oh, yes, yes," Sadler confirmed. "Jolly time on the old dark continent."

"Really?" the American tourist asked. "On Army business?"

"Quite," Sadler confirmed. "Down there observing the

Boers in their little tiff with the Zulus, you see. Ever *bean* to Africa, Mr? . . . Mr? . . ."

"Rothberg," the man replied. "Yes, I have, as a matter of fact. A couple of years ago . . . I really shouldn't tell you, I guess, but I was in Angola when I was in Delta Force. Fighting the commies and their Cuban advisors down there."

"Oh, how *veddy* exciting!" Rachel exclaimed.

Sadler raised his eyebrows and leaned forward, then in a stage whisper said, "I *say*, that must have bean *jolly* exciting! But I didn't think you Delta Force chaps were supposed to admit such things."

"Oh, Pinkie," Rachel said, causing Sadler to cast her a glance which seemed to say, "Pinkie?"

"Don't be silly," she continued. "If he cawn't tell a British awficer, whom *can* he tell?"

"Pinkie?" The man roared with laughter. "Pinkie?" he repeated, as he put his arm around Rachel's shoulder. "Look, honey," he said, placing his face close to hers, the smell of whiskey heavy on his breath, "why don't you dump this limp-wristed wimp and come with me tonight? We could have a hell of a good time."

She moved her face back from his and said, "Oh, I'm afraid I cawn't, you see, because Pinkie would cut your tiny *bolls* off."

"Now, why don't you take your bottle of wine," Sadler said, dropping his British accent and moving his face close to the other man's, "and bug off, before I shove it up your phony Delta Force ass!"

The man stood up, his face a bright red as he looked first at Birdie, then Rachel, then back to Birdie. "Why you godda—"

"Ah, ah, ah!" Sadler warned, wagging his finger at the man and narrowing his eyes, "you wouldn't want Pinkie to cut your balls off, would you?"

The man had snatched up the bottle of wine and stormed back to the bar with his friends.

Rachel and Birdie finished their drinks, then left and

walked, arm in arm, back to the hotel, laughing and continuing their charade as they walked.

"What time's your flight, Birdie?" Rachel asked.

"Two-fifteen," he answered, looking at his watch and standing up. "Guess I'd better check out of this place and get going."

She laid her clothes down on the bed, walked to him, and held out her arms. He embraced her strongly, and she kissed him lightly and said, "Thanks for everything, Birdie."

He smiled and said, "Hey, no problem. Maybe we'll have another job together, sometime. I'll see you in a few days."

"Bye. Have a nice flight home."

He left, and she went into the bathroom.

Half an hour later, as she dried and brushed her hair, she set up the satellite radio and called Fort Bragg. To her great surprise, Dave Ames answered her call.

"Brown, this is Ames," he said. "Long time no see."

The last she had heard about him several days earlier was that he had been sent to Fort Bragg for some involvement with a congressional secretary, and would probably be reassigned.

"Uh, Roger, Dave. Where are you?"

"Right here in the sit room," he replied. "When are you coming home, over?"

"Oh, sometime next week, I guess. Is the colonel there?"

"Just a minute and I'll see if I can run him down. Hey, I just sat in on the debriefing of Salem and the others, Rachel. They were really singing your praises. You're one tough lady!"

Tough, she thought. *I don't want to be tough.*

"I don't feel very tough, Dave," she said. "Just lonely."

"Well, I look forward to your getting home. Maybe we can do something about that. Hang on, and I'll get the boss."

While she waited for Garrett, she thought about what he had said. Lanny Cabe's report that Dave was to be reassigned was obviously incorrect, or he would never have been allowed to sit in on the debriefing of Salem's team. She was suddenly glad that Birdie had decided to go on back to the States.

In the situation room of the Delta Force headquarters, Wilton Garrett excused his subordinates from the room before calling Rachel on the radio.

"Brown, this is Garrett, over," she heard over the earphones.

"Roger, sir. Do you have an arrival time on Jensen yet?"

"Affirmative," her commanding officer replied. "He'll be in there tomorrow morning. He should be contacting you at your hotel at about nine o'clock your time. You are still in the Basil, aren't you?"

"That's affirm. Be advised, Sadler's on the way back there now—leaves Heathrow at fourteen-fifteen hours, over."

"Roger, copy, Cap'n Brown. Advise me after you talk to Jensen whether or not you want to do this job, over."

"Wilco, sir. Any further?"

"Negative. And you don't need to call back until after you make contact with Jensen. Also, you are to call no one except me on the radio until you return, acknowledge?"

"I understand, sir. Brown, out."

She tried not to speculate about the mission she would be briefed on by Sergeant Major Jensen. After she put the satellite radio away, she went down the street to the giant Harrod's department store to buy herself a decent winter coat, then caught the London subway to Trafalgar Square to visit the British National Art Gallery.

Harry Lawson's driver from CIA headquarters helped him carry the heavy box marked "Diplomatic Pouch, United States of America" from the government van to the ramp of the big C-5 Galaxy aircraft at Dover Air Force Base, Delaware.

"Damn, this thing's heavy," the driver commented. "What you got in here—gold?"

"Wish it was," Lawson replied, "but it's only some electronic gear for the station in Frankfurt."

He had a smaller diplomatic pouch as well, and after he showed the necessary paperwork and his diplomatic passport to the loadmaster of the huge cargo plane, he watched as the box with Ramirez's improvised bomb was strapped down in the nearly empty airplane. Then he took the smaller pouch with him and climbed the ladder to the passenger seats in the top of the C-5. He sat down and placed the smaller pouch in the seat next to him and stared at it for a moment. In it were the detonating device for the bomb, a pair of rubber gloves with Ramirez's raised fingerprints burned into them, and a small bottle of almost-instantaneous poison pills.

A crewman gave him and the other six passengers on the aircraft a safety briefing, then Lawson sat back and settled in for the long flight to Frankfurt.

At Washington National Airport, Sergeant Major Matt Jensen checked his suitcase and went to the gate for his TWA flight to Boston's Logan International, where he would change planes for the overnight flight to London.

He hoped that Rachel Brown would agree to go along on the mission. If not, he would have to rely on the CIA man, Harry Lawson, and he preferred to do the job with a Delta soldier. Besides, a woman would be much better cover to accompany him on the job he had to do.

Lawson and Jensen were both out over the Atlantic when Marlene Graf of the embassy of the Federal Republic of Germany paid a visit to the Georgetown apartment of Charlotte Black, a member of the staff of Congressman Wesley Bolton of Wisconsin.

After Charlotte gave Marlene the envelope she had taken from Harry Lawson that morning during a brief encounter in the theater of the National Air and Space Museum, she opened the bottle of wine Marlene had brought with her. While she did so, the German woman read the contents of the envelope which she was to pass on to her KGB contact when she met him on Sunday.

It was an excerpt from the fictitious statements of Emilio Ramirez, who was believed by the Soviets to be under interrogation at Eglin Air Force Base, Florida.

According to the excerpt, Hakim Nidal had requested Ramirez to provide him with "a certain instrument of mass destruction" for an extremely large amount of money. Ramirez had not actually sold the device to Nidal, but had agreed, for half the sum of money, to arm and plant the bomb for him somewhere. Once it detonated, Nidal would pay Ramirez the balance of the money.

"Under continued interrogation," the report said, "the subject became evasive, then incoherent. Continued interrogation was deemed inappropriate and was curtailed for the night.

"When attempts were made to wake the subject for continued interrogation the following morning, it was discovered that he had committed suicide by wrapping a piece of wire from the mattress of his bed around his neck, and twisting the ends of it, causing unconsciousness and subsequent death by strangulation."

The fictitious report went on to say that concurrent and subsequent interrogation of the woman who was captured with Ramirez, a Nicaraguan citizen named Nadia Cruz, indicated that she was largely unaware of Ramirez's movements and his dealings with Hakim Nidal.

"Polygraph readouts confirmed the veracity of the woman's statements," the report continued. "The only item of significance in her statements was the fact that she believes Ramirez was in Europe during a week-long absence in November of last year.

"Interrogation of Nadia Cruz continues," was the statement with which the report ended.

Marlene folded the phony report up, put it back in the envelope, and put the envelope in her purse.

Charlotte Black handed her a glass of wine, sat down on the couch beside her, then leaned over and kissed her warmly on the lips.

"Now," she said, reaching over to unbutton her lover's blouse, "let me look at you, darling."

31

It was well before dawn on Saturday, January 18, when the C-5 with Harry Lawson and his two diplomatic pouches arrived at Rhein-Main Air Base near Frankfurt, Germany.

He was met by a fellow CIA officer from the Agency office in Frankfurt, who helped him load his pouches into a Volkswagen van. That done, the man drove him away from the security area in which the aircraft was parked.

"The C-130 that's taking you to Berlin doesn't load 'til seven, Harry," the man said. "How about some breakfast? We can get some at the transient hotel here on base."

"Sure," Harry answered, "as long as we can secure these pouches."

They pulled up to the entrance of the base hotel, which was guarded by Air Force Security Police. They took the pouches into the hotel entrance and set them down in front of the desk where a young woman was checking identity cards. When they showed her their diplomatic passports, she said, "Thank you, gentlemen."

"Will you keep an eye on these pouches for us while we get a bite to eat?" the man who had met Lawson at the aircraft asked.

"Sure," she replied. "Just leave them right behind the desk, here."

They went upstairs to the hotel cafeteria, which was open all night to serve the transient servicemen and women and their families traveling to and from duty in Europe.

After they got their breakfast trays and sat down in a far corner of the cafeteria, the other CIA man said, "So, what the hell are you doing in Germany, Harry? I thought you were chief of the Director's security these days?"

"Just a little courier detail in conjunction with an advance. Mr. Moore has a visit coming up over here, so the tech guys asked me if I'd courier in some stuff to the station in Berlin while I was arranging the Director's trip."

"When's Moore coming over? Strange that I haven't heard anything about it."

"Well, it's an unscheduled visit, I guess," Lawson lied. "So, what have *you* been up to, Paddy? Last I heard you were in Beirut."

"Yeah, what a rat fuck *that* was. I should have known from the first day I got there, that it was gonna be a wonderful tour. They issued me a pistol for self-protection, and while I was loading it, I put a round in the ceiling. Never heard the end of it."

Lawson laughed. "You always were a good spy and a shitty marksman, Paddy."

Three Air Force Security Policemen came into the cafeteria and looked around—a second lieutenant, a sergeant, and an airman. Spotting the two men in the corner, the sergeant nodded in their direction, and the lieutenant walked over to them with the other two following behind, their hands on their holstered pistols.

"Will you come with me please, gentlemen?" the officer asked.

"What's the problem, Lieutenant?" Paddy inquired.

"Just come with us, sir," he answered. "Now."

"Can't it wait until we finish our breakfast?"

The sergeant stepped forward and said, "You heard the lieutenant. *Now*, mister!"

The two CIA men looked at each other quizzically, then got up and followed the lieutenant, while the other two security policemen followed closely behind them. They walked down the stairs and out to the front entrance.

"Wait just a minute, Lieutenant!" Lawson demanded. "Where the hell are the two diplomatic pouches I left here?"

"That's just what we want to talk to you about. Now, get in the sedan," the young officer ordered.

"Just a goddamn minute!" Paddy demanded. "Those are diplomatic pouches of the U.S. State Department, Lieutenant. You'd better return them to us immediately!"

Holy Jesus Christ! Harry Lawson thought. *I should never have let those things out of my sight.*

"They've been taken out of here," the lieutenant replied. "You'll get them back in due course. Get in the sedan."

They were put into the back seat of a Security Police sedan, and the sergeant drove away, the lieutenant sitting beside him.

"Are you going to tell us what this is all about, Lieutenant, or do I have to get the people from the U.S. Consulate out here?" Paddy asked.

The officer said nothing, and they were driven to an isolated part of the flight line. There were two more Security Police sedans there, lights flashing, and a yellow crash truck. They were in a wide circle around the diplomatic pouches, which were sitting on the concrete with the headlights of the three vehicles shining on them. A young airman with a dog on a leash stood beside one of the sedans.

"Now, gentlemen," the lieutenant said, "I need to know what's in the pouches."

"No way, son. Those are diplomatic pouches, and what's in them is none of your business," Paddy replied.

"Well, I can tell you *one* thing that's in them," the Security Police officer replied. "Explosives. That dog over there is the best explosive sniffer in Europe, and he keyed on that big bag like I've never seen him do before."

"Look, Lieutenant," Lawson said, "there may very well be some explosives in one of them. They're for the American Consulate in Berlin, and there're probably some file destruction devices for the safes, or something. We both have diplomatic passports and I have courier orders." He pulled his passport and other paperwork out and handed them to the officer. "Your job is to *assist* me in getting the pouches moved, not *hamper* me."

The Air Force officer looked carefully at the passport and paperwork, then picked up the microphone of the police sedan's radio and called his headquarters. He explained the situation to the man on the radio there. "Roger. Just stay where you are," came the reply. "The major will be there in a few minutes."

It was fifteen minutes before an Air Force major showed up in yet another sedan with flashing lights. The lieutenant explained the situation to him, and the major walked to the pouches and examined them. Then he came to the sedan where Harry and Paddy were, examined their passports and the courier orders. Satisfied that they were legitimate, he said, "All right. Sorry for the problem, gentlemen, but the lieutenant was only doing his job. I'm sure you can understand that. And I must say, Mr. Lawson, that you'd be well advised to stay with your pouches from now on."

"Yes," the relieved Lawson replied, "you can rest assured that I will. Thank you, Major."

"One other thing," the major said. "If you're going on to Berlin on a U.S. Air Force aircraft, you're going to have to declare this as hazardous cargo so it can be handled properly. Either that, or let someone here examine the contents to assure us it isn't dangerous, and I don't think the State Department would take kindly to that."

"No, they sure as hell wouldn't," Paddy mumbled.

"We'll take care of it, Major," Lawson replied. "Just get us and the pouches back to the hotel where our vehicle is, please."

"Very well, sir," the major said. "Lieutenant, take 'em on back. Good job."

When they got back to the base hotel, they loaded the pouches into the van again. Paddy looked at his watch and said, "Well, old buddy, how we gonna get this fixed up in time to get you on that C-130 to Templehof? You've only got twenty minutes till it loads."

"We aren't," Lawson replied. "Take me over to the commercial terminal where they're *used* to diplomatic traffic. I'll take a commercial flight to Berlin from there."

It was ten minutes to nine that Saturday morning when Sergeant Major Matt Jensen called Rachel from Heathrow Airport to tell her that his flight to London had been a little late. They arranged to meet at ten-thirty at the Knights-bridge underground station, which was a short walk from Rachel's hotel.

Jensen stored his suitcase in a locker at the airport and made his way to the subway train. He was going on to Berlin that evening, whether she agreed to accompany him on the mission or not. He studied his tourist map of London as he rode toward the center of the city, and when the train got to Green Park, he got off and walked to the Knightsbridge station. En route, he reassured himself that he was not being tailed by anyone, timing his arrival at the station for exactly ten-thirty.

When he saw Rachel, she smiled and walked toward him, but he scratched his right ear to indicate that he was not under surveillance.

Damn! she thought to herself. *I haven't been checking to see if I'm clean or not.* She walked on past Jensen without speaking, scratching the back of her neck to indicate that she didn't know if she was being followed or not.

He followed her at a distance as she took a circuitous route into Hyde Park, mentally scolding herself for not having taken evasive measures earlier to detect anyone who might be following her since she left the hotel. Finally, when she was satisfied that she wasn't under surveillance, she scratched her right ear and waited for Jensen to catch up to her.

"Hello, ma'am," he said when he reached her.

"Hi, Matt," she replied as she shook his hand. "Let's walk through the park here, and you can tell me what this job is all about."

He pulled his wool scarf up around his neck and shoved his hands in his pockets. "It's a very important mission, Captain Brown," he began.

"It's Rachel, Matt."

"OK, Rachel it is," he said. "The first thing I have to tell you, Rachel, is that the boss said I have to explain a couple of things to you before I can tell you about the mission."

"What's that?"

"Well, the first thing is that, if we get caught at what we're

295

doing," he said, stopping to look her in the eyes, "we have to commit suicide."

She studied his face for a moment, then asked, "How?"

"Pills," he answered. "I'll pick them up when we get where we're going."

"And, where's that, Matt?"

"I can't tell you that, yet."

"Well, what do you think the chances are of our getting caught?" she asked.

"Personally, I think it's highly unlikely that we will, unless we really screw up," he said as they resumed walking. "But there's always that chance."

"Matt, in your mind, is it *really* an important job?"

"You bet it is," he replied, "The most important one *I've* ever had. Ever *will* have, I imagine."

They walked along in silence for a while, then she stopped and looked at him. "That's good enough for me. I can do it, if I have to. What else?"

"If we do get caught, they'll deny that they knew anything about what we were up to—"

"They?"

"The government. The unit. Everybody. They'll even tell our family, friends, the news media, that we were nothing but a couple of outlaws—two traitors who went nuts over drugs or money or something. And they'll have all the evidence they can manufacture to back it up."

They started walking again, and she said, "Plausible denial. It figures. I mean, if they expect us to kill ourselves, then it's obviously so they can deny knowing what we were up to, or why."

Once more, they were silent for a while until she spoke.

"Well, if I'm dead, I really won't give a damn what they say about me, will I? 'Nobody said it was gonna be easy,' right?"

"You want a little more time to think about it, Cap— Rachel?"

"Nope. So, where are we going, and what are we going to do when we get there?"

"You're sure?" he asked. "I mean, if it comes down to it—even though I honestly think it's unlikely—and you can't take your own life . . ."

"You'll kill me? You'd better, Matt. Because if you hesitate, *I'll* kill *you."*

He looked at her for a long moment, then said, "We're going to Berlin, Rachel. We're going to pick up the nuke we found in Washington, rearm it, and try to get it into East Berlin."

"My God," she muttered. "Why the hell do they want us to do *that?"*

He sneezed, and she said, "Gesundheit."

"Thank you. Once we get it in place, they're going to tell the Soviets that Valenzuela—Ramirez—put it there, so they can find it and disarm it."

"Jesus! No wonder they're going to deny any knowledge of us, if we get caught," she commented. "But how the hell are we going to manage to get it into East Berlin?"

"I don't know if we *can* manage it, Rachel. But if we can't, if the risk of getting caught is too great, we're supposed to find a place along the Berlin Wall to put it. *Wherever* we put it, it has to look as if it's been there since November, though."

He sneezed again, and she said, "Nasty cold."

"Yeah," Jensen replied. "No wonder, with all the changes in climate I've been through lately. And lack of sleep."

"Well, when are we supposed to get to Berlin?" she asked. "And when do we have to have the thing in place?"

"We'll go to Berlin tonight. We're to get it emplaced as soon as possible, but no later than Monday, day after tomorrow. We'd better head toward your hotel, so you can check out and we can get back to Heathrow. We have a Pan Am flight at four-ten."

As they walked through Hyde Park toward Knightsbridge, Jensen explained to Rachel the other details of the mission.

When they got to the Knightsbridge underground station, she said, "Why don't you catch the tube on out to Heathrow from here, Matt? Buy the tickets, get yourself a cup of tea, and something for that cold. I'll meet you at the Pan Am check-in counter no later than three o'clock."

"Yeah, I think I will," he said. "Be sure to call the Ranch and tell Garrett you've agreed to go."

When she got back to her hotel, Rachel set up the radio and called Garrett.

When he came on, she said, "I've linked up with Matt Jensen, sir, and he explained the situation. I'm going with him."

"Roger, Captain Brown. Thank you. Now, you need to delete the code from your radio and find somewhere in London to leave it. Can you do that?"

"How are we going to communicate with you, over?"

"You won't—not until you get back to London, anyway. Then just give me a phone call with an open code phrase, like, 'the package has been delivered,' or something."

"Why bother, sir? If you hear from me, you'll know it's been delivered. If not, this is the last conversation we'll ever have, over."

"Roger, Rachel. If you need something in Berlin, Matt knows how to get in touch with Harry Lawson there, over."

"All right, boss. I'll delete the code from this thing, leave it in the long-term baggage storage at Heathrow, and mail you the receipt, then. Anything further?"

"Negative further, Captain Brown. Good luck. I'll see you in a few days."

"Roger, sir. See you around Tuesday or Wednesday . . . and sir, I just want you to know that this is the best job, with the best men on the planet, that a woman could ever have."

"Understand, Captain Brown. When you get back, I've got another mission for you. I need you to survey someplace for us to conduct hot weather training. You know, a week or so in the Virgin Islands or Tahiti or somewhere."

"Can do, sir. Can I take someone along to help?"

"Who do you have in mind, over?"

"I'll let you know when I see you next week."

"Roger, Captain Brown. This is Garrett, out."

She took off the earphones and laid them down, then pressed the control and escape keys on the keyboard of the portable computer into which the satellite radio transmitter circuitry was integrated. The radio thus rendered unusable, she packed it away, then packed her clothing and checked out of her hotel.

32

Harry Lawson arrived in Berlin before noon, and was met at Templehof Airport by a member of the CIA station in that isolated West German city. They retrieved the diplomatic pouches directly from the cargo hold of the Boeing 727 and loaded them into the man's Mercedes sedan. He took Lawson to the small safehouse near the Tiergarten section of the city, and left him there.

"Anything you want me to take in to the station?" the man who dropped him off asked.

"No, thanks," Lawson replied. "I'll call if I need anything."

"OK. Everything you should need is here. You say you'll be here till Tuesday?"

"No later, I hope. Is that VW van out front the one I'm supposed to use?" Lawson asked.

"Oh, yeah. I almost forgot," the man said. "Here are the keys."

His escort departed then, and Harry Lawson lay down to take a nap while he waited for Matt Jensen to telephone the safehouse—a call he didn't expect for several hours. The diplomatic pouches were on the floor beside him.

In Alexandria, Virginia, Marlene Graf met her KGB handler that morning in a store in Landmark Plaza, just off Shirley Highway. She passed him the envelope with the phony report of the interrogation of Emilio Ramirez and his pregnant girlfriend, Nadia Cruz. He waited until he got back to the Soviet Embassy to read it, then drafted a message relaying its contents to the chief of the KGB in Moscow.

It was dark when the telephone rang in the safehouse where Harry Lawson lay sleeping. It rang three times, then stopped. Exactly one minute later, it rang twice more.

He got up, dragged the pouches into the bathroom, and closed the door. Then he left the safehouse, ensuring that the door was double locked, and drove into the city to pick up Matt Jensen and Rachel Brown from a preplanned spot near Templehof Airport.

When they were back at the safehouse, he showed them the diplomatic pouches. After he helped Matt carry the larger one back into the bedroom, he broke the seal on the pouch, and they removed the box containing the small but heavy, unarmed nuclear bomb. Jensen opened the box, and the three stood there looking at the stainless steel cylinder for a minute.

"I'll need something to wipe it completely clean with," Matt said to Lawson. "Alcohol, or ammonia, or something like that," he added, clearing his throat.

"You sound terrible, Matt," Rachel said. She put her hand, then her wrist, to his forehead. "And you've got a high fever. Why don't you take some aspirin and go to bed? We can start on this thing in the morning."

"Yeah, I think I'd better. Let me check the other pouch first, though."

Lawson broke the seal and took from the pouch the two small boxes, which were taped together. Jensen cut the tape with his penknife, and opened the smaller box, finding a pair of rubber gloves wrapped in plastic, and a small bottle with four capsules in it.

In the other box was the firing mechanism for the bomb, an open-end wrench of the correct size needed to screw the bolts into the bomb casing, and a tube of superglue.

"That should do it," Jensen said. "Now all we need to do is find a place to put the damned thing."

"And get it there without getting caught," Rachel added.

"Yeah. Well, let's get some sleep, Rachel. Tomorrow's gonna be a busy day."

"Let me get you some aspirin, first, Matt," she said, opening her suitcase. She gave him three, and he took them and went to bed in the room with twin beds where he and Lawson would sleep.

"Are you hungry, Rachel?" Harry Lawson asked.

"Yes, I could use something to eat," she replied. "Want me to fix us something?"

"Why don't we go find a gasthaus and get some good German food?" Harry suggested. Except for a snack on the airplane, he hadn't eaten since his breakfast was interrupted by the security police at Rhein-Main Air Base.

"Oh, I think I'd better stay here with Matt," she said.

From the bedroom, Jensen said, "Don't be silly, Rachel. I'll be fine. You and Harry go have yourselves a good meal."

"Are you sure, Matt?" she called.

"Of course. Go on, now. Just make sure you lock me in this place with that stuff in the other room."

They found a nice little restaurant a short distance away, the Baerchen Haus, and ordered *Jaegerschnitzel* with green salad and beets. Harry ordered a bottle of dry Rhine wine, and the waitress poured them each a glass.

"Well, Miss Brown," he said, raising his glass to her, *"willkommen in Berlin."*

"Danke schön, mein Herr," she responded, and took a sip of the tasty wine.

"Have you been to Berlin before?" he asked.

"Yes. I visited a friend who was stationed here about, oh, two-and-a-half years ago. I spent two weeks here."

"Did you get over to the East at all?"

"Yes, I did," she said. "What a miserable, dreary place."

"Yeah, I know. Makes you glad to live in a free country, doesn't it?"

"It sure does. Especially when you think that East Germany has the highest standard of living in the Soviet Bloc."

"Is that why you're in the line of work you're in?" he inquired.

"Yes, I suppose that has something to do with it. That, and the brother I lost in Vietnam."

"Oh, sorry. I wasn't aware of that," Lawson said. "How long have you been in the job you have now?"

"About two years."

He topped off their glasses of wine and said, "Well, from what I've seen the last week or so, it must be exciting. I have a lot of respect for you and the people you work with."

"It's not usually as 'exciting' as it's been lately, Harry, thank God. But, yes, it is interesting, most of the time. And thanks for the compliment."

The waitress brought them their dinner, and they ate in silence for a while.

"How come an attractive woman like you isn't married, Rachel? Or are you?" Lawson asked.

"Oh, I don't know. Waiting for Mister Right still, I guess," she said. "What about you, Harry? Are you married?"

"Divorced," he replied. "Since last summer."

"Kids?"

"Yeah. A little girl. She lives with me," he said.

"And who takes care of her while you're running around the world like this?"

He smiled. "My boss and his wife. My parents have both passed away, so they've become sort of her adopted grandparents."

"Well, that's really nice. How old is she?"

"She'll be six next week," he said. "On the twenty-third. Hope I'll be back home by then."

"Of course you will," Rachel said. "You're going back when we do, aren't you?"

He looked at her for a long moment. "Yes, I am, if it goes well."

They continued to chat over coffee after they finished their dinner and the bottle of wine. Eventually, Rachel looked at her watch and said, "We'd better get back and check on Matt, Harry."

He paid the bill, and when he was helping her into her coat, she said, "Thank you very much for dinner, Harry. It was delicious."

"My pleasure," he replied. "And thanks for the good conversation. I really enjoyed it."

On the way back to the safehouse, he said, "Rachel, do you get up to the Washington area much?"

"Now and then," she said.

"Well, maybe we could have dinner and go to a show or something, next time you're up that way."

"Why, thanks, Harry. Yes, I think I'd like that."

When they went into the house, she checked on Matt. He was burning up with fever. "Maybe we should get a doctor out here to have a look at him," she whispered to Lawson.

"I don't need a damn doctor," Jensen mumbled. "Give me a couple more aspirin. I'm sure I'll be OK by tomorrow morning."

He was somewhat better in the morning, and while Rachel fixed a breakfast of ham and eggs from the food with which the safehouse kitchen was stocked, he and Harry cleaned the bomb vessel off with some ammonia-based cleanser they found in the bathroom.

"All right," Jensen said. "From now on, nobody touches this thing without these fingerprinted gloves on."

After breakfast, Matt dressed in the Army green uniform he had bought at Fort Myer. It was the uniform of a second lieutenant, with a 3rd Infantry Division patch on the left shoulder.

"Why the uniform?" Lawson asked.

"So I can conduct a recon in East Berlin," he replied. "Under the Four Powers Agreement, American, British, and French soldiers can visit East Berlin just by walking through Checkpoint Charlie in uniform. The Russians can come over to this side, too, and we can't do a thing about it. As far as the Russians and East Germans are concerned, I'm just another second looie from the 3rd Division, up in Berlin for the standard orientation tour they're all encouraged to take."

"Don't the American MPs at Checkpoint Charlie check your ID card and orders, though?" Rachel asked.

"Got 'em right here," he said, producing an ID card and

phony orders from the inside pocket of the uniform jacket. " 'Second Lieutenant Walter L. Shumate,' it says here."

"Walter Shumate?" Rachel laughed. "Not *that* name, again."

"Yeah," Jensen replied, "I asked Garrett why he used Walt Shumate, and he said it was all he could think of at the time."

"That's the name all these guys use when they're trying to hustle women in bars," she explained to Harry Lawson.

"Well, let's get on with it, Rachel," Jensen said. "You can drop me off near the checkpoint, then go ahead and recon those areas around the wall I showed you on the map."

She drove to Friedrichstrasse, near Checkpoint Charlie, as Matt gave her directions and rehashed the rest of the plan. If Matt was successful in finding a suitable place in East Berlin to plant the bomb, Harry Lawson would arrange to get him one of the so-called G-2 cars from the Berlin Brigade. The G-2 cars routinely drove around East Berlin with uniformed U.S. Army drivers, to assert the Allies' right to do so, as well as to spot East German and Soviet troop movements around the city. It was one of the duties Jensen had when he had been stationed in Berlin several years earlier. He would load the bomb in the trunk of the car and drive it into East Berlin.

Rachel, meanwhile, would rent a car and drive to one of the checkpoints between West Berlin and East Germany proper, where she would pose as an American civilian tourist taking a tour of East Germany. Her car would be searched, in all probability, but all that would be found was normal luggage. She would then drive into East Berlin from the East German countryside, where there were no checkpoints, and rendezvous with Jensen in a secluded area of the city, where they would transfer the bomb to her car.

That done, either she would emplace the bomb, if the location Jensen found made that feasible, and return to West Berlin; or she would spend the night in East Germany while Jensen returned to the West, changed into civilian clothes, and entered the East as a tourist in the manner

Rachel had. Then, the two of them would emplace the bomb and return to the West by separate routes.

"Of course," he remarked as she approached the point where he was to get out and walk into the East for his reconnaissance, "I may get lucky and find a suitable place where I can just stop the G-2 car, plant the bomb, and haul ass back here. Anyway, wish me luck. Pull over right here, and I'll get out."

"I'll pick you up here at five-thirty," she said. "Good luck, Matt."

He got out and she drove away toward the first of the places he had pointed out to her on the map.

The American Military Policeman at Checkpoint Charlie snapped to attention and saluted Jensen as he approached the guard shack there.

Matt returned his salute and handed the MP his bogus ID card and orders. The soldier handed them through the window of the guard post to the sergeant on duty there, who logged in Second Lieutenant Walter L. Shumate, along with his phony Social Security number and unit of assignment.

"How long will you be over there, Lieutenant Shumate?" the sergeant asked.

"Until about dark, I guess," Jensen replied. "Something like five-thirty."

"Roger that, sir. I'll log you in to return by seventeen-thirty. If you're not back by that time, a patrol will be dispatched to look for you. Please don't let that happen, sir," he said, grinning, "or it's highly unlikely that you'll ever make first lieutenant.

"Now, sir," he continued, "I'm required to advise you of the following."

The sergeant began a litany of warnings about what not to do, and what to do in case of a problem.

It included such prohibitions as exchanging dollars or West German marks for East German marks, drinking more than a single alcoholic drink, photographing uniformed personnel or buildings bearing German Democratic Republic or Soviet flags—"except for the Brandenburg Gate, which is OK.

"And remember, sir," the Military Police sergeant concluded, "if an attempt is made to apprehend you, demand to see a Soviet Army officer. The Russkies will take care of you, because they don't want to lose their right to come over *here* and snoop around without being hassled by us mean-assed American MPs. Any questions, Lieutenant?"

"No," Jensen said, then coughed hoarsely. "I think you've covered everything pretty well. Thank you."

The sergeant and the junior MP snapped to attention and saluted sharply. Jensen returned their salutes and walked past the glaring East German guards who, as they always did when an American officer entered the East, followed his every step with binoculars fixed intimidatingly on him until he was past the checkpoint and out of sight around the corner.

He felt very woozy, so when he got over to Unter den Linden, he bought a glass of lemonade with the East German marks Lawson had given him, and took three aspirins.

Two amateurish surveillance men—he couldn't tell whether they were East German or Russian—followed him for a while, and he made no attempt to lose them. It made no difference to him whether they stayed with him or not, as all he was doing was looking. He tried to walk quickly to the areas he wanted to reconnoiter, but he was sweating profusely from a raging fever. He felt himself becoming markedly weaker, and had to stop and sit down to rest several times.

"This is no damn good," he finally mumbled to himself, and stumbled back toward Checkpoint Charlie.

I'll just have to rest up until tomorrow, he thought, *and tomorrow, I'll have Lawson get me a G-2 car. Then I'll just put the bomb in the trunk, ride around over here until I find a place to plant it, then go the hell home.*

He crossed back into the West, and the MP saluted and said, "You didn't stay very long, Lieutenant . . . Say, are you feeling all right? You're pale as a ghost."

"Yeah, I guess I've got the flu or something. Where can I get a taxi?"

"Right over there by that little museum, sir."

"Thanks," he said, and returned their parting salutes. He tried to determine where Rachel would probably be, so that he could take a taxi there and intercept her. He guessed she would probably be in the French sector, so he got into a taxi and headed that way.

His guess was correct, because he saw her driving slowly past an area parallel to the wall that has divided the city since 1961, near a location at which he felt he might be able to conceal the bomb, if he couldn't find a suitable place in the East. He rolled down the window of the taxi, leaned out, and flagged her down.

She pulled over, and he paid the taxi driver and got out, then climbed into the Volkswagen van beside her.

"What happened?" she asked.

"Sick as hell," he replied. "Take me back to the safehouse. I'm gonna lie down here in the back."

He crawled into the back seat and lay down, shivering with fever.

"I'm going to take you to the Berlin Brigade dispensary," she said.

"No! No, ma'am. Just take me to the safehouse. If I don't get better, Harry can get an Agency doctor for me."

"Well, all right. But if you're not better by this evening, I'm going to damn well *order* you to see a doctor."

She took him back to the safehouse. Harry Lawson answered her knock at the door and said, "What's wrong?" as he saw Matt leaning heavily on her arm.

"He's sick as hell, Harry. Help me get him in bed."

Once Matt was in bed and wrapped warmly up, she said, "Can you get a doctor out here, Harry?"

He thought a moment, then said, "I don't know, Rachel. I mean, I'm sure I can, but it's liable to compromise the mission. Nobody knows there's anyone here but me. They think I'm going around the city caching some stay-behind equipment in case the Big War ever starts."

"Shit!" she exclaimed. "Well, we're going to have to do *something*. . . . Look, if nothing else, I'll just take him to the Army dispensary later. Right now, I'd better go find a place to put that damnable bomb, since it looks like I may have to do it by myself. If he gets worse before I get back, just call a taxi and *send* him over to the Berlin Brigade dispensary, all right?"

"Yeah. There's a pharmacy just down the street a little way. I'll go down there and get a thermometer. What else should I do?"

"Oh, I don't know. See if you can get something into his stomach. Something like chicken soup. And plenty of liquids. I'll see you later."

Rachel went back out to the van. She realized that she needed to concentrate on the mission, since she might very well have to find a suitable site for the bomb, and place it there herself, since Jensen was so ill. She studied the map he had given her, then started the van and drove away. A short while later, she was at the River Spree, the wide river which runs through the divided city. In places, the river forms the boundary between East and West Berlin.

Although it is inaccessible from the East because of the formidable Berlin Wall and its sensors, mined strip of earth, patrol dogs, and surveillance cameras and towers, the River Spree can be reached from West Berlin in places. Where it flows from the West into the East, and back again, there are underwater barriers to prevent divers from escaping the oppression of the communist East to the freedom of the West.

But there is nothing to prevent a diver from swimming from West Berlin up to the underwater barriers which form the East-West boundary beneath the dark waters of the Spree.

Several canals—the Landwehr, the Tetlow, the Westhafen —go back and forth beneath the Wall's twenty-eight-and-a-half-mile length, as well.

Rachel reconnoitered each of these locations, looking for one where she felt Jensen would be able to enter the water undetected by observers from either side of the former German capital city. Only one appeared usable. It was in the center of the city, just north of the Brandenburg Gate, near the restored Reichstag building. She got out of the car to check it out on foot. The best location to enter the water was at a spot on the bank of the canal where there were three white, wooden crosses. Each bore the name and date of death of a person who had died while trying to escape to freedom by swimming across the canal. Rachel decided the place was unsuitable, after all.

She drove to the southwest corner of the walled-in city, to Wannsee, where the Berliner Forst borders the waters of the Havel River and the Tetlow Canal. There, Koenigstrasse crosses from West Berlin into the city of Potsdam over a bridge known in the West as "Freedom Bridge," for it was here that the captured agents of the Free World and the Soviet Bloc were usually exchanged during the occasional "spy trades" which were conducted during the Cold War.

Just north of the bridge, a narrow road looped from Koenigstrasse through the wooded park beside the Havel River. Rachel parked the car and reconnoitered the area on foot.

"Just right," she said. And symbolically, it was the sort of place worthy of such a historical act as she and Jensen were about to perpetrate.

33

Rachel located a sporting goods store off the Kurfurstendamm that sold diving equipment, and went in. When she found a salesman who spoke English, she told him that she was going on a Mediterranean vacation and wanted to buy some scuba diving equipment to take with her.

He asked her a number of questions that only an experienced diver would be able to answer, so she said, "Oh, I'm not a trained scuba diver yet. I'm going to learn when I get there."

"Ah, I see," the salesman said, "then you just want the basic equipment?"

"Yes," she replied. "You know, tanks, mask, fins—that sort of thing."

He sold her a single tank, regulator, mask, fins, weight belt, and upper body wetsuit, all of which he helped her load into the van.

Almost as an afterthought, she said, "Maybe I'll get a chance to test it in the embassy swimming pool before I leave tomorrow night."

"That would be a good idea," he said, "and if something fails to work correctly, bring it back here. And, of course, be sure to have the tank filled with air first."

"Air? You mean it's not already filled?"

"Oh, no," he said.

"Can you fill it here?" she asked, thinking, *Damn, Brown. A lot of good all this gear would do you if you tried to dive with an empty air tank.*

"No, we have no compressor here. But I can give you the address of a place where you may get it filled, if you wish."

"Yes, would you please?"

The salesman wrote an address on a slip of paper and explained to her how to get there, then warned, "And be certain to drain the tank before you take it to the airport. It's not allowed to be flown by aircraft unless it has been emptied."

"Of course," Rachel said. "Thank you very much."

She stopped by the address the salesman had given her and had the air tank filled, then went back to the safe house.

It had begun to snow heavily by the time she got there, and when Harry Lawson opened the door for her, she said, "Boy, it's really coming down, isn't it?"

"Yeah," he said, "and according to the radio, it's supposed to do this all night."

When she got inside, she discovered that Matt Jensen was considerably better. His temperature had fallen to just two degrees above normal, and he had eaten a bowl of soup that Harry Lawson fixed for him.

"Matt," she said with excitement in her voice, "I think I've found just the place to put it."

She sat down on the bed and unfolded the map. Pointing out the site she had found, she said, "Right here."

He looked at the map, then thought about it a moment.

"Yeah," he said. "Yeah. Freedom Bridge. If I can get it out in the water far enough, that might be just the place."

Rachel grinned and said, "No problem. I bought a set of scuba equipment."

"You did? Hell, that's perfect then, Rachel," Jensen said. "Well done!"

Harry Lawson looked over her shoulder at the map. "In the water?" he asked. "Is the thing waterproof, though?"

"We can *make* it waterproof easily enough," Jensen said, sitting up in bed. "Harry, what I need you to do is go find a couple of good, thick plastic bags big enough to put the thing in. And I mean really *thick* ones, and some good quality glue that will seal them shut. And, let's see, some nylon straps or belts, for a carrying handle."

"I can do better than that," he said. "I can get an underwater cache container from the Agency station. It'd be ideal."

"But wouldn't that make whoever finds it realize that *we* put it there, and not Ramirez?" Rachel asked.

"Hell, Rache," Jensen said. "If the guy can get a nuclear bomb, he sure as hell should be able to get an underwater cache container."

"Anyway," Lawson added, "you can order them through those survivalist magazines. It's no problem."

"When can you get one?" Matt inquired.

"Right now, if I want to. The people here think I'm putting in caches, anyway. It wouldn't be an unusual request at all."

Matt thought a minute, then said. "All right. Let's do it tonight, while we've got this snow to cover us. Where's the scuba gear, Rachel?"

"Out in the van."

"Let's bring it in here so I can test it—oh, hell—did you think to get the tanks filled?"

"Tank," she replied. "It's a single tank. But, yes, I did get it filled."

"Harry, why don't you go get the container? Rachel and I will test the gear, then arm the bomb and get it the hell out of here. And the sooner the better, as far as I'm concerned."

"Anything besides the container?" Lawson asked as he pulled on his overcoat.

"Let me think," Jensen said. "Did you get a compass, Rachel?"

"No, I didn't," she replied.

"I can get one," Lawson said. "You want the wrist type, right?"

"Yeah. It would be nice to have a wetsuit, but I can do withou—"

"I *got* a wetsuit," Rachel interrupted. "And fins."

"Great!" Matt said. "OK, let's get with it."

Harry and Rachel brought the scuba gear in from the van, and while Harry went after the underwater cache container and a compass, Jensen tested the gear.

"Good quality gear," he said. "You must have paid a bundle for it."

"Yeah, he really took me for a ride," she replied. "Once he found out I didn't know anything about diving, he only showed me the most expensive stuff."

"You've never done any diving?"

"Oh, I've done a little shallow water diving with friends before, but I've never received any formal training."

Jensen stood and immediately leaned forward and put his hands on his knees and lowered his head.

"You OK?" Rachel asked.

"Yeah. A little woozy, that's all. I'll be all right."

She felt his forehead with her hand. "You still feel awfully feverish to me."

"Well, I'll feel a hell of a lot better once we get rid of this thing," he said as he walked to the box containing the vessel of the bomb and opened it.

He opened the smaller box, took out the rubber gloves with Ramirez's fingerprints on them, and pulled them on.

Their mood became somber as he took out the timing device and detonators and examined them. The timer, its self-contained battery still working, showed that it was still set to go off while the President of the United States was delivering his annual State of the Union address.

"Four days, nine hours, five-and-a-half minutes," Matt said as he stared at the timer. "Now, let's see if I can reset this thing like Fox showed me."

He took the firing mechanism into the kitchen and set it down on the table. With difficulty because of the rubber gloves he was wearing, he took a pencil point and pressed the tiny set button. With the point of another pencil, he pushed the days button six times. The timer now showed ten days, and just over nine hours.

"Close enough for government work," he muttered. His orders were to plant the device with approximately ten days left before it would detonate.

"Rache," he said as he took the device back into the bedroom where the body of the bomb lay in the carrying container, "now comes the hairy part."

"What can I do to help?" she asked.

"Just stand over there and hold your breath," he said.

He laid the firing device on the bed, then took the wrench and removed the plastic screws from the threaded holes in the vessel into which the blasting caps would be placed. He picked up the firing mechanism and untwisted the wires of each cap. Slowly, he reattached each wire to the timing device, then connected the wires to the two small batteries which were glued to the square of plywood beneath it.

Next, he carefully inserted one of the caps into each threaded hole in the bomb. With his fingers, he screwed in first one of the bolts through which the firing wires ran, then the other. Picking up the wrench, he next screwed each bolt firmly into place.

"Take that superglue please, Rachel, and put a blob on the back of this piece of plywood."

When she had done so, he pressed it against the stainless steel container and held it there for a minute or more, until he was certain that it was firmly affixed. Then he stood, looking at the now-armed nuclear time bomb as he pulled off the gloves.

"We need some padding now," he said, wiping his sweaty brow with his handkerchief.

She reached over to the bed and picked up a pillow. "What about this?" she asked, holding it up.

"Let me see it," he said. He pulled the case off, unzipped the cover, and pulled out the foam rubber pillow.

"Perfect," he said. After he had split the end of it open with a knife, he put the fingerprint gloves on and pulled the split foam rubber pillow down over the top of the bomb and the firing mechanism, then glued it to the steel vessel. Finally, he took another pillow, split it, and pulled it over the bottom half of the bomb.

The potentially devastating nuclear time bomb was now entirely encased in foam rubber, and from the outside, appeared as harmless as the inside of a long sofa pillow.

"Well, there it is," he commented. "All wrapped up and ready to go."

Rachel stood looking at it, slowly shaking her head.

"Whoops," he said, and ran into the bathroom. As another result of his illness, Jensen had developed diarrhea. When he returned from the bathroom, he was pale and sweating. He went to his bed and lay down. Rachel got the thermometer and had him put it into his mouth.

"You're burning up," she told him as she felt his forehead. She went to the bathroom, wet a washcloth with cold water, and placed it on his forehead. When she looked at the thermometer, it read nearly one-hundred-four degrees.

"When was the last time you took some aspirin, Matt?" she asked.

"Several hours ago," he replied weakly.

She got three more aspirin and gave them to him with a glass of water.

"You'd better lie there and rest. And I think we'd better

wait until tomorrow night to put the bomb under the bridge."

"No," he said, "we can't afford to."

"Why not?"

"Because, Captain, we've got the snow tonight. If we wait, it'll probably stop, and our footprints will show where we went into the water. Somebody's liable to investigate."

She thought about it for a while. He was right. If they didn't do it tonight, the snow wouldn't cover their tracks, and anyway, they were both anxious to get it over with and go home.

"I guess you're right," she said. "But you'd better let me swim the goddamned thing out to the bridge."

"We'll see," he said.

Harry Lawson returned as she was bathing Matt's arms and forehead with a wet washcloth.

"How is he?" Lawson asked.

"A little better," she replied. "His temperature was up to a hundred and four earlier, but it was back down to under a hundred and two a few minutes ago. Did you get the container?"

"Yeah, an old one that's been used before," he said. "I figured that would be better, since the thing was supposed to have been planted months ago. Got a wrist compass, too."

"Good," she said. She looked at her watch. "It's only six forty-five. Let Matt get some sleep. I don't think we should try to go before at least ten o'clock."

They went into the kitchen and sat down at the table.

"Well, the bomb's all armed and padded," she said.

"It is? What's the timer set on?"

"Right now, I guess it's down to about ten days and six or seven hours," she said.

He made a note of that, and the current date and time on a small slip of paper from his wallet.

"Would you like something to eat?" she asked him.

"No, thank you. But go ahead and get something for yourself."

"No, I couldn't eat right now. How about a glass of wine, though? One won't hurt."

"I'll get it," Lawson replied, and when he returned to the table with two glasses of *auslese,* he said, "You know, I've been thinking, Rachel. *I* had better go try to put the bomb in. Matt's much too sick. And weak."

"Wouldn't work, Harry. Suppose you got caught?"

"That's why I brought that little bottle of pills."

"No, that's not what I mean. You *know* the KGB knows you're Moore's boy. They'd raise a stink the U.S. would never live down."

"Well, maybe," he replied. "But I'll just make sure I don't get caught."

Rachel reached out and took the CIA officer's hand in hers. "No, Harry Lawson, you know better than that. It's risky enough for the ol' U.S. of A. as it is. I mean, they've already figured out how they'll deny us, I'm sure. Let's just stick with the plan."

He placed his other hand on hers. "I guess you're right," he said. "You'll be careful though, won't you, Rachel? I'd hate for you to break your promise to go out with me next time you're in D.C."

She smiled and said, "I promise I'll keep our date," then withdrew her hand from his and picked up her glass of wine.

They sat there making small talk for more than two hours.

Around nine-thirty, Matt Jensen came in and said, "Let's get this damned job over with."

They placed the nuclear device in the underwater cache container, then Matt Jensen pulled the wetsuit on over his torso, and put a sweater, jeans, and dark blue jacket on over it.

Rachel put on jeans and a sweater as well, and the new winter coat she had bought in London.

"We about set?" Jensen asked.

"One second," she said. She went to the small steel box and took out the bottle of suicide pills. She handed one to Matt, who put it into the pocket of his jacket. She put another in the pocket of her coat.

"All set," she said, trying to force herself to smile.

They loaded the scuba equipment into the van, then the cache container. Jensen strapped the diver's compass onto his wrist while Rachel went back into the safehouse and got two towels and a blanket.

Harry Lawson stood in the two-inch-deep snow and held out his hand to Matt Jensen. "Good luck, Matt," he said.

"Thanks, Harry. See you in a couple of hours."

He held out his hand to Rachel, but she embraced him, kissed him on the cheek, and said, "Have some coffee made when we get back, will you, Harry?"

"Coffee, my ass," Matt said. "You'd *better* have a bottle of good whiskey."

They got into the van, Captain Rachel Brown in the driver's seat, with Sergeant Major Matt Jensen in the seat beside her.

She started the Volkswagen, and with a final wave to Harry Lawson, the two Delta Force soldiers, with an armed nuclear bomb on the floor behind them, drove away down the snowy Berlin street.

34

On the way to the park near the West Berlin foot of Freedom Bridge, they said little. Rachel noticed that Matt was shivering, but knew that it was from the fever wracking his body, not fear of swimming the bomb to a spot beneath the bridge.

He sneezed, and a moment later said, "Oh, great . . . damn!"

"What's wrong?" she inquired.

"I just crapped in the damned wetsuit, I think," Jensen muttered, then, "Think, hell—I *know* I did."

She had no appropriate response, so said nothing.

When they turned onto the road near the foot of the

bridge, she drove past the spot she had selected to park, then turned around and drove back to it, the side door of the van away from the road.

Through the heavy snowfall, they saw a couple strolling arm in arm toward them from up the road, so for several minutes they sat there in the darkness.

Rachel touched Matt's forehead as he sat shivering with his neck hunched down into his shoulders. His fever was terribly high.

"Are you going to be able to make it, Matt?"

"Yeah, of course I am." He looked all around, and seeing no one, climbed into the back and picked up the scuba gear. He opened the side door and carried it off into the park. Rachel got out and went around to the side of the van and pulled the cache container to the edge of the door by the carrying handles. A moment later, Jensen returned, and together they carried it to the spot surrounded by bushes where he had put the scuba gear.

Quickly, he got out of his clothes, except for the wetsuit, and standing barefoot in the snow, donned the scuba equipment. He was breathing in short gasps.

"OK," he said, his lips trembling from the combination of the freezing cold and his illness.

He laid the swim fins atop the underwater container, and they picked it up between them by the carrying handles. When they got to the edge of the narrow open stretch between the park and the riverbank, they set it down, and he pulled on the swim fins. With his wrist compass, he took a reading from their location to the floodlit center of the bridge, and set the bezel ring of the compass so the luminous indicator was fixed on that azimuth.

He looked at Rachel, and they reached down, picked up the bomb and, as he high-stepped with the swim fins to avoid tripping, they walked to the edge of the river. Matt set the container down on the bank and walked straight into the cold, dark water until it was thigh-deep, and Rachel heard his breath escape from his lungs. He lay back in the frigid water a moment, the coldness of it slapping him like a heavy blow. He surfaced, put the regulator into his mouth, pulled the mask over his face, and kneeling in the water, grabbed a handle of the container. He pulled it into the river and disappeared quickly beneath the calm surface of the Havel.

With her feet, Rachel swept away the swim fin prints in the snow, and moved back into the bushes at the riverside edge of the park. She looked at her watch. It was 10:53 P.M.

In the frigid depths of the river, Matt Jensen held the carrying handle of the container in his right hand, and kept the luminous dial of the compass on his left wrist in front of his face. Aligning the needle of the compass with the preset azimuth, he paddled with nearly numb legs toward the center pylon of the bridge.

In spite of the wetsuit, which kept his torso fairly warm, he shivered as he swam, and his head ached as if it were splitting open. His arms and legs lost all of their feeling, and in spite of the total darkness surrounding him, there was a sensation of sparks of white light in his eyes.

He concentrated on holding onto the handle of the bomb's waterproof container with his numb right hand, and on keeping his legs moving. Fortunately, the slow current of the Havel helped move him toward the bridge as he did his best to focus his blurred vision on the compass dial.

He could feel his heart pounding wildly, and he couldn't seem to suck enough air into his lungs through the regulator of the scuba system. He thought he was going to suffocate, and nearly panicked at the thought, then said in his mind, *Breathe slowly, Matt. Long, slow breaths, now. Come on— kick, kick, kick, inhale—kick, kick, kick, exhale.*

Suddenly, he felt totally disoriented, unsure of which way he was swimming, incapable of aligning the compass needle. He looked wildly around him several times before noticing a faint patch of light above him and to his right.

With weakening kicks, he swam the bundle toward the light, barely able to keep his blurred mind working. He bumped into something with his left wrist and reached out to feel it. *A stone wall,* he thought, *no, the bridge pylon.*

He rolled onto his side, looked above him toward the surface of the river, and saw dim lights almost directly overhead.

This must be it, he thought. *It has to be. I can't go on anymore.*

He tried to release the handle of the container, but the numb right hand which grasped it wouldn't uncurl, so he reached down and peeled it open with his left thumb. The underwater cache container with the nuclear time bomb inside it rested on the bottom of the Havel River.

Suddenly light-headed from a burst of adrenaline at the realization that he had made it to the center of the bridge, he giggled into the regulator. He looked at his wrist compass and aligned it on a back-azimuth of the one he had used when swimming toward the bridge. He turned and began kicking his way back toward the riverside park.

Rachel stood in the park, hugging herself against the cold as the heavy snow continued to fall around her. It had already almost totally obliterated the footprints she and Matt had made down to the river. For the tenth time, she looked at her watch. It was seven minutes past eleven.

How long will it take him? she wondered. *I should have asked him how long he thought it would take. Suppose he can't make it?*

She pulled off her glove and reached into the pocket of her coat, touching the suicide pill with her fingertips before quickly withdrawing her hand. Was she supposed to take her life if only *he* was caught, or if he drowned while emplacing the bomb? Of course not—they couldn't expect *that,* could they?

Again, she looked at her watch. Eight past eleven.

Beneath the surface of the frigid river, Matt Jensen was growing ever weaker. He had no idea how long he had been in the river, how far he was from shore. His bowels emptied into the crotch of the wetsuit again, and his legs were so weak that he wasn't even certain he was making any headway.

With difficulty, he brought his left wrist up in front of his mask, saw that he was generally on course, then let the arm relax and drift back to his waist. *Come . . . on . . . come . . .*

on, his mind urged with each weak kick. He exhaled, and couldn't seem to get himself to take another breath, then, from the back of his mind came a vision of the bomb behind him detonating in a flash of heat and light.

His whole body jerked at the burst of thought, and he realized that he had probably been momentarily unconscious.

From the last shot of adrenaline his body could muster, he felt strong enough to go on for a few more strokes. *Come . . . on . . . come . . .*

He felt no pain now, no cold. He was without feeling. He reached to his waist, his numb fingers unfastening the weight belt, then the waistband of the scuba tank. He rolled onto his back, shrugged weakly, and the tank came off. As he sucked in one last breath, the regulator was pulled from his mouth. He went limp, exhaled, and blacked into unconsciousness.

On the shore, Rachel was terribly worried. She was checking her watch several times each minute now, and the rest of the time was staring at the spot where he had entered the water eighteen minutes before.

The big flakes of snow would hit the surface of the river and for a second, lie there, then melt away. She was unable to see more than thirty or forty feet through the heavy snowfall and darkness.

"Come on, Matt. Come on," she whispered to herself.

She looked at her watch again, then out into the river. Something in the peripheral vision of her left eye caught her attention. She stared for several seconds in that direction, then saw something on the surface of the water. *The scuba tank!* It was on the surface, drifting slowly toward the bridge. Then, closer to her, she saw something else on the surface. It moved slightly. She ran to the bank of the river, and there it was. A body? Matt!

She tore her coat and gloves off, pulled the shoes off her numb feet, and plunged into the water. The shock of it robbed her of the ability to breathe, but she stroked toward the body of her fellow soldier, no more than twenty-five feet away. Her wool sweater suddenly seemed to weigh a ton, so she ripped it off over her head, then stroked on toward the unconscious body whose blond head made her certain it was Matt Jensen.

Rachel grasped him, rolled him over onto his back, then seized the collar of the wetsuit and began to swim to shore.

"Don't be dead . . . don't be dead," she blurted with each breath she exhaled, stroking as hard as she could with her free arm, until finally, her feet touched the bottom of the riverbed. She dragged him up onto the shore and felt for a pulse in his neck, but her fingers were too numb to have felt even a strong one. She picked him up, his weight barely noticeable to her adrenaline-filled muscles.

When she got to the van, Rachel laid him on the floor behind the front seat, then frantically dried off his arms, legs, and head with the towels she had brought. She wrapped the blanket around him, and wearing only wet jeans, a bra, and socks, ran back to the riverbank.

There, she pulled on her coat, picked up her shoes and gloves, and ran to the spot in the bushes where he had removed his clothes. She scooped them up, then ran to the van and threw them into the back seat. Placing her face near his open mouth, she felt a slight touch of warmth from his shallow breath. She pulled the blanket off of him, took his penknife from his pocket, and cut the wetsuit off him. After she wiped the messy feces from his crotch with one of the towels, she put his jeans and sweater on him, and then his shoes, then wrapped him up in the blanket again.

He moaned, and Rachel whispered, "You'll be fine now, Matt. You did it. I'm going to get you to a hospital. Just hang on, Matt. Hang on."

She rolled her wet socks off and pulled on her shoes, then jumped into the driver's seat and started the van.

Quickly, she checked the map of Berlin, then put the Volkswagen van into gear and tore off down the slick street.

By 1:00 A.M. on Monday, the twentieth of January, Harry Lawson had begun to worry.

Maybe, he thought to himself, *they decided to wait until later in the night to try to put the bomb in place.*

He paced the floor of the safehouse, thinking of all the things that could go wrong. It was an awfully risky operation, at best. When he had said that to Jason Moore, the Director of Central Intelligence, several days earlier, Moore had smiled and said, "Yes, Harry, it is. But as Henri Bergson said, at about the time I was born, 'The greatest successes have been for those who accepted the heaviest risks.'"

"But that was before nuclear weapons had been invented, sir," Lawson had responded at the time.

"That's true," Moore replied. "And the awful threat of those weapons is why we *must* try to do this."

Well, maybe so. Maybe if the very worst possibility occurred, and the weapon detonated—then at least the thousands of lives lost would surely lead the world to the realization that nuclear weapons were *already* out of control.

"Don't you understand, Harry?" Moore had explained. "This homemade bomb—this terrible, frightening tool of mass destruction—is not something *we* built, *we* planted in the Capitol of the United States, to destroy almost the entire government. It was put there by a single, insane individual. Where and when will the *next* one be put, if we don't get these satanic things under control—eliminated?

"Yes, it's risky, Harry, to be sure. But, goddamn it, I'd rather have it go off in Berlin than in Washington, as it might very *well* have done. And if these two young people—and maybe you, yourself, Harry Lawson—if you or they happen to get caught and have to *die* to make the world understand that nuclear weapons are no longer just in the hands of responsible governments, then it's a sacrifice well worth making."

It made sense when he thought about it, and Harry said, "I understand, sir. We'll get it done and we'll be back in a few days to tell you about it."

Now, he wasn't so sure about the "we" part.

* * *

It was almost 2:00 A.M. when he saw the Volkswagen van pull into the snow-covered driveway of the safehouse.

"Thank God," he muttered.

He opened the door, watched Rachel get out, and saw her go around to the side of the van and take an armful of items out of the back. He went out to help her, and seeing her disheveled and shivering, and that Jensen wasn't with her, said, "What happened, Rachel? Where's Matt?"

Lawson took the smelly bundle of towels and the torn-up wetsuit from her as she replied, "He nearly died, Harry. He may die yet. But he did it. He's in the hospital, but he *did* it, and we didn't get caught!"

"Oh, God, Rachel. I was so worried about you. But you *did* it! And you're here!"

He dropped the armload of soiled material and embraced her, and she began to weep. "It's all right now, sweetheart. It's over. You did it, and it's all over. Come inside now."

He recovered the towels and wetsuit, and they went inside. In a daze, she unbuttoned her coat and took it off, then slumped into a chair and pulled off her shoes. She was wearing only her damp jeans and a bra, so he went into his room and got her one of his sweaters, and a towel from the bathroom, as she sat there rubbing her numbed feet.

She unfastened her bra and dropped it on the floor, then pulled his sweater on.

"Get me a dry pair of pants, Harry, please. And do you have any heavy socks?"

He found a pair of jeans in her suitcase, and some panties, which he handed her before going into his room to get her a pair of his wool socks.

When he came back, she was pulling the jeans on. Then she sat down again, and he said, "Tell me what happened, Rachel."

As she did so, he knelt in front of her and put the socks on her cold feet, then got a blanket, wrapped it around her, and sat beside her while she finished telling him what had happened.

"I took him to the emergency room at the hospital and

told them that we were skating and he fell through the ice. I claimed that I couldn't get him out for ten or fifteen minutes. You should have seen him, Harry. He was completely blue."

"Christ, I guess so. Will he be all right?"

"I don't know. He seemed to be coming around, but he was still only semiconscious. And he was so sick before he went into the water. I just don't know. They seemed pretty worried about him. They had an oxygen mask on him, and IVs in both arms. They asked me where his identification was, and I said that it must have fallen in the water when I was getting him out. I didn't know what else to do. They asked me for my ID, too, and I said I'd have to go get it. I guess I'd better take my passport and go back. . . . Can you go with me?"

"There's no need for you to go back, Rachel. Who'd you tell them he was?"

"Shumate," she answered. "Lieutenant Walt Shumate, like it says on the ID card he used to get through Checkpoint Charlie."

"Good," Harry said. "I can call the Chief of Station and tell him to fix it so they won't ask any questions, or try to notify his unit or anything."

"Will that work? I mean, won't he want to know who it really is?"

"Not when the Director's personal assistant tells him to do it. And the people at the hospital won't think it's that unusual, either. This damn town's so full of spooks, that they won't think twice about it."

He dialed the chief of the CIA station in Berlin, and when the man answered, he said, "Sorry to bother you this time of night, Bill. It's Harry, from J.M.'s office. . . . Yeah, look there's a guy in intensive care at the Army hospital named Shumate. See that he's taken care of—no questions or any of that. . . . Right. . . . OK, Bill, good. And thanks. If he isn't doing well, call me right away and let me know, will you? . . . Thanks. I'll call your office in the morning."

He hung up, and to Rachel said, "He's going to send his

deputy down there right away to baby-sit Matt. He'll call here if there's any change. Now, I've got one more call to make."

He called the international operator and asked for a number in Philadelphia. When it went through, the Philadelphia telephone automatically transferred the call through to another number in northern Virginia.

"Hello, it's me," Rachel heard him say. "The order has been placed with the German firm. You can expect delivery in ten days. We'll be home in a day or two. Good-bye."

He hung up, then pulled an uncorked bottle of Henkel Troken *Sekt* out of the refrigerator. He brought the bottle and two tulip-shaped glasses back into the living room where Rachel, now warm and elated at the completion of the mission, smiled at him.

"That was Director Moore," Lawson explained as he poured her a glass of the sparkling wine. "He was so pleased he could hardly speak. All he could say was, 'Thank God. Thank you. Thank God.'"

35

On Monday morning, the Director of Central Intelligence had a personal letter, in Russian, delivered by courier to the chief of the KGB at the embassy of the Union of Soviet Socialist Republics in Washington.

The note read simply, "It is in the best interests of the people of our two great nations and world, for you to meet with me alone this afternoon at three-fifteen at the statue of *Giant Rising from the Earth* on Hains Point in Washington, the District of Columbia."

By noon, there were KGB agents all around the Hains

Point area. They saw nothing suspicious, other than a number of drug deals being made in the parking areas there, and reported that fact back to the Soviet Embassy.

At ten minutes past three, Jason Moore, the head of the Free World's largest intelligence agency, parked a battered, old Chevy Nova in the parking area near the cast aluminum statue and got out. He was wearing faded jeans and a Navy pea coat, and he walked slowly over to the portion of the statue which consisted of a giant hand rising from the ground.

Three minutes later, after a family of tourists had taken several photographs of each other cavorting on the unusual statue before getting into their car and driving away, a lone man approached Jason Moore.

"Mr. Moore?" the man asked with a perfect American accent.

"Yes," Moore replied. "I'm Jason Moore."

"What did you want to talk about, sir?"

"I don't want to talk to you, Ivan Golovkov," the Director of Central Intelligence said, noting with delight the surprise in the eyes of the number two man in the Washington bureau of the KGB at the sound of his own, true name. "I will speak only to Vasily Marchenko, your superior officer."

The Russian said nothing for a moment, then said. "Very well, Director Moore. But I will have to be here as well, to translate for him. His English is rather poor."

"Bullshit, Golovkov. He speaks English as well as you and I do. Now, quit fucking around and go get him."

The Russian walked back to a Buick Regal sedan with two other men in it, and after a moment, the one in the back seat got out, and walked over to the elderly chief of American intelligence.

Moore held out his hand to his Soviet adversary and as the Russian shook it, said, "Hello, Vasily."

"Good afternoon, Jason," the senior KGB officer in Washington said. "This must be terribly important."

"It is," Moore replied, then reached into the pocket of his pea coat and turned on the small transistor radio he had there. "Forgive me, Vasily," Moore said as rock and roll music began blaring from his pocket, "but this is too sensitive for your very capable officers and their electronic ears to hear."

He turned and walked past the statue, with the KGB officer walking beside him, listening intently. Once, the Russian stopped abruptly and looked at Jason briefly before saying something, then walking on.

The men conversed for less than three minutes, then the Soviet official took the hand Moore offered him, shook it warmly, turned and walked away.

Moore watched as the two Russians in the Buick sedan jumped out and opened the door for their superior. Fifteen seconds later, the car drove away, with another sedan carrying four more men following it at a discreet distance.

Moore got back into the old Chevy and headed for his headquarters in Langley, Virginia. A silver Oldsmobile with three KGB agents followed him until he turned off the George Washington Parkway. He rolled down the window of the Chevrolet and waved to them as they sped past. They pretended that they didn't see the old intelligence czar wave.

Harry Lawson drove Rachel Brown to Berlin's Templehof Airport to catch the midday Pan Am flight to Frankfurt.

"You take good care of Matt, Harry," she said as he stopped to let her out of the car at the entrance of the terminal.

"He'll be fine, Rachel," Lawson said. "I'll have him home in a couple of days."

They had gone by the hospital hours earlier to check on "Lieutenant Shumate."

The nurses had refused to even acknowledge that they had a patient named Shumate, until one of them had gone to Matt's room and brought the Deputy Chief of Station back to the desk. The man recognized Lawson and said, "They're OK," so the head nurse let them pass and go to Matt's room.

He was rather woozy, but in good spirits. When he, Harry, and Rachel were alone, Matt asked, "How the hell did I get here, anyway? The last thing I remember, I thought the damned thing went off. Then I realized it *couldn't* have, or I wouldn't *be* here. What happened?"

"You got to the surface, somehow," Lawson explained, "and Rachel swam out and pulled you ashore, then brought you here."

He looked at her with glazed eyes for a long moment, then said, "Rachel, you're something else."

"Hey!" she said, smiling. "'Nobody said it was gonna be easy.' Did you get it where you wanted to put it?"

"I *think* so," Jensen said with slurred speech. "If I ended up back where I started, I *must* have. Anyway, if it ain't where it's supposed to be, I'm *damned* sure not gonna go back and *move* it."

"Look," she said, "I'm going to head back to the Ranch, if it's all right with you. Harry has promised he'll take care of you, but he thinks I ought to go on back and let his boss—and ours—debrief me."

Matt took her hand. "'Course, Rachel," he said. "I'll probably be ready to travel by tomorrow, myself. You get on back and get the party started. If I'm not back in a few days, it's just 'cause I've let ol' Harry here drag me off to . . ."

Jensen drifted into semiconsciousness as a result of the drugs he'd been administered, and Rachel leaned over and kissed him on the cheek.

"He'll be OK, thank heavens," she said, smiling at Harry.

"Thanks to you," Lawson declared.

"We'd better get on back to the safehouse and pick up my stuff," she had replied, "and let him rest."

Now, they got out of the van and he came around and took her suitcase from the back. He flagged a porter, and gave the man a twenty mark note as he took the suitcase. "Pan Am nach Frankfurt," he said. The porter moved off toward the Pan Am check-in counter.

He took Rachel's hands in his and said, "Don't forget, now. Next time you're in Washington . . ."

She reached up and kissed him on the lips. "I won't forget, Harry. Thanks for everything. I'll see you real soon."

The CIA officer watched her as she walked away, looking for all the world like an athletic young tourist headed for a skiing vacation in the Alps or a diving holiday in the Caribbean.

In Cyprus that Monday afternoon, the Greek Cypriot police came to the conclusion that someone—Israel's Mossad being the prime suspect—had killed or captured Hakim Nidal and his two bodyguards. The tan Mercedes Benz sedan Nidal had rented in Larnaca was discovered in a parking lot in Nicosia, its floorboard stained with blood and brain tissue. Their fingerprint experts were unable to help solve the mystery, for the perpetrators of the deed had wiped the car clean.

They issued a press release stating simply that Hakim Nidal, staying at a hotel in Limassol with a Libyan passport in the name of Salim Nir, had been abducted and possibly murdered, along with two other members of the pro-Iranian Hezbollah faction, by unknown persons.

Rachel Brown waited until she got to London to call Wilton Garrett in his office at Fort Bragg.

"Hi, it's Rachel," she said when he answered. "I'll be getting to Dulles late tonight."

"That's the best news I've ever heard," Garrett replied. "What time will you and Matt be getting there?"

"He's not coming for a couple more days. He had a bad case of the flu or a relapse of malaria or something, and then he was skating on thin ice and fell through it, so to speak. Anyway, he had a bad case of hypothermia, so Harry's going to stay with him 'til he's well enough to travel."

"Well, I'll pick you up at Dulles myself. I'm sure J.M. will want to talk to you."

"Right. I'll be there at, let's see, ten-fifty tonight. See you then."

She went to the long-term baggage storage office in Heathrow Airport and told the man there that she had lost the receipt for the personal computer, Sony Walkman, and umbrella that she had stored. After he checked her passport and got her to sign a receipt form, he gave the items to her, and she checked them with her other baggage.

She was one of the last passengers to check in for the flight, and the young man at the ticket counter looked at her approvingly, then said, "I'm going to put you in first class, Miss Brown. We've several empty seats there, and I'm afraid we're overbooked in economy."

"That would be wonderful," she said, smiling. "Thank you very much."

Most of the passengers had already boarded the flight by the time she got to the gate, and she sat down to wait for the first class passengers to be called to board the L-1011 airliner.

A man hurried into the lounge a minute or so behind her. She had seen the same man earlier, at the Frankfurt airport, and again on the flight to London. Was it just a coincidence, she wondered, that he was again on the same flight as she?

The man, about forty years old and nicely dressed, glanced at her, then handed the agent his boarding pass, and went onto the airplane. The first-class passengers were invited to board a moment later, and she went aboard to find that the man was already there—and in the seat beside the one she had been assigned.

"Hello," she said, then sat down in the seat beside him.

As the stewardesses gave their safety briefing and demonstration, she wondered who the man was, now convinced that it was more than just coincidence that he was there.

She decided that she would do her best to find out what he was up to. When the safety briefing was finished, she held out her hand to him and said, "How do you do? My name is Rose Bryan."

He shook her hand briefly and with a British accent, said, "How do you do? My name is David Lamb."

"Are you going to the States for business or pleasure, Mr. Lamb?" she asked him.

"A bit of both, actually," the man replied.

"What sort of business are you in?" she inquired.

"Uh, military equipment sales," he responded. "And what about yourself, Miss Brown? Have you been in Europe for business or pleasure?"

"Aha," she thought. *He called me Miss Brown, but I introduced myself as Bryan.* Now she knew that he was not only following her, but knew who she was, as well—at least what her name was. Why was he following her?

She answered his question by saying, "Business. I've been on a photo assignment in Germany for a travel magazine."

"I see," he replied.

A stewardess offered them champagne, and they both accepted. "Would you like to take off your jacket, sir, and let me hang it up for you?" the stewardess asked.

"Oh, no, thank you," he replied. "I'll just wear it, thanks."

It must have been very warm in the tweed jacket the man was wearing, and Rachel looked closely at it. There was a barely noticeable bulge under his left arm, and Rachel thought, *The bastard has a weapon!*

"Are you staying in Washington, Mr. Lamb, or just changing planes at Dulles?" Rachel asked him.

"No, I'm flying on from there," he answered. "What about yourself?"

"I'm going on to North Carolina," she said.

"Not to Fayetteville, by chance, are you?" he asked.

"No. No, I'm going to Raleigh-Durham. Why did you say Fayetteville?"

"Because that's where I'm headed. I'm trying to sell some military kit to the Army at Fort Bragg."

Clever, Rachel thought. *He assumed I'd be going to Bragg, so he made up that cover story to have a reason for going there, too.*

She wondered if the man intended to do her harm—kill her, perhaps, or kidnap her. Did he know about the mission? Was he KGB, perhaps intent upon torturing information from her? Thank God that Colonel Garrett was going to be at Dulles to meet her, and that she had led the man to believe she was going on from there.

"Raleigh is near Fort Bragg, also, isn't it?" he asked her.

She thought, *I'll let him think that I'll be an easy target in*

*North Carolina, so that, hopefully, he'll plan on doing then
whatever he has in mind.*

"Yes," she said to him, "in fact, the Raleigh-Durham
airport is almost as close to Fort Bragg as the airport that
serves Fayetteville."

"Really," he commented. "Perhaps I'll go there, then. I'll
be able to hire a car there, won't I?"

"Yes, of course," she replied.

"Is someone meeting you there?" he inquired.

"No. I'll take a taxi from there," she said.

"I'd be happy to give you a ride," Lamb offered.

"Well, thank you. That would be very kind of you,"
Rachel said.

She thought, *That should make him think his job's going
to be easy.*

No longer worried about him, she took out the book she
had bought at Heathrow. It was entitled *Mike Force,* and
was about the Special Forces unit her brother had been
serving with in Vietnam when he was killed, and it kept her
entertained—except while she watched the in-flight movie
—until the aircraft landed at Dulles Airport.

David Lamb sat beside her in the mobile lounge that took
the first-class passengers from the airplane to the international arrivals gate. His bag came off the carousel before
hers, and he got into the foreign passenger customs line. She
recovered her bags and was through customs just ahead of
him.

She went out into the international arrivals waiting area,
and was relieved to see Garrett waiting for her just beyond
the waist-high posts through which arriving passengers
walked as they left the customs area.

As she approached her commanding officer, Rachel put
down her computer case and rubbed her left eyelid with her
index finger then scratched her forearm with one finger,
Delta Force signals which meant, "I'm under surveillance
by one armed male."

Garrett nodded, and as she picked up her bag and walked
toward him, Lamb caught up to her and said, "Let me help
you with your bag."

She let him take her suitcase, then said, loudly enough for Garrett to hear, "Why look at this! My editor's here to meet me."

Putting her bag down, David Lamb said, "Hello, Colonel," and held out his hand to Garrett.

"Hello, Major Lamb," Garrett replied, shaking the man's hand.

"You *know* this guy?" the startled Rachel asked.

"Sure," Garrett replied, "Major David Lamb, British S.A.S. We asked the Regiment to have somebody cover you from Frankfurt back to here, because of all that classified material you're carrying."

"Well, I'll be damned," she muttered at the realization that Lamb was a member of Delta's sister unit, the 22 Special Air Service Regiment, and not a KGB agent bent on doing her harm.

"Why didn't you just *say* so?" she asked him, adding, "I thought you were one of the bad guys."

Lamb smiled, "Yes, I was afraid that, when I slipped and called you Miss Brown, you had burned me. Sorry, but if we had been hijacked, I didn't want you to know me. That ticket agent really put me in a bind when he upgraded your ticket to first class. If it hadn't been for that, I don't think you'd have ever known I was covering you."

"Well, thank you very much for doing so, Major Lamb," she said.

Garrett picked up her suitcase, and said to David Lamb, "We have some business here in Washington tomorrow, David. Are you going to go on to Fort Bragg tonight?"

"No, I've got to go to the embassy and turn this bloody thing in," he said, patting the pistol beneath his jacket. "I'll be going on down there tomorrow."

"We'll see you there, then," Garrett said.

"Thank you again," Rachel said to the British officer.

"Pleased to have done so," Lamb said, smiling. "See you at Fort Bragg, Captain Brown."

Garrett drove her straight to CIA headquarters, where Director Jason Moore was waiting for them.

A MISSION FOR DELTA

The Director shook Rachel's hand warmly with both of his when Garrett introduced her to him.

"I'm very, very pleased to meet you, Captain Brown," Moore said sincerely. "Your sergeant major is going to be fine, by the way. I just spoke to Harry a few minutes ago, and he said they'll be leaving Berlin the day after tomorrow.

"Now," he said, sitting in a chair opposite her and leaning forward to listen attentively, "please tell me how you two managed to get the device emplanted, and exactly where it is."

After she told him the story, he got up and took a map of Berlin from the top of his desk and handed it to her.

"Let me make certain I have the right bridge," he said.

"Right here, sir," she said, pointing to it. "It's on the south side of the center pylon, in the underwater cache container Harry got for us."

"And as far as you know, the scuba gear was dropped here, near the West Berlin bank of the river?"

"Yes, sir. The only other thing we left behind was my sweater, which I had to pull off when I went in after Sergeant Major Jensen."

"Yes, well, I don't see any problem, then, Captain Brown," he said. After a moment, he said, "Captain Brown, you deserve a medal for what you've done—you and Sergeant Major Jensen both. Very large medals. But you'll never be awarded them—not for *this* operation."

He placed his hand on her shoulder. "Instead, Miss Brown, you and Jensen will have to be satisfied with the secret knowledge that what you have done may lead to the eventual saving of thousands, perhaps even millions, of human lives. You may very well have provided the catalyst for a Soviet-American agreement which will put an end to the nuclear madness that threatens this planet. This nation, and all of mankind, if our plan works, owes you fine soldiers an immense debt.

"Perhaps one day, many, many years from now, you'll be given the place in the history books you deserve. But, meanwhile, this secret must remain with the five of us who know it; we three in this room, and the two men in Berlin."

"I understand completely, Director Moore," Captain Rachel Brown replied.

"Oh, there *will* be a sixth person aware of what you've accomplished, Captain. I'll tell the President tomorrow."

"You mean the President doesn't already *know* about the operation?" she asked.

"Not the phase you've just completed," Moore replied.

"Mr. Moore," Wilton Garrett said, "while you're briefing the President, would it be possible for you to surface another issue?"

"What's that, Colonel?" the Director of Central Intelligence asked.

"The American servicemen still carried as missing-in-action in Southeast Asia. I promised Sergeant Major Jensen that I'd see what could be done to try to get the issue on the front burner."

Moore looked at him and smiled. "Well, there *are* still a few leads over there that haven't been resolved yet, Will. Maybe your man Jensen would like to go back out that way with a reconnaissance team to confirm or deny them?"

"Every man in the Delta Force would jump at the opportunity, sir," the Delta commander replied.

"And woman," Rachel added.

"I'll see what I can do, then," Moore said. "Now, you take good care of this fine young officer, Will, and excuse me, please. I've still got a bit of work to do."

On Tuesday morning in Potsdam, East Germany, a team of Soviet Navy commando divers arrived on the bank of the Havel River. They entered the river across from the West Berlin park where Captain Rachel Brown of the U.S. Army's Delta Force had waited anxiously for her teammate, Sergeant Major Matt Jensen, to emerge from the icy river.

Within an hour the Soviet divers had departed, taking with them a heavy object in a waterproof cache container which they had recovered from the river bottom beneath the center pylon of the bridge.

That evening, the Foreign Minister of the Soviet Union left for hastily arranged meetings in Washington with officials of the United States government. News media reports speculated that the meetings might be related to a break-through in U.S.-U.S.S.R. negotiations on some major issue —possibly strategic nuclear weapons reductions—which the President was expected to announce during Thursday night's State of the Union address.

On Wednesday evening, the U.S. Secretary of Defense departed Washington for Brussels, where he briefed his NATO counterparts on the discussions with the Soviet Foreign Minister.

While he was doing so, Matt Jensen and Harry Lawson shook hands at Dulles Airport.

"Thanks for taking care of us over there, Harry," Jensen said.

"You and Rachel did the hard part, Matt," Lawson replied. "Thank *you.* And give her my love when you get to Carolina, will you?"

36

At eight o'clock on the evening of Thursday, the twenty-third of January, several Delta Force soldiers were gathered with their friends—mostly active and retired members of the U.S. Army Special Forces community—in the Green Beret Sport Parachute Club. Command Sergeant Major Dick Salem walked into the old World War II building which served as the clubhouse and ordered a six-pack of Miller Lite to share with his subordinates and friends.

Retired Sergeant Major Ben Dennis, an old friend of Salem's from their days in the 1st Special Forces Group on Okinawa, said, "Where you been, Dick? Long time no see."

"Over at the stockade, trying to sort through all the paperwork Rob here keeps piling up on my desk," Salem replied, indicating Master Sergeant Rob Small, who had also served with Dennis on Okinawa.

"Hey, Joe," Birdie Sadler said, helping himself to one of the beers the Japanese-American bartender had brought over. "How 'bout turning up the television so we can hear what the President has to say?"

Joe turned up the volume on the big TV mounted above the bar, and the men fell silent to listen to the State of the Union address.

"The state of the Union today," the President began, "is one of freedom, strength, and hope."

In her condominium at Woodlake Resort just north of the Fort Bragg reservation, Rachel Brown was on the telephone with the Delta Force operations officer, Major Dave Ames.

"Thanks, Dave. I'd like to go," she said. "But I've invited Harry Lawson and his little girl to come down here for the weekend. Maybe I'll do the next one with you."

Dave had invited her to go down to Georgia with him to take part in a triathlon on Saturday, but Harry had called her earlier, and she invited him to bring his daughter to Woodlake for a weekend of relaxation.

She hung up the telephone and sat down to listen to the address her commander-in-chief was delivering.

"I am pleased to report that the General Secretary of the Soviet Union has agreed to a summit meeting here in Washington in the near future," the President was saying. "We are optimistic that, by that time, we will have completed the negotiations necessary to take the first major step toward eliminating many of the terrifying nuclear weapons which threaten not only our two great nations, but the rest of the world as well."

In Delta's Woodlake safehouse not far away, Santos Baldero sat with his arm around Nadia Cruz, listening to the President and translating his words into Spanish for her.

"In addition, we have pledged to sign an agreement to

cooperate in the elimination of another of the scourges of the modern world—international terrorism."

In the situation room of the former Fort Bragg stockade which had been converted to his headquarters, Colonel Wilton Garrett and Delta's intelligence officer, Major Jim Greer, were going over recent intelligence reports dealing with the possibility that American servicemen were still being held prisoner in the jungles of Southeast Asia.

Garrett had received instructions from the Chairman of the Joint Chiefs of Staff that afternoon, to develop a plan for reconnaissance teams to infiltrate the areas where the reports indicated small numbers of Americans might still be incarcerated after being captured during the Vietnam War.

Greer looked at his watch and said, "Let's take a break, boss, and listen to the State of the Union address."

In his on-post quarters, the weak but recovering sergeant major of Delta's Detachment E-1, Matt Jensen, sat with his wife and two daughters watching television.

"The issue of our prisoners-of-war and missing-in-action from the Vietnam War," the President was saying, "has dragged on far too long. During the coming year, I pledge to the families and loved ones who continue to yearn to know the fate of these brave Americans, that I will take whatever steps are necessary to resolve this issue, once and for all. The resolution of this matter, and of the other Americans being held against their will around the world, is something our people want and deserve, and I know that I will receive full, bipartisan support in these efforts."

Matt Jensen looked at the clock above the television. It was eight twenty-five on Thursday evening, January the twenty-third. He smiled, and hugged his wife closer to him.

Epilogue

On the morning of Friday, January the twenty-fourth, Major Dave Ames was waiting at Delta headquarters for Colonel Garrett to arrive. The building was nearly empty, since Garrett had declared the day a training holiday for the Delta Force, but he had called Ames the night before to tell him he would be needed to assist in planning an upcoming operation.

While he waited for his commander, Dave sat in the reception room, thumbing through a two-day-old copy of the *Washington Post*.

"Oh, my God," he muttered as he read a small article in the Metro area news section of the paper.

Women Found Drowned in Potomac

The bodies of a Capitol Hill secretary and an employee of the West German Embassy were discovered Tuesday night on the rocks of the Falls of the Potomac. Charlotte Black, a staff assistant of Congressman Wesley Bolton (D-Wisconsin), and Marlene Graf, a West German woman, were found by a Great Falls couple who were searching for their lost dog.

Both women were fully clothed and bore no signs of struggle, and police speculated that they had fallen into the river as they hiked beside the falls, which were raging as a result of the melting snow . . .

Rachel Brown had decided to relax on her day off by reading Charles Reade's *The Cloister and the Hearth*, a romantic novel of medieval times which she had not read since she was a student in college. She poured herself a cup of coffee, and curled up on the couch in her lakeside condominium, then opened the book and began to read.

"Not a day passes over the earth, but men and women of no note do great deeds, speak great words, and suffer noble sorrows. Of these obscure heroes, philosophers and martyrs, the greater part will never be known till that hour, when many that are great shall be small, and the small great; but of others the world's knowledge may be said to sleep: their lives and characters lie hidden from nations in the annals that record them. . . ."

Printed in the United States
30801LVS00006B/7

9 780595 165254